
★

She skipped down the tall, dirty stairs, and right into the corpse that lay across the path....

The deceased was Cameron Dessay, one-time Anglo-French wunderkind of Comparative Lit and relative newcomer to the English department. Known simply as "De-sigh" among a sizable proportion of the female student body, Cameron had been not only a brilliant researcher, but charming—in multiple languages. However, the pale, fine-featured face that had inspired so many hopeless aspirations now lay unnaturally still, the glossy black locks matted with blood that had flowed from a small but distinct wound in the bare, white throat.

Unable to speak as she was ushered back into the house, Dulcie slipped from shock into a dank, wet pool of guilt. She had not been one of Cameron's admirers.

No matter what she had thought of her dashing colleague, this was not how she wanted to remember him. But when she closed her eyes to block out the image, it only grew stronger in her mind. The cut looked so small and strange, so wrong in that smooth white skin. His green eyes frozen, like glass.

★

Previously published Worldwide Mystery titles by
CLEA SIMON

MEW IS FOR MURDER
CATTERY ROW
CRIES AND WHISKERS
PROBABLE CLAWS
SHADES OF GREY

GREY
MATTERS
CLEA SIMON

W☉RLDWIDE®

TORONTO • NEW YORK • LONDON
AMSTERDAM • PARIS • SYDNEY • HAMBURG
STOCKHOLM • ATHENS • TOKYO • MILAN
MADRID • WARSAW • BUDAPEST • AUCKLAND

For Jon

Recycling programs
for this product may
not exist in your area.

GREY MATTERS

A Worldwide Mystery/February 2012

First published by Severn House Publishers.

ISBN-13: 978-0-373-26786-6

Printed in U.S.A.

Acknowledgments

Writing is essentially solitary. Creating a book, however, is not. Friends, family and colleagues come together with support, encouragement and advice, and I would be remiss if I didn't thank everyone who has put up with me during this process. First and foremost, my deepest thanks go to my fast and careful readers: Naomi Yang, Brett Milano and, of course, Jon S. Garelick. My agent Colleen Mohyde, and the wonderful folks at Severn House, including editors Amanda Stewart, Rachel Simpson Hutchens and Claire Ritchie all helped bring Dulcie to life. And sister writers and artists, friends and family—including Lisa Susser, Caroline Leavitt, Vicki Constantine Croke, Karen Schlosberg, Fran Middendorf, Chris Mesarch, Iris Simon, Sophie Garelick, Frank Garelick, Lisa Jones and Ann Porter—all lent their good spirits. Thanks as well to Jon for putting up with the charred artichokes and countering with stories of Cheever and Naipaul. You make everything seem possible.

ONE

The apparition remained silent, but its speaking eyes saw far. Green eyes, cool as emeralds, stared into her own, summoning images of the sea beyond the borders. Of the forest, far away. Of a key to secrets lost. Of another, gone before…

'WHY DON'T YOU JUST say something?' Dulcie Schwartz sighed and slumped back against the wall. 'Anything?'

It was no use. The plump black and white kitten sitting opposite her looked up with wide green eyes. 'Kitten?' The green eyes blinked, and that was it.

With another, larger sigh, Dulcie pulled herself to her feet. Just this morning, she had been sure something was going to happen. A third-year grad student, she'd had sections to teach and hadn't been able to stick around. But all day, through Dickens and Poe, she'd been thinking. Waiting for the moment she could run home. And an hour ago, she'd broken away, postponed a tutorial with three students who didn't seem to care much, anyway, and thrown herself on to the floor to be at eye level with the tiny tuxedoed beast. The kitten had stared at her with such concentration, she'd felt certain they were going to have a breakthrough. Then, nothing.

'That's fine, then. Play dumb.' Sliding a full book bag on to her shoulder she gave the small feline a parting look. 'But don't think this is the last of it.'

Buttoning the heavy wool duffle coat she'd dug out of storage only two weeks before, Dulcie clumped down the stairs to the apartment's front door. If she'd looked up as she fished her keys from her pocket, she might have seen the kitten tilt its head as if listening to something in the silent flat. She might have seen the tiny cat jump up and hurry to the head of the stairs, the better to view Dulcie's red-brown curls disappearing through the door's small window. If Dulcie had glanced back just then, she might have seen the kitten's small pink mouth open in a soft 'mew.'

But Dulcie Schwartz had other things on her mind. At ten of four on a Monday afternoon, the Cambridge dusk was already settling in, and she was late meeting her adviser. Only the day before, he'd left a message that he was filing an end-of-semester performance review—and that he expected her to be able to show 'significant progress,' although he'd neglected to elaborate on what exactly that meant. He'd also moved their meeting again, away from his convenient and perfectly lovely office in Widener to his Tory Row house, another ten minutes away. As the Cyrus Professor of the Eighteenth Century Novel, William A. Bullock had one of the choicer library offices, high enough in Widener's subterranean warren to have an actual window. But no, Dulcie muttered as she raced toward Harvard Square, that wasn't good enough. What had he said?

'I want us to be able to speak in private, Ms Schwartz.'

She knew the real story. A complete nicotine fiend, the professor wanted to be able to smoke without setting off any of the library's super-sensitive alarms. And so she trudged across the muddy Common and up Brattle, lugging a bag full of books and fully aware that yet another sweater would be saturated with smoke, her nose stuffed, and her throat hoarse before she got home that night.

Pushing open the small wooden gate, Dulcie hurried up the garden path. Garden! A bunch of cracked flagstones led the way past an overgrown holly that, by virtue of its evergreen foliage, managed to snag her year-round. Whenever she read of a haunted castle or some mountainous keep, Dulcie pictured Professor Bullock's townhouse, the end of a long row of darkened brick that bordered on a shadowy alley. The urban address—not to mention the proximity of neighbors—didn't quite mesh with her Gothic fancy, but the gloomy aspect of the building fit the bill. Victorian brickwork, ornate but soiled, it positively glowered, overshadowing that poor front yard and the tiny, barren space out back. In any other century, it would have been haunted, Dulcie thought with a flash of interest. And if any of her favorite authors had written about this house, the holly would be reaching out to grab her—and closing up behind. But this old house just wasn't that interesting, and Dulcie snuck by without any pulls or runs, climbed the slate stairs, and rang the bell, only ten minutes late.

'DULCIE!' THE PROFESSOR'S EYES lit up as he opened the door, letting her into the front hallway. 'What a surprise!'

'We had an appointment,' said Dulcie, before catching her own tone—and his sarcasm. 'I'm sorry I'm late.'

'Of course, of course.' The professor headed back down the long, dark hall, leaving Dulcie to hang her own coat on the decrepit coat tree by the door. One of these days, its curved wood branches would collapse, dropping the odd assortment of sweaters and windbreakers that always seemed to be there on to the threadbare Oriental runner. For now, it only sagged a bit more, and Dulcie turned to follow her mentor into the back room that acted as his combination home office and library. Polly, the onetime grad student who now served as his part-time housekeeper, seemed to have contained the worst of the professor's habits to this office-slash-den.

Professor Bullock's office was an academic's hideaway, a throwback to an earlier era. Bookshelves ran up every wall, which between the dim lighting and the constant fog of tobacco seemed to be even taller than they probably were, reaching to an unseen—and doubtless smoke-stained—ceiling. A series of lamps, some precariously perched on piles of books, shed strategic shafts of light on the professor's stained blotter and one shabby reading chair, its armrests pockmarked with small burns. No computers had infiltrated this bookish retreat, nor any other sign of the last century, really. This was Bullock's refuge, his escape from modern times. Even the one window, which looked out on to the tiny, shadowy back garden, was dimmed with nicotine residue, the ivy that climbed up its protective grill further obscuring the outside world. And not even the prolific ashtrays—Dulcie counted six—seemed adequate to catch the stray leavings from decades of smoking. If the professor were truly some kind of hoary beast in disguise—and Dulcie, looking at his bushy white eyebrows and thick beard, secretly thought it likely—this was his lair, which, she admitted, was probably why she felt a frisson of fear at bearding him here.

'You don't mind, do you?' he'd said, pulling out his pipe before she could answer. Not that she would have. Her room-mate Suze might roll her eyes, but Dulcie knew how much of her fate depended on this man. Besides, the pipe was a good-faith gesture. Professor Bullock had been trying to quit cigarettes for as long as she'd been at the university. Smiling her assent, Dulcie lifted an opened journal from the wooden chair facing the desk and took a seat, waiting as her mentor got the tobacco started. He seemed to be savoring it, and she sat as patiently as she could while he smoked and stared at the grimy window.

'I was wondering if we could talk about my latest research?' Clearing her throat, Dulcie found the courage to speak up. For several months now, she'd been honing an idea—a new reading of a lesser known Gothic novel. *The Ravages of Umbria* only survived in two fragments, and most scholars dismissed its be-leaguered heroine and lurking ghosts as so much two-hundred-year-old trash. But Dulcie had fallen for the spunky Hermetria and, more importantly, had a theory about the resolution of the heroine's dilemma that no other scholar had yet suggested. According to Dulcie, the orphaned heroine hadn't been undone by a nasty ghoul or some fortune-hunting suitor, as would have been common for a book of its time. Instead, Dulcie believed, the heroine's supposedly faithful attendant Demetria had betrayed her—and the author had hidden the clues to this surprise resolu-tion in the attendant's overwrought speeches. The interpretation was totally Dulcie's—and something of a breakthrough—and she had spent the last few months compiling evidence from the text to support her idea. At one point, only a few months ago, Professor Bullock had been encouraging. Had even thought her thesis would be publishable. Recently, however, he had seemed to lose interest. 'Here,' she said. 'I've made a bunch of notes.'

Angling one of two desk lamps to see better, she pulled a bunch of papers out of her bag, determined to take the lead. To actually get some substantial feedback from the tenured scholar after weeks of dithering. Dulcie knew that her thesis was undoubtedly secondary in the professor's life to his own great work, but, well... 'Faint heart never fair doctorate won,' she murmured to herself, as she placed a heavy book next to the papers. 'There's a phrase here that I'm curious about,' she added in a more audible voice. 'I seem to recall reading it elsewhere, and it's kind of unusual.' She thumbed through the book. 'Here it is, "Cool as emeralds." It's really quite a striking image. Original, I think, but it made me wonder about precedent, and I was considering if I should do some biographical research. There's an interesting essay here, in the Gunning text—'

'Gunning? Bah. A hack. He's just a condenser, a collector, a...oh, hell, what do you call it?'

'An aggregator? A collator?' Dulcie jumped in before the professor could get more upset. 'Well, yes, he does collect previously published material, but—'

'Compiler. A damned anthologizer. Bah!' Bullock broke in before she could finish and began shuffling the papers on his desk. Dulcie fished her own pages out and placed them on top. They were virtually the same notes she'd dropped off the week before; she'd never heard back from him about them. But if he really wanted to see what progress she was making, she'd load him up with copies till his desk collapsed. 'Where's my damned pen?'

'Here, sir.' Dulcie automatically handed him her own: a refillable fountain pen. Her favorite.

Bullock grabbed it, gave it a cursory glance and tossed it down. 'That's not a real pen, and it certainly isn't mine. And why are you bothering with biography, anyway?'

It wasn't really a question, but she wanted to make her case. 'Well, so little is known about the author of *The Ravages of Umbria*,' she began, retrieving her pen. It was tricky, sometimes, filling in her adviser while they both pretended he had read her work, and his little fit of pique hadn't made her any more relaxed. 'After all, only some of the text remains, and we don't know if the author wrote anything else.' Dulcie's area of expertise, the Gothic novels of the eighteenth century, was peopled by an odd set of characters—impoverished noblewomen, mad monks, the occasional ghost—but none of the heroines she read about ever had to deal with the self-satisfied academic. 'And there's one theory, put forth in Chapter Five here—'

No use. Bullock was waving his pipe and had scooped up her papers with a loud grumble. 'Nonsense! Context is simply an excuse. Coward's way out.' He rumpled up the papers and leaned back in his chair, before tossing them back down again. 'It's all in the text—or it's nowhere.'

Dulcie sighed and sat back in her own chair. Bullock was on a roll. Famous for the book he'd written more than twenty years before, the white-haired professor started on about syntax and rhythm. Which was all well and good, but Dulcie had heard him give this lecture before. At least three times in this office, as well as once a semester when he kicked off 'The Great Novel,' the survey course almost every undergrad ended up taking. Plus, she knew that if she opened up the copy of his masterwork, *Unlocking the Great Books,* that sat prominently displayed, cover out, on the shelf behind his desk, she could read the same speech, word for word.

She knew she shouldn't complain. The course based on 'Great Books'—'Doorstoppers,' as some university wag had dubbed it—had largely paid for her graduate education; the class always needed section leaders. But she was working on her doctoral thesis now. She'd been hoping for something a little more in-depth.

'And so, young lady, the best advice I can give you is to scrap your research.' Bullock tapped his pipe to empty it, getting as much ash on the desk—and Dulcie's notes—as in the ashtray. 'And that hack Gunning. Forget the facts…' Dulcie could have finished the sentence with him: 'and open your ears.'

Did he even realize how repetitive he had become? As Dulcie took the proffered pages—unread, but well wrinkled—she examined the equally creased face of her mentor. He'd been brilliant once. She'd read his book as an undergrad. They all had. And when he'd singled her out for attention as a grad student, she'd been flattered beyond belief. He certainly looked the part, with the beard and the tweed, his hair just long enough to evoke his early days as a sexy semiotics crossover, back when the boundaries between linguistics and literature were still fluid. Rumor was that the aging institution was working on a great new idea. A new book that would break the field wide open again. Dulcie was no longer sure she believed in it—or in him. Just looking around his cluttered office provided ample evidence. The man was comfortable. Dug in. He had no reason to start anything new.

But Dulcie had work to do. She had settled on her thesis topic only that summer after uncovering what she believed was the hidden subtext in its flowery prose, and she was desperate to get her ideas on paper. Even without Bullock's 'status report' deadline, she wanted to get started before another scholar stumbled over what she considered her breakthrough.

But before she could air her own theories, Dulcie had to be able to base her thesis in good, solid scholarship. She'd been making notes for months now, jotting down the linguistic discrepancies between the heroine and her sidekick. She'd even gone back to a bunch of the book's contemporaries, trying to find out what the author might have been reading and what might have influenced her. This was important, even if it wasn't progress of the sort that Professor Bullock wanted. No matter what her mentor said, she needed to find out more about the author of *The Ravages* if she was going to write her own work with any kind of authority.

Maybe the key was, like those other clues, in the text? That emerald reference seemed to echo in her mind. Perhaps there were other phrases like that one, other images that would lead a careful reader back to the truth. She'd been so focused on the new kitten lately; maybe she'd missed something. And so, without waiting for the professor or his aging waif of an assistant to show her out, she shoved her papers back into the bag, along with the three books she'd been hoping to discuss and the laptop with all her notes. Hefting it all on to her shoulder, she let herself out the heavy front door. Had Hermetria felt like this, when she left the castle keep up on that Umbrian mountain? Had she breathed the free air with relief, before descending the romantically rocky equivalent of the professor's slate stoop?

She must have, Dulcie thought. Because Hermetria was really just like her. A woman against the odds, destined to triumph. And with that happy thought, she nearly skipped down the tall, dirty stairs, and right into the corpse that lay across the path.

TWO

The deceased was Cameron Dessay, one-time Anglo-French wunderkind of Comparative Lit and relative newcomer to the English Department. Known simply as 'De-sigh' among a sizable proportion of the female student body, Cameron had been not only a brilliant researcher, but charming—in multiple languages. However, the pale, fine-featured face that had inspired so many hopeless aspirations now lay unnaturally still, the glossy black locks matted with blood that had flowed from a small but distinct wound in the bare, white throat.

Unable to speak as she was ushered back into the house, Dulcie slipped from shock into a dank, wet pool of guilt. She had not been one of Cameron's admirers. Besides her basic distrust of Cameron's playboy reputation, there was the class issue. Cameron had come into the department last year, but everyone knew his heart was in English-French comparative literature, just as everyone knew that Comp Lit looked down on the English Department as simplistic. Archaic. And possibly stupid. The straight English Lit types had rallied back, pooh-poohing the Comp Lit types as dilettantes, with Cameron as their poster boy. A lightweight who drove around in a fancy car and dressed better than any grad student had a right to. A hedonist. A cold, dead… No, no matter what she had thought of her dashing colleague, this was not how she wanted to remember him. But when she closed her eyes to block out the image, it only grew stronger in her mind. The cut looked so small and strange, so wrong in that smooth white skin. His green eyes frozen, like glass.

'Miss? Are you okay?' The uniform who had walked her back into Professor Bullock's house looked worried. Dulcie nodded and tried to smile. 'It's only that you're awfully pale.'

'I always am.' Dulcie tried to reassure the young cop. Still, she took his advice and put her head down between her knees. Spots appeared—the same shape as that wound—and she blinked them away, staring at the book bag that she'd dropped as he led her to a seat. Was that…? Yes, she reached beneath the bag's closing flap and pulled out a single white whisker. The kitten must have gotten into the bag overnight. Dulcie twirled the stiff strand as her breathing became easier. During their few months together, that kitten had already managed to get into everything, she thought, smiling to herself. The whisker—or thoughts of the inquisitive young cat—had banished the spots, but Dulcie kept playing with the long white hair, her head down over the bag. That young cop had his pad out. He was going to start asking questions, and right now she was happy just to breathe.

'Excuse me.' She heard the uniform stand up and step away. Good. There wasn't much she could tell him, anyway. Cameron had just been…there. She closed her eyes. 'Ma'am?'

Dulcie looked up, but the cop wasn't talking to her. Out in the hallway, some murmuring was met by a shriek and a thud. Conquering her own queasiness, Dulcie ran to look.

'No! Professor!' Three uniformed cops gathered around a slumped form, surrounded by books. Of course Polly Heinhold, perpetual grad student and Bullock's part-time housekeeper, would be a fainter. Skin so pale she was almost translucent, colorless eyes always rimmed in red, Polly looked like one of the ghostly spirits from Dulcie's novels. Dulcie might be fair-skinned, more prone to freckle than to tan, but Polly was spectral, with white-blonde hair that hung as lank as seaweed. The older woman served as a cautionary tale, too. Rumor had it that Polly had been in the graduate program for at least seven years, which meant that any academic status she'd once had was now iffy, if it existed at all. Instead, somewhere along the line, all those endless meetings had morphed into her doing errands—and then laundry. Departmental rumor had it that she rented a tiny garret over in Davis Square, one of the few neighborhoods grad students could still afford alone. But for all intents and purposes, her life was here, in Professor Bullock's house, and had been for the greater part of a decade. And while nobody dared to ask, there had been no hint of a thesis in that life—or in the works—for many of those years. *There but for the grace of God go I,* thought Dulcie, and went to help the poor woman.

'Polly? Are you okay?' Pushing her way between the uniforms, Dulcie reached the seated woman and helped her up. 'Let's go sit someplace more comfortable, shall we?' Although the older student—if student she still was—stood a good three inches taller than Dulcie, she felt light as a feather. Or maybe, Dulcie thought, feeling the pale woman's arm, a bat's wing. 'When did you last eat, Polly?'

'The book…' A limp hand reached out for a volume that lay face up, its pages slowly turning.

'We can pick those up later.' Dulcie closed the offending volume and helped the other woman over to the sitting room.

'The professor! The professor!' Sinking down into a motheaten settee, Polly looked around frantically.

'He's fine, Polly. He's in the back.' Actually, Dulcie didn't know where the police had taken the professor. He'd shown up not when she first screamed, but after she had scrambled back up the steps, ringing the bell and pounding on the tall wooden doors furiously; then he'd gone to call 911. Still, since the cop had seated her in the front room, his office seemed like a good bet.

'Miss, do you mind?' Dulcie looked down to a hand on her upper arm. Her cop—the young one—was pulling at her gently. 'If you're up for some questions?' She looked back at Polly, who seemed able to sit and willing to stop shrieking. An older cop stood waiting for her.

'Sure.' Dulcie let herself be led into the kitchen, which someone—undoubtedly Polly—had kept reasonably clean. 'May I have some water?'

The officer jumped to fill a glass for her, and then refill it. Dulcie hadn't realized how thirsty she was. But the drink, and the distraction of Polly, had her feeling a bit more like herself. It didn't help the young cop, though.

'All I can tell you is it—he—wasn't there when I came in.' She'd said this a dozen times already. 'And the professor was alone, I think. I mean, he let me in and I didn't hear anyone else in the house. Yes, we were in his office.' She paused for a moment to consider the impact of her words. 'The office is in the back, under the stairs. So I guess I would have heard if someone had come down them. We talked for about an hour, and then, well, then I found him.'

The memory took away her newfound calm. Cameron hadn't been her favorite person by far. But to see him so still, so cold… Dulcie bent forward again.

'Miss, are you all right?'

The world was getting smaller and Dulcie closed her eyes. It didn't help, and the dizziness made her gasp. But just then she felt a brush against her ankles. A soft and comforting touch, like a cat leaning in to be stroked. Automatically, Dulcie opened her eyes, but saw only her own feet and the big black shoes of the cop. She sat up.

'Did you see a cat in here?'

He looked at her with suspicion. 'Miss?'

'I could've sworn I felt a cat go by. You didn't see anything?'

He shook his head, and called out, keeping his eyes on her all the while. 'Sylvio? Sylvio? Can you come here a minute? I think this young lady needs a ride home.'

It wasn't until he had walked her up to her door, rang the bell, and handed her over to Suze's care that Dulcie realized she didn't have her own key. She'd left her bag at the professor's house.

THREE

'AND PROFESSOR BULLOCK doesn't have a cat, right?'

Dulcie was lying on the sofa, the kitten on her stomach, as Suze grilled her. Dulcie would have objected, except that Suze had fussed so when Dulcie came in, escorted by a cop who double-parked his cruiser in front of their apartment. Not usually the maternal type, Suze had insisted that Dulcie lie down and now the two of them were eating ice cream out of soup bowls; Dulcie to get her blood sugar back up, Suze in solidarity. So even though her roommate was acting more like the third-year law student she was this fall, rather than the friend she'd been for years longer, Dulcie took it. With a large spoonful of rocky road.

'I'm sure, Suze,' Dulcie said, once she had swallowed. Scooping up a little bit of the melting ice cream, she held out her spoon. The kitten licked at it and took off, as if spooked by the cold sweetness. Dulcie watched the little cat leap for the coffee table and not quite make it, hanging on for a moment of startled silence before falling and bounding back out of the room. Usually, the kitten's antics amused her, but today the kitten's clumsiness only served to accentuate the difference between its youth and an adult cat's dignity. When she looked up, she saw how Suze was watching her, not the kitten. Her normally fastidious roommate didn't even comment when Dulcie then used the utensil to dip into her friend's favorite, mint chocolate chip. Swallowing a lump in her throat that the ice cream couldn't explain, Dulcie ventured a question: 'Do you think it could've been Mr Grey?'

Suze took a conveniently large mouthful of the ice cream and used the opportunity to look over at her friend. Mr Grey had been Dulcie's beloved pet, an intelligent long-haired stray who had adopted her as an undergrad, and who had come to live with the two friends until his death the previous spring. Although Suze had been fond of the handsome feline, Dulcie had been his person—and it was Dulcie who believed that the spirit of the great grey cat still talked to her, showing up at moments of crisis to give comfort and suitably feline cryptic advice.

Dulcie thought back on that moment, the passing brush of fur that had calmed her when panic had started to overwhelm. The whisker she had found had a logical explanation, but that moment of contact had been just as real. She looked up at her roommate. 'I know you're skeptical, but don't you think it makes sense? I was in trouble, so maybe he appeared again.' She pictured Mr Grey, the slanted black-lined eyes and pointy face, more Siamese than Persian. How easily she could imagine him looking at her, elegant white whiskers perked up in a feline smile. 'He knew I needed him. And you're going to get a cold headache if you keep taking spoonfuls that big.'

'I think you had an awful day.' As a law student, prevaricating came naturally to Suze. 'You found one of your colleagues dead—murdered—and then you had to be grilled by the police, with nobody there to support you but your thesis adviser. Who is, if you don't mind me saying so, practically useless.' Dulcie nodded, but didn't interrupt. Suze continued. 'All of that has to have been a horrible shock, so I believe that you think you felt a cat.'

'But you don't believe it was Mr Grey.' Dulcie looked down. The tiny kitten had reappeared and was trying to climb up her legs, using her claws to rappel up Dulcie's jeans. She reached down to hoist the kitten to her lap. The little animal seemed to be trying to entertain, but as adorable as the black and white creature was, it—she, Dulcie corrected herself—still couldn't replace Mr Grey. That dignified feline had been more than a pet. He'd been her constant companion, able to read her mood if not her mind, through years of academic and personal struggle. In some ways, his absence had only made him a more tangible presence in Dulcie's life. No matter what Suze believed, Dulcie was convinced he came to her, sometimes as a presence, sometimes just as a voice, when she needed his wise feline company. Sometimes, Dulcie suspected, the kitten could talk, too. If only she wanted to...

Not that Suze was having any of it. 'I know you loved Mr Grey, Dulce. He was a great cat.' She paused, and Dulcie waited for the inevitable. When it came, her roommate at least had the grace to soften her voice. 'You know, Dulcie, if you could let go of him, just a little, you might find yourself falling for that little girl on your lap.' She took another bite of ice cream, smaller this time. 'You might even give her a name.'

FOUR

As much as she wanted to stay in bed the next morning, Dulcie dragged herself out. She'd slept badly, her dreams bringing her close enough to see glowing cat's eyes—Mr Grey's eyes—and to hear two words—the key—but nothing more. She'd woken herself up trying to talk, to ask what that meant. Desperate to reach out to her one-time pet. But she'd been as mute as the kitten who had taken Mr Grey's place, and he'd disappeared, those glowing gold-green eyes fading into the dark. She longed to recapture the dream, although she suspected that its message had more to do with her research frustrations than anything personal. But the departmental secretary had stressed that attendance at the emergency meeting was mandatory, using an excessive number of exclamation points for emphasis. Besides, Dulcie needed to get her bag back.

'Better to be there than be talked about. Right, kitten?' The kitten, who was taking an early morning bath, did not look up.

As she made her way into the Square, Dulcie juggled her travel mug and dug her cell out of her pocket. At least that hadn't been left behind! But the one voicemail waiting was from Chris, not Professor Bullock. Her boyfriend had called pre-dawn, probably as soon as he'd gotten her message. She'd have preferred to have him run to her rescue. But like most of his colleagues in applied mathematics, her studious beau had a tendency toward the nocturnal, an inclination that the department preyed on. For the past few weeks—since midterms, really—he'd been up most nights in the computer lab. Like her, he was just scraping by and serving as the on-duty expert during those overnights paid pretty well. Besides, he'd explained only a week before as he left after another late dinner, this was the lab's down time, when he could get his own work done fastest. But Dulcie suspected that her lanky sweetheart was also just a softie for the undergrads who gathered there, bleary-eyed and frantic, desperate for his help.

'Dulcie! How are you?' The concern in his voice warmed her almost as much as the dark roast. 'I just got your message and it's…damn, it's nearly five. I'm so sorry.' Another voice interrupted and she heard Chris's muttered response. 'Look, I'll try you again at a better hour. Or call me!'

'Hey, Chris,' she said as her own call went straight to voicemail. 'Thanks for your call. I'm off to the big departmental meeting. I swear, if they say anything about grief counseling, I'll throw something.'

Dulcie hung up. That bit of bravado helped and she turned down Dana Street with a little more lift in her step. Despite the economy, this academic neighborhood, right outside the Square, had been spruced up in the past year, its old clapboards boasting new paint and fancy trim. Well, if the neighborhood could put on its bravest face, so could she, Dulcie told herself. Still, having an actual boyfriend—someone who was physically present—would have been better. Some days, she felt like the heroine in *The Ravages of Umbria*. Hermetria had been haunted by a friendly ghost. Did that keep her warm at night? As Dulcie climbed the stairs to the refurbished colonial that served as the English Department's headquarters, the lack of sleep and accompanying self-pity led her to one strong answer: No.

The ancient but quite reliable departmental coffee maker was hard at work as Dulcie entered, and she refilled her mug before joining her peers in the back conference room. A dozen students, all in varying states of wakefulness, sat around a long, oval table. No Professor Bullock. On the near side, a bleached blonde with two nose piercings looked up and waved.

'Hey, Trista.' Dulcie sidled over to the chair her friend had held for her. 'Bother, I was hoping Bullock would be here.'

'Really?' Trista asked with surprise, but then leaned toward her friend. 'How are you?' Dulcie was about to respond when she realized that all eyes were on her. Before Trista could press her, though, Martin Thorpe, the acting chair, came in. More stooped than usual, Thorpe cleared his throat, then looked down at the bundle of papers in his hands as if they had shown up of their own free will. Dulcie had never studied with the balding scholar—his specialty, Renaissance English poetry, made her grind her teeth—but today she felt sorry for him. Tenure and staffing were hard enough without throwing murder into the mix.

'Good morning.' Thorpe looked up from the papers. Nobody corrected him, and he continued. 'Thank you for coming in, all of you. Especially you Americans.' He looked around and nodded at a few of the gathered students. Of course, Dulcie realized, picking out her colleagues. 'Origins of Colonial Style: The Puritan Sermon' met Tuesdays at ten.

'I thought, ah, we should have this meeting because of, ah, recent events.' Thorpe's eyes dropped to his papers again, his throat working like he'd been asked to swallow a Norton's anthology. Trista raised her eyebrows at Dulcie, and Dulcie kicked her friend under the table.

'Some of you have probably heard of the unfortunate demise of Cameron Dessay yesterday.' He glanced around the table. So did Dulcie, and noticed how many of her colleagues quickly looked away. Despite his easy manner, Cameron hadn't had many close friends in the department. 'We are all saddened by the, ah, loss of such a promising young scholar.'

Trista kicked Dulcie back.

'And, of course, the department will be organizing some kind of memorial, a commemorative service of some sort, to be announced later. We are also—' here, Thorpe looked around with a little more focus, perhaps expecting help from the assembled scholars '—coordinating with Mr Dessay's family in terms of the actual funeral and possibly a memorial scholarship to be created. We will be posting information as all of this comes together, and either I or Nancy will be emailing you all.' Nancy, the plump and competent departmental secretary, nodded.

'The timing of all of this is, of course, very unfortunate.' Even Thorpe seemed a bit embarrassed by that, but his attempts to recover were worse. 'I mean, death in one so young is always unfortunate. But death this late in the semester—'

Someone coughed, and the beleaguered chairman gave up. 'What I mean is, Cameron had a full course load. And I need to redistribute it among you.' A low groan rose from the assembled students. Thorpe stood straighter, now that he had a purpose, and looked around. 'Shall we begin?'

Twenty minutes later, Dulcie thought she'd gotten lucky. Either because of the obscure nature of her specialty or its growing unpopularity among undergrads, she'd avoided any extra tutorials. She'd only been given one assignment—a senior named Raleigh Hall. 'Sounds like a prep school,' Dulcie had muttered to Trista. Raleigh was working on her undergraduate honors thesis, and, unless she complained and found another scholar to take her on mid-year, Dulcie would step in as her adviser.

'Do you think he was light on me because, you know?' Dulcie leaned over to Trista as the group broke up. She didn't have to explain more: In the mysterious ways of social groups, the news that Dulcie had found the body seemed to have spread.

Her friend shrugged. 'Who knows? Some of these undergrads can be real handfuls, though.' Trista paused, then smiled. 'Hey, maybe Bullock will drop that ridiculous progress report thing now. I mean, threatening to jam you up with the grant committee was just unconscionable. He better than anyone else should know you've got to do a ton of research before you start writing, right?'

She looked over at her friend for confirmation and Dulcie nodded, resigned. Trista was deep into her own thesis, 'Characterization through Metaphor in Late Victorian Fiction,' and ever since Dulcie had told her about Bullock's new requirement, she had pronounced the whole idea ridiculous. ('We're finishing our post-grad education, and he wants us to check in every ten pages?') 'It's just not fair,' she protested now. 'Not that any of this is.' She'd groaned softly when Thorpe had handed her two more sections for the Dickens survey course, but accepted it with outward grace. At least, as she'd put it, nobody was 'checking up on her.' Now the two joined the small crowd milling by the coffee machine, waiting for the next pot to brew. Dulcie snagged the last cinnamon donut hole—Nancy must have sent a work-study student out for more—and sagged against the wall.

'Wait here.' Trista grabbed her friend's travel mug and moved in for the fresh brew.

'You okay?' Her place was taken by Lloyd, Dulcie's office mate. Lloyd the Long-Suffering, as Trista had dubbed the chubby little man, was also an eighteenth-century specialist. Considering his specialty was criticism and satire, he might have been more chipper. But he also served as Professor Bullock's research assistant, which explained the name.

'Yeah.' Dulcie was noncommittal. She didn't know how much any of her colleagues knew.

'Must have been rough.' Of course, as Bullock's boy, Lloyd would have heard everything.

Dulcie looked over at Lloyd. They'd been sharing an office since the beginning of the year. With two desks in one tiny space, they took turns seeing students. Still, they'd both been in their shared cell long enough to partake in some confidences, too. Long enough for Dulcie to realize that being closer to the tenured professor was not necessarily a good thing.

'It was horrible,' Dulcie said, her voice low, and immediately felt better. Confession was good for the soul. 'I just don't want everyone asking questions.'

Lloyd looked around. Three of their colleagues were discussing the proper ratio of grounds to water for yet another pot of coffee. 'I don't know if there'll be any questions. Cameron wasn't what you'd call one of the guys.' He turned back to her, and Dulcie was struck by how tired he looked. Granted, Lloyd was always pale; he was nearly as fair-skinned as she was. But today he looked positively unhealthy, the rings sinking deep and dark around his eyes, his plump cheeks sagging. 'They're probably all wondering if Bullock did it.'

'Really?' She thought of his temperamental outbursts, when he'd thrown down her pen, and toyed with the idea. The thought was perversely cheering, and not just because the professor had become such a lax adviser. 'Anything I should know?'

Lloyd shrugged his rounded shoulders. 'The usual gossip.'

Dulcie hesitated. She knew the rumors. Given how close the professor kept Lloyd, many in the department assumed their relationship was more than simply professor and assistant. Knowing Lloyd, she didn't believe that love was a factor, but she'd never dared ask. 'But he couldn't have,' she said finally, the truth of her words sinking in. 'I mean, think about it. He was meeting with me. I'm Bullock's alibi.'

Trista must have gotten through to the coffeemaker, because she pushed a full mug into Dulcie's hands. 'You're Bullock's alibi?' She was also chewing on a donut hole. Maybe Nancy had a secret stash. 'I guess that's why the cops are questioning everybody.'

'Huh?' Lloyd looked up, startled.

'Yeah, I just heard from Joel and Tina. Nobody's really talking, but from what they gathered, Cameron wasn't robbed or molested or anything. He still had that fancy watch on, too. So they're thinking it wasn't a random mugging.'

Lloyd looked at Trista, and then they both turned to Dulcie. The impact of Trista's discovery countered all the good the hot coffee had done her, and she slumped further against the wall. 'So Cameron knew his killer,' she said, her voice flat. 'And maybe we do, too.'

FIVE

'WELL, WHAT ABOUT that Polly woman? Couldn't she have been involved?'

Dulcie didn't like to be needy, but after the meeting she'd called Chris back. She'd caught him just waking up, and as soon as he heard the strain in her voice, he suggested they meet for a late breakfast at the Greenhouse.

The Greenhouse was as close as Harvard Square came to a diner, its low prices and breakfast all day somehow surviving even as other student-oriented outlets gave way to pricey boutiques. And usually Dulcie enjoyed its hearty, if greasy fare. Today, however, food hadn't had much appeal, so she'd been toying with a muffin as Chris talked. Forcing herself to swallow a dry-as-dust mouthful, she shook her head. 'Polly was out. Doing errands, I think. She'd have let me in if she'd been around.' In her mind, she could still hear the washed-out blonde's strangled scream. 'She saw Cameron, too.'

'Yeah, but who's to say that she didn't stage that?' Chris gestured with a fork full of pancakes. 'That she didn't kill him and then get lost for a while?'

'Not likely.' Dulcie thought of the wan assistant and tried to explain. 'You might as well sic a scared rabbit on someone.'

Chris continued shoveling syrup-soaked pancake into his mouth. On most days, Dulcie was frankly envious of his capacity. If anything, her tall boyfriend was too skinny, while Dulcie was, well, curvaceous. But today neither of them was thinking much about food. Even as he ate, he kept his dark eyes on her, pushing the question.

'Besides, I'm sure she has an alibi.' Dulcie almost choked on the word and took a sip of her coffee while she thought. 'She only came in after—you know. Poor girl.'

Chris paused for breath, fork in air. 'Dulce, you were the one who found him. A certain amount of shock, of post-traumatic reaction, would be normal.'

'I know. Believe me, I know.' The moment came back to her—the intense stillness of the scene. The calm as her own mind began to shut down at the sight. The white face, the blood. And just as the dizziness threatened to overwhelm her, she recalled once more that brief touch of fur. Her late cat had been there with her, and she had felt safe because of him. Despite the horror of the day, that one touch had stayed with her. Polly didn't seem to have anything in her life like Mr Grey. Nothing that gave her such comfort. She thought about explaining this. Suze hadn't believed her about the spectral pet, and she'd been hesitant to tell Chris about the latest visitation from Mr Grey. They hadn't been together that long. 'But there was something else.'

They both paused as a waitress refilled their mugs. 'Yes?' Chris looked over, waiting. He'd been in therapy ever since his mother had been diagnosed with cancer, and some of the habits had worn off. At least the twice-weekly sessions had made him a good listener.

Still, Dulcie hesitated, recalling the day before. What had really happened, anyway? All she could say with certainty was, as she had been sitting there, trying to answer the policeman's questions, the other woman had come in and collapsed with more than the expected thump.

'Polly had just arrived with a load of books for Professor Bullock.' As she thought back, Dulcie could see the older woman, collapsed. 'Nice ones, for his private library, probably. And she dropped them.' She saw the image of leatherbound spines piled haphazardly on the floor, of pages splayed open. She was the professor's servant in all but name, and for a moment Dulcie glimpsed her own future. But no, she had Mr Grey. That, ten years' grace, and the doctoral thesis that Dulcie was determined to finish before her grants ran out. She made a mental note to call Professor Bullock again. The Gunning anthology was a library book. And the heavy volumes that Polly had been carrying?

'Bullock cares quite a lot about his private library. I know it's not her fault, but I bet on top of everything else, there's going to be hell to pay for dropping all those books.'

SIX

CHRIS HAD LAUGHED, shaking his head as Dulcie explained how persnickety her thesis adviser could be about his collection, much of which consisted of rare first editions. And Dulcie had been grateful. Chris cared about her, she knew that, and if he sometimes threw a psychotherapy phrase at her, it was just because he cared. But right now she needed some distraction from the reality of the murder. She needed to get back to work. He'd walked her over to Widener after their shared meal. They'd been on the wide granite steps, making plans for the evening, when Dulcie's cell had rung.

'Nancy?' The departmental secretary's voice brought it all back for a moment. 'Is everything okay? Has something else—?'

'No, no. I'm sorry, Dulcie. Everything's fine.' The motherly secretary was quick to jump in. 'It's just that I've received a call from Raleigh Hall. Cameron's student? She'd heard the news and wanted to find out what was happening. I wanted her to have a sense of continuity, and so I told her that you'd be calling her soon. Would you, dear? She sounds a little frantic.'

'Sure.' The flash of fear vanished, but it had chased away the warm feeling from the Greenhouse for good. 'I'll call her now.'

'Trouble?' Chris was watching her closely.

'A new student. Undergrad. We're splitting up Cameron's workload and I got her.' She forced a smile on her face. 'It'll be fine. And you should get back to the lab.'

'I can hang, if you need me.' Chris wasn't fooled, and Dulcie felt her smile becoming genuine.

'Thanks, sweetie. Really, I'm fine. Taking on a new student is a drag, but it's got to be done. I'm just going to call her and see if I can flush out Bullock, get my bag back. And then I'm going to spend the afternoon in the stacks, where no computer dude dares follow.'

Chris's thin face split into a real grin. 'Don't dare me, Dulcie Schwartz! But this time, I'll let you go.' He leaned in for a kiss and Dulcie watched him lope off toward the Science Center, waiting until he'd slipped past the white-steepled church before punching in the numbers of her new charge.

'Hello, Raleigh?' The automated voicemail gave no sign if the recipient was male or female. 'This is Dulcie Schwartz calling. I'm going to be your adviser, at least for now…' Dulcie quickly gave her own phone number and her office info, and hung up, grateful for voicemail. After yesterday, she really needed a day in the stacks. But just as she pushed open the big glass doors, the sound of an old-fashioned phone rang out.

'Miss?' The guard gave Dulcie a pointed look, and she nodded. Kicking herself for not turning the phone off, she turned back to the door, dug the offending implement back out of her pocket and, taking a deep breath, answered. If she was going to have to deal with a grief-stricken student, she may as well get it over with.

But the voice that greeted her was both more distraught and more familiar than expected. 'Dulcie, thank the Goddess I've reached you.' Dulcie sank down on the top step and looked out over the Yard. This could be a while.

'Hi, Lucy. What's up?' Lucy—Dulcie rarely called her mother anything else—was prone to premonitions, dreams, and other psychic disturbances. Despite the rarity of these various portents having any basis in real life, Lucy never failed to get worked up about them.

'Where are you? You're not home, are you, Dulcinea?'

Living in the commune, as Dulcie still thought of the Oregon arts colony where her mother had settled, Lucy had little concept of cell phones. Or of the demands on her daughter's time. 'No, Mom. It's three hours later here, and you didn't call me at home. I'm in Harvard Yard.' She looked out over the spread of lawn and the intersecting paths that guided students and tourists alike under the now-bare trees. 'I'm on the steps of Widener, if you must know. I was about to do some work.'

Guilt didn't have any effect on Lucy. 'That's a library, right? I knew it. I've been having this dream. More like a vision, really…'

Dulcie rolled her eyes. Recently, Lucy's premonitions had focused on Dulcie's chosen field. She didn't know if her mother resented the research that kept her in Cambridge, away from their carbon-neutral community, in some delayed form of empty-nest syndrome, or if there was something else at play. Sometimes, she admitted to herself, Lucy was even right. But then, stopped clocks were right twice a day, too.

Lucy continued talking. 'So, in the dream, it's something about the books—or, rather, one specific book. You're writing about one particular book, aren't you, dear?'

'Yes, Lucy,' Dulcie confirmed, hearing the resignation in her own voice. With any prompting Dulcie would have gone on about *The Ravages of Umbria.* She'd originally thought that as a single mother (Dulcie's dad had taken off before she turned five) Lucy would love a story about a beleaguered heroine who triumphs. Particularly one who communes with various spirits. But Lucy had heard it all before, and obviously failed to retain it, so Dulcie just let her go on.

'And it's an old book, too?'

'Yes, Lucy.' Dulcie couldn't resist. 'Most scholars think it was probably written around 1790 and published in London, probably in serial chapbooks—'

'Yes, yes.' Lucy was already interrupting her. 'That must be it. Because the book in the dream is very old, dear. And it's in very bad shape.'

Dulcie waited. She wasn't going to explain that the main sixty-page fragment of *The Ravages* really had more going for it than most modern novels.

'Yes, it's in very bad shape.' Lucy was obviously consulting notes, and if Dulcie's memory served, her mother's midnight handwriting was even worse than her scrawled daytime penmanship. 'And the disrepair is what's fooled everybody. Because, you see, Dulcie—oh, I'm sorry to be the one to tell you, dear!—there's something wrong with the book. I believe it's fake. And, well, there's something else—something about poking about being wrong or even dangerous...'

'Mom!' That did it. 'You're talking about research, about my life! Look, I know you believe in your dreams. But I'm a scholar, and it's my research that tells me they're real. I mean, I've read about them. Looked up their provenance, their history, in order to verify they are what they say they are, and—' Dulcie was well launched into a spirited defense when a tone broke in. 'Look, Lucy,' she recovered herself. 'Thank you for your concern. I know you love me and you mean well. But, please, leave my discipline to me, okay? I've got another call. I've got to go.'

Without giving her mother a chance to respond, Dulcie clicked through to the other call. 'Yes?' She heard the snappish tone in her own voice and hoped it wasn't Chris or Suze or, Goddess forbid, Professor Bullock.

'Dulcie? Dulcie Schwartz?' The female voice sounded young and a little uncertain.

'Oh, this must be Raleigh! I'm so glad you called back.'

'No, I'm sorry. This is Ms Schwartz, right? This is Detective Carioli, with the Cambridge Police Department. We'd like to ask you to come into the precinct office in Central Square. We have a few questions.'

SEVEN

BY THE TIME DULCIE finally got into the stacks, she felt like hiding. The call from the police had been the final straw, driving home the horror of the last twenty-four hours, and although she had agreed to come in the following morning, she was tempted to break her word. If only she could burrow into Widener like some scholarly squirrel, dig deep into the subterranean levels of the library and stay safely pocketed away until spring.

But as she rode the elevator down to Level A, she realized such a plan—tempting as it was—was flawed. Not only did library staff come around at closing, making sure that neither the frantic nor the merely absentminded got locked in. Dulcie had responsibilities. Would Suze remember to feed the kitten? Would Chris?

With a sigh that was matched by the subdued hum of the library's ventilation system, Dulcie stepped out of the elevator and into her world. Here, amid the approximately 3.2 million books, manuscripts, letters, and other carriers of the written world, Dulcie was at home. It was ironic, she thought, as she walked by a cluster of study carrels and nodded to a fellow scholar. Lucy had raised her as a child of nature, boring into her only child the necessity of appreciating the old-growth forest that surrounded their Pacific Northwest commune. But even though her mother had rejected almost all the teachings of her own East Coast upbringing, somehow she had instilled in her daughter a love of literature. Although most of the family's books were housed in the communal kitchen-slash-living space, Dulcie had rarely been without one, and some of her fondest memories were of long afternoons spent reading on a mossy hillock, the small, constant noises of woodland creatures going about their lives all around her. She loved the woods, all right, but as a place to get away from it all—and read.

Just then another student scurried by, nodding briefly on his silent way up toward seventeenth-century criticism. Well, maybe this particular little ecosystem wasn't that different, she realized, as she made her own way to Professor Bullock's office. Despite a hand-lettered card posting office hours that included, yes, Tuesdays, the door was locked, its pebbled glass window dark. Of course, Dulcie could have kicked herself. She'd meant to call him before coming in. But since she was here… Five more minutes through the subterranean haven and she was turning into her favorite aisle.

'Hello, old friends!' Speaking softly to the rows of gold-embossed spines, Dulcie felt her shoulders relax and her breathing grow more regular. 'And how are you today?' Leaning forward, she inhaled the scent of old leather. The library's climate control kept decay at a minimum, and any volumes showing signs of the dreaded red rot, which turned leather to dust, were quickly whisked off to the conservators. Still, something of age lingered here, as sound and true as those long-ago stately redwoods.

Or were they? Dulcie found herself reaching for a familiar volume when she stopped, hand barely resting on the dark blue spine. The book she'd been about to remove was only about a century old, a compendium of critical essays about the novels of the century before. The books Dulcie had at home were all modern reprints. In the past few months, Dulcie had been able to read one of the few remaining copies of *The Ravages of Umbria.* Harvard, of course, had managed to beg, borrow, or steal both segments and now had them secreted away in one of the locked areas where only authorized scholars could go. But by the time Dulcie had gotten in to see those pages, their eighteenth-century lettering rendering the words nearly incomprehensible to a modern reader, she'd already been a believer, a convert to the cause.

Maybe it was because of her own past, but the idea of a verifiable history—a provenence—had a special allure for Dulcie. In so many ways, Lucy had tried to re-create a history for herself and her daughter, particularly once Dulcie's father had left their Oregon community for an Indian ashram. Desperate for some kind of roots, Lucy had cobbled together a mishmosh of mythology and traditions, abandoning her Philadelphia mainline origins to pick and choose among Native American religions. Dulcie understood her mother's impulse—Trickster's rituals were a lot more appealing than debutante balls, and her mother really did practice an ecofriendly lifestyle. But the patchwork of beliefs, none of which really fit a fair-skinned and freckled brunette, had left Dulcie feeling somewhat disconnected. Fate was the trickster in her life; by choice, she'd have opted for a straight narrative.

Still, thinking of her mother made Dulcie smile. Lucy tried so hard. And at times her visions reflected a sounder basic intuition than Lucy herself would ever credit. She'd liked Suze right away, and she'd never questioned Dulcie's attachment to Mr Grey—not even when that attachment grew to include the grey cat's ghost. Which led Dulcie to wonder: what if Lucy's dream about her book had some validity?

No, she shook the thought loose and pulled the book from its shelf. Only this time, instead of flipping directly to the one essay she'd been working on—'Italian Meters Transposed into Late 18th Century English Popular Fiction'—Dulcie turned to the front matter. The volume she held had been published first in 1893, by a house in London that was now long gone. The essay she had been meaning to look up was a few years older, and had originally run in a scholarly journal based in Edinburgh, a university town that made Cambridge, Massachusetts, look like a young upstart. This had to be credible, didn't it?

It was no use. All Dulcie could see were the gaps in the book's history. A publisher who no longer existed. A scholarly article written by a source long dead, and based in another city, to boot. Centuries of discussion of the minutiae of a work, by academics who had inherited the idea of the work's authenticity along with their musty books and black robes.

But there was a way out. When Dulcie had expressed her interest in the unknown author of *The Ravages*, it hadn't been because she doubted that such an author existed. Instead, she'd been curious about the mind behind such a lively adventure. So many of the Gothic novels had been predictable. An embattled heroine. An evil prince or monk or a scheming relative. A ghost or two… Just like today's popular fiction, the novels that got passed from hand to hand in the late 1700s had a standard repertoire of thrills and chills, usually leading to a happy ending. But what had grabbed Dulcie about *The Ravages* was the key relationship in the book and how it was revealed. If, as her thesis was arguing, the real nature of the noble Hermetria and her backstabbing buddy Demetria was hinted at throughout in the way the two spoke, then the author had been both smart and more savvy than many of her peers. Dulcie wanted to know that author and, in return, give her a name. But if Lucy's dream had any basis in fact, that search took on a greater import. People faked books all the time. Pastiches could be simple homages to older styles. They could be reworkings, postmodern takes on classic themes. Or they could be scholarly fraud. Dulcie swallowed, hard. If *The Ravages* wasn't as old as everyone believed—wasn't in fact a real Gothic novel—it wouldn't matter why it had been created. That fact alone would discredit it as a serious object of study. Would mean the loss of everything Dulcie had done thus far. Three years of reading and research, three months already of focused note taking…

Unless, a nasty thought rose up like a spark, there was a hoax of some sort—and Dulcie uncovered it and made her literary reputation by revealing the awful truth. She'd be a heroine in a way, the defender of the canon… No, she stamped the thought down. *The Ravages* was so good, so real. Was it too real? Too perfect? The thought flared up again, and Dulcie saw herself delivering the death blow via her groundbreaking thesis. Dulcie the Debunker. It would be difficult for a graduate student to have that kind of impact. It might take years more work. But could it be done? No, she shook her head sadly. Maybe it could, but not by her. She wasn't Bullock. She wasn't anybody. And besides, Dulcie adored *The Ravages*. To destroy its reputation would be too painful.

And besides, what about Mr Grey? As silly as it seemed, Dulcie found the thought of her late cat comforting. He'd been an ordinary cat in his lifetime. He didn't speak; he certainly didn't study. At most, he encouraged her first tentative explorations of what would become her area of concentration by curling up at her feet as she read. But since his death last spring, his spirit had made itself known to her in a variety of ways, always coming through when she faced some kind of crisis. A soft voice, firm and assured. The tickle of whiskers against her face. The brush of a tail, as she'd felt only the day before. Suze might not believe, but Dulcie did. And if she'd been chasing a specter, Mr Grey would have let her know, wouldn't he? Unless, of course, that had been why he had made himself known to her yesterday, as she sat in her thesis adviser's home. After all, Cameron had already met his fate by then, and so the feline ghost hadn't needed to warn his one-time human of any danger.

Or had he? Suddenly, Cameron's still, pale face flashed before her eyes again, the stacks before her growing faint. He had been killed, possibly by someone he knew. Who she might know. Who might still be around...

It was all too much. Dulcie's concentration was shot and not even the cool, quiet of Widener was going to help. She needed to get her bag back, to at least follow up on the idea of identifying the author of *The Ravages*. On top of everything, she realized she was hungry. That coffee with Chris had been over an hour ago, and at the time she'd been too preoccupied to do more than pick at the muffin on her plate. She needed to get some food, some fresh air, and maybe a fresh perspective.

EIGHT

THE BRIGHT AFTERNOON and a falafel onion wrap had Dulcie feeling like herself again, and as soon as she had licked her fingers clean she'd pulled out her cell phone and punched in the number of the Bullock residence. But instead of hearing Polly's breathless voice, the great man himself answered.

'Dulcie, of course!' He'd sounded almost warm as she'd explained her lapse with her bag and asked if she could come by. 'I'll be in for the rest of the afternoon. Lovely to see you.'

Grief affects people in strange ways, she thought. Had the professor been close to the handsome young student? Maybe simply the shock of being involved in a murder had opened him up. With vague thoughts of a more receptive thesis adviser, Dulcie happily trotted the half mile up Brattle to her professor's house. The sun was bright, a few red and gold leaves still colored the sidewalk, matching the brick of the Tory Row houses. The air was chilly rather than cold. Bracing and—

And then she saw it. The dark green holly that so recently had concealed Cameron's body. The day dimmed, and Dulcie found herself leaning against a bare elm. Unbidden and unwanted, the image of Cameron's face came back to her. He had been so pale. Bloodless. But there had been something—blood? dirt?—on the side of his face.

Dulcie gulped in air, slumping against the tree. What hadn't she noticed yesterday? How had the young scholar even died? With that thought, she began to feel a little better. Curiosity had always been her strongest trait. Maybe that's why she bonded so well with cats. And with that thought, Dulcie pulled herself to her feet and walked the last half block up to Professor Bullock's house.

'Come in, come in.' The white-haired professor opened the door himself, ushering Dulcie back into his office. For a moment, as her eyes adjusted to the dim and smoky light, she wondered if perhaps he'd forgotten her phone call. Maybe today she'd have the thesis meeting she'd hoped for yesterday. 'Here are your things.'

Dulcie's bag lay on her chair. The copy of her thesis chapter, printed out for the professor to read, lay on top. As did a fat leatherbound book. She bent to read the title—something on the later metaphysical poets.

'Please, please.' He motioned for her to pick up the heavy volume. She did so and looked at him, waiting. This wasn't her area of interest. Wasn't even her period.

'Did you want me to read something in this, Professor?' The book weighed several pounds. But the antique binding—tooled leather gilded with gold leaf—had seen better days. Knowing how the professor felt about his books, she'd be reluctant to take it home.

'What? Oh, not necessary.' He had already moved on, and was thumbing through a file he'd picked up from the windowsill. Dulcie stood waiting, more than a little confused, watching as the ivy outside tossed in the wind, casting decorative shadows from its ironwork grill. The professor kept reading, and she wondered if he'd forgotten her. After a moment's silence, she bent to place the book ever so carefully back on the chair.

'Oh, no. That should go immediately.' She had his attention now.

'Professor?'

'Look at that binding. The corner, badly damaged.' He waved toward the book and Dulcie turned it over, holding it closer to the lamp on Bullock's cluttered desk. 'That's got to go to Gosham's right away.'

Understanding flooded over Dulcie. Gosham's was a bookbinder and book repair specialist in the Square, and Dulcie was being given an errand.

'Is Polly not around?'

'Called in sick. Vapors, or something.' The professor made another vague gesture, waving away all kinds of feminine sensitivities. 'Left me totally in the lurch.' With that he turned away, leaving Dulcie to place the book—very carefully—in her bag. Poor Polly. Yesterday's events must have been too much for her. Unless, Dulcie thought as she let herself out, Polly was smarter than she'd given her credit for, ducking out just when Dulcie was likely to be around. As she picked her way carefully down the steps, keeping her eyes up and away from the holly, Dulcie wondered. Was she being groomed to be Polly's successor?

Despite that unpleasant thought, Dulcie didn't much mind the errand. Gosham's was legendary. Roger Gosham, who had supposedly trained in Germany and Eastern Europe, was the department's unofficial go-to guy. Although faculty had access to the college conservator, those who could afford it took their private treasures to Gosham's, and Dulcie had never been.

Ten minutes later, Dulcie was less enthusiastic. The book was heavy, and Gosham's—on the far side of the Square—was a third-floor walk-up. Climbing stairs curved with wear, Dulcie tried to recapture the adventure of the errand. Gosham's was a throwback, a remnant of the era when Harvard Square hadn't been dominated by pricey boutiques and chain sportswear shops. Even this stairway, she thought, wouldn't have survived in one of the newer rehabs. Hermetria, exploring the castle keep, might have made her way up just such an aged stairwell. She might have been grateful for such a smooth brass railing, particularly where the black treads had worn away. Wasn't there a passage in which one of the ghosts exhorted the heroine to draw on her inner strength? Could she have been climbing a stairwell at the time?

It was a hard sell, and Dulcie was left with a new respect for Polly by the time she'd reached the top landing. No wonder the other woman always looked tired! Catching her breath, she looked around. One door was blank, a faint shadow where a name had been removed. The other wooden door still had its original label: 'Gosham's Rare Books' in gold leaf, outlined in black. Dulcie reached to trace the old-fashioned lettering, still clear and proud, and then knocked softly beneath it. When no answer was forthcoming, she pushed gently. The door opened, and once again, she was in a magical land.

Gosham's wasn't large. Dulcie stepped into a front room that couldn't have been bigger than twelve by fifteen. But it was beautiful, a gem of a workroom set up high in this nondescript Harvard Square building. The late afternoon sun streamed in the big front windows to light up a wooden contraption as big as a desk. A large corkscrew on top, leading down to a flattened block, suggested an ancient torture device, but Dulcie knew she was looking at a letter press, a basic technology that had remained unchanged for centuries. Behind it, by the window, a large work table was laid out with tools that Gutenberg would have recognized: a variety of awls and scalpels, their worn wood handles in sharp contrast to their polished metal blades. A smaller press and something that looked like a guillotine sat on a second table, which topped a chest of drawers. Drawn by the beauty of the ageless equipment, Dulcie stepped forward into the room and bent to read a label on one of the drawers.

'May I help you?' The voice was gruff, and Dulcie jumped. An older man stood in the doorway to her left. He was wiping his hands on the apron he wore and looking at Dulcie with a rather stern expression.

'Oh, I'm sorry! The front door was open.' She motioned to the door behind her. Of course, it had been unlocked because someone had been working. The man crossed his arms and waited. 'I'm Dulcie Schwartz. I'm one of Professor Bullock's students?' She heard the rise in her own voice and kicked herself. Just because she'd been startled was no reason to feel cowed. 'He asked me to bring a book to you.'

The man nodded, but continued to stare. 'You're new.'

'No, I'm one of his doctoral students. Polly, his regular assistant, wasn't available.' The man kept staring at her, which gave her the opportunity to study him right back. Fortyish, probably, with grey amply sprinkled in his too-long wavy hair. He had the kind of wide-set eyes and large mouth that were probably once considered handsome. At this point, Dulcie found his unbroken gaze disturbing. It was time to turn the tables.

'And you are?' She leaned forward slightly, prompting him to answer. Suddenly the craggy face broke into a big grin revealing large, yellow teeth.

'Gosham. Roger Gosham.' He held out a hand and Dulcie took it. Whatever he'd been wiping off had left it dry and warm, with calluses that reminded Dulcie of Mr Grey's paw pads. 'Welcome to my lair.'

That was it, Dulcie realized. Between the hair, the teeth, and the generally lupine attitude, the older man resembled nothing so much as a werewolf. He led her into the back room, around a stack of large boxes. Behind them, rows of leatherbound books in various states of assembly covered another long wooden table top. In one of her books, Roger Gosham would be some kind of enchanted knight, forced to live apart because of some lycanthropic curse. But before she could follow the fancy any further, she realized she had a role to play. The bookbinder was standing by the table, waiting, and so—feeling more than a little like Little Red Riding Hood—Dulcie reached into her bag and carefully, with both hands, removed Professor Bullock's damaged book. One corner was definitely crumpled, she saw as she handed it over. The top of the spine folded on itself in a way that couldn't be doing the ancient leather any good.

'Oh, my.' Gosham took the book from her, his voice growing soft with concern. 'Oh, oh, my.'

Cradling the injured volume in one large hand, he used the other to hold the front cover partially open. 'Do you know how this happened?' He looked up for a moment, then focused again on the book.

'I believe it was dropped,' said Dulcie, and watched the wolfish man wince. Muttering something under his breath, he brought the damaged book over to one of the work tables.

'The spine.' He sighed audibly. 'And I believe this signature will have to be re-sewn, too.' Clucking his tongue softly, he propped the book cover with a block of wood, holding it partly open. With one large hand he smoothed a page back, leaning close to examine the joint where it was bound to its neighbor. 'Oh, my.'

Dulcie stood silent and transfixed. She could leave now, she suspected, but she was witnessing a transformation. The wolfish man had become as gentle as a lamb, and the attention he was giving the old volume warmed the young scholar's heart.

'Is it fixable?' Her own voice sounded too loud, but she wanted to know.

'Yes, yes.' He didn't look up. 'Of course. It's just such a pity.' He reached for a small bag—it looked like a sandbag—and laid it on the page to hold it open. 'The glue was barely dry.'

'It's new?' Dulcie knew her question made no sense, but then neither did the bookbinder's statement.

He looked up sharply, a trace of the wolf flashing in his eyes. 'Of course not.' Dulcie took a quick step back, and Gosham's expression softened. 'I simply meant that this was newly repaired.' He forced a small smile. 'I'd only handed it over to Polly yesterday.'

Of course, this must have been one of the books she'd dropped in the entranceway. 'I'm sorry,' she answered, moved by his tone.

He waved her sympathy away. 'No matter. This is what I do. She usually comes by once a week, you know.'

Dulcie muttered something noncommittal and watched him get back to work. The stacked boxes hinted at a move. Was he being priced out of Harvard Square? He wouldn't be the first, she thought, with regret. Seeing how he handled the book, reaching first for one wooden-handled tool and then rejecting it for something with a flat, rounded blade, rather like a spatula, she could see he was a true craftsman. And though a little old for her, not an unattractive man.

'So, where is our Polly today?' Gosham was still bent over the book, but a slight tightness had crept into his voice. Dulcie had a feeling that the question was more than casual.

'She's out.' Dulcie didn't know if word of Cameron's death was common knowledge yet. 'Out sick.'

'Nothing serious, I hope?' The bookbinder looked up and Dulcie realized how large his deep brown eyes were. 'Not home in bed with an early flu or anything?'

'No, she's fine.' Dulcie realized she was making no sense. 'She's just taking the day off.'

He nodded, looking a little thoughtful. 'Maybe I should bring this one back myself, when it's done. Check in on her.'

As he spoke, an idea began to take root in Dulcie's mind. It was probably a fiction, she told herself. That was a hazard of the trade—all those years spent in books—but the more she thought about it, the more she hoped it was true. Was there something going on here between the artisan and the academic? She took a fresh look at Gosham's big, muscular frame, the gentle way his large hands cradled the book in front of him, and felt warmed by the thought. Why shouldn't the quiet assistant have a little romance in her life? Just as quickly, another thought came to her. Had she deprived Polly of a chance to see her love?

'I'm sure that's not necessary.' Dulcie spoke quickly, eager to make up for any misstep. 'I bet she'll be back at work tomorrow and will come by as soon as she can. Just to check in.'

'Sly little minx,' he said, as much to himself as to her, and returned to work. The comment only confirmed Dulcie's impression that there was a connection between the two—and that she had not been the expected visitor this afternoon. After a few more minutes of watching him work, Dulcie excused herself. Gosham muttered something, not even looking up, and Dulcie took off, warmed with the feeling of a job well done.

But any hope Dulcie had of sharing her speculative gossip faded when she got back to the Central Square apartment she shared with Suze.

'Anybody home?' As she let herself into the front door of the duplex, Dulcie looked up the stairs that led to their first floor.

At the top landing, a little face looked down. 'Hey, kitten. Is it just you?'

But if she expected an answer, none was forthcoming. Instead, the kitten waited until she'd climbed up before throwing herself at Dulcie's shins.

'Hello to you, too, little one.' Dulcie dropped her book bag and reached for the kitten. Plump as the kitten might be, compared to Mr Grey the tiny black and white cat barely made a handful. She pressed the little body to her face and heard a purr—but nothing else. 'You ever going to talk to me, kitten?'

A wet nose pressed against her cheek as she carried the kitten into the kitchen. 'Suze?' she called, before spotting the note on the fridge:

Totally forgot Jeremy's birthday dinner, the note read. She tried to place the birthday boy. Jeremy? Wasn't he someone's roommate? That was it, she thought. Jeremy lived with Suze's boyfriend, Ariano. *So sorry to leave you alone! Call or come join us—Burrito Villa—if you want!*

'Bother.' Dulcie sank into a kitchen chair, depositing the kitten on the table in front of her. Burrito Villa was back in the Square, and while that was usually a manageable hike, tonight she didn't feel like tackling it again. It wasn't that she needed the company. Considering what had happened the day before, she felt surprisingly good. It's just that she really could have used someone to talk to. And more and more often, she admitted to herself, Suze was not around. 'It's the university,' her roommate had explained only the week before. 'I've got to get away. I know you see your future in academia, Dulcie. But for me, it feels like some kind of very nice, very safe chrysalis. It's served its purpose, and I'm ready to break out.'

Suze had meant well, and Dulcie could see the truth in her friend's words. Even her choice of a boyfriend—Ariano, a non-academic—reflected her movement away from the tidy world that Dulcie loved. That they both had, for close to seven years. But Suze was moving on, and Dulcie felt abandoned.

In front of her, the kitten started to wash.

'JOIN ME IN DUNGEON?'

The strange text-message invitation, tendered as it was by Chris, had considerable appeal. Although the idea of crashing someone else's party hadn't interested Dulcie, as the evening had worn on the apartment had grown a little too quiet for comfort. She'd tried settling in on the sofa with the Gunning, but the tight type and myriad footnotes had soon made her eyes heavy. Even when she exchanged the heavy research work for something lighter, the magic just wasn't there. As much as she didn't want to admit it, the last forty-eight hours had taken their toll. 'Maybe,' she'd texted back, but whatever reply she was hoping for, all she got was silence.

'At least you're here.' She looked over at the kitten, who was busy battling one of Suze's shoelaces. 'Why don't you come read with me?' Cats don't usually come when called, but when Dulcie grabbed her worn copy of *The Ravages of Umbria* and lay back down on the sofa, she was pleased to feel a light thump as the kitten landed by her feet. 'Good girl.'

This was how it used to be with Mr Grey. She could think of him these days without even tearing up, and as his successor kneaded a pillow, Dulcie dove into her book. Not for the plot this time, although the adventure of beleaguered Hermetria and her duplicitous sidekick Demetria could usually suck her right in. Now she wanted to focus on the language. What were the hints—the idiosyncrasies—that might lead her to uncover the novel's anonymous parentage? Were there any regional phrasings or odd colloquial bits? What about the landscape? Despite the gaudy cover illustration, there were no real mountain peaks in Umbria, no castles secluded on crags. Could they be a clue that perhaps the author had lived in a wilder area? Dulcie put down the book and looked over at the kitten.

'It's hopeless, isn't it? The author was probably sitting in London the entire time.' The kitten only blinked and then, suddenly, took off. Dulcie heard a thud and wondered what the feisty little creature had knocked over this time. When no howling followed, she dismissed it. This cat was crazy, and she had work to do.

A half-hour later, no further crashes had interrupted her and Dulcie had been able to trace the phrase that had popped up in her dream. Although in her sleep, she had placed the 'emeralds' in her late cat's eyes, the word popped up in an entirely different context. Opening the second remnant of *The Ravages,* it seemed to follow a visitation by a spirit, one of the many ghosts that haunted Hermetria's ancient home. This one may or may not have been friendly, but Hermetria had faced it down with her usual aplomb:

Such visitations taxed her not overmuch, drawing as she did upon an inner strength as cool as emeralds, as supple as the sword drawn from its sheath...

No wonder she'd missed it. It was an unusual phrasing: strength was usually described, even then, in terms of metals or of stone, not precious gems. Dulcie made a note of it and started leafing back, looking for other recurrences. The phrase had surfaced in her dream for a reason, and Dulcie wanted to believe that it was more than simply the way it evoked Mr Grey's eyes. But another hour passed with no further discoveries. The fragments weren't that big, and at times like this the magnitude of what had been lost was disheartening.

And so when Chris called to suggest again that she abandon her studies and come join him in the subterranean computer lab, she was tempted. He'd be on duty for several hours yet—as the semester drew to a close, the undergrads grew increasingly desperate—but there were no rules against a quiet visit. Or against the visitor bringing pizza.

Which was why Dulcie found herself buttoning her coat and detaching the kitten from her scarf—'Sorry, baby, I'm going to need this'—and heading out into the frosty November night.

'My heroine!' Chris looked up from his terminal with unfeigned happiness. All around him, bleary-eyes looked up and blinked.

'It's only pepperoni.' Dulcie blushed. 'And it's probably

gotten cold.' But she let herself be properly hugged and kissed before Chris opened the box and started separating the slices. Despite the chill outside, the pizza had retained enough of its warmth to be appetizing, and the company was warmer still. Until, that is, Dulcie started telling Chris about her latest fears.

'I mean, Lucy's pretty nutty. I've told you about her "psychic" dreams, right?'

Chris nodded and grunted something, his mouth full of cheese.

'But I've got to wonder. I mean, could it be a coincidence that right now, I'm looking into the provenance of *The Ravages?*' Dulcie was trying not to take a third slice and kept on talking. 'And, you know, when Mr Grey came to me again, in Professor Bullock's home—'

'Mr Grey?' Chris swallowed hard. 'You heard Mr Grey's voice again?' He knew about her spectral pet. And although she couldn't tell if he completely believed her, he had always been supportive. And so Dulcie continued.

'I didn't hear him, not exactly. But I felt him brush against me.' She closed her eyes to better recall the soft touch of fur. 'He didn't head-butt me like the new kitten does—and he certainly doesn't take off like a crazed thing and wreck the place. But sometimes, when he'd walk by, he'd just brush his tail against my shin. And I can't help but wonder. I mean, at the time I thought it was because of what had happened. Because of Cameron, you know. But maybe it was about the book. Maybe Lucy was right.'

She opened her eyes. Chris was staring at her. He'd even put his unfinished slice back down on its paper plate.

'Oh, Dulcie, you've had a miserable couple of days, haven't you?' He reached forward and took her hand. 'And I've been no good at all, tucked away here. Working all hours.'

Something was off. 'Yeah, it's been pretty bad. But I know you've got to work.' She looked around at the students at their terminals. She was suddenly pretty sure they were all eavesdropping. She lowered her voice. 'But it's not like I'm imagining all of this.'

'I know Lucy called.' His voice was low, too. Comforting. The voice one would use with an invalid. 'And she has a way of getting under your skin.'

Dulcie gasped. What Chris had said was right, but why he'd said it was all wrong. 'You think I'm losing it.' Heads popped up and then quickly ducked back down. 'You think I'm freaked out by Cameron and I'm putting it all on *The Ravages*.' He didn't respond. 'You don't believe in Mr Grey!'

She was nearly yelling at this point, and Chris leaned forward to take her other hand. Dulcie pulled it back. 'No, I don't need this.' Suddenly, the third slice had no appeal. 'I'm going home.'

'Dulcie!' It was too late. She was heading toward the door, and Chris, she knew, was on duty till midnight at least.

Suze wasn't home yet, but Dulcie decided not to take any chances. Instead, she dumped her bag in the living room and climbed the second stairway to head straight to bed. 'Nobody believes me. And I don't know what to believe, either.' She was talking to herself as much as anything. But as she kicked off her shoes and climbed into bed, she couldn't help but hope...

'There, there, little one.'

Could it be? The same calm, deep voice she'd so missed. The voice that Mr Grey had used to communicate with her from beyond. 'These are trying times, and not everyone is ready to accept what you and I understand to be true. After all, not everyone knows what we know.'

'Oh, Mr Grey! I'm so glad you're here again.' She relaxed against the pillow, ready for a good heart-to-heart. 'I've missed you so much! And I'm really worried about my thesis.' But the voice didn't stop.

'I know we expect better from her, but really, look what she's working with.'

Dulcie sat bolt upright. There, in her bedroom doorway, sat

the kitten. The little tuxedoed cat was staring straight ahead—at the empty space at the top of the stairs.

'She'll come along, little one. She simply has to learn to trust herself. Give her time.'

NINE

It wasn't that Dulcie didn't trust the Cambridge police. Despite an upbringing that leaned heavily toward anarchism, or at least distrust of what Lucy deemed 'the dominant paradigm,' Dulcie was essentially a law-abiding type. She wouldn't, for example, use her cell phone in the library, and she was relatively good about throwing a quarter into the departmental coffee fund. But she was on her guard the next morning as she walked up to the imposing stone building that houses Cambridge's finest.

'I'm here to see Detective Carioli.' She tried to keep any quaver out of her voice. Suze had stayed over at her boyfriend's, which meant that Dulcie was here without advice of counsel. She knew, as well as if Suze had shared a morning cup, that her law-school roommate would have told her not to come in without a lawyer. But calling on the school's legal clinic had seemed like an unnecessary hassle this early in the morning. Besides, there was no way Dulcie could be considered involved in Cameron's murder, was there?

Unless, of course, she'd killed Cameron on her way in, and then met with her adviser to establish an alibi. Or she'd paid a hitman... As her mind started flying off into the various possible scenarios, she imagined what Lucy would be saying.

'It's not that the police are bad, dear. It's just that for so-called peace officers, they have a tendency to lean toward violence. That kind of conflict breeds bad karma.'

But just as she caught herself from answering her mother's argument out loud, Dulcie heard her name. A stout woman in plainclothes, her iron-grey hair just touching the tweed collar of her jacket, stood by a doorway. Dulcie jumped up and followed the older woman past a board full of notices. None of the sketchy faces looked like anybody she knew. The theft notices were another matter, and Dulcie would have liked to have read those, particularly the one from the Harvard Square jeweler whose name she recognized. But as she paused, she became aware of the other woman waiting, and so she turned and they continued on, neither of them speaking, into the back warren of offices.

'Coffee?' Those first words were offered with a smile, but Dulcie was hesitant.

'Sure,' she said after an awkward pause. To refuse might look suspicious. 'Milk and sugar, please.'

'Coming right up.' The officer sounded cheery, but as she stepped out of the room, Dulcie made a point of surveying her surroundings. She'd sat in a broken plastic chair that pinched her thigh, but no other chair offered itself—except for the wooden one behind the desk. Was this some new kind of interrogation technique? For the umpteenth time since she'd stepped in, she'd cursed herself for not taking Suze's advice. She could've woken up a few minutes earlier or postponed the interview.

'Here we go.' The stout detective's tone was cheery as she handed a heavy white mug over to Dulcie, sipped at her own and settled into her own chair. 'If you've got to come in here, the least we can do is give you coffee.'

'Thanks.' Dulcie sipped the hot brew suspiciously. Why was this detective being so friendly?

'So, Dulcie Schwartz.' The officer flipped open a file and raised her eyebrows. 'Seems you've been in to talk with us before.'

It wasn't a question, but Dulcie nodded. The murder of her summer subletter had taught her more about the workings of the Cambridge police department than she cared to remember. Detective Carioli read for a few moments, then closed the folder with a little grunt. 'Well, that was interesting.'

Dulcie waited. If nothing else, Suze had taught her to keep her mouth shut.

'So, would you walk me through Monday afternoon again?'

Suze had also taught her to keep her answers short and factual, which was a challenge for anyone who lived in novels. But by the time Dulcie got up to her finale, when she was banging on the professor's door with the bottom of her fist while yelling herself hoarse, she felt like she'd kept her story as straightforward as possible. Still, she had the sneaking suspicion that the detective was trying not to chuckle as she shuffled some papers.

'Thanks for—ah—filling in the details.' She was definitely suppressing a smile. 'But I still have a few more questions.'

Dulcie waited.

'How long do you think you waited before Professor Bullock opened the door?' Dulcie shrugged and thought back. It probably hadn't been more than five minutes. 'And what was the professor's relationship with the deceased? According to what you observed, please?'

'I don't know that he had one.' Dulcie wasn't sure how much about the academic world this detective knew. 'You see, although they were technically in the same department, they were in really different areas. Entirely different centuries.' She smiled, and hoped that her words didn't sound condescending.

The detective nodded. 'And personally?'

Dulcie opened her mouth and then closed it. Nobody really knew about the professor's private life. The only gossip had speculated about Polly and, more recently, Lloyd. 'Well, Cameron was known as a ladies' man.' She spoke without thinking and bit her lip, remembering the first time they'd met. It had been a departmental mixer, and he'd been charming, asking Dulcie all about herself. She'd been flattered that he'd known about her adventure the previous summer, and a little flustered—until he moved on to their more attractive colleagues. That had broken the spell, leaving Dulcie with the impression of an experienced flirt who knew full well the extent of his powers. Still, a pretty boy could swing both ways. 'You don't think...' She paused, unsure of how to phrase the question. 'You don't think that Cameron and the professor...? I mean, I was there...'

The detective was looking at her, not smiling, as all the possibilities began to run through Dulcie's mind. A thwarted pass. A broken heart. 'Maybe there was someone else. A third party?' She was creating a fiction, something Suze pointed out that she often did. And at the thought of her law-school roommate, Dulcie finally shut up. Several long moments passed before the detective spoke.

'Just as a matter of course, given the nature of the wound and all, may I ask you, Ms Schwartz, if you have ever carried a knife?'

'A knife?' She shuddered, thinking about that incident over the summer. 'No. Never.'

'What about Professor Bullock?'

By the time Dulcie left the office, she had the distinct impression that Detective Carioli had found her amusing. And that Professor Bullock was a suspect.

'HEY, LLOYD, HAVE YOU ever noticed anything hinky about Professor Bullock?' Dulcie had picked up a sandwich and chips at the Union and had half finished the tuna rollup by the time she found her colleague in the tiny office they shared.

'Oh, don't tell me that's all starting up again.' Lloyd looked up from his desk, his face as white as the papers piled before him.

'What do you mean?' Dulcie collapsed into her own chair, opened up the bag of chips and pushed them toward Lloyd. 'Again?'

Her officemate grabbed a handful and considered while he crunched. 'I've worked for the man for, what, three years? Anyway, I still can't tell you the truth.'

'Can't, or won't?' Dulcie was joking, but the look Lloyd shot her as he reached for more of the chips was serious. 'What?'

'It's not funny, Dulcie.' Lloyd looked like he'd swallowed a bug, rather than salt-and-vinegars, but when Dulcie didn't apologize, he kept talking. 'You really don't know?'

Mouth full of the last bit of sandwich, she shook her head.

'Well, you know that *Unlocking the Great Books*, his defining work, came out, what? Twenty years ago next year? And that he's supposedly been working on his next book ever since?'

Dulcie nodded again. This was departmental lore.

'Well, ever since I became his research assistant, people have been hounding me, trying to find out what the next book is on.'

Dulcie murmured. She had to admit that she, too, had been curious.

'I mean, he's got me researching everything. Etymology to usage, Continental colloquialisms, you name it. So, no, I have no idea what the new book is on. Or even if he's started writing.'

'There can't be that much pressure on him.' Dulcie put her feet up. 'I mean, he's not like one of us. He's a university professor.'

Lloyd was shaking his head. 'I don't know, Dulce. Even endowed chairs are getting a little tighter. I think there may be more heat on Bullock than anyone knows.'

'Come on. I can see how he's putting pressure on himself—'

Lloyd cut her off in mid-sentence, rolling his chair over to hers as if even their tiny office wasn't secure. 'It's not just self-inflicted, Dulcie. Nancy has let some things drop. They're pressuring old Bullock. They want him to retire. The minute his title changes to "emeritus," he frees up a ton of cash.'

'No!' Dulcie stared at her officemate's pale face and felt her own color drain away as he nodded slowly. 'This isn't imminent, is it?' She could hear her voice cracking. If Bullock left before her thesis was finished, she'd be essentially orphaned. From the grim set of Lloyd's mouth, she knew he'd had the same thoughts.

'That's just it, Dulcie. I don't know.' He pushed back to his own desk. 'That's one big reason I've been putting in the hours. He's always had some student do his dirty work, but if I can help him get moving…'

He didn't have to finish the thought. His career, even more

than hers, was tied to the professor. With a sigh, he went back to grading papers while Dulcie mulled over what he'd said. For a few minutes, the soft scrape of his pencil was the only sound in the office.

'And now the cops are asking about him.' The words slipped out, but they had an electrifying effect on Lloyd.

'You serious?' He started up, the papers in front of him once again forgotten. 'About Bullock specifically? In what way?'

Dulcie thought about what the detective had asked her. 'I don't know exactly.' She looked over at her officemate, searching for the words. How do you ask a colleague if his mentor has ever seemed murderous? 'He's never seemed, I don't know, odd to you?'

'No more than usual,' Lloyd said, his voice falling.

Dulcie wondered how long he'd been at those papers. 'Junior essays?'

He shook his head. 'Midterms.' As Dulcie watched, he ran one hand through his thinning hair. She bit her lip. Most of the student midterms had been graded weeks before. 'Bullock held these up for some reason. Wouldn't hand them over. And I, well, I figured I'd help him any way I can.' He answered her unspoken question.

'So there is something going on!' She craned her neck over to look and was a little taken aback when Lloyd slapped one hand down on the closest paper.

'Who are we to question the gods?' The humor in Lloyd's voice softened the blow, but he'd noticed how she had recoiled. 'I'm sorry, Dulcie. I've just got to plow through these.'

'No problem.' Now that she was sitting here, she wanted to tell him all about her morning. He was close enough to Bullock that maybe he could shed some light on what would make the professor a suspect. But in the moment as she gathered her thoughts, Lloyd had gotten back to work. Whatever he was scrawling in the margin might not be legible, but at least the graduate student was giving the paper more attention than the professor ever would.

WHEN THE KNOCK CAME on the door, they both jumped.

'Come in,' Dulcie called and stood to greet the guest—and ended up craning her neck. The tall, slender woman who waltzed into the tiny office looked as out of place as a swan in a duck pond. 'May I help you?'

'I'm looking for Dulcie Schwartz?' The voice was low and as warm as her golden skin.

'You found her.' Dulcie pointed to the one guest chair. Behind her, she could hear Lloyd shifting. She'd have to get rid of this visitor quickly and let her officemate work in peace.

'I'm Raleigh Hall,' said the bronzed beauty, as she lowered herself into the chair with the grace of a model. 'I've come to talk with you about my senior thesis.'

'Raleigh. Of course.' Dulcie blinked. At five-five, she'd gotten used to most of the student body being taller. But undergrads were not supposed to be this self-assured. Or this gorgeous. 'I left you a message.'

'Yes, I got it, and I thought it would be best if we met as soon as possible.'

Behind her, Dulcie heard Lloyd cough. 'I'm sorry. I'm afraid we're disturbing my colleague here.'

'Not at all.' Lloyd squeezed by Dulcie's desk and extended a hand to the undergrad. 'Lloyd. Lloyd Pruitt. Doctoral candidate in eighteenth-century prose.'

Raleigh smiled, her chestnut hair falling across her face. 'Pleased to meet you, Lloyd.' She took his hand, and Dulcie noticed the shimmer of pearl polish on her tapered fingers. 'Don't you work with Professor Bullock?'

'Oh, y-yes!' Lloyd almost stuttered, and Dulcie was amused to hear her colleague's old speech defect—gone for years—reawakened by the presence of this girl.

'We should talk sometime,' the undergrad was saying. Lloyd stood transfixed, as Dulcie reached for her coat.

'Anyway, Raleigh, why don't we go grab some coffee?' She ushered the willowy girl out in front of her. Turning back, she raised her eyebrows at Lloyd. 'Back to work, Lloyd,' she stage whispered. She'd been about to add something more. Something about how maybe the tired-looking scholar should try to finish by midnight for a change. Should maybe come out with his fellow students for some beer and socializing once in a while. But the look on his pale face stopped her. She'd expected him to look smitten. Shocked, maybe, or awed. What she saw was fear.

TEN

WHATEVER WAS GOING ON with Lloyd, however, was none of Raleigh Hall's business, and Dulcie hurried the undergrad out of the Commons and into the bright, cold day.

'Kate's?' she suggested. The coffeehouse wouldn't be too crowded in the middle of the day and it was only half a block from Harvard Yard.

Raleigh nodded and buttoned up her coat. 'I'm really glad you could see me so soon.'

'Hey, that's my job.' Dulcie put on her warmest smile as she looked up at Raleigh. Maybe the pretty young student had an undergraduate's nerves after all. 'To help you get your thesis done.'

'Well, I'm glad.' The taller girl's longer legs had Dulcie scrambling to keep up, but when she saw Dulcie puffing she paused. For a moment, they both looked in a store window. High-end knits, imported and dyed into a rainbow of hues. But even as Dulcie pulled her own rather scratchy hat down over her ears, she realized the younger woman was still talking. 'Because, you see, I want to get my first draft finished in time for my sponsors to read. I've submitted a chapter as an essay to the *Modern Languages Review,* and I believe I'm a strong candidate for the Krullworth Prize, and you know how political that can be.'

Dulcie made herself close her mouth. Publication in the *Review* was usually reserved for graduate students or post-grads, an honor that almost guaranteed a fellowship—if not the offer of a teaching job. And the Krullworth Prize was the most prestigious award given to undergraduates. 'You know that students in all disciplines will be competing for the Krullworth?' she managed to say. 'Not just English.'

They were walking side by side through the Yard now, the bright sun occasionally broken by the shadows of the bare trees around them. Raleigh had once again pulled ahead, but Dulcie had the distinct impression that the younger woman had rolled her eyes.

'I'm fully aware of the competition for the Krullworth.' The younger girl turned to glance down at Dulcie. 'But I also know that the last two have gone to abstract mathematics and paleo-physiology. So Cam and I knew that this year the judges would want to consider the humanities.'

'Cam?' It just slipped out.

'Cameron. You know, my thesis adviser?'

'Ex-thesis adviser,' Dulcie muttered. Her colleague's face flashed into her mind. Not as he had been: handsome, and, yes, a bit manipulative. But cold and white, with that smudge of dirt and blood on his face. 'But wait.' She shook her head to clear it and nearly sent her hat flying. 'This year? What do you mean?'

The younger woman looked over, her eyes wide. 'I took two semesters off, didn't it say in my files?'

Dulcie shook her head. They'd reached Mass Ave and stood, waiting, while a crowd of Japanese tourists piled into a bus. 'I haven't had a chance to read your file yet. I'm sorry.'

'Well, what have you been doing?'

'I've been a little busy.' They stepped around the last of the tour group and up to the curb, just as the light gave them the okay to cross. Perfect timing, thought Dulcie. She was very tempted to give the younger student a piece of her mind, but not when she had to use all her breath to keep up.

'Well, you can catch up on your own time.' Raleigh stepped into the street. 'But basically, I'm looking at the postmodernist novel-drama interplay from a semiotics standpoint.'

'Wait.' Dulcie grabbed her student's sleeve, stopping them both in the middle of traffic. 'This is an undergraduate thesis? In the English department?'

'Well, yeah.' A car honked, and the two kept walking. 'I started out in philosophy, but then I met Cam and he convinced me that what I was doing would really stand out in English. I mean, aren't most of the theses just more re-readings of some old texts?'

Dulcie bit her lip and then made herself take a breath. They'd reached the coffeehouse, but she was no longer convinced she could sit down with this woman. 'Something like that,' she managed to say.

'Well, that's what Cam said, anyway. And so when he suggested I wait a year, I…oh, I'm sorry.'

To Dulcie's horror and surprise, the pretty undergrad suddenly put her mittens up to her face and started to sob.

'It's so terrible,' she managed to say. 'I'm sorry.'

'No, it's fine. There, there.' Dulcie reached up to pat the slim girl's shoulder with one hand, while rustling around in her pocket for a clean tissue with the other. 'It's okay.' She had no idea what to say. Mr Grey would have been so much better at this. He, at least, could have leaned in, offering his soft, warm bulk for comfort. In lieu of a similar act, Dulcie found a tissue that looked clean enough and handed it over as she ushered her student to a table. Raleigh wiped her eyes and blew her nose. When she looked up, she was trying to smile. The attempt made her look younger, and Dulcie dismissed her earlier reservations.

'Raleigh, if you don't mind me asking, when did you last have something to eat?'

'Oh, I had an egg-white omelet for breakfast—' Dulcie cut her off and ordered two bowls of split pea soup and an oversized chocolate chip cookie to share. Maybe Mr Grey had taught her something about creature comforts after all.

Twenty minutes later, Raleigh had resumed her equilibrium and Dulcie had eaten most of the cookie. But along the way, Dulcie had also gotten the rundown on the willowy senior, if not her thesis. The pampered only child of a bi-coastal couple, Raleigh Amesbury Hall had whizzed through some of the finest prep schools in the world. Whizzed through—or burned out of.

The slender brunette blushed slightly as she described running off for a weekend with her Classics tutor at Everett. But from the way she described her career, Dulcie began to understand her confidence. This young woman had long been the most brilliant star in whatever firmament shone overhead. Probably the prettiest, too. Dulcie also had the sense that she hadn't ever really lost anyone before. Not to murder, at any rate.

'I am sorry, Raleigh.' She poured the last of the organic peppermint tea into her student's mug. 'This has been a huge loss for all of us.'

'Well, yeah.' Her voice had gotten soft. 'Of course, Cam was a bit of a dog.'

'Oh?' Dulcie hadn't heard any negative gossip about her late colleague. Women tended to like him, but as far as she knew, he hadn't been breaking any hearts. Then again, if he had a tendency to hit on undergrads, he'd have wanted to keep that secret. Such relationships were considered a serious breach of ethics. 'Raleigh, was there something going on with Cameron?'

'God, no. He might have impressed other girls, but, really, I'm so over that whole routine: staring into your eyes and acting all solicitous.' She fiddled with the handle of her cup, and Dulcie felt herself blush. 'Although, I have to admit, I do think those rules about students and teachers are way out of date.'

Dulcie kept quiet. This girl had already confessed her past. But just then another thought crossed her mind. 'You're not… There's nothing going on with Professor Bullock, is there?'

To her great relief, the younger woman laughed, throwing back her head and revealing perfect teeth. 'The old Bull? God, no.' Her humor was contagious, and Dulcie found herself giggling along. Of course not. If Bullock was involved with any of his students, it would more likely be an older one. One of the graduate students who was already spending hours with him. Was already beaten down by his will. Her mind flashed to Polly and, regrettably, to Lloyd. But Raleigh had started talking again.

'I'll tell you, though, Cam thought something was wrong with the old guy.'

Dulcie looked at her, her own thoughts joining with what the younger woman was saying. She sipped what was left of her own tea, loath to voice her suspicions.

Raleigh leaned forward. 'Plagiarism.'

Dulcie choked and the two spent the next few minutes with tissues and glasses of water, Raleigh patting her tutor's back until the erring tea had been redirected.

'That's unthinkable.' Dulcie whispered the second word. It was, she thought, the only appropriate one for the sin that Raleigh had mentioned. 'It's just not possible.'

'I don't know for sure.' Raleigh shrugged and slipped back into her seat. 'Cam wouldn't tell me exactly what he was thinking, just that something was up with the old guy. But Cam was really sharp about people, and he was sure of it.' The pretty brunette considered Dulcie. 'You'd better watch out that he doesn't pull a fast one on you.'

'Why? What do you mean?' Dulcie was still reeling from her last suggestion. It fit too well with Lucy's last dream. And from what Lloyd had said, the professor might be that desperate.

'You know.' Raleigh had the grace to look abashed. 'The typical professor thing?' She even kicked at the ground.

'No, Raleigh.' Dulcie tried to concentrate on what the undergrad was saying. 'I don't know what you mean.'

'Well, that he might do what they say professors do.' She looked up, finally, her face serious. 'That he might just steal his students' work.'

ELEVEN

As DULCIE WATCHED her new charge take off into the Cambridge afternoon, she felt the energy drain out of her. Had she ever been that confident? That smart? Young Raleigh was not what Dulcie had expected, and any fleeting fantasy of a close mentor-student relationship was fading as quickly as the autumn light. It wasn't only the younger woman's looks, though if she were being completely honest with herself Dulcie had to admit that the senior's willowy beauty made her feel both shorter and chubbier than usual. It was that air of entitlement. What had she said about 'old books'? Dulcie had spent her academic life in just such worn-out pursuits. Had felt like she'd *found* herself deep in the stacks. And that comment about Professor Bullock? No, it couldn't be. Or, Dulcie thought as she shrugged on her own coat and prepared to face the chill, if it was, it just might be too late.

What exactly was the professor working on? Dulcie made a mental note to grill Lloyd further, wondering again at her officemate's apparent discomfort in the presence of the beautiful young student. Well, thought Dulcie as she shrugged her heavy bag back on to her shoulder, maybe that wasn't so odd. How often does someone like Lloyd see a beauty like that? She couldn't be sure of Lloyd's orientation, but if any part of his connection with the professor depended on... Dulcie didn't even want to go there.

Instead, she watched as the lithe undergrad gradually blended into the rush-hour crowd and then made her own way back into the Yard. Dulcie couldn't have said exactly why she didn't want to walk with her new student, but she knew she needed the time alone. Even with all the leaves fallen, Harvard Yard was a beautiful place. This late in the afternoon, the buildings cast long shadows across the grass, the bare trees stark against a deepening blue sky. But the New England fall was winding up. A cold gust prompted Dulcie to turn up her collar and stirred the remaining leaves. Letting her feet wander, she watched one errant oak leaf as it flew into a corner, joining a small pile that had gathered between the steps and the bike rack by Emerson. The leaf—and the wind—settled, and Dulcie was startled to see the pile move. A squirrel, cheeks extended with bounty, popped out and she laughed out loud.

So much for nature in the city! As much as she missed the quiet of the forest, Dulcie didn't regret coming East. After years of Lucy's hodge-podge spirituality, Dulcie found the business-like hustle and bustle of Cambridge a welcome relief. Life made sense here. Physics had more weight than metaphysics. But sometimes she missed those little touches, the preparation of animals for winter. As she took a step toward the leaf pile, the wind picked up again, swirling the pile into a dust devil of browns and golds. And one bright touch of red. There! Was that a maple leaf? The swirling dust got into Dulcie's eyes and she blinked, quick tears forming. Through the tears, she tried to focus, wanting to catch that one last touch of October's brilliance. Just as quickly, Dulcie saw another flash, this time grey. But too big to be that squirrel. No, through her bleary eyes, it looked like a cat. A large grey longhair, diving on to the leaf pile as Mr Grey had so often done, for play as much as for prey. Dulcie wiped her hand across her eyes. Mr Grey? Could it be? But when she looked again, the vision was gone. The pile of leaves once more still.

Was she seeing things or had Mr Grey appeared to her, once again, in a vision? Lack of sleep and way too much caffeine made the former more likely, Dulcie realized as she set off once again across the Yard and toward the apartment she shared with Suze. But as she walked, she saw another flash of red as bright as that leaf. No maple, though, this was a bright beret. A pretty thing, perched on a pale figure whom Dulcie recognized.

'Hey, Polly!' Dulcie waved at the familiar figure. 'Wait up!'

A wan face turned toward Dulcie and then turned away.

'Polly!' Holding her bag to keep it from slamming against her side, Dulcie trotted after the older woman. The assistant kept walking, face down, only that red cap marking her out in the dying light.

'Polly!' Dulcie caught up to her and put her hand on the other woman's arm, pausing to catch her breath. 'I guess you didn't hear me.'

'What? Oh, no.' The older woman looked even more washed-out close up, the bright hat only accenting the lack of color in her lank blonde hair and the faded camel of her coat. 'I guess I'm rather preoccupied.' She forced a thin smile.

'I don't blame you.' Dulcie smiled back. 'But I'm glad to see you're up and about.'

Polly nodded and started to walk again, her long coat flapping against her legs. Dulcie struggled to keep up.

'I wanted to touch base with you.' Even from the side, Dulcie could see the look of pain that crossed the older woman's already ashen face. 'I'm sorry. I should've asked. How are you?'

'I'm fine. Thank you.' Polly looked over and Dulcie saw the deep rings around her eyes. 'I mean, as well as can be expected.'

Dulcie nodded. She'd been there, too. 'I'm sorry you had to come back when you did.'

'He needs me.' Her answer was immediate and rather sharp, her thin lips compressing so that even the little bit of color in them drained away.

'Of course.' Dulcie was quick to reassure her. 'But, well, he's not totally helpless. He was capable of opening the door, you know.'

'I was on errands for the professor.' An edge had crept into Polly's voice, and Dulcie tried to think of how to backtrack.

'I know! I saw the books.'

Polly shook her head. 'I can't believe I dropped them. They'd just come from Gosham's, too.'

Dulcie smiled and decided against telling the older woman about her own trip there. 'I'm sure he's grateful.'

'Who, Mr Gosham? He should be.'

Dulcie had been thinking of the professor, but clearly Polly had other ideas.

'Professor Bullock is an esteemed client. Having a recommendation from the professor is enough to make a man like Gosham. Not that he truly appreciates the patronage.'

Dulcie looked at the other woman as they walked. Was she witnessing the result of a lover's spat? Or was Polly's loyalty to the professor so complete that she couldn't give any part of her heart to another man?

'I'm sure Professor Bullock appreciates your loyalty,' she started to say. Dulcie didn't want to think about Raleigh's accusation, but she couldn't resist. 'You must be such a help with his research.'

Polly glared. 'The professor is quite capable of doing his own work,' she snapped. Almost immediately, she softened. 'I'm sorry. It's just been a horrible, horrible week.'

'And it's only Wednesday!' Polly didn't so much as smile. Dulcie longed to touch the other woman. But the way Polly was walking, holding herself so tight and upright, it would have felt awkward. Besides, they'd reached the Quincy Street exit. Dulcie's path took her off to the right. Polly, clearly, was going back to the professor's house. 'I think we've all been through the mill.'

That won Dulcie a small smile and the two parted ways. After a few feet, though, Dulcie turned back. Had that vision of Mr Grey been a sign of some sort? Had she even seen a cat at all? Watching Polly walk away, she noted her bright beret again. So colorful, and really so unlike her usual attire.

'Hey, Polly!' she yelled down the street. The other woman turned. 'I like your hat!' And at that, Polly bent her head further into the wind and scurried away.

TWELVE

By the time Dulcie got home, dusk had settled, and with it a nippy cold. November had arrived in earnest.

'Suze! I'm home!' As Dulcie entered the postage-stamp-sized foyer, she heard music. 'Suze?'

Peeking over the top step, a small black and white face stared down and mewed. 'Hey, kitty.' Dulcie peered up as the small cat raced down the stairs, tumbling the last few steps in her haste. 'Hang on.' Dulcie scooped the kitten up and carried her up the stairs. 'What's your rush?' She smiled down at the little animal. 'Did you have something you needed to tell me?'

The kitten mewed again, squirming, but Dulcie set her down as another, louder voice called out.

'Coming!' A flurry of footsteps brought Suze down from the top floor. From the Harvard Swim sweats, Dulcie figured her roommate had either been napping or getting ready for a run. 'You wanna hit the river?'

The latter. But despite her roommate's best intentions, Dulcie had already collapsed into a kitchen chair. 'Susan Rubenstein, are you trying to get me to exercise?'

Suze had her leg up on the other chair by this point, but turned her head with a smile. 'Never too late to start! Besides, I figure with the week you've had…'

'Ben and Jerry is all the therapy I need.' Even watching Suze stretch was making Dulcie tired. 'From the cops to my new student—'

'Cops?' Suze stood up straight. Of course, Dulcie realized, she hadn't told her 3L roommate about the meeting. 'Don't tell me—'

'Don't worry, Suze! I'm not a suspect.' Dulcie didn't add 'this time.' They both remembered what had happened only a few months before. 'I was meeting with Professor Bullock when, um, when it happened.' Somehow, Dulcie still couldn't get herself to say 'murder.' 'They just wanted some background.'

'Background?' Suze pulled the other kitchen chair out and sat down, looking as intent as a cat.

'About Professor Bullock. Which is odd, 'cause if he's my alibi, then I'm his, right? But they were asking about his relationship with Cameron.'

Suze raised an eyebrow. 'Relationship?' That was enough. If Suze ever became a prosecutor, she'd be known as the strong, silent type. Dulcie spilled: The detective's vague insinuations, Lloyd's casual recital of department rumors. Cameron's recent switch to the much less glamorous department. By the time she got up to Raleigh's accusations, Dulcie herself was beginning to wonder.

'But really, Suze, there's nothing there. The only things we know are true are that he hasn't published in about twenty years, he works his assistants too hard, and, well, maybe he's not holding his weight in the department.'

'Why was Cameron coming to see him?' Dulcie shrugged. Suze thought for a second, and spoke again. 'Or, maybe, what had they been talking about?'

'Had?'

'Think about it, Dulce. You said Bullock let you in, right? And his slave girl, or whatever he calls her, wasn't around. So how do we know that he wasn't meeting secretly with Cameron? Then, I don't know, he lets you in and Cameron leaves by a back door. There's got to be a back door, right? And meets his end as he's coming around the house to the front gate.'

'But why?' Dulcie wasn't going to argue with the mechanics of it. 'What's the motive?' As she asked the question, the image of the dead man leaped into her mind and she forced herself to picture him not as she'd last seen him, but as he'd been in life. Cameron Dessay: playboy. There'd been one other time, early in the fall, when she'd felt his allure. He'd been driving past, hurtling down Broadway as she trudged along the steamy sidewalk. He hadn't noticed her, of course, but Dulcie's eye had been caught. He'd been in a cute little convertible, racing green, easily the nicest wheels of any of the grad students. There had been a blonde by his side, and they'd both been laughing, hair blown back by the breeze. For a moment, Dulcie had wished herself into that car, so cool and carefree. But while all that flash might have impressed his fellow students, it would have been small change to a professor who lived on Tory Row. 'And besides, even if Bullock wanted him dead, who would he have do the actual killing?'

Her own words made her cringe. Suze seemed less bothered. 'Bullock's got enough lackeys.' She was up and stretching again. 'Maybe he had one of them waiting. Maybe there was someone lurking in the holly as you walked in.'

THIRTEEN

WITH THAT UNSETTLING THOUGHT, Suze took off for her run and Dulcie contemplated dinner. Earlier in the fall, she and Chris had developed a comfy routine. Mary Chung's and a DVD, then reading for both. And a squabble, like the one last night, would have been resolved before the next order of takeout. But tonight, she knew, Chris would be working again, Dulcie was on her own.

'What's it going to be, kitten?' The little tuxedoed cat had followed her into the kitchen, sitting by her feet as she and Suze had discussed the aspects of the case. Now she looked up at her human and gave an almost imperceptible chirp.

'Dumplings? What a brilliant idea.' Calling in her order, Dulcie opened a can for the kitten. By the time she'd returned with the takeout—including some extras to heat up for Chris as a peace offering if he could come over later—the kitten had finished and sat, diligently working one white front paw over her face.

'Just like a grown-up cat!' With a pang, Dulcie found herself thinking about Mr Grey. The beautiful long-haired grey had just shown up one day, already a full-grown cat, ready to watch out for her in exchange for kibble. This kitten was a different matter entirely. Tiny, dependent, and frenetic in a way that Dulcie didn't understand. Is that why she didn't feel the bond that she'd felt with the large grey?

'Maybe, in time…' Dulcie didn't realize she'd spoken out loud until the kitten tilted her head up, bath interrupted. 'I'm sorry, kitten. That's not very fair to you, is it?' The small creature stared, her large green eyes quizzical, and Dulcie reached for her. 'At the very least, we can get some work done, don't you think?'

But the kitten had other ideas. Clambering up on to the kitchen table, she sniffed the bowl that had so recently held soup dumplings. Then, seeing Dulcie's books, stretched out her small claws to scratch.

'No, kitten!' Dulcie held the young cat's paws, removing her claws from the leather bindings. 'Those are from the library.' Anyone in her household was going to have to learn proper respect for books, particularly those that came from Widener. To reinforce the message, Dulcie pulled the volume toward her. *Berlette's Biographies,* the top who's who of English arts and letters. Well, maybe the kitten had a point. Maybe Dulcie should quit spending so much time trying to figure out who had hated Cameron Dessay enough to kill him and more time trying to work out who had actually authored the work she was writing her thesis on.

Two hours later, Suze had returned and taken off again, muttering something about a Constitutional Law study group. The kitten had completed three crazed laps of the apartment and then fallen asleep. But Dulcie was still sitting at the kitchen table, wide awake. Not that she'd been idle: working through the kitten's putative scratching post, she'd read through the biographies of the more famous writers and moved on to the smaller ones, the 'she-authors' who wrote so many of the popular works of the time. Some of these were well known: Ann Radcliffe, for example, had been the Danielle Steele of her day, churning out best-selling page-turners even as the critics snubbed her. Others were less well known, the educated daughters of mill owners or shop keepers who wrote one romance or adventure and then settled into a life of domesticity, their one brush with public fame tucked away like a keepsake. But Dulcie had always had a different idea about the author of her favorite work. *The Ravages of Umbria* had never won the acclaim of *The Italian* or *The Castle of Otranto.* Hadn't even been written about at the time of its publication, as if it were truly beneath even the critics' notice. But the sixty or so pages that survived showed a style and verve that very few of its contemporaries could match. Yes, it had ghosts, a ruined castle, and at least two romantic entanglements. But there was more. Surely, such a smart and subtle author couldn't have disappeared.

Unless…Dulcie started flipping back pages. What if the author of *The Ravages* hadn't disappeared? What if she—or, yes, possibly he—had published other works, under a different name? Maybe some better-known author had wanted to shed the conventions, to write something a little bit subversive. Wouldn't that be reason to publish pseudonymously?

'It's still done today. Isn't it, kitty?' Dulcie watched the tiny thing yawn, and then go back to sleep. 'Well, I'm intrigued, anyway.'

An hour later, and the idea had gone sour. None of the possibilities—Dulcie thought of them as her suspects—had long enough gaps in their timelines. Nobody who could have pulled off *The Ravages of Umbria* seemed likely to. And those lesser authors, the ones who wrote one book and disappeared, well, they just didn't have the skills, did they? Dulcie looked at the kitten, who had turned her back to the books.

'Time for ice cream?' The kitten looked up and for a moment Dulcie waited, holding her breath. Just one word… But the only reply was a very quiet 'mew.'

FOURTEEN

By the time Dulcie dragged herself out of bed, she was already late. Chris had failed to appear, though his midnight call had sounded both sweet and stranded, with no mention made of their tiff. She'd finished the dumplings, then, and the combination of the doughy wrappers and the spicy dipping sauce had probably contributed to her evil dreams. Throughout the night, she'd found herself in a windswept wasteland, alone except for some spiked bushes and the disturbing smell of smoke. Each time, she was holding a book—*The Ravages,* she assumed—and in each iteration the dream followed the same plot. 'The key,' she'd hear, although each time the voice seemed further away. 'The key to secrets lost.' She'd start turning the pages, looking for something, she wasn't sure what, as the wind tossed the pages before she could read them, stinging her eyes with the suggestion of ash. 'The key...' And then that wind, howling and cold, would rip the book from her hands, and as she dived for it, scratching herself on barbed leaves, she'd find herself face to face with Cameron, cold, white, and dead.

'Enough already!' she'd yelled after the third time she'd woken up, sweating and tense, at some pre-dawn hour. She'd sat up with a start, eager to shake off the horror of that sight, the dead eyes so close to her own. The movement had been enough to dislodge the kitten and as she saw the small tail dip over the side of the bed, Dulcie had to wonder. Those scratchy bushes—was this kitten developing some bad habits?

'Look who's talking.' The voice startled Dulcie awake. It was the same voice she'd heard in her dream, only closer.

'Mr Grey?' She looked around the small bedroom, seeking the grey cat. But everything was grey in this light, the muted glow of the moon or, more likely, a nearby streetlight, casting shadows. Did something move by her desk? Was that the kitten, there, by the waste basket? Or was it her old friend, back to offer comfort and a soft purr?

Silence greeted her, and a sudden memory of Mr Grey's sensitive ears. If she'd yelled like that when he was around, they would have flattened out. He would have left the room. The little kitten probably felt the same way.

'I'm sorry I yelled.' Dulcie felt a sudden stab of remorse. 'I guess I'm not much fun these days.'

'Dulcie, Dulcie.' A soft thud on the foot of the bed announced the arrival of a larger feline than the one she'd chased away. 'Will you never learn?'

'You don't mean the dumplings, do you, Mr Grey?' As much as she wanted to reach out, to feel for the long, soft fur, Dulcie held back. A wave of fatigue washed over her and she lay back down. Somewhere, at the foot of the bed, a rhythmic motion like a cat kneading had started. Along with the quiet hum of a purr, the effect was hypnotic.

'No, Dulcie, not the dumplings.' She longed to sit up, to pull the heavy grey cat toward her and hold him once more. He must know about her thesis troubles. If only he weren't so cryptic. If only she weren't so sleepy. 'We're trying to help you, but you've got to do your part, too, Dulcie. You know what makes a heroine.' He must have heard her, but before she could respond, the voice came back. 'Now you must learn to trust yourself.'

What did self-confidence have to do with her thesis? With *The Ravages of Umbria?* With anything?

'Rest now, Dulcie. You'll need your wits about you if you're going to find the key.'

THE KITTEN WAS SLEEPING on her pillow when she'd woken the next time, the weak November sunshine flooding the room.

'Watch it, kitty.' She'd been careful to move around the kitten, her little mouth slightly open as she slept on. 'Sorry about last night.'

In response, one small white paw twitched, but that was all. And Dulcie did her best to shower and dress quietly, slipping out of the room without disturbing the feline further.

FIFTEEN

'SO, WHERE'S THE BEEF?' Lindsay Potter was Dulcie's least favorite student. A smart modernist with a tendency to mistake advertising slogans for real writing, Lindsay tended to dominate Dulcie's Thursday tutorial.

'Good morning, Lindsay.' Dulcie dropped her bag and put her travel mug on the table. 'Good morning, Greg. Good morning, Karen.' She unbuttoned her coat and hung it on the hook at the back of the door. The departmental office had a coat closet, but Dulcie had been running so late, she'd simply bounded up the stairs to the second floor conference room. No time to ponder last night's dream, she'd barely managed to refill her mug from downstairs. 'I hope you've all been able to do this week's reading?'

'Never mind the reading.' Lindsay wasn't letting go. 'I want to know about the murder.'

Dulcie opened her planner and used the moment to think. When she looked up, three eager faces were watching hers.

'Well?' Lindsay seemed to be speaking for all of them. 'Spill.'

A bitter taste that couldn't be blamed on the departmental coffee rose in Dulcie's throat and she struggled to keep from making a face.

'I gather you've heard about Cameron Dessay's death.' She decided to keep it simple. Clinical. 'Yes, one of our graduate students was killed on Monday. No, I don't know anything about the investigation.'

'I heard you were the one who found him.' Greg seemed to have finally found a topic that interested him.

'I really have nothing more to say on this subject.' Dulcie pulled the planner close and tried to summon a sense of authority. Was this what Mr Grey had meant about trusting herself? 'Please, people, we have work to do—and limited time.'

As Greg and Karen pulled out laptops, she heard Lindsay muttering.

'Yes?'

'Nothing.' The blonde junior started chewing at the end of her pen. 'Only, yeah, why can't we talk about this? It's more relevant to our academic career than any of this stuff.' Her gesture could have encompassed the books that Dulcie had pulled from her bag, the table where all their notes now lay opened, or the English Department itself.

'More relevant than character development in the late-eighteenth-century novel?' Dulcie started to chuckle. 'I don't think so.'

Her students didn't even try to stifle their groans. Not one of them shared her interest, but all of them needed a pre-1850 tutorial in order to qualify for honors.

'Would you rather be in Lippcott's tutorial?' Dulcie felt a spasm of disloyalty. Earl Lippcott couldn't help it. A Chaucerian, with a special interest in the minor poems, he was known for his extreme shyness. Anyone who had listened while he stammered and blushed through a reading of even the most decorous of the *Canterbury Tales* would think twice about spending any serious study time with the man.

'I'd rather be working on something relevant.' Lindsay spat out the last word. 'Golden Age detective fiction, maybe.' She said it like a challenge, and Dulcie fought down the urge to bark back. Thinking of Mr Grey helped, and as she did, an idea came to her.

'If you're interested in detecting,' she said, starting to pull stray thoughts together. 'I have an idea.' What had she been telling Lucy? 'Why don't we talk about provenance? So much of what we're reading this semester comes to us with questions. Which versions are the best ones, the ones the author intended? How do we decide on an author when authorship is disputed?'

For a moment, Lucy's second warning flashed through her mind. How 'poking about' could be dangerous. But Dulcie shook her head. That was just Lucy, wanting her daughter to believe. To have some kind of spiritual attachment. Well, she had faith in research. 'How can we research this?' She addressed her students. 'How can we prove the authenticity of anonymous writings?'

Lindsay snorted, but Greg and Karen looked intrigued, so Dulcie kept talking. 'For better known works, we have a clear history. We know something about an author. We have the publication history, sometimes even the first reviews. But what about the works that didn't take off? Or the ones that only exist in fragments?'

'Like *The Rampages of Austria*, you mean?' Lindsay's voice had taken on a mocking tone.

'Like *The Ravages of Umbria*, yes.' Dulcie fought to hold her voice steady. She was the adult here. But as Lindsay sat up to speak again, Dulcie jumped in. Why risk a battle? 'This is a legitimate scholarly topic. After all, there have been some famous frauds.'

'Such as?' If that was the best the blonde junior could come up with, Dulcie could cope. At least she had the attention of her other two students.

'Well, like that Shakespeare play.' Karen was into it now. 'The one that was supposedly found in an attic?'

'If someone named Will Shakespeare even wrote those at all,' Greg chimed in. 'After all, he was barely literate.'

'Wait a minute.' Dulcie found herself smiling even as she interrupted. Her students might have the facts wrong, but this was the most animated she'd seen any of them. 'Shakespeare wasn't illiterate. He might not have had much formal education, but he could clearly read because we know he could write.'

'Unless the plays weren't by him!' Greg was getting excited. 'And it was all a great big conspiracy!'

'Well, what do we mean by "author," anyway.' Karen's postmodern bent was showing. 'I mean, if the Earl of Whatever really wrote *Hamlet,* then maybe he was Shakespeare. At least in terms of what the name Shakespeare signifies…'

And they were off.

SIXTEEN

By the time the tutorial broke up, some ninety minutes later, Dulcie's head was spinning. Somehow the discussion of provenance had turned into a debate over the definition of authorship and whether a work could actually be considered 'written' if it drew on earlier works.

'At least they're thinking,' Dulcie said to herself, as she clumped down the stairs.

'Students?' a familiar voice asked. Trista was holding an empty coffee pot. 'Don't be too sure of it. And if I make more…'

'Yes, I will. Thanks.' Dulcie filled her friend in on the tutorial. Trista's response—complete with groans and eye rolling—was gratifying. She and Dulcie had bonded sophomore year during Introductory Anglo Saxon. They'd since moved on to separate specialties. Despite her post-punk piercings and bleached blonde hair, Trista was a pure Victorian at heart. But neither had much use for the latest trends.

'I mean, if you deconstruct a book, what do you really get?' Trista filled two cups with the fresh brew.

'Paper?' Dulcie was joking, but only partly. 'Leather bindings?'

'Hmm, now that sounds interesting.'

But Dulcie didn't rise to the bait. 'Hey, Tris, what do you know about Roger Gosham?'

'You are not—?' Trista raised one pierced eyebrow.

'No, no,' Dulcie was quick to reassure her. 'Chris and I are tight. I mean, unless he's got someone else tucked away in the computer labs…'

'Chris? Nah.' Trista sounded so sure that Dulcie found herself relieved. Funny, she hadn't even realized she was worried. 'But why do you ask about that bookworm, accent on the "worm"?'

'He seemed cranky, but why do you say that?' Dulcie looked at her friend. 'I mean, Bullock swears by him.'

'Well, of course.' Trista seemed content to leave it at that, but Dulcie was waiting. 'He's a total brown nose, Dulcie. Have you ever seen him with any of the senior faculty? It's "Of course, Professor," and "Yes, Professor." Complete toady.'

'Well, he does depend on them for income.' More than most of her classmates, Dulcie knew the pinch of poverty.

'Yeah, and he's making a good living at it.' Trista wrinkled up her nose.

Dulcie thought about the boxes. 'I don't know. What with rents being what they are, and the economy…'

'That one? He'll be fine.' Trista leaned in. 'I hear he's expanding, taking over the entire top floor of the building. I guess maybe that would make him a good catch. Only, there's something about him. Maybe it's mold.'

With a laugh, Dulcie downed her coffee. Trista's gossip did explain the boxes, and maybe he would be a good mate—for Polly. But until either of the interested parties said anything, she'd keep her theories about Polly and the grouchy bookbinder to herself. But while the tutorial had at least engaged her students, it hadn't helped her with her own nagging question. What if *The Ravages of Umbria* really was, somehow, not what it seemed? She needed some guidance and if Roger Gosham genuinely did have all the expertise that Professor Bullock seemed to believe he had, maybe he'd be able to shed some light.

Still, Trista's words carried a warning. If Gosham truly owed his success to Professor Bullock, he'd undoubtedly share any news with his best client. She'd have to find a way to ask without asking. Maybe she could use her connection to Bullock as an entree. She could find a way to run another errand. If she had to, she'd explain to Polly afterward, and apologize if she'd stepped on any toes.

SEVENTEEN

'HEY, LLOYD, WHAT CAN YOU tell me about Bullock's rare book collection?' Ten minutes later, Dulcie was back at the Student Union office.

'What do you mean?' The face that looked up at her was more worn than the day before, prompting Dulcie to wonder if her fellow grad student had left the cramped space in the interim.

'I'm not sure. I'm looking for something that might need some work. Something that just isn't what it should be. Something off.' Dulcie noted with alarm that Lloyd had grown paler still. 'Lloyd, are you okay?'

'I… What do you mean "off," Dulcie?' His voice had a tremor in it. 'Please, tell me what you mean.'

'Nothing, Lloyd.' She started poking around in her bag. Raleigh's warning flashed through her head, but concern for Lloyd trumped gossip. 'Have you eaten today? I think I have some of the Chips Ahoy left from the other night.'

'No, I'm fine.' He shook his head at the offered cookies, which were pretty much crumbs after a few days in Dulcie's bag. 'I'm just tired.'

Dulcie sat on the edge of her own desk and nibbled at one of the broken bits. They still tasted good. 'I didn't mean to startle you. I'm just, well, I'll be honest. I'm having some doubts about the provenance of *The Ravages* and I thought it might be useful to speak to that book-repair guy, Roger Gosham. And Trista says that he worships the ground that Bullock walks on, so I thought if I arrived on an errand from the professor, well, it would make my life easier.'

Lloyd nodded and took a piece of cookie. 'Good idea. Gosham's kind of a legend in the field, I gather. Really picky about what he works on—and who for.'

'Yeah, I gather he owes his success to Bullock.' Dulcie's mind flashed to Polly. Maybe if the professor wasn't paying so much for rare books, he could afford to give that poor woman a raise. She mentioned that idea to Lloyd, only to have him snort in derision.

'Bullock? He hoards like some mythical dwarf. If I didn't have my grants…' He left the sentence unfinished. 'But why the worries, Dulcie?'

Dulcie chewed and hesitated. Most of her friends knew her background. But Lucy's special brand of psychic nuttiness had been shared with only a few. 'Have I ever told you about my mom?'

Lloyd smiled and reached for the cookie bag. 'The good witch of the Northwest? Yeah. Is this one of her prophecies?'

Dulcie nodded, relieved. 'I wasn't sure if I'd told you about her. But, yeah, Lucy had a dream.'

'And you've started writing in earnest, so this hits on all your anxieties.' He looked up so suddenly that Dulcie wondered if he'd bitten his tongue. 'Maybe that's it, Dulce. Maybe your mom is psychic, but not in the way she thinks. Maybe she's picking up on your fears.'

'Wow.' Dulcie savored the idea. 'That would be great, wouldn't it? But what about you? Why did you tense up when I asked?' She could see Lloyd drawing back and considered sharing her student's suspicions. 'Come on, Lloyd. You can tell me. Is something up with Bullock?'

Lloyd nodded. 'I swear, he's getting worse.' Her officemate lowered his voice. 'Sometimes, Dulcie, I think he's losing it. He called me at home last night at some godawful hour. I'd been in bed for hours.'

'What an invasion of privacy!' Dulcie looked suitably shocked. She'd noted Lloyd's choice of words, and although she couldn't imagine Lloyd being in bed *with* anyone, the trespass was unforgivable. Sleep itself was precious. 'He couldn't have waited till morning? He couldn't have emailed?'

'Please.' Lloyd didn't have to say anymore. Professor William Alfred Bullock did not use email. Dulcie doubted he even typed. 'And get this. He told me—I kid you not—that he wants me to start researching some rare text. An Elizabethan romance or something!'

'Huh?' This wasn't what she'd expected.

'I know! Not even his period!' Lloyd was still whispering, but the color had returned to his cheeks. 'He's being all mysterious about where he got it, acting like it just turned up in his collection, and now he wants me to drop everything and get to work on it. And this after he's had me working nonstop on the notes for the new Smollett edition. I mean, he's supposed to have turned in the foreword months ago.'

He sat back and the two friends mulled over the craziness of bosses.

'Senior faculty.' Dulcie broke the silence at last. 'I guess they really are free to follow their fancies. And it's our job to try to keep up.' She looked around the tiny office. It looked comforting. Homey. Raleigh's guesses might be off target, but that didn't mean Dulcie shouldn't start reading her student's thesis project, or get back to work on her own. But that question—and Lucy's call—still rankled.

'Speaking of, I think I'll head over there. Beard the lion in his den.' She pulled the heavy book bag back on to her shoulder. 'Want me to tell him anything? That you've discovered Sir Walter Raleigh's diary or something?'

Lloyd smiled and shook his head. 'I'll figure it out, Dulcie. Actually, I'm hoping that if I don't mention it, he forgets about it. I don't think he even remembers where he got it, if it exists at all. Maybe it was all a dream. He's been getting a little, well, less reality-based as time goes on, if you get my drift.'

'As if he ever was, Lloyd.' Dulcie smiled and headed for the door. She hadn't even taken off her coat.

EIGHTEEN

SHE HEARD THE PROFESSOR before she saw him. Halfway up that short walkway, eyes focused on the front door, Dulcie heard what could only be described as a roar. For a moment, she hesitated. What if the killer had returned and was now wrestling with the aged academic? What if her mentor had gone into a wild, murderous rage? Would she be finding Polly's body next, lying arms akimbo among the fallen books?

Shaking that all-too-believable image from her head and taking a deep breath for courage, Dulcie climbed the stone stoop and rang the doorbell. Inside the heavy oak door, chimes—and more roars—rang out.

'Hi, Dulcie,' Polly answered, looking no more flustered than usual. 'I'm, um, I'm not sure the professor is receiving visitors.'

She stood in the doorway as another roar made the wan assistant wince. Dulcie wondered once again about her mentor's temper. He wouldn't actually hit Polly, would he?

'Where the hell is it?' The roar had words now, either because Polly was holding the door to the solid brick house open or because Professor Bullock had gathered his thoughts. 'The bloody thing was on my desk not two hours ago!'

Dulcie tried to look over Polly's shoulder. There was no sense in pretending she hadn't heard the outburst. But the assistant stood her ground. 'Has the professor lost something?' Dulcie asked.

Polly paused, perhaps questioning where her allegiance lay. Looking down, she began picking at a loose thread that held a mismatched button on to her sweater. Maybe she has only just realized it doesn't match, Dulcie thought. She doesn't have to be embarrassed about her clothes in front of me. For a moment, Dulcie wondered about reaching out to her, about sharing her own stories of coming East with little more than homemade sweaters and the Riverside Shakespeare. But another roar from the back room interrupted her—and pushed Polly into a decision. She nodded, as if answering her own question, her colorless lips tight. 'A letter opener. His letter opener,' she corrected herself.

'Was it valuable?'

Polly shrugged thin shoulders. 'I don't know. Maybe. It was part of a set. A gift from when he spoke at McGill. The North American Academic conference, '83, I think?'

Dulcie nodded, not surprised that the conscientious assistant knew the origin of every item in the professor's office. 'Do you think I can get in to see him?'

Polly wrung her hands and dared a glance back over her shoulder. 'Do you, well, do you think maybe you could come back?'

Dulcie hesitated. While not as afraid of the professor's wrath as Polly evidently was, she wasn't keen on aggravating the professor further. For a moment, they both stood there, Polly clearly wishing she could close the door.

'Look, Polly,' Dulcie finally resolved. 'Why don't you let me in? We'll sit for a few minutes. If he calms down, great.'

Polly wasn't convinced. 'You didn't have an appointment.'

Dulcie gave her a look that made the older woman twist her hands again.

'Oh, come in,' she finally decided. 'You're letting all the heat out, anyway.'

'Thanks, Polly.' Dulcie gave the pale woman a big smile as she followed her in. For a moment, they both stood in the entrance to the sitting room. Dulcie hesitated because of the memories. Polly looked in at the antique furniture and arrived at her own decision.

'Let's go back to the kitchen.' She started off down the hallway. 'So much warmer, don't you think?'

'Sure.' Dulcie started to follow when a thought came to her. 'Hey, Polly, you know, you might be able to help me.' Whatever she had become, Polly Heinhold had once been a scholar, too. 'I'm trying to figure out a question of authenticity.'

'Oh?' For a moment, something flickered in the older woman's eyes and Dulcie regretted not asking her earlier. 'Are you working on a disputed text?'

Dulcie hedged. She didn't want the subject of her thesis to be disputed. It wasn't, really, except in her own mind. 'It's complicated. You see, it has to do with my thesis.'

'Tell me about it!' Polly surprised her by letting out a laugh. 'Theses! Oh, man, I could write a book!'

This was a new side to Polly, and Dulcie looked up in wonder. Was this what the older woman had been like at Dulcie's age? Before starting to work for Professor Bullock? Was the professor some kind of psychic vampire, sucking the life out of his assistants? Would Lloyd be his next victim? Would she?

Before Dulcie could even begin to frame any of these questions, her cell rang. Lindsay, from her junior tutorial. These students ignored office hours but they expected Dulcie to be on call 24-7. She let the call go through to voicemail, but the moment with Polly was lost as the doorbell rang again. From inside the house, the chimes sounded deep and loud and Dulcie wondered how the professor could ignore them. He must just be used to Polly answering the door, she realized as the older woman did indeed trot back down the hall. There, standing on the stoop, was Roger Gosham.

'Great!' Dulcie started back down the hall in Polly's footsteps. Now she wouldn't need the introduction. But within five steps, it became clear that there was something going on between the two at the door.

'Rog—Mr Gosham!' Polly nearly stuttered, and for a split second Dulcie thought again of Lloyd. 'What are you doing here?'

'You should know…' He saw Dulcie and his tone lightened. 'I believe in service to my best customers!'

'But, but, we have no books for you today, Mr Gosham.' Polly was wringing her hands again. Dulcie looked on. Was she witnessing the tail end of a romantic spat? Or was something darker going on? Perhaps some kind of competition, vying for Professor Bullock's favor?

'I've brought one, Polly.' The gnarled bookbinder held out a package wrapped in brown paper. As Polly unwrapped it, Dulcie was sure she was holding her breath.

'Oh!' She sounded startled and Dulcie, looking over, recognized the title.

'That was fast!' With a cheeriness she didn't feel, Dulcie dived in, eager to defuse the situation. 'I brought that over on Tuesday, Polly. You were out, and the professor asked me to take it. I'm sorry.'

They both turned to stare at her.

'I mean, I didn't mean to get in anybody's way.' Now she was the one stammering.

'Oh, you didn't!'

'Not at all, so glad to help.' Polly and Roger Gosham fell over each other trying to reassure her.

'But while I'm here—' Gosham smiled '—I was wondering if I could pick something up.' His large, yellow teeth were positively wolflike, but maybe some women liked that. The comment had not been directed toward her.

'I don't know what you're talking about.' Polly blushed and turned away. Dulcie felt like a third wheel. As unobtrusively as possible, she started to edge away from the couple. She could wait in the kitchen.

'Now, don't play coy with me.' Behind her, Dulcie heard a slight scuffle and, possibly, a slap.

'Go away.' Polly was whispering. 'The professor could come out at any moment.'

'Okay.' Gosham didn't sound pleased. 'But I'll be back.'

At the sound of the door opening, Dulcie figured it was safe to look up. But although Gosham was indeed standing in the open doorway, the first thing she noticed was Professor Bullock, standing in the entrance to his office, his white hair disheveled and his eyes wild.

NINETEEN

'Professor!' Whatever had been going on with Roger Gosham, Polly's attention had turned entirely to her employer.

'Polly.' Bullock nodded and absently ran a hand over his hair, smoothing it back into some semblance of normalcy. 'Gosham. Glad you're here.'

The bookbinder stepped toward the professor, but turned one last time to Polly. Dulcie didn't know if he was readying a kind or cutting remark, considering what she'd just heard. But she did see her moment of opportunity.

'Professor, Mr Gosham, if you have a moment?'

The professor looked at her and blinked.

'No, I don't have an appointment, Professor.' Dulcie scrambled for an explanation. 'But something's come up.' Both men were looking at her now, and Dulcie had the distinct impression that Polly was relieved. She, however, had to figure out what to say. 'It's about a book.'

'Yes?' It was the professor who had spoken, but Gosham was staring at her.

'I'm having a problem I'm wondering if maybe one of you can help me with.' Dulcie paused, trying to figure out the best way to phrase her question without revealing all of her doubts. 'It's a question of authenticity.'

'Authenticity!' The professor's eyes lit up and he repeated the word as if it were exactly what he'd been meaning to say. 'How fascinating! Do come in, Dulcie.'

Right behind her, Roger Gosham started to speak, but Professor Bullock waved him away. 'We'll talk another time, Roger. Grateful that you came down here. Polly?' The professor barely turned to acknowledge his faithful assistant. 'Give Gosham the Reynolds, will you?'

Dulcie looked back at Polly and at Gosham, who shrugged. The Reynolds was the volume that the bookbinder had just returned. With an answering shrug of her own, Dulcie turned and followed the professor into his office.

'Have a seat, have a seat.' The professor was being unusually courtly, but as Dulcie looked around she realized she'd have a difficult time obliging. Along with the usual scholarly clutter— the piles of books and journals, dog-eared printouts and scribbled notes—the large dim room was witness to a rampage. The professor's search for his missing desk set seemed to have had him turning over furniture as well as upsetting some of the older, and taller, piles of books. Dulcie righted a lamp as she made her way over to the usual guest chair. An opened magazine lay face down and she closed it, placing it on the floor beside her as she took a seat.

'Sir? Did you find it?'

'Find what?'

Dulcie blinked. Surely, he must have realized his cries of dismay were audible. 'Your letter opener?' He stared at her, his face blank. Maybe Polly had it wrong. On Tuesday, he'd been complaining about a missing pen. 'Or was it a pen? A missing pen?'

'What? My pen?' Bullock reached among the papers on his desk. 'It's right here.' He reached for something on the desk, dismissing her concern with a small wave. 'So, are we talking authenticity in terms of actual authorship or in terms of an intrusive editor? A suspect edition, perhaps?'

Dulcie looked. The pen in the professor's hand was a common ballpoint. Something odd was going on, and suddenly she didn't want to share her fears. Still, he was looking at her, his blue eyes piercing.

'Well, I was wondering about authenticating a lesser known work, actually.' She was hedging and he knew it. His bushy eyebrows rose. 'I mean, we accept so much at this point and we don't really question the veracity of books once they've entered the canon, do we?' She was waiting for him to slap her down. After all, earlier this week, he'd nearly laughed her out of the office for her curiosity about an author.

Much to her surprise, he seemed to be considering her question. 'Interesting,' he said, leaning back in his chair. 'Do you have a particular work in mind?'

'Well, of course, I'm thinking at least a little about *The Ravages.*' Saying that much wasn't giving her suspicions away. He had to know that any questions would touch on her thesis. 'After all, there are several versions of the surviving manuscript—of the surviving fragments, I mean. How do we know which version to trust?'

She was stalling. In truth, one of the best known studies of *The Ravages,* out of Berkeley, had already dissected the slight variations about five years before. It had attributed the minor changes to either subsequent editions or unauthorized reprints, much as Shakespeare's works continued to change over the centuries, with editors modernizing spellings and adding stage directions. But how could she say that she was beginning to doubt that *The Ravages of Umbria* was even written in the late 1700s? That it might in fact be a hoax? Some later scholar's idea of a joke? She might as well question her entire discipline. 'What if a book isn't what it seems? I mean, faked texts are being exposed all the time.' There, she'd said it.

'You're thinking like a scholar, Dulcie.' The professor chuckled slightly, startling Dulcie, who thought she was doing anything but. 'In fact, I may have an interesting case. A previously undiscovered work.' He got up and started looking through his bookshelf.

'I was thinking more of falsified texts,' Dulcie said. But the professor was on a roll. Browsing through the shelves, he pulled one book and replaced it, then another. 'Professor?'

With a shake of his head, he turned around. 'Nevermind. This is off the point for you, Miss Schwartz. I think you have your hands full with *The Ravages.*'

'But I was talking about *The Ravages*—'

Bullock interrupted her. 'Now, now, let's not go off on tangents. We'll meet when you have your next chapter ready. Ask Polly to schedule something.' She was being dismissed.

'Okay.' She stood up. 'Thanks, Professor.' But Bullock remained deep in thought. Only as she let herself out did she see him start rustling through the papers on his desktop again. She could have sworn she heard him say something about a pen.

'Polly?' The assistant was taking an uncharacteristic break, sitting on the front room's settee, her head in her hands. 'Are you all right?'

'Yes, yes.' She jumped up and grabbed Dulcie's coat off the overburdened coat tree before Dulcie could reach it herself. 'Lost in thought.' She forced a smile as she stood there, smoothing down her skirt with nervous hands.

Dulcie wondered again about the assistant's involvement with Roger Gosham. Clearly, something was amiss. Dulcie could relate: it seemed like she and Chris barely saw each other these days. But that was end-of-the-semester craziness. Polly seemed to be insecure enough to blame herself.

'He's lucky, you know.' Dulcie leaned toward the older woman, feeling a surge of sisterhood. 'You're quite a catch.'

Polly gasped and jerked back, her eyes glazed with horror.

'Polly? What is it?' Dulcie reached for Polly, her hands barely making contact with the other woman's bony arms before she pulled free and ran into the kitchen.

'Polly?'

Behind the door, she heard the other woman sobbing.

TWENTY

'POLLY?' DULCIE LEANED against the kitchen door, speaking as softly as she thought would still be audible. 'Whatever I said, I'm sorry.' There was no response. 'Would you like to talk?'

The door stayed closed and after a few more tries, Dulcie stepped back. That brief moment when Polly had started to talk about research had made her feel like they had a bond. Sisters in academia. But clearly Dulcie had overstepped. Not all relationships were like hers and Chris's. To be honest, she wasn't even sure what theirs was like anymore. It was time to leave.

But as Dulcie started buttoning her coat, she looked around. Even with the professor locked in his office and the assistant in the kitchen, Dulcie had a strange sense of being not quite alone, as if some other presence remained—and was trying to reach out to her. After the earlier hubbub, the old brick townhouse was quiet. No street noise made it up here and the high walls, lined with books, acted as additional insulation. So what was that feeling? She was beginning to get ever so slightly creeped out when she remembered that missed phone call. Of course, conscience was a funny thing. And nobody would mind if she checked her messages, would they? Sure enough, Lindsay's call had been far from urgent. Something about wanting a recommendation for a program next summer. Mystery solved, Dulcie turned the phone off. She'd deal with it in the tutorial, maybe try to teach these kids about boundaries.

But as she tucked the cell back in her pocket, she found herself looking around. Something was drawing her, she could feel it. All those books—they were like so much catnip to a scholar. Floor to ceiling built-ins, with additional volumes and strange curios taking up any extra space, they gave the old house the feeling of a treasure room, a scholar's den. Knowing she shouldn't, and that she certainly didn't want to be caught, Dulcie walked softly, almost tiptoeing, back down the hall and into the sitting room. Behind the settee, tall windows let in the last of the afternoon sun. Half-opened lace curtains kept the light off the books that flanked the far wall, and it was to those shadows that Dulcie gravitated. *Humphrey Clinker,* a biography of Aphra Behn, short works by Smollett: all earlier than Dulcie's beloved Gothics, but still her century. Essays on Fielding and, yes, finally, a collection of critical pieces on Gothic great Ann Radcliffe. Had she read that one?

Reaching for the volume, Dulcie had to squeeze a bit. An oversized leather armchair was pressed close to the shelves, leaving a space only big enough for someone Polly's size to slip through. The coat added a few inches, of course, but Dulcie made a mental note to start doing sit-ups again, as she pushed in. The book was just slightly out of reach.

A clattering of metal made her jump back, scraping the big chair on the hardwood floor.

'Damn! Sorry!' Dulcie reacted automatically, looking down to where the chair's thick legs had left a scuff on the polished wood. 'Oh, hell.' Spitting on her finger, she bent to rub at the spot, hoping to erase the evidence before anyone came to investigate. Nobody did and after a few seconds she gave up. The floor wasn't in pristine shape, anyway. But as she was pulling herself up—the coat was heavy as well as bulky—a glimmer caught her eye. A miniature sword, no more than ten inches long, lay half under the chair. That must have been what she'd brushed against, the noise that had made her jump.

Dulcie reached for the little sword, wondering where to replace it. It seemed an odd curio, more fitting for a professor of the Romantic nineteenth century than Bullock. In her hand, it felt strangely heavy, its curiously worked handle held some kind of inset stone, dark in the shadow of the chair. In *The Ravages of Umbria,* Hermetria saw a sword, but it was a phantasm, a vision sent by the ghost of the old family retainer. This little weapon,

Dulcie ran her finger along one edge, was quite solid. And surprisingly sharp.

Of course! The realization hit her like a flash of sunlight reflected off the blade's surface. She'd found Professor Bullock's missing letter opener.

'A letter opener,' Dulcie corrected herself, unaware that she'd spoken out loud. For all she knew, Bullock had one for each room. Still, this little doodad had the look of a cherished piece: the molded curlicues in the hilt picking up the shapes outlined on the pommel. This could very well be the one the professor had misplaced, and Dulcie stood to leave. If she dared to knock on the professor's office door, she might win herself some credit with the tenured grouch.

Or, she realized, she might simply annoy him. The combination of the sword-shaped opener and the closed door combined and Dulcie saw herself in armor, bracing to take on a dragon in its den. 'Wrong period,' she joked, to give herself courage.

But as she started toward the hallway, a strange sound stopped her. It wasn't loud, but Dulcie had grown so used to the silence that the sound—a light tap—was quite distinct.

'Polly?' Dulcie heard her voice crack. Stepping into the hall, she saw that the kitchen door was still closed. So was the professor's office. And somewhere, down below her, she heard what was most definitely a footstep.

'This is ridiculous.' She was speaking out loud to give herself courage, but even as she said it, she realized she was gripping the little sword. Most likely, Polly had recovered her composure and was now down in the basement, doing the professor's laundry or darning his socks or something. Or maybe the professor himself had emerged and gone off to seek some old draft of an article, kept in a storage area below.

'Professor?' It had to be Polly. There was no way the professor could have gotten past her so quietly. Maybe there was a service stairwell, leading directly down from the kitchen. Dulcie peered down the hallway. 'Polly?'

Just then, she heard a sniff. The unmistakable sniff of someone who has been crying and wants it to be noticed. The sound of Polly, coming from inside the kitchen. Dulcie looked down at the tiny sword in her hand. Despite its weight, it was a curio. A letter opener.

'Run, Dulcie! Get out of there!' Even before she heard Mr Grey's voice, she knew that something was wrong, very wrong. Dropping the pretty toy, Dulcie spun around toward the front of the house, threw the heavy door open, and ran out to the street.

TWENTY-ONE

'Wow, I GUESS YOU PUT YOUR foot in it.' Suze's voice on the phone was only partly comforting. Dulcie had jumped when her cell had rung as she walked back through Cambridge Common in the fading light. But hearing her roommate—and talking about dinner plans—had started to bring her back to reality.

What had happened at Professor Bullock's house had not made any sense. But as she gave the facts to Suze, at least it seemed a lot less scary than it had only minutes before.

'You mean, with Polly?'

'Yeah. I mean, who knows what's going on with her. She sounds a bit ghoulish.' Suze chuckled. 'Hey, maybe the professor really is some kind of vampire! Maybe you heard Lloyd, chained up in the basement.'

'Very funny.' The fright had worn off, leaving Dulcie edgy and a little sick. Just then, she got the double beep of an incoming call. She checked: Raleigh Hall. With only the smallest ping of guilt, she ignored the student and flipped back to Suze.

'As long as you're working on your thesis, I think you'll be safe.' Suze had obviously kept on talking. 'But actually, I was thinking about that letter opener.'

'Why? What do you mean?' Maybe Dulcie had missed something.

'The professor's?'

'No, I know.' Dulcie pictured the miniature sword. She'd meant to put it back on a shelf, but she couldn't remember if she had—or if in her rush, she'd just thrown it back to the floor. Well, if it was in the middle of the room, the professor or Polly would find it. 'But what about it?'

'Think about it, Dulcie.' Suze had listened with interest as

Dulcie had described the pretty piece with its fanciful design. 'Cameron was stabbed, right? Maybe you just found the murder weapon.'

Dulcie caught her breath, as Suze continued with the kind of good, practical advice she could be counted on for. Dulcie should call the police. She should tell them about the letter opener, about the suspicious behavior. Since she'd already touched the thing, she should consider retrieving it. But as Suze went on with her sensible list, Dulcie started remembering everything else that had happened since she and her roommate had had a real heart-to-heart. She hadn't gone into detail about her talk with the police, for example, which meant that Suze didn't know that the police were already considering Professor Bullock—her thesis adviser—as a suspect. Dulcie had no urge to protect a killer, but she couldn't just blindly do anything that would sink him further. Besides, what Suze was saying about the letter opener didn't make sense.

'But, why?' Before her roommate could start listing motives, Dulcie finished her thought. 'I mean, why would someone have left it there after, well, you know?' She paused. There was something else she hadn't mentioned: Mr Grey had led her to that letter opener. And Professor Bullock had said it had been lost. Maybe he'd wanted it lost. 'You think, maybe, that it wasn't really lost? But that I was supposed to find it?'

EAGER TO EXPLAIN HERSELF, Dulcie gave Suze the rest of the story, about the strange lure of the library and that voice, that last warning to flee, that had sent her stumbling down the stairs, running until she reached the open space of the Common, where Suze's call had found her.

The silence on the line lasted so long that Dulcie checked to make sure they were still connected.

'Suze,' Dulcie said finally, kicking at a small pinecone. 'You think I'm losing it, don't you?'

'I think you're under a lot of stress,' said Suze, the perpetual diplomat. 'But, you know? I also think there may be something to this. Like, maybe, Mr Grey is coming to you for a reason. Not to point out clues, but maybe…' Here she paused, and Dulcie waited, wondering just what her hyper-rational roommate would say. 'Maybe Mr Grey is appearing to you,' Suze started talking again, 'because you're in danger.'

TWENTY-TWO

THE PROMISE OF EGGPLANT lasagna went a long way toward mollifying Dulcie after that bombshell. Dulcie hadn't been quite sure that her roommate believed in the feline ghost, and to hear that she had—and that she took the warning seriously—shook Dulcie to the core. Luckily, although Suze had neither a huge range of recipes nor enough time to cook on a regular basis, occasionally both urge and opportunity coincided.

'You need some good home cooking. Well, some home cooking at least,' Suze had said. 'And I need to do something brainless and immediately gratifying.' Suze had gone on to explain about an ongoing study group report on the implications of some Supreme Court ruling or other. 'Call Chris, too. I'll be making enough to freeze, but you know it's better fresh.'

She had called while the sauce was simmering, and while they talked had begun layering the pliant pasta into the large, square bake pan the roommates had found at a yard sale only a month before. Just the sound of Suze's prep work did a good job of calming Dulcie after the fright of the afternoon, and she promised to be home in time to enjoy the final masterpiece while it was still hot.

'Want me to pick up anything?' The idea of a real meal with friendly faces had buoyed Dulcie considerably. 'Some more of that Algerian red?'

Suze made a gagging noise. 'Just bring Chris. I'll tell Ariano to pick up some wine.'

As they signed off, Dulcie had to fight the slight sinking feeling she'd had at the mention of Suze's beau. Ariano was a perfectly nice guy. He and Suze had met during her summer internship in Washington, and he'd followed her up north, trading in a Georgetown University job for one at Harvard, handling information technology for the university libraries. Which meant that he could help out when the roommates ran into computer problems. Plus, as one of the few gainfully employed men in their circle, Ariano was the source of much superior vino.

'May the days of Algerian plonk be over!' Dulcie called out to the yard in an attempt to rally her feelings that only succeeded in scaring a squirrel. It was just that after the last few days, Dulcie would have liked to have Suze to herself. Especially, she admitted to herself, because she knew Chris wouldn't make it.

'Hey, Chris?' Her call had gone straight to voicemail, and although she left the relevant details—lasagna, decent wine, love and affection—she felt her good mood draining even further away. 'If you really can't get away, let me know?' Talking to voicemail was like pouring that wine down the drain. 'Maybe I can bring a plate over.'

Hating the pleading sound in her own voice, she clicked the phone shut. She'd reached the Union by then and after one glance up at the warm red of the bricks, decided to stop in. Thursday afternoons, Lloyd had office hours and she ran the risk of disturbing him during a student conference. But these days, students usually emailed or called, and he used the time to catch up on his own work; they both did. And sometimes an interruption would be welcome.

Dulcie felt her spirits lifting as she descended the steps toward their office. So what if Chris wasn't available? She had other friends. Besides, Lloyd might be able to cast some light on Professor Bullock's odd behavior. The more she thought about it, the more the visit to the professor's townhouse seemed like a bad dream. A crazy professor, his haunted assistant, and some strange sounds in the basement… It was all beginning to sound like one of her books. Yes, that was exactly the kind of plot device that would have her undergrads rolling their eyes. But maybe, mused Dulcie, for her it made sense. When one spent so many waking hours among the ghosts and haunted castles, why wouldn't ordinary life start to show signs of the paranormal?

Plus, Dulcie admitted, ghosts were somewhat less scary—and a lot more fun—than many human motivations. Would anyone really care about Hermetria, for example, if the poor young woman was only dealing with loneliness, bills, and the care and upkeep of a drafty old castle? Dulcie felt a pang of remorse; the way she was thinking, she might as well be her mother, viewing the world as filled with her portents and omens. Well, she'd call Lucy later tonight. Maybe by then Lloyd would have some insight on the mysterious book that Lucy had warned her about.

But as she turned down the hall of offices, she saw neither Lloyd nor Raleigh, nor the open, welcoming doorway she'd expected. Instead, an impossibly thin young woman in a long suede coat slouched against the wall like a super-chic faun.

'Oh, hello.' The thin girl's greeting sounded strangely like a reprimand.

'Hi.' Dulcie was confused. 'Are you waiting for Lloyd?' The girl shrugged, lanky blonde hair obscuring her face. Dulcie reached for the doorknob. Midterms were over, but maybe a particularly difficult assignment had his students queued up.

'It's locked,' suede girl said, just as Dulcie tried the door. 'Don't bother.'

Dulcie fished out her key and opened the door. Not until she switched on the light and saw the empty space, both desks as cluttered as always, did she realize she'd been holding her breath. No, there was nothing strange here. Except for Lloyd's absence.

Dulcie turned and realized that the skinny girl had followed her in. 'Did you have an appointment?'

'He's supposed to be here now.' The girl strolled over to Lloyd's desk and with a bony hand, nails bitten to the quick, began poking through his papers. 'I'm in his class.'

'Do you mind?' Dulcie tried to put some authority in her voice. The combination of whine and nosiness wasn't attractive. 'I'll have to ask you to leave those alone.'

Something must have worked. The girl looked up, a spark

in her hooded eyes. 'Oh, you're the other grad student. Dulcie Schwartz?'

Dulcie blinked and the girl nodded toward the sign on the door. Of course.

'You're the one with the ghost stories.' Lloyd's student leaned back against his desk, appraising Dulcie. 'Funny, I thought you'd look different.'

'Black hair and lipstick?' Dulcie had been through this before. 'Funereal attire? Unearthly pallor?'

The other girl shrugged, overplucked eyebrows arching.

'Wrong Gothic. Like Lloyd, I specialize in the fiction of the eighteenth century. Not rock and roll.'

'Pity.' The girl pushed off the desk and sauntered toward the door.

'Shall I tell Lloyd you came by?'

The girl half turned and looked back over one suede shoulder, her shadowed, angular face as glamorous and dismissive as a movie star's. 'Whatever.' And she was gone.

DULCIE CLOSED THE DOOR behind the skinny student and sat down at her desk, more to reassert her claim on the space than to get anything done. In front of her, a pile of student papers silently loomed, and she pulled them toward her. There was no visible dust on them, not yet, but their very presence served as a reproach.

'Imagery in the Sermons of Jonathan Edwards.' Great. More burning insects and fiery pits. Dulcie flipped through the three-pagers to find five more iterations of the exact same title. No wonder she hadn't been able to start on these. Couldn't her students at least pay lip service to originality? She closed her eyes, the mound of papers before her becoming something more lofty and yet strangely welcoming. If only the only task before her was to scale a mountainous peak, like the ones surrounding Hermetria. Never mind that there were no rocky crags in Umbria, not like the ones depicted in *The Ravages,* anyway. For a moment, she let herself imagine being locked away, in a 'lofty retreat, poised as it were, like a cloud atop the mighty precipice.' Then she'd be able to get some work done.

How was she supposed to work on her own thesis when she had a full section of English 10 students, most of them clueless freshmen? Not to mention three very clued-in junior tutorial students, who had no respect for her. And now one supremely confident senior, who seemed to expect Dulcie to drop everything and help her with her undergrad thesis.

She opened her eyes with a start. Is that what Cameron had done? Given her extra attention? Dulcie let the papers fall back on to the desk, momentarily forgetting her more onerous duties. She—and the police, apparently—had been focused on where Cameron had died. Specifically on the professor. But Cambridge wasn't that big a city and if someone had a personal grudge, it would have been easy to follow the handsome grad student across the open Cambridge Common. It certainly would have been easy enough to see an opportunity in the overgrown front yard of the brick townhouse.

Had Cameron angered someone with his attentions to Raleigh Hall? Any kind of involvement between a tutor or teacher and a student was strictly forbidden, and Raleigh had denied any relationship. But she did seem to be quite familiar with her former adviser. Not to mention that Raleigh was an older undergrad, probably more like Cameron's peer than his protégé. Plus, Dulcie had to admit, both Raleigh and Cameron were gorgeous. Perfect physical specimens. They'd have looked great together.

Dulcie thought back to the gossip she'd heard about her late colleague. Cameron Dessay had certainly invited lust. 'Byronic' was the term most often bandied about, at least by the English Department. With his black curls and fine-featured face, the other departments probably just called him 'dreamy.' Had he been linked to anyone, male or female? Graduate or undergrad?

Dulcie tried to picture Cameron as he had been. Tall, slim, but with a lean grace that hinted at muscle underneath. That dark hair almost too long against his fair skin. She could almost visualize him, driving in his little convertible, his arm around someone equally slender and pale. A blonde? A brunette? It was no use. The more she tried to focus, the more she saw him as he'd last appeared—too still. The blue-white skin specked with blood.

She pushed herself from the desk. She wasn't going to get anything done here. As a last-minute thought, she stuffed the English 10 papers into her bag. Maybe after a few glasses of wine, she'd be able to stomach grading them.

TWENTY-THREE

'HONEY, I'M HOME!' Dulcie called up the stairs.

'Dulcie?' The voice that called back was male, but the face that peered down at her was female and covered in fur.

'Kitty!' Dulcie mounted the steps and picked up the kitten, carrying her into the kitchen despite some squirming and an annoyed mew. 'Hey, kitty, what's wrong?' The kitten stared up at her, but said nothing as Dulcie set her down. 'Wow, Ariano, what's that?' Suze's boyfriend was standing over the stove stirring something that smelled faintly of vinegar, pepper, and some unidentifiable herbs. Dulcie pushed by. 'Smells wonderful.'

'Watch it!' Suze's stocky beau held up a wooden spoon defensively and Dulcie backed off. 'I just burned the skin off these peppers and they are super hot. But there's bread and cheese on the table.' He pointed with the spoon and Dulcie cut herself a wedge of cheese. At her ankle, the kitten chirped softly and so Dulcie broke her off a piece, too.

'I'm drawing the line at the stuffed peppers. You know, you spoil that creature.' Dulcie looked up, but Ariano was smiling.

'She wouldn't like them, anyway.' In truth, the kitten had only licked at the proffered treat, intent instead on rubbing against Dulcie's leg. But as a peace offering, Dulcie sliced more of the cheese, something hard and crumbly, and offered it to the chef. 'Where's Suze?'

'She's off to Christina's.' Ariano laid the cheese on some bread and munched happily. 'Somehow it seems you two had run out of ice cream.'

'Horrors.' Dulcie cut herself another slice of the dry, salty cheese and offered another to Ariano.

'No, thanks. I want to save my appetite.' He turned back to

the stove top and his peppers. 'Suze didn't think you'd be back before seven.'

Another mouthful of bread and cheese kept Dulcie from responding, and Ariano didn't press her. She looked over his shoulder, watching as he split the softened peppers and spooned a chopped meat mixture inside. It smelled delicious and she wondered if the fragrance alone could account for the kitten's burst of affection.

'I should learn to cook,' Dulcie said, as much to herself as to Ariano. He smiled and kept spooning. She didn't voice the end of her thought—'might as well, I've got no future in academia'—because the kitten, at just that moment, had thrown one small paw over her foot and bitten it.

DULCIE DIDN'T NEED the small, sharp pain to put her off balance. A half-hour earlier, she'd been in the library. Deep in the stacks, she'd hoped to find the solace that her office hadn't provided, or at least to shake off the strangeness of the day. Of the week, really.

Maybe it made sense that everything was spooking her. After all, she'd found the dead body of one of her colleagues only three days before. But in the past, the library had been a source of comfort for her. Even this past summer, when trouble—in the form of a crazed hacker—had followed her down to Level A, that basic sense of security hadn't really been ruptured. This was her turf, her safe place.

And so, after leaving her lonely office, Dulcie had come to Widener, heading directly to the lower level she knew best. Shrugging off any leftover hesitation—and the guilt over those ungraded papers—Dulcie had deposited her coat and bag at an empty study carrel and set off to work. Her idea, which had seemed so smart out in the light of day, was to do a bit of detective work. By comparing some of the more arcane descriptions—*The Ravages,* like all the Gothics, was full of flowery language—she'd hoped to track down some clues as to the unknown author's identity. Maybe not a name, but a location. An age. Maybe a phrase that would help trace her to a particular school.

Not that the author was likely to have gone to school. Odds were, Dulcie's nameless heroine had been home educated. Just as likely, she'd read all the same books as her colleagues, and lifted from the best of them. But in the back of Dulcie's mind had been something—some clue—that she'd read a few months back and not made a note of. Something to do with the rhythm of the words or their order. If she could find that phrase once more, and link it to a known writer, she'd thought, she just might have something to work on.

But a string of words, no matter how distinctive, can be difficult to find. It wasn't that Dulcie had to look through all of Widener's three million-plus books, but just for her period alone, the Brits filled more than two aisles of floor-to-ceiling metal shelves. Halfway through late 1790s fiction she still hadn't found the elusive phrase. And as she'd turned the corner, beginning to entertain the idea of giving up, she'd been surprised to see Polly, staring at the shelves.

'Hi, Polly!' The other woman had jumped. Dulcie had spoken softly, but in the quiet of the library, her greeting sounded loud, even to her. 'Sorry.' She dropped her voice even more. 'What are you looking for?'

'Oh, nothing.' Polly had looked down at the floor as Dulcie sidled up to her. Even in the constant temperature of Widener, Polly still wore her long wool coat, buttoned to the neck.

'Moving into the Romantics, are we?' Dulcie had looked up at the shelves, spotting a collection of Coleridge. Beside her, Polly had shuffled, hands in pockets. 'I'm sorry.' Dulcie had stepped back. 'I'm disturbing you.'

'No, no, it's fine.' Polly had moved back, too, and bumped into the shelf behind her. 'I'm just returning… He—' She stammered, and then had seemed to gather herself together. 'Cameron was interested in some of the poets.'

'Ah.' At that, Dulcie had looked again at the blonde assistant. Her hesitation spoke more loudly than her actual words, making

Dulcie think once more of her late colleague. Had she seen him with a blonde? Could it have been Polly?

Polly glanced at Dulcie, then resumed staring at the floor. In that brief moment, though, Dulcie got an impression of tired red-rimmed eyes. Had Polly been crying?

'I think we all miss him.' She'd spoken as gently as she could and reached out. But as soon as her fingers touched the rough, pale wool, Polly pulled back.

'It wasn't like that.' She sniffed.

Dulcie waited, summoning up an image of Mr Grey. He could sit for hours, his presence alone calming. What would he have made of the handsome, mercurial Cameron? Again, the word 'Byronic' came to mind. Well, maybe at some level, she had re-called one of her brilliant colleague's interests. Had Polly been another?

But the assistant had been working up to something. Her hands had come out of her pockets and she reached to touch a book. Just a touch, one finger on the gold-leaf of the spine, but that was enough. Then she stepped back and turned away.

'Polly?' Dulcie hadn't wanted to lose her. 'Is there something you want to talk about? Is it about Cameron?'

'Cameron.' Polly sighed and turned back, but she was look-ing at the books, and Dulcie couldn't read her face. 'Cameron knew I liked pretty things.'

As Dulcie watched her walk away, her leather flats slapping softly on the metal floor, she'd found herself wondering. Chris had voiced his suspicion right from the start, and Dulcie had dis-missed it for lack of motive. But what if there had been a motive, something to spark the bloodless Polly to action? Had she under-estimated Polly's amorous appeal among the Cambridge literati? Roger Gosham's craggy face came to mind, but maybe there was a reason Polly had been fighting with him. Maybe she'd rejected him. Maybe she'd moved on, or hoped to. Just then, Dulcie felt the unmistakable touch of fur, the soft touch of a cat twining around her ankles. But when she had looked down, she'd seen nothing. She was all alone.

TWENTY-FOUR

AFTER THAT, WORK HAD BEEN impossible. And even though she'd spent another twenty minutes sitting on the metal floor, trying to conjure the spirit of Mr Grey, she'd neither felt nor heard any sign of her beloved pet.

'What is it?' She'd spoken softly into the deep library quiet. 'Are you trying to warn me about Polly? Alert me?' Bullock's assistant had been sobbing in the kitchen that afternoon, and Mr Grey's message then had not been at all ambiguous. 'Am I supposed to comfort her?'

Maybe that was it. The woman was clearly suffering. Any relationship with Cameron had probably been all in her head, but that didn't make it hurt any less. Plus, Dulcie remembered with a pang of guilt, Polly had seen the body, too. That image was still haunting her, and Dulcie suspected she was a bit tougher than Polly.

'Poor girl.' Dulcie had pulled herself to her feet. 'I'm sorry, Mr Grey, I missed my cue. I should have tried to make her talk.' As she'd brushed off her jeans, Dulcie looked again at the book Polly had touched. Byron, all right, but later—at least twenty years—than the surrounding books. So Polly had pulled a book and misshelved it. She was upset, and it was easy enough for Dulcie to take the pretty little volume back to the correct era.

After that, however, Dulcie couldn't focus. Between Polly and Cameron, and the mixed messages from Mr Grey, her own nameless heroine, the author of *The Ravages of Umbria,* seemed insubstantial.

'I should be able to do this,' Dulcie had told herself, trying to recall her earlier plans.

Language, wasn't it? Clues in the scenery or in some pouffed and powdered phrase?

Which is why she ended up at home, earlier than expected.

'SO, YOU WANT TO TALK ABOUT IT?'

Ariano's voice broke through the haze of Dulcie's thoughts and she looked up, startled.

'You've been rubbing your foot for five minutes now, and I'm starting to get worried.'

Ariano smiled and Dulcie found herself smiling back. With his neat beard and that wide grin, he looked handsome—almost, for a moment—and Dulcie found herself suddenly understanding her roommate's attachment to the hefty systems guy. His eyes twinkled when he smiled like that, and Dulcie found herself staring into them, trying to make out if they were grey or blue.

Cameron's eyes had been green. The thought wiped the smile off her face with a sudden wave of dizziness.

'What? What did I say?' Ariano's smile was gone now. 'Are you all right?'

'No, it's nothing.' Dulcie steadied herself, leaning back against the counter. 'The kitten nipped me, that was all.' But that bite, while it hadn't punctured the skin, had broken into her self-pity and gotten her thinking again. What was the phrase she'd been trying to track? 'As cool as emeralds.' Where had she heard it? Was it even in *The Ravages of Umbria,* or had she conjured it in some fevered nightmare? She pushed herself upright. 'I've got work to do.'

Her excuse was lame, and she knew it, but she headed toward the stairs. 'Give a yell when Suze comes home, will you?' she called down, before stumbling into her own room to lie face down on the bed.

TWENTY-FIVE

'YOU'RE NOT STILL MAD, are you, Suze?' Dulcie was washing dishes while Suze wrapped up the leftover lasagna and peppers.

'Never was, kiddo,' her roommate replied, reaching for another plastic container. 'I just wish, well, you know.'

'Yeah, I should've either never touched the letter opener or I should've taken it with me.' Dulcie started on the wineglasses. 'And, yeah, if I talk to the police again, I promise I'll tell them. But you can't really think that Professor Bullock…'

Suze shoved the last dish into the refrigerator and began counting off reasons. 'You've said he's been acting strange. You've also said that he might be about to be kicked out. That could make someone desperate. Plus, who knows what was happening with Cameron? I mean, if that guy was as bright as everyone says, then maybe your professor was stealing his work.'

'Poor Lloyd.' Suze looked over sharply at Dulcie's non sequitur. 'No, really, Suze,' Dulcie tried to explain as she filled the baking pan with soapy water. 'No matter how you slice it, he's going to suffer. Either the professor is on his way out, which is bad for Lloyd. Or he's going to keep his chair, but maybe by plagiarizing student work, which is also bad for Lloyd. And, well, I can't help but wonder if there is something else going on.'

'You mean with the professor? Is Lloyd gay?'

Dulcie shrugged. 'To be honest, I don't know. He's just Lloyd. But he might be. And Professor Bullock has never been romantically linked to anyone. Not even Polly, and she practically lives with him. If there was someone else in the picture—if there had been something going on between the professor and Cameron—it would explain why Lloyd has been stressed out recently.'

'You do realize how wildly unethical that would be.' Suze grabbed a dish towel and started to dry. 'A professor and his grad student.'

Dulcie shrugged and took up the other towel.

'Plus,' Suze said, pointing a newly clean wineglass at Dulcie for emphasis, 'you do realize you've just come up with a motive for Lloyd to have murdered Cameron, don't you?'

'SHE HAS A POINT, YOU KNOW.' When Chris called, an hour later, Dulcie had filled him in.

'Lloyd is not a murderer.' Dulcie was in no mood to be reasonable. Not only had Chris called, instead of showing up, but now he was attacking her officemate. 'He's my friend.'

'Think about it, Dulce. Even if there isn't anything inappropriate going on with the professor, he might have been jealous. Everyone says that Cameron was brilliant and handsome. And Lloyd's, what?'

'But I know Lloyd.' Dulcie paused and pondered her own statement. It wasn't exactly true. 'I mean, I've worked with him for years. And he's not unattractive.'

'Oh?' Chris packed a lot into that one syllable.

'Well, hey, I never see you anymore.' Dulcie was teasing, but she heard the edge in her voice.

Chris did, too. 'That's not fair, Dulcie. You know the drill. I've got to be here. These students are my responsibility.'

Dulcie bit her lip. Yes, grad students did have to be accessible to their students. But it seemed like Chris had been working awfully long hours. 'Every night, Chris?' It just slipped out.

'Dulcie, I've got a plan. This will all be worth it, really.'

Dulcie didn't respond. What was there to say?

'I don't like to think of you alone with any of these guys. That professor. Lloyd…'

'Next, you'll be wanting to lock me up in some mountain keep.' She was trying for humor, but it fell flat.

'Now, Dulcie, that's not fair. There's been a murder, a real one. Not some wild imagining from one of your books.' Before she could respond, Chris backtracked. 'I mean, I love your books. I know you're devoted to them, and you're going to be a great scholar, Dulcie. Just, well, be careful, will you? At least until whoever did this is caught?'

'I will.' She sighed. 'But I miss you. And we saved some of the lasagna for you, too.'

'Thanks, Dulce. I know it'll be great the next time I can get over there. Hey, pet the kitten for me, will you?'

But the tiny tuxedoed cat was nowhere to be found.

TWENTY-SIX

A MOUTHFUL OF FUR WOKE Dulcie the next morning. Sometime during the night, the kitten must have fallen asleep on her pillow. Now the little creature was dead to the world, barely stirring as Dulcie slid her over to the empty side of the bed. Chris's side. Well, end of the semester was always crazy. If she could focus, she'd be working that hard, too. Dulcie thought of the student papers still in her bag and promised herself that she'd get to them today. In the meantime, she showered and finished the coffee Suze had brewed.

Another full pot later, the papers were done. Dulcie knew she'd catch hell for her comments. As she became less certain of her own thesis, she grew crankier with her undergrads. But she'd tried to compensate by grading high on the curve. That was all these kids cared about, anyway.

Heading into the Square, she decided to swing by the departmental offices. Her section didn't meet till Monday, and Dulcie knew that some of her more anxious students would want to pick up their papers before then. Maybe if she emailed them that the papers were with Nancy, she wouldn't have to talk to them.

But if she thought that the old clapboard would offer her a respite, she was mistaken. As soon as she pushed open the front door, the volume greeted her.

'No!'

'What?' At least five of her colleagues were squeezed into Nancy's office, another four or five talking loudly by the coffee machine. Promising herself more caffeine as soon as she dropped the papers off, Dulcie made for the departmental secretary's door.

'Was anybody hurt?' The question stopped Dulcie cold, and five sets of eyes turned toward her. 'Dulcie!'

'What?' Her voice came out breathy, the papers temporarily forgotten. 'Has there been another—?'

'Oh, no, no, no!' Plump, efficient Nancy somehow pushed her way out of her desk and ran over to Dulcie. 'Nothing like that.' She maneuvered Dulcie into the chair that held the door open. The room had begun to spin, but Dulcie recognized Trista's voice as she pressed a paper cup of water into her hand. 'Just a break in.'

'Here?' Dulcie looked around. The little green house was the center of the department, but beyond a few computers there wasn't much to steal. Even the coffee machine was outdated.

'Nuh-uh.' Trista sat on the floor beside her. 'At Bullock's! Someone broke into Professor Bullock's house.'

The noise in the basement. But the professor and Polly had both been home. 'When? Yesterday?'

Trista shook her head. 'Last night. Word is, someone snuck in and then started looking through the place late at night. Professor Bullock woke up and heard something, but his blundering around must have scared them—him—' Trista paused '—or her, off.'

Dulcie blinked. 'Wow, I was there yesterday.' She'd finished the water and found the world holding still again. 'I mean, earlier. And I heard—something.' She couldn't explain about Mr Grey, but maybe she didn't have to. 'I wonder if I heard the burglar?'

'The cops will want to talk with you. They're talking with everyone who had access to the professor's house.'

Dulcie nodded, taking it all in. She'd find out soon enough if she was a suspect. 'Did they get away with anything?' She thought of the letter opener. If that was evidence in a bigger crime…

But Nancy had taken over the story. 'A book, I think. It's hard to tell, because the police are being very closed-mouthed, and the professor is quite shaken up, as you'd expect. But I think a book.'

'The professor's library…' Dulcie said. She didn't have to finish. They all knew. 'But what's the market for a rare book? I mean, where could it be sold?'

'I bet there are collectors.' Jamie, a Renaissance scholar, piped up. 'The prices for some of those early quartos are through the roof.'

Roger Gosham would know, thought Dulcie. But in the meantime, Jamie's specialty sparked a memory. 'Lloyd said the professor had found something. Something new. Maybe Elizabethan?'

Jamie shook his head. 'Not likely. I mean, we'd have heard of it.'

Dulcie shrugged. 'Where is Lloyd?' Shrugs all around.

'Probably off researching a footnote,' said Trista, not without sympathy.

'Yeah, Bullock's next great work.'

But Dulcie wasn't so sure. She wanted to trust her friend, but as Suze and Chris had noted, he might have motive. And he had been missing yesterday afternoon.

TWENTY-SEVEN

DULCIE LEFT THE PAPERS WITH Nancy and headed for the office. With any luck, Lloyd would be there, a ready explanation at hand. Maybe he could tell her more about the professor's stolen book. If, in fact, the book was really gone and hadn't simply been misplaced like the pen and the letter opener before it.

But as Dulcie clattered down the Union stairs, she was in for another surprise. The lithe and impossibly chic Raleigh Hall was uncharacteristically slumped against her office door.

'Raleigh, I'm so sorry.' Dulcie caught her breath, suddenly aware of her fly-away curls and the quick pace that had undoubtedly reddened her cheeks. 'I got your call.' She stopped. Truth was, she hadn't even listened to her voicemail.

'It's okay.' The undergrad waved away her concern.

'And I still haven't read your notes.' Dulcie rushed out the words, desperate to get her confession on the table.

'Oh, it wasn't about that.' The tall undergrad stepped back, reassuming her sylphlike grace and letting Dulcie unlock the door. Still no sign of Lloyd. From what Dulcie could tell, the office hadn't been touched since yesterday.

'But, um, you wanted to see me?' Being shorter, rounder, and admittedly unprepared, Dulcie tried to salvage what little authority she could muster. She walked around to the back of her own desk and gestured to the office's one guest chair. 'Would you like to take a seat?'

But despite her best efforts to conjure the aura of a Bullock, or even her own undergrad advisers, Dulcie noted that Raleigh wasn't paying attention. Instead, the willowy senior was standing over Lloyd's desk and was blatantly picking through his papers.

'Um, Raleigh?' Dulcie heard her own voice cracking a bit. 'May I help you?'

'Oh, no, I'm fine.' She had cleared away Lloyd's desk and stood with her head twisted, reading his desk calendar.

'Raleigh?' Dulcie started to stand up. What was it about undergrads these days? 'Um, I think that's private?'

'Oh, not to worry!' Raleigh stepped back and opened her own bag. 'I just wanted to drop this off. It's all good.' She leaned forward as if to read something written on Lloyd's desk blotter, and then pulled a small package, wrapped in brown paper, out of her bag. She placed it on Lloyd's desk and, with a wave, walked out the door.

It's all good? That was the best an English honors student could do? With no other outlet, Dulcie vented her irritation on her own desk, aggressively neatening a pile of books that had been threatening to fall over since the semester's start. What the hell did that mean, anyway?

'Maybe more than you know.' The voice sounded calm and close, as if someone were speaking right behind her left ear.

Dulcie sat up with a start. 'Mr Grey!'

'You don't need to get so worked up, Dulcie.' There was a hint of a reprimand in the voice. The threat of claws under the velvet fur.

'I know, Mr Grey.' Dulcie slumped back in her seat. 'I just...' She paused to think. 'I feel guilty. I haven't really been doing my work, you know?'

In response, she heard a purr. 'So I hear-rr-rr...' For just a moment, she had a flash of the long-haired grey cat, circling a spot on Lloyd's desk, as if to settle down for a nap. And one word: 'Focus.'

'On what, Mr Grey? Is it something on the desk? Something that Raleigh saw?' Dulcie stood up but hesitated, unwilling to disturb her late pet, even if he was now invisible. 'What did she leave, anyway?'

'Dulcie, Dulcie.' The voice was softer now. Mr Grey was either fading away or slipping into sleep. 'Be careful, prying can have consequences. Knowledge must be used wisely. Haven't you learned anything?'

'What, Mr Grey? What am I supposed to have learned?' But some indefinable tang in the air—a slight staleness or settling of the dust—let her know that he was gone. She was left alone in the office, with a mysterious blotter and still no Lloyd in sight.

TWENTY-EIGHT

'WHAT WAS SHE LOOKING AT?' Forgetting her own sense of personal space and blatantly ignoring Mr Grey's warning, Dulcie pushed the papers on Lloyd's desk back. His blotter, like hers, was a big calendar of the month. Like hers, it was covered with coffee rings. Unlike hers, classes and sections had been marked in a neat block print.

WAB 2-5. WAB 10-1. Well, that was pretty clear. Lloyd was trying to keep track of the hours he spent on Professor Bullock's projects. MLRdead! was obvious, too. Even though she hadn't had anything to offer to the prestigious *Modern Languages Review,* Dulcie could not have been unaware of the deadline, coming up next week. Hadn't Raleigh said she was going to submit something for the journal?

'Dream on.' Dulcie was about to give up, when she noticed another notation, very small and tucked into several corners of several days: R. She read and then saw again, R. R. R.

Was this what Raleigh had been looking at? If so, what did it mean? For one horrid moment, Dulcie worried that her quiet officemate had become a stalker. Raleigh was a lovely young woman, but out of Lloyd's league.

No, she shook her head. Truth was, she didn't even know which way Lloyd's preferences lay—and, besides, she had only introduced the two of them a few days before. But what else could R mean?

She looked at the package that Raleigh had left. Neatly wrapped in brown paper, its folded ends taped up, it looked vaguely familiar. R. Of course! Roger Gosham. As Dulcie had already found out, Professor Bullock would blithely assign his errands to anyone at hand.

Dulcie itched to open the package. It had already been un-wrapped once: the marks of old tape could be seen under the new. If only the wrapping were a little looser. But the image of Mr Grey came back to her. What was she supposed to have learned? Not to poke into other people's belongings? No, cats as a whole—and Mr Grey had been no exception—were not big on privacy. It had taken Suze months to get used to the way the big grey cat would slam the bathroom door open with his body when he wanted to come in.

The vision had been curling up to sleep. To sleep on the problem? Is that what Dulcie was supposed to do? No, she shook her head. She'd been ignoring too many of her responsibilities these days. In fact, she could only hope that her brain was making some subconscious connections while she'd been so distracted. Otherwise, she'd be so far behind that she'd have to work through Thanksgiving and the upcoming semester break.

Thanksgiving. Dulcie slumped back on her desk. Strange that she hadn't thought of it before. Growing up, it had been a strangely ambivalent holiday. Back in the commune, the third Thursday in November was either the 'Day of Shame' or 'The National Apology for European Imperialism,' depending on which clique was running the discussion group that month. But something of Lucy's Eastern background must have remained. Even in the lean years, before Lucy's macramé hangings started selling, her mother had managed to follow up the commune's massive guilt fest with some kind of celebratory meal.

'It's only right that we honor Mother Gaia's gifts,' she'd tell her young daughter, justifying the fuss to herself as much as to Dulcie as she'd lay out a 'harvest-time feast' of squash, corn, and nutty whole grains. 'And besides, our ancestors helped ex-terminate the more grateful and earth-conscious people who had lived here before. We owe it to them to keep some of their home cultures alive.'

Those gatherings had been fun, and the food surprisingly tasty: Lucy's friend Nirvana made a mean carob pie. And since she'd gone off to college, Dulcie had learned to enjoy more mainstream celebrations, too, regularly heading down to New Jersey with Suze. It had been a few years since Dulcie had been back to Oregon to celebrate. But although Lucy always told her about the gatherings—the big circle to ask forgiveness, the re-blessing of the community's sacred ground—she suspected her mother missed her. Well, maybe sometime in the future she'd be able to afford cross-country airfare. She pictured driving up to the community from some West Coast teaching post, along with Chris. No, she made herself drop the image. That was planning too far in advance.

What she should be doing now was looking for Lloyd. She picked up the rectangular package and turned it over in her hands, putting it back on the desk with great reluctance. Or maybe she should be talking to Roger Gosham.

TWENTY-NINE

ANOTHER VISIT TO Roger Gosham's workroom was long overdue for a multitude of reasons, Dulcie told herself as she locked up the basement office. Even without that mysterious package, he might have something to tell her about Lloyd. He might be able to identify the professor's missing book. Hell, if he would only give her some pointers about how to authenticate *The Ravages of Umbria,* she'd consider herself amply rewarded. Even if the craggy bookbinder was his usual gruff self, he would remember she came from Professor Bullock, wouldn't he?

Steeling herself for the confrontation, she made her way to the Square and up the worn steps to Gosham's. Somehow, the stairs seemed steeper than they had the other day. The three flights endless. Dulcie paused on the second-floor landing to catch her breath. Lucy, she realized, would see an omen in this. Some evil spirit holding her back. Dulcie was more likely to credit the series of comfort meals she'd been enjoying since Tuesday. Or, conversely, the lack of lunch. The fact that she hadn't had anything to eat since last night's lasagna indulgence—one tiny muffin didn't count—seemed a lot more likely than a vengeful spirit. But since she was in the Square, she could easily stop at Lala's afterward, and that thought cheered her enough to ascend the remaining flight.

Once again, the hallway was empty, a dirty skylight high above shedding only faint light on the top landing. Once again, a strange fatigue—almost a reluctance—settled on Dulcie. Crediting the lack of protein, Dulcie went up to the first door on the right, the one with GOSHAM'S FINE BOOKS painted on it, and knocked.

'Hello? Mr Gosham?' When nobody answered a second

knock Dulcie let herself in, and once again found herself unaccountably cheered by the sunny workroom. Maybe it was the contrast to the dim hallway and its steep stairs. Maybe it was the archaic tools, the smell of leather. This airy aerie was a temple to books, a fitting tower for treasures, even if the keeper could be a bit of an ogre.

'Anybody here?' Dulcie walked over to the table under the wide windows and was about to pick up an awllike tool, its wood handle worn smooth with wear, when a familiar, deep voice interrupted her.

'Can I help you?'

Dulcie stepped back and found herself excusing Gosham's grammar. ('It's the colloquialism, and that is how language changes. Besides, he's a craftsman.') When she looked up, she realized the large man was staring at her, his dark eyes intense.

'I'm sorry. I was thinking of something else.' She smiled and cringed a little. Dulcie hated when she fell back into girly behavior, but something about this big man elicited just that. 'I'm actually here with a research question.' He kept staring. 'You know I'm working with Professor Bullock?'

Gosham grunted and nodded. At least he looked a little less threatening, so Dulcie continued. 'I was actually meaning to talk to you the other day, when you came by the professor's. I'm looking into the question of authenticating manuscripts. Books, really.'

'Oh?' The big man's voice had grown soft. 'Do tell.'

Dulcie smiled. All she needed to do was engage this man in his area of expertise. 'It sounds silly, I know.' There she was, doing it again. She tried for a stronger tack. 'I mean, I've got a horrible suspicion that something I'm working on…' She paused, reaching for more authority. 'Something I've been working on with the professor is a sham.'

'I don't believe it.' Gosham pulled himself up. He was, Dulcie noticed, quite tall and well built. 'I have nothing but the greatest respect for Professor Bullock. His scholarship is impeccable. His library, one of the finest in North America.'

'Well, it's not from his library, exactly.' She was getting into messy territory. She hadn't even told the professor her suspicions, and she didn't want them coming back to him via Gosham.

'But you think something is wrong?' He walked toward her and leaned against the table, his arms crossed. 'And you're working with him on it?'

This was the tricky part. How could Dulcie even begin to explain about Lucy—or ask Gosham to keep her inquiry secret? 'Not exactly,' she struggled for an explanation that would pass muster. 'It's just that someone said something.'

He was looking at her intently. She must sound as batty as Lucy. It was time to change the subject. 'You must know an antique the moment you get it, right?'

'Well, I do work with my share of rare books.' She had hit the right note. Gosham almost swaggered as he walked off toward the second table and carefully lifted the book that had been lying there. It was bound in turquoise leather, the lettering on its spine gold. 'Look at this. Teal Morocco, uncut. Hand-lettered. But stored horribly.' He gently flipped the book over, cradling its smooth leather in his large hands. 'I'm doing what I can.'

'What's the book?' Dulcie craned to read the gold lettering on the spine.

'What? Oh, Keats.' He ran one thick finger over the lettering and Dulcie read, 'Endymion.' With a start, she realized that the poem meant nothing to Gosham. For him, text was filler. All he cared about was the binding; the book as an object. Her heart sank. He wasn't going to be able to help her authenticate *The Ravages of Umbria*. An individual copy, perhaps, but not the words, the story. The author.

But he might be able to help her understand what was going on with Lloyd. 'Mr Gosham?' He had replaced the book on the table, and looked eager to get back to work. 'I share an office with Lloyd Markson.'

Gosham glanced back at her, his face blank.

'Professor Bullock's assistant? His other assistant, that is. The grad student who does most of his research.'

Gosham nodded, but had moved on to another book. Dulcie felt her time running out.

'He's working with the professor on something new, supposedly. A rare text. And, well, I heard there was a break-in at the professor's house, and it's gone missing. And, well, I was wondering if you'd heard anything about it.'

'What? Are you asking if I'm a fence?'

Dulcie blinked. The image didn't scan.

Gosham must have seen her confusion. 'A point man? A dealer in stolen artifacts?' He slammed his hand down on the work table. 'Do you know what my reputation is, young lady?'

'Yes.' Dulcie tried to backtrack. 'I know Professor Bullock trusts you implicitly.'

The bookbinder seemed mollified. 'Well, that's a relief. No, I hadn't heard anything about a robbery.' He paused, a thoughtful look on his face. 'Is this about Polly? Did she suggest you talk to me about a theft?'

'No, not at all.' She stepped back from the intensity of that stare. 'Why would she?'

The big man shrugged. 'No reason.' He'd turned away again, so Dulcie couldn't see his face. But even he seemed to realize that this answer didn't suffice. 'It's just that she, well, I don't know if you know, but she's been very upset. Ever since that young man—what was his name?—was killed.'

'Cameron, you mean. Cameron Dessay'

'Cameron Dessay.' His voice was flat. 'Yeah. I think they were close.'

Aha! Dulcie decided to press for more. 'And so were you two, am I right, Mr Gosham?'

'What is it to you?' He was back to his gruff self and didn't even look up.

'Well, I'm just saying…' Dulcie didn't actually know what she was saying. Or why she was prying for that matter. Maybe it was the lack of romance in her own life recently. Maybe it was that spark she had seen in the usually drawn assistant. She tried to picture what Mr Grey would say—or do—but only got a sense of fur being ruffled. A tail lashing in anger. Gosham's manner, no doubt. 'I know she was over here a lot.'

Gosham grunted, which Dulcie took as an acknowledgment. She wandered back to the work table. Next to the awl was some kind of chisel, the metal end shiny with use.

'She was here the day Cameron was killed, wasn't she?' She touched the awl. Its handle was black with use. 'Tuesday afternoon?'

'She came by, sure.' Gosham's voice was softer. Was it sad? Dulcie couldn't tell. 'Just to pick up some books, though. I had them all done up and she insisted on unwrapping them, every one. Like I'd have given her the wrong ones for the professor.'

Yes, sad. He must have felt wounded by her lack of trust. Dulcie recalled the neatly wrapped package she'd seen. What a contrast to the pile of books, scattered every which way on the floor after Polly had dropped them!

'Is that why you two fought?'

'We didn't fight.' Gosham's voice was even, but Dulcie felt tension rising. 'We aren't fighting. We talked. Briefly. And then she left.'

'That quickly?' Polly had been gone for at least an hour. Of course, she could have had other errands in the Square, but Dulcie was betting on something personal. Had Cameron come between them? If so, had he angered another lover or rival, as well?

'That quickly. I was working that day. Why?'

'I'm just wondering.' The roll of brown paper was affixed to one end of the table. 'She wasn't at the professor's when I got there, and she didn't show up for at least an hour.' Dulcie reached toward the roll and brushed against a palette knife, spotted with disuse. It started to roll, and she grabbed at it.

'What are you doing?' Gosham got it before she could, catching the blonde wood handle just as it fell from the table. 'God help me.' He shoved the tool in his pocket and turned away. 'Are you another one like her?'

'What? No.' A faithless woman? A meddler? Dulcie started after him, determined to get some answers. But when she reached for him, for the worn plaid flannel of his shirt, he spun around and glowered down at her.

'I don't need another interfering woman.' Dulcie could feel his breath on her face. His eyebrows, this close up, bristled like the fur on an angry animal. 'In my studio.' Dulcie stepped back, but he stepped forward, keeping pace. 'In my life.'

Dulcie stumbled back until she felt the door behind her, pulled it open, and fled.

THIRTY

WHAT WAS THAT ABOUT? Dulcie didn't stop to think it through till she had a counter seat at Lala's and a three-bean burger in front of her. Only then did her heart slow its pounding enough for her to summon logic.

Something had gotten Roger Gosham angry, and that something seemed to concern Polly. If that something involved romance, it certainly wasn't running smoothly. Could Gosham have seen Cameron as a romantic rival and killed him? Dulcie took a bite and chewed over both the burger and the thought. The timing seemed off. He'd been angry at Polly, but he'd let her go. If he'd been the type to lash out in jealousy, wouldn't he have gone for her? Or at least tried to catch them together? And besides, he'd given away a perfectly good alibi. From what he'd said, it seemed likely that the bookbinder and the assistant had spent more than a few minutes together on that fateful day.

Dulcie dragged a french fry through the hot sauce and tried a different tack. Maybe Polly had been the one furious at Cameron. Maybe the handsome grad student had toyed with her, turned his high-powered charm her way and then dumped her. Or at least fouled her more promising romance with the bookbinder. So, she'd come home, stabbed him. And then what? Walked around the block to waste time before her dramatic entrance?

Dulcie ate the fry without really tasting it. No, it didn't seem likely. Still, something was odd. If only she actually had the psychic skills that Lucy claimed, life would be so much easier.

As if on cue, Dulcie's phone rang: Lucy, or at least the community center phone. But just as she was about to pick it up, a hearty slap on the back nearly knocked her off her chair.

'Dulcie!' She turned to see Jerry, Trista's boyfriend. And, yes, just behind the gangling mathematician, her petite friend. 'Long time, no see!'

'Hey Jerry, Trista.' With a twinge of guilt, Dulcie pocketed the phone. 'What's up?'

'What's up with you?' Jerry reached across the counter for a menu, while Trista rolled her eyes.

'Really, Jerry. You're going to get the three-bean burger with fries and extra sauce. And I am, too.'

'I might go for cheese, this time,' said Jerry, even as he conceded defeat by placing the menu back on the counter. 'But, hey, what've you been up to?'

'I've been around.' Since the semester started, Dulcie had been busy. But she'd been trying to keep up with her friends. 'Have I missed anything?'

'Only one of the best dinners ever!' After sports, Jerry liked food. And Trista.

'Jerry's exaggerating, Dulce. And I think everyone understands that you didn't want to come out Tuesday.' As Jerry gave the long-suffering waitress their order, Trista came around to Dulcie's other side, nabbing a stool that had just opened up. 'But when Chris showed up, we really thought he'd have brought you along.'

Chris? What dinner was this? 'Suze had left me a message.' She tried to recall. Wasn't that for Ariano's roommate?

'Never mind.' Trista looked distracted, and Dulcie had the distinct impression that she wished Jerry hadn't mentioned it. 'You are coming out tonight, though, right?'

'Darts.' Dulcie nodded, glad that she remembered. Friday night. The People's Republik would be packed, as the English Department faced off against History and Lit. 'You think we have a chance?'

'Course we do!' Jerry put his arm around his petite girlfriend. 'Trista's got the best arm in the state.'

'Order Fifty-three?' A shout went up from near the cash register, and Jerry slid off the stool.

'You're not staying?' Dulcie realized, with regret, that she'd really wanted to talk to her colleague outside of the departmental offices.

Trista smiled, but shook her head. 'I've got my junior tutorial in five. Not that they care if I'm there or not.'

'Tell me about it.' Commiserating felt good, but as Trista shouldered her own bag, Dulcie reached out for her. 'One sec, Trista. I'm curious, do you have any thoughts on authentication?'

'You mean like documentation?' Trista raised one pierced eyebrow. ''Cause I'm an expert on notes and trivia. Once you get into late Victorians, man, I swear they never threw anything away.'

'Well, sort of.' Trista was a friend, and she only nodded when Dulcie told her about Lucy's dream. 'And so, I'm wondering, you know, if maybe I have it all wrong.'

'Dulcie?' Dulcie didn't realize she was looking down at the menu, her head hanging lower as she talked, until she felt Trista's hands on her shoulders. 'Do you hear yourself?'

'What?' She looked up. Trista was staring at her, ignoring Jerry.

'You've had a hell of a week. Now, I know about Lucy.' She raised her hand to stop any protest. 'I know. But really, what I think we're dealing with here is a super bad week, coupled with a thesis adviser who can't keep his act together long enough to find his pen set, or whatever.'

'I don't know, Tris.' Something was just not right, and Dulcie knew she hadn't really explained it.

'Look, Dulce. It's all a question of context. Think of everything that's happened.'

'But Bullock always said…' She could hear him in her head. He'd never thought much of *The Ravages*.

'Look, the man hasn't written anything of his own for more than twenty years. Forget about him. He's jealous. And, I mean, he's a murder suspect.' Trista paused, momentarily lost in thought, her tongue darting out to play with the ring on her lip. 'Hey, you don't think…'

She paused so long, Dulcie wanted to shake her. 'What?'

'Maybe Professor Bullock is hiding something. And maybe he's trying to gaslight you.'

'Great.' Dulcie did not really think it likely that her thesis adviser, the Cyrus University Professor of Eighteenth Century Literature, would stoop to driving her mad. There were, after all, simpler ways to destroy her career. But when she'd pointed this out to Trista, her friend had made mince meat of Dulcie's theories.

'No, really, it makes sense.' Trista actually sounded excited by the concept. 'I mean, as far as anyone knows, he sucked the life out of poor Polly Heinhold, and it looks like he's going to do the same to Lloyd.' Dulcie flashed to Lloyd's latest complaint, the new discovery that threatened to derail months of work. It was possible.

'I'd say it's probable!' Trista kept on. 'I mean, who else is in his sphere of influence?'

'I'm hardly—' Dulcie threw some bills down to cover her own lunch and followed her friends to the door.

'But you are!' Trista interrupted, as Jerry held the door. 'You're doing new and exciting research in his field.'

'Unless I'm barking up the wrong tree entirely!'

The three were shouting over traffic, and as they slipped inside Harvard Yard, Dulcie missed Trista's words.

'What? Wait up!'

But Trista was dashing up the steps of Sever. 'I said— context!' she shouted back. 'And don't forget—darts!'

Dulcie watched her friend disappear inside. Trista's suggestion, as odd as it was, had been strangely heartening. *Maybe I'm not paranoid after all.* She smiled at the thought. *Maybe my professor is out to get me.*

But even as she stood there, a cold blast—and the memory of her mother's latest missed call—swept that idea away. Trista might think she knew Lucy, but her suggestion ran counter to everything Dulcie's mother had ever taught her. Although she was always ready to attribute just about anything to the supernatural, Lucy never did like to assign negative motives to a person. 'It's the Threefold Law, dear. What you believe of others comes back to haunt you,' she'd say. 'Closeness breeds power, and you must always use that for good.' And that was one lesson, Dulcie thought, that usually made sense.

Still, there was something odd going on with the professor. If only she could talk to Lloyd. Walking slowly over toward the library, Dulcie chewed over her officemate's strange disappearance. Trista had talked about context. Lloyd not being there was out of place, as much as Raleigh poking about—and as that neat package in their overcrowded office. A leaf blew by, impossibly red. It skittered across the pavement to the bare dirt, just low and fast enough to tempt a playful feline. Mr Grey would have been on it in a minute. She could picture that: her sleek grey cat, chasing the last of the autumn beauty. She watched the leaf fly, as if evading those velvet paws; a jewel against the dull November setting. Like that emerald, in a way. The one from her dream: images of the sea beyond the borders. Of the forest, far away. She smiled. Imagery from *The Ravages* always had that effect. The leaf skittered away and Dulcie watched it, before turning again toward the library.

Nobody liked *The Ravages*. Readers had been looking at *The Ravages* for centuries and disregarding it until Dulcie uncovered its secret. The book was a mystery, partly by intent and partly due to history. Because only part of the book had survived, nobody had known the identity of the 'jealous spirit' who had preyed on the heroine. And Gothic literature being what it was, everyone had looked to one of the ghosts floating around. Although, really, in retrospect, why would a ghost care about a beautiful young woman or what remained of her wealth?

No, it had fallen to Dulcie to uncover the clues hidden in the characters' speeches. While other readers had just rolled their eyes at one more overwrought Goth, Dulcie had looked further. She'd been the one to realize that Demetria—the side-kick—wasn't all she pretended to be, and that the clues were in her speeches—in the author's cunning use of language.

Dulcie had been so proud of herself and even Professor Bullock had been impressed. And so she had set out to make her case, to compile the linguistic evidence that would support the flash of insight. But now everything was cast in doubt. Only a few months before, Dulcie had felt like such an accomplished scholar. She'd spotted the gem that the critics had missed. The bright spot in the cold dead yard. The witty, wonderful manuscript that nobody had ever noticed before. An irresistible lure to a young academic, just starting out and eager to make her mark. And just maybe, Dulcie realized, too good to be true.

THIRTY-ONE

CHRIS HAD NOT BEEN MUCH HELP.

'Oh, sweetie, I'm sure that's not the case.' His voice on the phone sounded just too far away. 'You're just…'

The pause gave him away.

'What?' Dulcie heard herself snapping as she sat up on her bed. 'Imagining things?'

'I didn't say that.' Chris had tried to argue her down, but by that point the only thing that might have worked was a warm hug. A cold phone was not a good substitute. It didn't help that on the walk home, she'd found herself recalling things Chris had said the previous summer. Then, she'd been the victim of a computer virus. Originally inserted through her computer, it had nearly brought down the Harvard library system before Chris and his buddies had helped unravel its poisonous 1s and 0s.

The virus, he'd said, wasn't that sophisticated. The university had been alerted when it kept trying to enter through various firewalls again and again. But it wasn't until Dulcie had helped uncover the source—her laptop—that the impromptu IT security team had been able to dismantle it. For some reason, a phrase he'd used last summer trying to explain the computer bug came to mind. 'Anomalous coding.' Was that it? She remembered the warmth that had existed between them then, the pride with which he'd explained his find—the one stray piece of coding that had threatened both the Harvard libraries and Dulcie's nascent career.

'It's elegant coding, really.' His voice had been full of admiration, once the virus was located. 'Not complicated, but really quite beautiful, if you look at it.'

To Dulcie, it had all sounded as horrid as an invasion of

beetles, although she admitted that some of her colleagues over at the Museum of Comparative Zoology would probably find them beautiful, too. Once they were dead and pinned to a card. As it was, the memory kept replaying in her mind. What if she'd gotten the wrong message from those wonderful lines? What if the beauty was really a sign that something was wrong?

What if she'd been duped?

'I just don't know, Chris.' She heard herself getting weepy and lay down once more, reaching for the old quilt that Lucy's Wiccan circle had made for her.

'I know.' Chris sounded confident, but so far away. 'I trust your instincts even if you don't.'

His words sounded so much like those of Mr Grey that Dulcie wanted to believe him. But how could she? Dulcie pulled the quilt up higher. Lucy had meant to embroider a grey wolf in its center. Despite her own childhood in Philadelphia, Dulcie's mother insisted on the wolf as her spirit guide. To Dulcie, the pointy-eared creature looked more like a cat.

'Why don't you go out tonight?' Chris was still talking. 'Isn't this Trista's big chance at the darts tournament?'

Dulcie sniffed. 'Uh-huh. But I was hoping, you know…' She didn't want to say it.

'I'll come if I can get out of here.' That didn't sound very reassuring. 'I tried to catch up with you the other night, you know. At that party?'

'Oh, yeah.' Great, so she wasn't only alienating her friends, she was missing opportunities to see her own boyfriend. 'Jeremy's shindig?'

'Yeah, you'd taken off from the lab, but I was hoping you'd show at some point.'

You could have come here. She didn't say it. Already, she was being whiny. 'Yeah, sorry.'

'Dulcie?' He sounded sad. 'I'm just working, you know. I want to be with you. It's just—well, there are things I have to do.'

'I know.' She didn't, really. They were both broke, but Chris had never worked such long hours before. *That you know of,* she didn't need a ghostly cat to correct her. She and Chris had started dating during the summer, when the demands of class-work and students were at their lightest. How did she know what his schedule was like during term time? They were both grad students; she was lucky that none of her students needed her to be available round the clock. And, she had to admit, she was a little more needy than ever before—with reason. 'But would you try to come over to the People's Republik later?' She paused, not sure how else to make her claim. 'I'll definitely be there.'

'I will, Dulce.' He hesitated. 'And I promise, this is just for now. There's a situation.'

She waited for him to elaborate, determined not to pester him.

'I love you, Dulcie Schwartz.'

And before she could respond, he was gone.

Buoyed by his final declaration, Dulcie realized that she did not need the nap she'd been planning. Instead, if she was going to go out, she needed to shower and change. As she got out of bed, she pulled the quilt back to make the bed. It was so Lucy, really, she looked down at it with that mixture of warmth and humor that only her mother could evoke. The stitching, while heartfelt, was amateur. Some of the patches puckered slightly, and no amount of ironing would make it lie completely flat. Still, as she reached down to straighten it out, she had to admit a fondness for the homey piece. And as she did, she was sure that the wolf—the cat, as she preferred to think of it—winked.

THIRTY-TWO

'SOMEONE'S IN A GOOD MOOD!' Trista looked up as Dulcie came into the bar. She nodded, knowing the broad grin on her face had been absent lately.

'Yeah, I might be meeting Chris later.' She walked up to the table where Jerry was pouring from a communal pitcher.

'Chris is coming?' He looked up as he handed her a full glass. 'I thought—'

'That's great.' Trista cut in, pushing herself by Dulcie and jostling her beer.

'Wait, what's going on?' Dulcie put her glass down and, at a loss for a napkin, licked the cold beer from her hand. 'Jerry?'

'My dimwitted boyfriend is jealous.' Trista spoke loudly enough for Jerry to hear. 'He was hoping to pick up some extra hours in the computer lab. But Chris needs them.' That was directed at Jerry, who nodded. He didn't look that displeased to be at a bar, instead of at work.

'What do you mean? He's not in any trouble, is he?' Dulcie knew well the round of grants and scholarships, and how precarious funding could be.

'No more than the rest of us.' Trista emptied her glass. For a tiny girl, she could drink. 'Which is why I'm really hoping to get top prize tonight.'

TWO HOURS LATER, SHE HAD, but the fifty dollars were being spent on multiple pitchers. The grad student crowd had grown, with nearly every face from the department crowding around the long, wet table that they'd commandeered earlier. Everyone except Lloyd, Dulcie noticed.

'Has anyone seen Lloyd?' Between the jukebox and the riotous cheers accompanying the runoff matches, she had to yell to be heard.

'Lloyd?' A huge pair of glasses with a tiny person attached blinked back at her. Sarah, a medievalist, Dulcie recalled. 'You mean, Bullock's boy?'

Dulcie nodded, biting her lip. If Lloyd wasn't careful, he was going to become the next Polly. 'He's got his own work, you know.'

Sarah turned back toward her, her glasses catching the light from the bar. 'I hear he's been helping the professor put his house back in order.'

So much for Lloyd's own thesis. Well, they all needed to get paid.

But Sarah was still talking. 'I wonder if he's trying to take over Cameron's role, I mean, now that it's open.'

Dulcie spun around, but with the colored light sparkling off Sarah's oversize frames it was hard to read her face. 'What do you mean?'

The medievalist shrugged. 'Just saying.'

'But Cameron wasn't working with Bullock.' Dulcie struggled to make sense of the claim. Between the beer and the lighting, she was feeling a bit muddled. 'He'd only just come over from Comp Lit. He was in an entirely different period.'

'He was doing something with Bullock!' Sarah's voice had started to grate, too. 'I remember him asking about his hours and stuff.'

'He was? They were?' She shook her head to clear it, but that only started it throbbing. Tiny pinpricks started behind her eyes, like little claws just beginning to make themselves felt. Just then three of the bar's execrable pizzas arrived, and Dulcie was jostled aside as the darts team and its cheerleaders fell on the greasy pies.

Five minutes later, only three sad-looking slices remained, and Sarah had gone off. Dulcie found herself next to Trista, pepperoni and mushroom in hand. Those tiny claws were still digging in, and she chewed on the slice, hoping that food would ease the pressure in her head.

'Did you hear anything about Cameron working with Professor Bullock?' Dulcie took another bite. She hadn't eaten since lunch, and mushrooms were a vegetable, weren't they?

Trista shrugged, her mouth full. 'Wrong period.' She wiped her mouth with the back of her hand.

'That's what I thought.' Dulcie looked at her crust, thinking to discard it, and instead took a bite. 'But Sarah was saying something about Cameron.'

'Sarah.' Trista rolled her eyes and reached over for one of the remaining slices. She looked up at Dulcie, who nodded. What the hell, it was Friday.

'What does that mean?' The cheese on the second slice had congealed and Dulcie had to grab it to keep it from sliding off.

'Cameron?' Trista was having her own problems, but managed to bite through the hardened topping. 'She was jealous.'

'But she's a medievalist.' It was the beer, it had to be. She closed her eyes and flashed back in time. When she'd sleep late—or too late for her hungry cat—Mr Grey would swat her, gently, to wake her. Had he ever used his claws?

She opened her eyes to see Trista was shaking her head, slurping down the rest of the slice. 'That hit the spot.' She wiped the crumbs from her hands, then turned back to Dulcie's question. 'I wouldn't sweat it, Dulce. I mean, I don't think it was academic. Maybe she saw them talking, who knows? But for Sarah, it was personal.'

Behind Dulcie's eyes, the claws took hold. Trista continued talking. 'Cameron was a bit of a masher, you know?'

Dulcie shrugged. She'd felt the force of his charisma, and she knew the other women talked about him.

'He'd hit on almost anyone. Act all fascinated about everything—your life, your work. And those eyes…' Trista got a faraway look, and Dulcie was tempted to tell her to stop. The pain was getting too intense. But then her friend snapped back. 'Hey, maybe he'd sweet talked the Old Bull. He could've. There was something off about him, though. You know? Like he was into the power trip of it all.'

Dulcie nodded. 'I think so. I think he manipulated his tutee. You know, the undergrad I'm now working with?'

'Raleigh Hall? Senior hot shot?' Trista seemed doubtful.

'Yeah. I know she looks older, but I'm getting the sense that she's sort of messed up.' Dulcie explained about the delayed thesis and about Cameron grooming her for the university's most prestigious prize. The pain came and went, right behind her eyes. 'I know she's smart, but I think he set her up for disappointment. Maybe, from what you're saying, he had other reasons, too.'

'There's definitely something going on with that girl. She's been showing up all over.' Trista glanced past Dulcie. 'And now you can ask her yourself.'

Dulcie turned toward the entrance, just in time to see Raleigh push open the door, the auburn highlights in her perfect hair set off by the light from the street. 'Just what I need,' she groaned. 'Work.'

'Is she that bad?' There was no way they could be overheard from this far away, but Trista leaned in, anyway. 'I'd heard she was quite bright.'

'Yeah, she is.' Honesty compelled Dulcie to continue. 'And, truth is, I haven't even read what she's written already. I'm getting as bad as Bullock.' She turned again to look. Raleigh had been swallowed up by the crowd. The pain had settled into a dull ache, leaving Dulcie feeling drained. 'I just want to work on my own stuff, you know?'

'Tell me about it.' Trista nodded slowly. 'All the kids care about these days is hypertext and postmodern staging.'

'Semiotics and signifiers!' Dulcie warmed to the theme.

'Does anyone give a damn about books anymore?'

'I do!' The two women looked up in surprise. Lloyd stood there, smiling. 'Did I miss anything? I mean, besides an old-fashioned gripe session?'

'I won at darts!' Trista preened.

'Score one for the bookish set!' He seemed jolly.

'I'm so glad to see you!' Dulcie felt herself cheered by the sight of him, at least until her own questions came rushing back. 'Hey, you weren't at your office hours. Raleigh dropped by—'

'I know, I know.' Lloyd made a face. 'Believe me, I heard about it. She had something for me. But I got the call from Bullock, and when Bullock calls…' He shrugged. Trista, meanwhile, had poured him a glass from one of the fresher pitchers, and put it in his hand.

'So, you got it, right?' He took a hefty swig and nodded.

Dulcie waited, but he seemed intent on his beer. Finally, she moved on. 'So, were you helping him clean up?' She'd get back to the book later.

'Yeah, he's sort of helpless these days.' He looked around. 'But I think I did some good.'

'What do you mean?' He smiled and lifted his glass to someone across the room.

'I got him to drop that stupid claim.' He refilled his glass and stood up. 'Now, if you'll excuse me?' And with that he disappeared into the crowd.

THE CROWD HAD THINNED OUT by the time Chris showed up, taking Lloyd with it and leaving Dulcie to wonder what he'd meant by that last statement. At least Raleigh had gone, too. Though when Dulcie mentioned this to Trista, her friend had given her an odd look.

'You've got to get over that girl, Dulce. She's not the threat you think she is.'

'I don't think she's a threat, exactly.' Dulcie stopped herself. What Trista had said had some weight to it. Here she was, doctoral candidate, afraid of an undergraduate. 'Not exactly.'

'She's a fact of life, girl.' Trista put her feet up on the table, just as Jerry and Chris returned with another pitcher—and another pizza.

'I don't think I can.' Trista pushed herself away from the table.

'Well, I haven't eaten.' Chris tore a slice off the pie and

offered it to Dulcie. She shook her head. Chris seemed not to notice her weight, but bad bar pizza at 1 a.m. could have unintended consequences.

'Your stomach is on a different timetable than mine.' She smiled to soften the words.

'I know, sweetie, and I'm sorry.' With two more bites, he finished the slice and reached for another. 'I know you're feeling needy and I've not been there. But I promise, this is just for now.'

Dulcie nodded. So much of their lives felt temporary. Until the end of the semester, or until the thesis was done. 'I'm glad you're working, Chris. Really, I am. It's just that I feel so blocked.'

'You're still worried about *The Ravages?*'

She nodded. 'What if there's a reason that nobody else solved the mystery?'

'Sounds like fear of success to me.'

It was the beer. The headache. Lloyd's enigmatic parting shot. The entire miserable week, but just then Dulcie couldn't take any more. 'It's not "fear of success," Chris!' She heard the edge creeping into her voice, but for once, she didn't try to stop it. 'And I'm not needy, I'm lonely. It's not post-traumatic ideation or any of your high-concept therapy terms.'

Chris had put his slice down and his mouth hung open, but Dulcie wasn't stopping. 'And maybe I really do have a problem. A real problem. You yourself said that whatever sticks out might be wrong. Might be, I don't know, suspect. You're allowed to have problems. But me? No, it's all in my head.'

She felt the tears starting and needed, quite suddenly, to leave. She grabbed up her coat and turned for one last parting shot. 'I know you think I'm obsessing over nothing, Chris. You've made that clear. But this isn't something I made up. It's not a ghost story. It's my life!'

HER EYES BLURRED BY TEARS, she pushed open the door and rushed out on to the street. She'd so looked forward to tonight.

To seeing Chris. As she pulled her collar up and started along Mass Ave, his declaration of love seemed like it belonged to another world. She let the tears flow.

Something grabbed her arm and she whirled around, ready for a fight.

'Whoa!' It was Chris. He backed off, hands up in surrender. 'Dulcie, I've been calling after you. I'm sorry—I had to grab Jerry for a minute there. But, hey.'

Dulcie stood her ground.

'Look, Dulcie, I'm sorry.' He ran his hand through his hair, pushing it back from a very white and tired-looking face. 'I've just been working crazy hours.'

She started to thaw, but the reference to Jerry struck a nerve. 'Why, Chris? Jerry started to say something earlier, and Trista stopped him. Is there something going on?' She didn't want to believe he was seeing someone else. But Trista's goofball boyfriend had been about to let something drop. 'Are you in trouble?'

'Only with you.' He grinned, and she noticed how thin his face was. How worn. 'Honestly, Dulcie, I've finally got the seniority to take all these hours, and I've just felt I should go for it. I mean, next semester, I'm going to have to start on my own thesis.'

She couldn't help it; she smiled back. 'Well, that will teach you.' She reached out to take his hand, and he pulled her toward him into a hug.

'Dulcie, you silly thing. I'm sorry for what I said back there. I've been spending so long analyzing student projects, I think I've forgotten how to act like a human.'

'No, you haven't.' She knew her response was muffled, pressed as she was against his wool Navy coat. So she hugged him closer before pulling back. 'But did you get enough to eat?'

'Me? You kidding?' They stepped apart and she looked up. Maybe it was the cold, but Chris seemed to have tears in his eyes, too. 'You wouldn't happen to have any of that lasagna leftover still, would you?'

'We just might, if you're lucky.' She took his hand and they started off toward her apartment. 'And maybe some of those stuffed peppers, too.' But as good as she felt, Dulcie couldn't help wondering. That pain, the touch of sharp claws, had struck midway through the evening and then disappeared. Had Mr Grey been trying to warn her of something? What had he wanted to alert her about, and did it have anything to do with Chris?

THIRTY-THREE

'So let me get this straight.' Chris was stirring the oatmeal the next morning while Dulcie filled him in on her suspicions. 'You think that Cameron might have been hitting on Polly and also Raleigh? And maybe also doing something with Bullock? And where does Lloyd fit into this?'

'I knew there was something strange about Lloyd.' Suze came down the stairs in her sweats and went straight for the coffee. Before long, the three of them were going over the possible permutations of Cameron's romantic involvements—as well as the nagging idea that something had come between Polly and Roger Gosham.

'He's just too, I don't know. Shut down.' Suze sounded as bothered by her lack of precision as by the concept. 'And you don't see it. You're a romantic.'

Chris just smiled as he got up from the table. 'She's a Goth, actually, but that just means she trusts emotions over reason, Suze. Anyone mind if I take the first shower?'

Once he had headed back up the stairs, Dulcie refilled her roommate's coffee and her own. Suze sat there, stirring her mug absentmindedly.

'What about that package?' Suze finally broke the silence to gesture with her spoon. 'The missing book?'

Dulcie had told Suze about the neatly wrapped book Raleigh had left on Lloyd's desk. Now she regretted it. 'That could have been anything.'

'But think about it.' Suze put her spoon down and started counting off on her fingers for emphasis. 'One, he tells you that the professor has him on some wild goose chase. Two, Bullock's house is broken into and the cause of that chase goes missing.

And, three, someone puts a book—a carefully wrapped book—on Lloyd's desk.'

'But Bullock has dropped the claim, or didn't file it.' Dulcie wasn't clear on the details. 'So the book wasn't stolen.'

'Maybe Lloyd hadn't realized that there would be a fuss. He's over there a lot, right? He could have slipped it back into the professor's library without the old man being any wiser. Or even better, convinced the old man that he'd simply misfiled it.'

'Motive, Suze.' Dulcie felt pretty confident about this. 'Lloyd had no motive.'

'On the contrary!' Suze was getting into this. 'He had every reason. For starters, with that mysterious book gone, maybe he could go back to work. I mean, back to the eighteenth century. And besides, this was a valuable book, right?'

'Lloyd isn't a thief.' Dulcie had to break in.

'Wait! Just give me a listen. I'm not saying he's a hardened criminal. But this book has got to be the cause of a lot of problems, right? And he is working for a pittance, so maybe he felt, I don't know, like the professor owed it to him.'

'You don't know Lloyd.' Dulcie wasn't sure how to explain. 'He's got scruples.'

'I listen to what you're telling me, Dulcie. And you've been telling me that he's stressed out, stretched to the limit—and recently he's begun acting a little odd. Like he had a secret.'

Dulcie shook her head. There was no point in arguing with Suze. If she ever went into trial law, she'd be deadly. 'Well, tell me this, then, Suze. Suppose he did take that book—or was given it.' What had Raleigh said about dropping it off? 'What would he do with it, anyway?'

'Sell it.' Suze said it like it was the most obvious thing in the world.

Dulcie couldn't help but laugh. 'I don't think an Elizabethan rarity fits the bookstore's definition of "used texts."'

'What about your rare book guy? He does more than repair books, right? He sells them. So, it makes sense he must buy them, too.'

'Suze, Professor Bullock probably bought that book from Roger Gosham. Gosham isn't going to buy it back from one of his students, especially without a provenance.'

'You sure?'

'About Gosham? Yeah, he worships Professor Bullock.' But something Lloyd had said sparked her memory. 'Though, to be honest, I think Lloyd told me that Bullock doesn't remember where he got it.'

'There you go, then. It's the only theory that fits all the facts.'

'Not really.' Chris came back down the stairs, toweling his hair. 'You're assuming a motive. The possible profit from a stolen book wouldn't be worth the risk to Lloyd.' Dulcie beamed up at him.

'Got a better one?' Suze was energized. Chris was always a better sparring partner than Dulcie.

'Maybe he borrowed it.' Chris poured more coffee into his cup and sipped it, leaning against the counter. 'He was supposed to be working on it for Bullock. Or maybe that girl Raleigh did, and asked Lloyd to bring it back for her. She's the entitled type, right? Or, get this, maybe she stole it—there was something in the paper about a wave of shoplifting in the Square. And then Lloyd found out and arranged to bring it back. Or, I don't know, maybe he did want it to disappear, maybe just for a while. He had reason. But then the professor freaked, and when Lloyd heard that the book was reported stolen, he brought it back and explained. I mean, Dulcie, did you ever actually see what was in that package?'

She shook her head.

'Maybe it wasn't even a book!' He drained his mug, triumphant, as Dulcie smiled up at him. 'It was a book, Chris. I know that wrapping—but I do like your logic.'

'That's my specialty.' He stood and put his mug in the sink. 'But now, I've got to get to work.'

Dulcie opened her mouth to protest, but stopped herself. Instead, she walked him to the top of the stairs and sent him off with a kiss.

'WHAT?' SUZE WAS WATCHING her as she came back into the kitchen.

'What what?' Dulcie turned toward the coffee pot, even though she really didn't need any more caffeine.

'There was something you weren't saying, when you were being all sweet to Chris. Is something wrong?' Suze took the pot and refilled her own mug. 'I mean, beyond him running off to work on a Saturday?'

'I don't know, Suze.' She turned toward her roommate, unsure how to explain. 'I just felt like i shouldn't push it. I think I was getting a warning from Mr Grey last night. And it started just before Chris came into the club.'

Maybe it was because she'd been out-argued by Chris, but Suze had a head of steam. 'Dulcie, do you hear what you're saying? I know you are having issues. But putting your anger off on Mr Grey?' As she got up, she looked over at Dulcie, and immediately her tone softened. 'I'm sorry. I really cannot imagine what this week has been like for you. And, yeah, I've noticed that Chris has been M.I.A., too. But I believe he's got a reason, whatever it is. And, well, Dulcie? Isn't it possible that you read the signs wrong? Maybe you just had a headache, a plain old vanilla headache?'

'Maybe.' With one more long look, Suze headed upstairs. As she heard the shower start, Dulcie poked her leftover oatmeal with her spoon. It had started to harden as it cooled, and looked no more appetizing than the cloudy day that stretched in front of her. 'Or maybe something really is going on. And nobody wants to tell me what it is.'

THIRTY-FOUR

NEW ENGLAND IN AUTUMN HAS its own particular kind of gloom. Everyone thinks of the foliage, those riotous weeks of September and early October, when each tree seems to be competing with its neighbor to be the most extravagant. In those heady early fall days, the chill in the air is welcome, the newly clear blue of the sky a stage-set backdrop to the impossible reds and oranges of the maples, oaks, and silver-barked beech trees. For Dulcie, that wild flurry of color coincided with the excitement of a new term, and the brightness of her adopted city perfectly complemented the feeling she had about coming to the university. This is autumn, the world seemed to shout. Can't you taste it?

But no matter how beautiful the season started, it always turned out the same by November. Just when the workload began to get heavy, the days grew grey, dull, and lifeless. It was enough to make one believe in the pathetic fallacy, Dulcie thought, as she descended the front steps. No Chris, no Mr Grey. Her new kitten wouldn't talk to her and her thesis was mired in, well, mire. Life was truly imitating art.

'Hey, Dulcie!' A friendly voice broke into Dulcie's gloom and she turned to see her neighbor Helene gesturing from her street-level front door. 'Have a minute?'

Dulcie found herself smiling. Her broad, and sometimes loud, neighbor had a heart even bigger than the rest of her. A city hospital nurse, she'd looked after Dulcie through the crises of the last summer, and Dulcie had come to appreciate the sweet woman behind the gruff manner. Since Helene had adopted two kittens, litter mates, Dulcie had found herself dropping by more often—the spunky felines doing more to bridge the town-gown gap than a dozen university symposiums.

'What's up, Helene?' Dulcie trotted down the three steps that led into the ground-floor apartment.

'I wanted to show you something.' Helene beckoned Dulcie back into the kitchen. 'Julius has a new trick.'

Dulcie had been planning on going to the library, and she seriously doubted that either Julius or his brother Murray had invented any original moves. But it was pleasant to be in someone else's life for a while, particularly when that life was spic and span, smelling vaguely of orange oil. 'So, where's the wonder cat?'

Helene turned toward Dulcie, a grin splitting her wide brown face. 'Check it out!'

She stepped back and Dulcie looked past her to the windowsill. There sat Julius, an orange tabby, proudly holding a pot holder in his mouth. At his feet, tucked into the sill, were a catnip mouse, a kitchen sponge, and a shredded piece of fur that had probably once been a toy mouse.

'He's a hunter-gatherer!' Helene sounded as proud as if her six-month-old kitten had mastered the piano.

Dulcie tried to smile, she really did. But looking at that marmalade kitten, his white legs just beginning to get that leggy adolescent look, she had to fight back the tears. Mr Grey had liked to fetch, too, bringing a wide assortment of items to lay at his human's feet. Another trait that his successor, the tuxedoed kitten, didn't seem to share.

'What?' Helen was suddenly hovering, her grin replaced by a look of concern.

'He's a great cat,' Dulcie said finally. 'He just reminds me of Mr Grey so much!' She found her smile and turned toward her neighbor. 'Which just means he's a super smart kitty. I'm so glad you have him!'

'I didn't mean to bring you down, dear.' Helene had heard it all. 'And isn't it good that all our cats are different? I mean,

Murray wouldn't know what to do with a cat toy if you threw it at him.'

Dulcie laughed at that and reached to pet the marmalade youngster. 'And my new kitten just likes to run around like crazy and then lie there, staring at me. I wish I could figure out what she's thinking!'

'Maybe she's saying, "When are you going to give me a name?"'

'All in good time, Helene.' Dulcie saw the other kitten, sacked out on Helene's sofa, and went over to rub his belly. 'But I'm in no rush.'

With another round of pets, she took off, trying to ignore the look of concern on her neighbor's face.

BY THE TIME DULCIE REACHED the Yard, the sun had almost broken through the clouds. The wind had picked up, as well, though, chasing the remaining leaves along the bare ground like scared prey. Dulcie tried not to think of her departed cat as she watched a pile of oak leaves swirl and settle, tempting any passersby to jump in.

'What would you have made of Julius?' The question came to mind. 'Or Murray, for that matter?' Mr Grey had had his lazy side, too. He was, after all, a cat, and could nap anywhere, anytime. But when he was awake, he had a certain alertness, an intelligence that shone in his green eyes. 'Emerald eyes,' Dulcie thought to herself, as she headed for the wide granite steps of the library.

Once inside, the chill of the day seemed to fall away. Widener was her home, the one place where she could really be herself. On a normal Saturday, she'd have preferred to be with Chris, walking by the river or taking in a movie. But as long as Chris was going to be distant, she was glad she was here. She had work to do, too!

Nor was she alone. With the semester coming to a close and the weather dismal, the marble-lined lobby of the library was serving as a refuge to other like-minded souls. Although the soaring ceilings—and the two guards—kept the hubbub to a minimum, Dulcie was aware of an un-library-like hum as she passed through the check point and made her way to the elevator. Three flights down, and she'd find the peace she craved. And maybe a few answers.

But although the stacks were significantly quieter than the lobby, they were hardly still. Soft footfalls padded up and down the narrow aisles, and Dulcie was aware of the motion-detector lights clicking on and off, soft but audible.

Tuning out the distractions, she started by pulling a copy of early feminist writings. The movement that so many thought of as a twentieth-century phenomenon had actually started two hundred years earlier, and the 'she-authors' of the time had played their part. Mary Wollstonecraft was the big name, her *Vindication of the Rights of Women* raising the cry when it was published in 1792. She'd even attacked other writers, Dulcie remembered, calling them to task for unflattering or overly pitying depictions of women in their books.

Wollstonecraft wasn't alone. There was one essay—Dulcie found herself skimming it again and smiled—that seemed particularly modern. 'A Call for Practical Education,' it spoke out against educating women solely for the roles of wife and mother. 'An idle mind is not merely an invitation to sin,' it read. 'It is a waste, displaying a rash disregard for the divine gifts with which, too, the female may be blessed.' The phrasing might be archaic, but the intent was cheering. As grateful as Dulcie was to have Chris in her life, she couldn't imagine a world in which her sole purpose was to please him.

But now Dulcie was looking for something else. That one phrase—'cool as emeralds'—had stayed in her mind and this morning it had reawakened another idea: one that she had put on the backburner recently.

The idea was simple: a corollary to her theory about the two main characters, Hermetria and Demetria. These two contrasting personalities may have been more than dramatic roles, Dulcie had begun to suspect. One strong and independent, the other an obsequious backstabber, they may have also reflected arguments about the nature of women in general from the author's day. If that phrase could not be found in other fiction of the era, maybe this was the reason. If Dulcie could prove that the author of *The Ravages* had instead used a phrase from one of those early feminist papers, she could argue that the novel's author had read them. Had thought like them. Maybe, even—if she could turn up the linguistic evidence—prove that she had been one of those strong women thinkers. It was possible. A lot of authors chose fiction to make their points, Dulcie mused. After all, more of the unknown author's contemporaries were likely to read a wild adventure filled with romance than a political tract. That was still true today, and it would make a bang-up secondary theme in her dissertation—if she could prove it.

But the fates were not with Dulcie. Although she knew she'd heard that phrase before—could almost place it—she wasn't finding it. And the fact that her mind kept going off on tangents, wondering about Chris and about Mr Grey, about Lloyd and Raleigh, didn't help.

Which at least partly explained why she started when, out of the corner of her eye, she noticed a pale visage, somewhat familiar, passing by. No, it wasn't one of Hermetria's ghosts, she realized. It was Lloyd, making an uncharacteristic appearance in eighteenth-century fiction.

'Lloyd!' Her stage whisper carried and he looked up. The rings under his eyes were dark against his colorless cheeks.

'Oh, hey.' He seemed distracted, busy with a book he had pulled from the shelf. A critique of Fielding, Dulcie noted, before getting back to the matter at hand.

'Lloyd, I wanted to talk with you last night.' She was talking normally now, her voice soft enough to be heard but not to carry through the floor-to-ceiling shelves. 'About the whole situation with Professor Bullock?'

'Not to worry.' Lloyd turned to the index, unconcerned. 'That's all taken care of.'

'What do you mean? You said he dropped the claim. Did you

mean about the stolen book?' He nodded, still reading. Dulcie wasn't appeased. 'Why?'

'It was all a lot of noise.' Lloyd closed the book and went back to browsing the shelves. 'Much ado about nothing.'

'Ha, ha.' Dulcie wanted him to look at her. Instead, he kept examining the shelves. 'Nothing was stolen, Dulcie. It's complicated, but just trust me on this one.'

She wanted to, really, but something didn't feel right. She looked at her officemate and then down at the book in his hand. 'Speaking of the bard, what are you up to down here? I thought you were on Elizabethan duty until further notice.'

He pulled another book down and, after a moment's hesitation, a third. 'Not anymore!' He turned to look at her, his pale face breaking into a smile. Dulcie could have sworn some color had come back into those cheeks. 'Like I said, it's all taken care of.' He squeezed by her and headed for the elevators. 'But I can't really talk now. I've got a big date to prepare for.'

Dulcie watched as the chubby scholar walked off, positively bouncing. She'd meant to work back to her serious questions. To ask him about the mysterious package on his desk. But by the time she found her tongue, he was gone.

THIRTY-FIVE

TOO DISTRACTED TO GO BACK to work, Dulcie followed soon after, checking out the collection of essays. But even as she found a seat in the spacious reading room, her mind raced. A date? Lloyd had a date? With whom? And how exactly had he resolved his conflict with Professor Bullock?

It was no use. How could she read about the intellectual callings of women when her own mind was stuck mulling over the social life of her officemate? Nothing for it, she decided, but to give in. The Science Center was just across the Yard. Maybe in the basement computer lab, she'd find both romance and the peace to pursue her mind's work.

As Dulcie crossed the Yard her mood lifted. The clouds were still skittering, a celestial echo to the leaves below, but the sun had broken through. And she was off to see Chris. On a normal Saturday, they'd be studying together. Why not today?

Just then a gust of wind hit, throwing up decidedly unromantic dust. Turning away, she wiped the grit from her eyes, and pulled her collar up. Why hadn't she worn a hat? That woman over there had been smart enough to—and with that thought, Dulcie recognized Polly, her bright scarlet beret standing out against the grey stone of University Hall.

'Polly!' Dulcie called and waved. The woman turned briefly and then hurried on. Well, the wind was picking up, and perhaps Dulcie had been mistaken. That was a handsome hat, but it was probably not the only one in Cambridge.

Her cheeks were stinging and her nose dripping by the time Dulcie reached the Science Center, and she paused on entering to wipe her streaming eyes.

'ID, please?' Guards were everywhere these days, but she

was used to it from the libraries. Still, as she handed over her university ID, she had to ask.

'Is there something special going on?'

'No.' The guard scanned the plastic card and handed it back. 'New policy.'

Curious, but perhaps just a sign of the times, and Dulcie descended down the curling stairs to the heart of the cavernous center: the computer lab.

'Dulcie!' Jerry looked up from the help desk. 'Welcome to the Underworld.' His big smile belied his words, but he furthered the illusion by leaning forward with a conspiratorial whisper. 'Don't eat anything down here, you know. Or you'll be forced to stay.'

'There are worse things.' She smiled back, her eyes already cruising the room. Row upon row of cubicles housed students, most working on laptops, some at university terminals that tapped directly into the school's mainframe. In one corner, two students leaned toward one screen, giggling. Otherwise, the vibe was serious. But not silent. Between the machines and the occasional mutter of hope or despair, the entire room hummed, low and steady. 'So where's Chris?'

'Chris?' Jerry looked confused.

'Yeah, you know.' Dulcie smiled, wondering at his bewilderment. 'Tall guy? Dark hair? Likes lasagna and the Red Sox?'

'Oh.' Jerry sat down and looked over at his terminal. 'He's not on till six. Didn't he tell you?'

'No, I just thought…' Dulcie paused, suddenly unwilling to let her dismay show. 'He must have.' She smiled again, although this time she had to force it. 'My fault. I must have gotten the days mixed up.'

'Good thing.' Jerry was looking over a schedule on his screen. 'I mean, he can't take all the hours.'

'Well, thanks, Jer.' Suddenly, Dulcie wanted to leave. The underground den no longer felt like a shelter and with a fast wave she was up the stairs, buttoning her coat as she went. But out in the Yard, again, she stopped. What was going on? Chris wouldn't have run off without a reason. He wasn't like that.

She paused to watch a squirrel and tried to think. Chris had had his secrets, when they first met. She'd run into him coming from the health services, from a therapy session, one night and uncovered the biggest. Unlike some of their happy-go-lucky classmates, he was dealing with some heavy issues. His mother, who had raised him after his parents' divorce, was battling cancer and a recurrence over the summer had sent him into a tailspin. But Sheryl was doing well now, her body clean of the invading cells, she'd said, the last time Dulcie had chatted with her on the phone. Well enough so that she was suggesting a visit over the semester break: Christmas on the Jersey Shore. 'Or Chanukah if you'd prefer,' she'd said. 'We can even make latkes.'

Dulcie had laughed, comfortable enough with Chris's family to explain about Lucy then, and Sheryl had brightened at the idea. 'Do you think your mother could come out? There's great healing energy on the beach.'

No, it wasn't Chris's mom. But something was up. The squirrel paused from its manic antics and fixed Dulcie with a shiny black eye. *Yeah,* she thought. *You're right.* She reached for her cell.

Chris picked up on the first ring and sounded glad to hear her.

'Where are you?' She hadn't meant for that to be the first thing out of her mouth. 'I was just at the computer lab. I thought I'd come and study with you.' She stumbled over her own words, trying to explain.

'I'm over at Winthrop House.' He sounded quite rational, and not at all ashamed. 'I guess I didn't tell you. I've put together a study group, some private tutees.'

'Oh.' That sounded reasonable. But why hadn't he told her? 'I didn't know.'

'I'm sorry, Dulcie. I've just been working so hard. I guess it just slipped my mind.'

She stood there, holding the phone. He sounded like Chris, but she had no idea what to say. Luckily, she didn't need to respond. Over the line she heard another voice—a woman's—and the sound of Chris muffling the phone.

'Look,' he came back on. 'I can't talk now, Dulcie. But our session will be over by three. Want to meet up after?'

'Yeah.' Her voice sounded weak, even to her own ears. 'I mean, yes. I'd like that.' But the day had lost its brightness once again.

THIRTY-SIX

Dulcie walked back through the Yard, kicking at leaves. But the nippy air was way too cold to let her spend two hours this way, and, besides, the squirrels were making her feel lazy by comparison. She knew her concentration was shot. What would the early feminists have made of this dilemma? Better she should focus on her other duties.

'I'll get Raleigh's notes and finally work through them,' she decided, turning toward the Union office. With Lloyd getting ready for his big Saturday night, at least she'd be able to concentrate there.

It was no good. Twenty minutes with Raleigh Hall's notes only convinced her that the young woman was as brilliant as she was beautiful. And that Dulcie was just not in a mood that promoted sisterhood. Suze would have been appalled, and probably could have talked her into a better space. But Suze wasn't answering her phone, either. And so Dulcie stuffed the papers into her bag, and hoisted the increasingly heavy load to her shoulder.

It was the weather, not her imagination. Or so Dulcie told herself as she stepped once more on one of the myriad walkways that crisscrossed the Yard. Clouds had once more rolled in, this time deepening the afternoon shadows and reminding Dulcie that snow would be coming soon. And not the pristine, silent snow of the Pacific Northwest. No, while Cambridge flakes came down as nicely and, truth be told, frosted the city quite beautifully for the first twelve hours or so of their presence, they never lasted. While the snows she had grown up with stayed beautiful, turning from white to blue as the daylight faded, here in the city it changed—and fast. Even before the first steps stopped crunching beneath her boots, Dulcie knew the white would be grimed with soot and grime. Soon the drifts would resemble lava flows, the streets filled with mucky slush. And Dulcie would wonder, once again, what she was doing here. She missed the trees. The quiet. Sometimes, even, Lucy.

Suddenly, a squirrel darted across her path, and Dulcie stopped short. The little animal stopped three feet away and stared, as if to reprimand her. And something in its piercing black eyes snapped Dulcie back to her youth. Growing up in the commune hadn't been all tofu and spirit circles. The more Dulcie got to know her college classmates, the more she recognized that the utopian ideals of sharing and respect were good ones—even if it meant being forced to come up with words of praise for Savannah's eight-bean casserole every new moon. Plus, all the hours she'd spent out in the woods were probably pretty healthy for a growing girl. At least, Dulcie hadn't worried about her weight then, though that may have been because everyone had been rather retro-shaggy and her ease with the communal animals had been considered as much of a social draw as Sirena's butt-length hair.

Nor had she been deprived, not in any real sense. Although their eco-friendly yurt had little room for private luxuries, or privacy for that matter, Lucy had always encouraged Dulcie's love of books and had even cleared out two shelves of crystals to make room for Dulcie's growing collection. True, she had tried at various times to push her daughter toward metaphysics. But when, at thirteen, Dulcie had laid down the law and firmly rejected the offer of yet another moonsigns guide, Lucy had seen the light. She'd given Dulcie her own Riverside Shakespeare, a last remnant of her own lost life, and encouraged her to take the biodiesel bus into town every week to visit the local library.

Dulcie smiled, remembering her first visit to Widener. She'd thought something was missing, and only later realized that it was the smell of cooking oil. Maybe that was why she loved Lala's french fries. That little library had been her first true love, long before Chris or Jonah, her faithless ex. Even before Widener. And when the local librarian had encouraged her to think of college, the die was cast. As much as Lucy sniffed at the idea of 'Back East'—she'd grown up on the Philly Main Line—she knew that the state schools weren't enough for her daughter.

'She's going to be a wise woman,' Lucy had explained to the community. 'A crone.' And if Dulcie had winced at those words, she'd been grateful, too. Lucy had always encouraged her to follow her own dreams. And her mother's greatest gift, after that complete Shakespeare, was letting her go. She wouldn't give up. Not now.

She looked at the squirrel, and the squirrel tipped its grey head up to stare at her. Then, with a flick of its tail, it was gone.

'Thank you!' she whispered. Maybe there was something to all this psychic stuff. But as she was looking around for another bit of animal inspiration, she saw a camel-colored figure, decidedly not rodentlike.

'Polly!' Striding along without a hat, the other woman must have been chilly. What had happened to that lovely beret? As Dulcie watched, the other woman moved quickly, her chin tucked into her collar and her pale blonde hair streaming behind her. 'Polly!'

Grateful for another familiar face, she trotted after her and found herself out on the street, just in time to see the older woman duck into an upscale stationers. Dulcie hesitated—something about the other woman seemed furtive, private—and then pulled the door open. A small chime went off and Dulcie found herself in a warm and well-lit space, surrounded by pricey pens and paper so creamy she longed to fondle it.

'May I help you?' The sales woman was wearing an ivory blouse that looked like silk. Surrounded by pens and ink, she'd managed to stay spotless.

'Just browsing.' Dulcie smiled at her, suddenly aware of her own flushed cheeks, the curls that were escaping every which way from under her own knit wool cap. 'Thanks.'

The store went back further than she'd noticed, and Dulcie

found herself drawn to a display of fountain pens. Maybe for the winter solstice, she could get one for Chris…

'That one is lovely, isn't it?' The sales woman had come up behind her. 'And quite a bargain. It's three hundred fifty. Reconditioned, of course.'

'Of course.' Dulcie swallowed. Chris wasn't a pen guy, anyway. She backed away from the case and saw Polly, far in the back, by a display of hand-blown glass pens and spherical paperweights. The latter were lovely things, little globes drawing the eye with color and light. Looking at them, Dulcie thought of Lucy and smiled. In Lucy's world, such a globe would be valued for its magic, as a focus for meditation—or a tool to gather psychic energies. Still, she knew her mother would secretly love such an object for its beauty, no matter what she called it. She moved closer, toward Polly, who held one of the smaller orbs in her ungloved hand and was running her thumb along its smooth surface.

'Pretty.' Dulcie found herself staring at it; a swirl of deep blue drew the eye in. But Polly must have been hypnotized, as well, because she started and put the paperweight down so quickly it made a noise.

'May I help you?' The sales woman was back again, this time giving them both a sharp look. 'Those are fragile, you know. Imported.'

'We're just looking.' Dulcie forced a smile. Harvard Square was becoming more like Newbury Street every day, with its pricey boutiques. 'Sorry,' she said as she leaned over to Polly. 'Didn't mean to startle you.' The face that looked back at her was paler than ever. 'Are you OK?'

Polly nodded, and Dulcie was left with a strong sense that she had overstepped as Polly reached out to touch the pretty thing again, her thin fingers trembling. But before she could, the sales woman swooped in and grabbed the little globe, wiping it down with a chamois before replacing it in the display. Clearly, these weren't real customers.

Dulcie had grown used to such treatment—in Boston if not in

scholar-friendly Cambridge. But Polly looked shaken, and Dulcie's heart went out to her. She reached for the older woman's arm and steered her away from the snooty clerk. Who needed an overpriced paperweight, anyway?

But Polly glanced back, and in that look Dulcie saw the hunger—for something beautiful, something precious. For just a moment, Dulcie saw a flash of the other Polly, the scholar who had spoken to her at Professor Bullock's. The woman she must have been ten, even fifteen years before.

'I'm sorry, Polly.' Dulcie felt for the other woman, her days spent in intellectual servitude. 'I didn't mean to interrupt. I think I've got a bad vibe today.' She tried to smile, to make a joke out of it. Polly could use some humor. 'Sales girls. Squirrels. I'm just hitting it off badly with everyone today.' No response. 'Man trouble.'

'Oh?' A bit of life came back into the pallid blonde's face, and Dulcie found herself breathing easier. It wasn't that she wanted to beef about Chris, but she felt better knowing that she'd found a way to reach Polly. She hadn't thought of her as the type for girl talk, but then, she had never bothered to inquire.

'Yeah.' She steered the other woman out of the store. The little chime sounded brittle this time, a curt goodbye. They stepped out on to the street, and when Polly turned toward Brattle, Dulcie kept pace.

'My boyfriend is acting weird.' It was an offering, an invitation to intimacy. But as the words came out, Dulcie realized it was also a relief to say those words out loud. Which was just as well, because as an opening, it was going nowhere. Polly kept walking, her head bent against the wind. 'Men,' Dulcie added, trying for sisterly camaraderie.

Polly glanced over, her pale eyes blinking beneath colorless lashes. Dulcie could have sworn her lips moved. But between the wind and the older woman's reticence, she missed it. 'Excuse me?'

'I said, you can't let them get anything on you,' Polly repeated, her voice sounding strained. She kept walking, and this time Dulcie had to struggle to keep up.

That wasn't exactly what Dulcie had been thinking, but then, she didn't know much about Polly's relationships. She started to trot to keep pace, and found her mind racing, as well. Could Polly be talking about Roger Gosham—or about Cameron? Or—another thought struck her—was Polly more than a house-keeper for the professor? The concept seemed so ludicrous, and yet so obvious, that she pulled up short. Suddenly, she remem-bered what Sarah had said at the pub. Cameron had been prying into Professor Bullock's life. Had he uncovered an inappropriate relationship? Had he been trying to help Polly? Had the profes-sor killed him over an affair?

'The bastard.' Luckily, they had reached the corner, where a dozen other pedestrians waited for the signal to cross. Several faces turned toward her, most as pale as her own, frankly curi-ous. 'Son of a—'

Polly turned to stare, her blue-grey eyes slightly distended, and Dulcie realized how crazy she must sound. 'I just mean, they are trouble, aren't they?' She tried to smile, to make it a joke. She needed time to sort this out. Could Bullock be in love? 'But they're human, too, right?'

Polly shrugged back, looking much less certain about the proposition. The light changed and the crowd moved into the street. Dulcie put her hand on Polly's sleeve and held her back.

'Polly, can you tell me? Is there something going on with Professor Bullock?'

Polly started like a spooked horse, and Dulcie fought back the urge to grab her. 'Polly? Please. I don't mean to pry—'

'Then don't!' The other woman turned on her, and Dulcie saw her lips start to quiver. 'I have nothing but respect for the professor. Professor Bullock is a scholar. Professor Bullock has an international reputation. And more than that, Professor Bul-lock is…he is the consummate gentleman.'

Dulcie let go and stepped back, shaking her head. She still wasn't convinced. 'I'm sorry, Polly. I only thought, the way you were acting...' Suddenly, Polly's words hit her. Something about the emphasis...

'It's not him, is it? Polly, tell me, did something happen with Roger Gosham?'

The thin woman turned away, but not before Dulcie saw her wince. Immediately, Dulcie felt a surge of sisterly anger and drew the taller woman in toward the shelter of a tobacconist's window.

'Polly, we should tell someone about this.' Up against the display of humidors, they were protected from the whipping wind. It almost felt private. 'If you're in an unsafe relationship—'

'No, no, it wasn't like that.' Polly looked panicked, and Dulcie held back, listening. 'Really. It was just a—a misunderstanding.' The pause before the final word made Dulcie hesitate. Was Polly lying out of shame or a sense of complicity? 'It was, well, it was complicated.' Polly looked so miserable that Dulcie didn't have the heart to push.

Polly looked in at a carving of an Indian holding a tobacco leaf and whispered to him. 'There were...other factors.'

'Cameron?' Dulcie said softly, watching the other woman as she nodded and bit her lip. Inside the store, a clerk had noticed them and started toward the door, a note of concern on his mustachioed face.

'But it's all worked out now,' said Polly, stepping away from the window. 'Hasn't it?' With a smile that did little to erase the sadness in her eyes, she reached into a pocket and pulled out the bright beret, fixing it on her head before walking off. Dulcie watched her go, with no heart to follow. That was one way of looking at it, Dulcie realized, and wondered again at the older woman's attachments.

THIRTY-SEVEN

SHE SHOULD HAVE FELT comforted, Dulcie told herself. Polly's strange comments had been, well, strange, but she should have felt better upon seeing Chris waiting for her at Lala's, where he'd managed to snag one of the few tiny tables. But she didn't, and even after they ordered, she found herself playing with the condiments—switching the hot sauce with the pickled peppers—and waiting for him to explain.

'What is it, Dulcie?' Chris took her hand, but she pulled away.

'Are you asking me what's wrong?' Dulcie heard a tone in her voice that brought to mind those peppers. 'Because if you are seriously asking me literally what this is…' She reached again for the small bottle.

'No, I know,' he said, taking her hand once more. 'Please. Tell me what's wrong.'

Dulcie felt miserable. How could she explain that she didn't feel centered anymore? That she didn't know what was safe?

'Dulce, please?' His face was sad, his dark eyes huge under those recalcitrant bangs. And she melted.

'Oh, Chris, I don't know what's going on.' She couldn't say 'lying,' she just couldn't. But after that horrible, horrible day when she found Cameron…after all the turmoil about Lloyd and Raleigh, Professor Bullock and her thesis. The new kitten, who wouldn't talk, and Mr Grey, who had also become so quiet. It all came tumbling out, in no particular order, until finally she got up to Chris, up to him not being where she thought he would be. The final straw for her metaphorical camel to bear.

'Oh, sweetie.' He lifted her hand to kiss it, and she thought she saw him smile. 'You have nothing to worry about. I mean,

Lloyd, I don't know. Nor that professor. To be honest, he doesn't sound like he's all there. But I'm all yours. Didn't I tell you that I love you?'

'Yes, you did.' She blushed. Somehow, she hadn't been able to tell him about her own feelings. Probably because he was never around long enough. And that thought sparked her anger all over again. 'But you're not telling me what's going on. Because, Christopher Sorenson, something is going on. I may not be psychic, but I can tell.'

He stopped trying to hide his grin. 'Speaking of psychic, have you spoken to Lucy lately?'

As if on cue, Dulcie's phone rang. She looked at it and then up at Chris. It was her mother.

'Mom?' Dulcie couldn't remember the last time she had called Lucy anything but Lucy. Then again, she couldn't remember when her mother's timing had been quite so on. Perhaps if Lucy wasn't psychic, Chris was.

'Dulcie, darling! I'm so pleased to have gotten you. Did you find out about that book yet? I really suggest you get rid of it, if you haven't already. I was meaning to tell you that you can't just throw it out. There's a key in it. Or maybe that's another book, I'm not sure. Just that there's a new message, "the key is in the book." But then there's the fake book. And that you've got to get rid of—'

'Lucy! Hang on.' Dulcie was laughing now. At least one thing hadn't changed. 'I'm still doing my research. And no, I haven't yet found the key to anything—or anything poisonous, either.'

'Treacherous, dear. Treacherous or maybe false.' Lucy, like her daughter, was a stickler for words.

'The treacherous book, then.' Her mind flashed to *The Ravages of Umbria*. 'About the key, I have some ideas. But, Lucy, I hope you're wrong.'

'We often wish for things, Dulcie. But unless we pay attention to the portents, we may never get them.'

'I am working, Lucy.' Whether because she wanted to prove herself to her mother or because she needed to get her own ideas straight, Dulcie found herself explaining her research to her mother. 'So, even if it's just for background, I'd like to find out who the author of *The Ravages* really was.'

Lucy was characteristically cryptic. 'Does anyone ever truly reveal who they are?'

'Who he or she is, Lucy.' Dulcie was beginning to regret her attempt to communicate.

'Don't be semantic, dear.'

'Pedantic,' Dulcie corrected under her breath. But Lucy's punctiliousness clearly only extended to her own concerns, and she was already rattling on about another message, something that had come up during a purifying circle. 'This question of identity, it's so important to you, Dulcie. I can see that.' Dulcie bit her tongue. 'I can see that, though I'm not entirely sure how it fits in. There are shadows, dear. Some things are not clear yet.'

That sounded to Dulcie like a recipe to get back to work. Unless Lucy had another clue. 'You can't tell me anything else, can you?'

'I wish I could, dear.' Lucy's voice faded out briefly and Dulcie had a moment's pause. Was she really talking on the phone to her mother, or was this some strange astral projection? The waitress came over with their plates. At least lunch was real. 'You know what you have to do. It's for you to uncover.' Her voice was fading, distant, reminding her vaguely of something. Some dream. 'You know what makes a heroine, Dulcie. Trust yourself.' Then her mother's voice came back, clear and strong. 'But that's not why I called.'

'Oh?' Dulcie waited. There must have been another dream. Or perhaps a vision, if Lucy and her friend Nirvana—aka Shirley—were doing peyote again. While she was waiting, Dulcie took a bite of her three-bean burger.

'It's about squash.'

Dulcie almost choked on her burger. 'Squash?'

'Yes, this year, the squash are just the most beautiful things you've ever seen. Butternut, acorn, those big green ones that I always forget the name of. The goddess has truly smiled on us, and I was trying to remember something.'

Dulcie, her mouth full, grunted.

'Do you prefer the squash baked with maple syrup or mashed?'

A wave of sadness swept over Dulcie, and suddenly the bite of burger was too big to swallow. After a moment, she managed, and found that her voice was cracking.

'Lucy, Mom, you know I'm not coming home this semester break, don't you? I'm sure I told you. Chris's mother invited us both down to New Jersey, and what with the shorter bus ride and us both being broke—'

'Yes, yes.' Lucy seemed unconcerned. 'You told me, dear. Sheryl sounds like a proper human, for a she-wolf.'

'A what?' Dulcie looked up. She hoped Chris hadn't heard that, but he seemed to be happily digging into his own burger. There was a spot of hot sauce on his chin, and she reached to wipe it off.

'She-wolf.' Lucy seemed to have taken Dulcie's question literally. 'And frankly, I'm jealous. You know, I've always felt a kinship with the grey pack. Though perhaps it makes sense. Wolves are very family-oriented, you know. And I do think that your Chris sounds like a very nice young man.'

'He is.' Dulcie might never understand her mother, but she was also never bored by her.

'So, tell me, which way do you prefer your squash?'

'Either is fine.' Images of a mushy care package filled Dulcie's mind. 'Baked, I guess.'

'That's what I thought, but Nirvana remembered otherwise. Now tell me one more thing, Dulcie, and I'll let you get back to that boyfriend of yours.'

Dulcie waited.

'Do you think he'd like my wheatberry casserole?'

'I love you, Lucy.' Dulcie knew if she didn't cut in, she'd be on for far longer than Lucy could afford. 'And I'm hanging up now.'

'Goodbye, Dulcie. And remember: the one who does the seeing may be just as important as that which is seen.' With that, Lucy hung up, leaving Dulcie shaking her head.

'What?' Chris looked at her.

Dulcie shook her head. How could she ever explain?

'Are you going to finish those fries?'

She pushed her plate over to him and watched as he wolfed them down.

THIRTY-EIGHT

THE TWO PARTED OUTSIDE the café, with plans to meet up again later. Chris had said he was working the night shift at the computer lab. And this time, he promised, he really would be there, and so Dulcie had agreed to come by around nine, with food for a break.

They kissed goodbye, Chris's smile as sweet as ever, but Dulcie was still not completely satisfied. The lunch—and the strange phone call from Lucy—seemed like a set-up, somehow. As if those close to her were planning something. That was probably her imagination, she acknowledged, as she made her way back to her office. But she couldn't help the prickly feeling, as if the hair were standing up along the back of her neck. Chris had not been completely straight with her, she felt, even if he claimed it had all been a mistake. And there was something else going on, she thought as she started across the Yard for the umpteenth time that day. Maybe it was this path, carrying her between Widener Library and the stark, old Memorial Church, but her thoughts seemed clearer here. Something was wrong. Chris was not the cheating type. She trusted him. But he was hiding something. Or at least, she corrected herself, he had not been entirely forthcoming.

Once again, a fat squirrel darted across her path, and Dulcie paused to watch it as it stopped at the base of an oak tree. Acorn in hand, it nibbled a little, then shoved the nut into its cheek, all the while staring at the human intruder.

'Don't worry, fella.' Dulcie smiled at the fluffy creature. 'I'm not going to steal your feast.' And with a flash, she realized what else was bothering her. Thanksgiving, as the college called it, was right around the corner. In previous years, she'd been happy to tag along with Suze to her folks' place in New Jersey. But this year, she'd received no such invitation. Suze was probably taking Ariano with her, and Suze's parents were conventional enough that the big Italian would undoubtedly be given the one spare room. And Chris's mother had invited Dulcie for the longer winter break—the solstice holiday, as she still thought of it—and that would be her chance to meet his family.

But Thanksgiving, however you termed it, was two weeks away, and nobody had even mentioned it to her. Watching the grey rodent stuff its face, Dulcie realized she would be alone while everyone else enjoyed a ritual dinner. Family, friends. Love. Suddenly the three-bean burger felt like a mistake, a lump in her stomach, and she trudged the rest of the way in a funk as grey as the skies.

IF WE CONSIDER THE precedents for such revolutionary theory...

Dulcie rolled her eyes at the overwrought prose, but still she had to admit it: Raleigh Hall was smart, and once she toned down the hyperbole, her undergraduate thesis really might be a prize winner. Just because the young woman was pretty—and tall and slim—was no reason to discredit her work. And so, making a few notes, she read on.

Discipline, that was the key. As she read, occasionally gnawing at the end of her pencil, Dulcie allowed herself to feel a little proud of herself. Here she was, abandoned and forgotten, and yet she was still getting down to work. Hermetria must have gone through similar days, alone in her mountaintop castle. Her best friend had proved faithless, too. Not that Suze was faithless, Dulcie corrected herself with a flash of guilt. Just preoccupied with her new romance. But Hermetria had managed to prevail, even sorting out her two suitors to find which one was true of heart. Had she made the right decision, going with the young, impoverished knight? Chris's face flashed through Dulcie's mind, and for the first time in a long time, she found herself questioning her own choices. She hadn't wanted to fall for the skinny computer nerd. He'd won her over with his kindness, his persistence. His attention. Had she been too needy recently? Had she leaned on him too much—and ignored Suze?

No, it was no use. Dulcie dropped the pencil. If she wasn't going to concentrate on Raleigh's paper, she shouldn't be marking it up. She'd only be making more work for herself later. And if she was going to start thinking about *The Ravages,* she may as well apply herself to her own thesis. She was Dulcie Schwartz, scholar. And if she was looking for any comparison to Hermetria, she should keep in mind that the beleaguered heroine had worked hard to make her own luck. Of course, she had had a friendly ghost on her side.

'Mr Grey.' Dulcie addressed the still air of the office. 'If you're out there, would you help me?' So many things seemed to be weighing on her, she didn't know what to ask for. But ghosts weren't like stars. You didn't make a specific wish, did you? No, Mr Grey had always been a source of comfort. Warmth, stability: that was what she needed now.

Would he hear her? She had to believe it, and so with a new determination, she fished the library book out of her bag. Somewhere in among these essays, she'd find some connection to *The Ravages.* And maybe a clue about its author.

The key, she was convinced, was in that one phrase, *cool as emeralds.* Though since her talk with Lucy, she couldn't help but wonder. *The key is in the book...*

But the small office was stuffy and warm. The heat had kicked in for real, with the fading of the day, and somewhere a radiator hissed gently, the steam coming out in small gasps: whirr...whirr...whirr... Dulcie felt her lids grow heavy, the book unwieldy in her hands.

Thump! It was the noise that woke her, the thud as the large volume slid from her lap to the floor. She reached for the book, which had fallen open, grateful that neither Professor Bullock nor Roger Gosham were there to witness it lying, pages open, on the dirty floor.

And as she picked it up, a paragraph jumped out at her:

The modern female must be strong, as cool as emeralds, and this strength she must utilize in furtherance of more than simply family or personal betterment. No, in order to better serve the society to which she is the rightful heir, she must draw that strength like a sword from its sheath, and wield it for the common good…

That was it! Dulcie couldn't believe it, and looked around for someone to share her good news. No Lloyd, but she'd tell Chris. He would understand. He knew how hard she was working. But first, she had to take notes. Dulcie couldn't understand why she'd had so much trouble finding this one quote when it was there all along.

'Thank you, Mr Grey.' She closed her eyes and imagined the satisfied way his eyes would close, his whiskers proud and alert. And with a similar smile, she flipped back to the beginning of the essay, the marvelous, wonderful essay. And she froze.

'Commentary on the Rights of Women,' read the title page. Below it, the publisher had conveniently printed the original publisher and date of first printing: November 20, 1840. This essay had been published a good forty years after *The Ravages of Umbria*.

Dulcie started and shook her head, confused. Could the essayist have picked up the phrase from the novel? But how? No critics had commented on *The Ravages* when it was first published, at least none that Dulcie could ever find. And too much would have passed since its initial publication for it still to be a hot topic in 1840. *The Ravages* had probably been forgotten by then—as if it had never been written.

And as that phrase took shape in her mind, the implications grew. Forty years—a lifetime. After all that time to have that exact phrase pop up? No, it was too little, too late. Too long after the fact to have been lifted from the original, as she knew it, and too close to be an accident. By the 1840s, Gothic novels had become the butt of jokes, of parodies.

Dulcie swallowed. Hard. She had found her proof all right. Proof that *The Ravages* was a fake.

THIRTY-NINE

A WAVE OF NAUSEA PASSED over Dulcie, leaving her weak and sweaty. No, it couldn't be. She closed her eyes and opened them again. Yes, it could. This was exactly what she'd suspected for a while now, what Lucy's strange dream had warned about. Suddenly the office was too small, too stuffy. She needed to talk to someone about this—anyone, but ideally someone who could tell her that she was wrong. That she hadn't just stumbled over damning evidence that *The Ravages of Umbria* was not the product of a later era. A pastiche or, worse, a spoof.

'Lloyd, where are you when I need you?' Dulcie keyed in his number on her cell, but only got his voicemail. Of course, the big date.

As she sat there, trying to think of whom else she could talk to, Dulcie was hit by how small a field she really worked in. Sure, the English Department was decent-sized. But Trista probably hadn't read anything this early since she'd passed her general exams. For Sarah the medievalist, this would be several centuries too late. For Jeremy—no, never mind Jeremy. He'd gotten so caught up in Anglo Saxon that he found Chaucer decadent. Which left…who? Professor Bullock? Dulcie shuddered. Yes, if push came to shove, she would have to talk to her thesis adviser. He had never really liked *The Ravages of Umbria* and had only approved her thesis because her supposed discovery meant it had a good chance of getting published. With this turn of events, he'd be positively gleeful.

'What a wonderful fraud, Dulcie!' She could hear him chortle. 'This will show them all!'

Sitting there, she could imagine him gloating, his heavy eyebrows no longer hiding the sparkle in his eyes. That one phrase was it: the missing link. Would it be enough to ensure an academic career? Or was Raleigh right? As much as she trusted the professor, she could easily imagine Bullock claiming credit. She'd be a co-author, the student he'd shepherded to a great discovery. Of course, it might still be enough.

But no, she didn't care. Finding out that *The Ravages* wasn't all she had thought was not like Chris debugging a program. It was more like discovering that there was no Santa Claus. Not even a beneficent Mother Time, as the gift-giving patron of the solstice holiday was known back on the commune.

Thinking of Chris didn't help. He would try to be comforting, but he was the source of too much uncertainty himself these days. Dulcie was in no mood for vague reassurances—or second-hand psychobabble. She needed to do some work on this, to see if there was a rational explanation for this late, and possibly fatal, reference.

Lloyd would have been the best source, as close to Professor Bullock as she could get without alerting her adviser to the issue. But he wasn't the only one. Hadn't Dulcie shared a scholarly spark with Polly not that long ago? And now that the two woman had bonded, however awkwardly, over men, maybe the older woman would feel sympathy for Dulcie's dilemma. The only question was, how to reach her? With a splash of shame, Dulcie realized she had never had a conversation with the woman except by accident. She had no idea if Polly had a cell or could take calls at the Bullock house. And at—she checked her watch—six p.m. on a Saturday, she might reasonably be assumed to have other plans. For all Dulcie knew, Polly Heinhold was Lloyd's hot date.

That thought made her laugh out loud, and the laugh brought Dulcie back to life. What she needed to do was to reach out. It wasn't that far to Professor Bullock's house. If she were lucky, this would all be cleared up before she was due to meet Chris.

CROSSING THE COMMON IN THE lengthening shadows, Dulcie found herself formulating excuses. After all, she wanted to speak to

Polly, not Professor Bullock, and on the off chance that the professor himself came to the door she didn't want to have to explain why. Should she give some girly excuse, claim that she needed to ask the other woman about clothes or a date? Once again, Dulcie found herself laughing, startling a jogger. Polly wasn't a bad-looking woman, just way too pale and worn for her age. With a little more color—Dulcie pictured that bright beret—she'd come back to life. But Dulcie was hardly the girl talk type. As the years had gone by, she'd become much more comfortable with her bohemian-by-necessity style, and she had enough male attention, even before Chris, to know that not every man wanted a model-thin woman. But the idea that she'd walk across town for fashion advice was ludicrous. And for any other words of wisdom, she had Suze. Suze had grown up in a conventional household and had pulled Dulcie out of more than a few social straits.

Nothing for it, she decided as she headed up Brattle. If Professor Bullock answered the door, she'd just wing it. But when she got to the row of brick houses, she hesitated. By now, the shadows of the day had lengthened, throwing the small front yards into shadow. Holly, dark and glistening, took on a menacing aspect, and Dulcie hesitated, her hand on the low iron gate, remembering.

'Cameron didn't die because of you.'

The voice came out of nowhere, causing her to jump. 'Mr Grey!'

'He touched many lives, but not yours.'

Dulcie blinked. There, on the high slate steps, sat a long-haired grey cat, his flag of a tail neatly wrapped around front paws. 'You were not part of this, Dulcie. And you are a scholar.'

'You're right, Mr Grey.' She pushed the gate forward and stepped in, hoping against hope that in a few steps, she'd be able to pick up her beloved pet once again. But as she walked forward a cold blast of wind rattled through the shrubbery, sending a rush of dust and leaves. Dulcie blinked against the onslaught. When she opened her eyes, he was gone.

His purpose, however, was clear. Mr Grey wanted her to investigate, and while Dulcie could only mull over the exact meaning of his message, she got the gist of it.

'But I am touched by this,' she was saying to herself as she reached for the brass knocker. Just then, the door swung open.

'Hello?' Dulcie stood on the stoop and called in. 'Professor Bullock? Polly?' Nobody called back, and for a moment Dulcie worried about what she would find. Cambridge was a city, and an open door could mean another break-in—or worse.

Then she remembered her vision of Mr Grey. He wouldn't lead her into danger. In fact, he was usually warning her away from it. An unlocked door was probably simply a sign of the professor's absentmindedness.

'Hullo!' She stepped into the foyer and looked into the study, where Polly stood apparently examining a shelf of books. 'Polly?'

'Oh!' The thin blonde whipped around, a spot of color coming into each cheek. 'I didn't hear you.'

'I'm sorry.' Dulcie smiled. 'I didn't mean to startle you. The door was open.' She stepped in and closed the door behind her, making sure she heard it latch.

'Professor Bullock.' Polly shook her head dolefully. 'He just ran out. I swear sometimes he's so preoccupied.'

'Really?' Dulcie was just making conversation, grateful for a simple solution to her dilemma. But Polly seemed to take her query seriously.

'Well, he's got a ton on his mind, you know.' The color in her cheeks drained away. 'His research is eating up his time. The new book is going to be tremendous.'

Dulcie nodded. She'd been hearing about the professor's 'new book' for as long as she'd been at Harvard. What concerned her now was something she'd noticed as the other woman had turned around. Dulcie really just wanted to get to the point, to ask Polly about nineteenth-century essayists who might shed some light on the strange connection between that one piece and *The Ravages of Umbria*. But she couldn't help but wonder why, as Polly had turned to greet her, she had seen the other woman slipping something into the pocket of her skirt. Something that looked suspiciously like the professor's fancy letter opener.

FORTY

It all happened so fast, Dulcie doubted her own sight. Could it have been some other trinket? A pair of sewing scissors? No, she'd seen the ornate hilt of the little sword. The glint of the green stone.

'So, did you want to leave a message for him?' Polly was standing there, waiting, and Dulcie realized that she must look like a dolt.

'No, no.' She quickly recovered. Whatever Polly had been doing, she had come here for help. 'I was actually hoping to run into you.'

Polly smiled ever so slightly, and the years dropped away. Dulcie began to see why men might have fought over her.

'It's an academic question, really.' She paused. How to explain without spilling her worst fears? 'A question of authorship. Are you familiar with the collection *Women Writing on Women, 1780—1840?*'

'The Gunning? Certainly.' Polly stepped into the hallway and motioned for Dulcie to follow. 'Would you mind? I was just cleaning up.'

Dulcie breathed a sigh of relief. Polly was straightening up! She probably pocketed the errant letter opener, meaning to return it to the professor's office. But now the older woman led her into the kitchen, where she put the kettle on the stove.

'Tea?' Without waiting for a response, she reached for a teapot on an upper shelf. Dulcie glanced at the clock. She had envisioned a short chat—a few questions, some quick answers, and then she'd be off. But this woman was clearly starved for company.

'Sure.' She settled into a kitchen chair and tried to plot out a line of questioning.

'Chamomile OK?'

Dulcie swallowed hard. Chamomile was one of Lucy's favorite cure-alls. But, hey, maybe Polly would cure what was ailing her tonight. She nodded and hoped her smile didn't look overly strained.

'It's interesting that you brought up the Gunning.' Polly brought over mugs and a plastic bear filled with honey. 'That was one of the first major collections of British feminist writings, you know.'

'I hadn't realized that,' Dulcie responded, half her mind on her own questions. 'But there is one essay in it—'

'Oh, yes,' Polly broke in. 'Although it wasn't published until, oh, mid-1840s, which is shameful, when you think about it. After all, many of the ideas espoused in those essays had been circulating for decades. But it was Horace Gunning who came up with the idea of anthologizing them, raising a subscription of more than five hundred for a first edition—'

'Actually, it was the date on one of them.'

'Really?' Polly poured more tea, and then continued as if Dulcie had never spoken. 'Gunning himself was said to have been influenced by his wife, an early follower of Mary Wollstonecraft...'

It was no use, Dulcie realized. Polly was on a roll. Either she had been denied a chance to discuss her favorite topics for so long that the pressure was unbearable. Or, and Dulcie felt a twinge of guilt at this thought, the older woman's loneliness was more complete than she had realized. When Polly finally paused to take a sip of her own tea, which had to be cold by then, Dulcie tried one more time.

'Polly, maybe you can help me.' She spoke quickly, hoping to get her question out. 'I'm worried because I found a phrase in an essay and it's the same as one in a book that was supposedly published at least forty years earlier.' She paused. Polly stayed quiet. 'And I'm afraid it's a fraud.' There, she had said it.

'Impossible.' Polly's pale face wrinkled up at the thought, and Dulcie felt a flood of relief.

'Really? Thank you.' Dulcie breathed easier than she had in an hour, and when Polly got up to heat more water, she vowed to do whatever was in her power to pay the older woman back. She'd have tea with her once a week. Even chamomile.

'Definitely.' Polly refilled the pot. 'Those texts were all authentic. I know some people have questioned his methods, but Gunning was quite rigorous in his standards, collecting original documents and comparing versions. By the second edition...'

Dulcie groaned and caught herself. Polly had misunderstood—and she was trapped. 'Would you excuse me?' The tea made a convenient excuse, but in truth she just needed a moment alone to figure out a better strategy or an escape. The hallway was dark; the early dusk had fallen. She'd been in this house often enough to know where the bathroom was, even in the shadows. But she wondered at the lack of light. Was the professor saving energy? Should they turn on a lamp, just to welcome him home?

On her way back to the kitchen, Dulcie looked again into the library. Maybe she could convince Polly to let her look at the professor's books. Bullock was no feminist, but in the interest of history, he undoubtedly had some other complete anthologies. There had to be an explanation. She reached to turn on the tall, ornate floor lamp and heard footsteps.

'Were you looking for something?' Dulcie turned to find Polly standing behind her.

'Oh, sorry.' Dulcie smiled to disarm the other woman, who had started to frown. Perhaps she felt Dulcie was brushing her off? 'It's just that I'm looking into an authentication, and I was wondering about other anthologies?'

'The Gunning is the definitive work. Alpha and Omega.' Polly stood, waiting for Dulcie to pass, back into the kitchen, but Dulcie couldn't resist one last glance at the crowded library. Only the dim glow of the street lights came through the windows, but as a car drove by, the flash of headlights sent a wave of illumination over the room.

'Oh, that's so pretty.' Before the light had faded, a flash of blue had caught her eye. Blue and a little gold, all set in a glass globe. 'Is this from that store?' She started toward it, and felt a hand on her upper arm.

'That's the professor's.' Polly pushed by her and drew the drapes. 'And since he's not here, I really couldn't allow—'

Just then, Dulcie's cell phone rang, startling them both. Although she didn't recognize the number, she flipped it open.

'Dulcie! Thank God I got you.' It was Raleigh. On a Saturday night. Dulcie's sense of relief turned to annoyance. Didn't students have any sense of boundaries? But before she could remonstrate, Raleigh broke in. 'You've got to help me. Help us. It's Lloyd. He's been arrested!'

'What?' Dulcie must have yelled, because Polly stopped short. But volume didn't work with Raleigh, who was too upset to make much sense. Finally, Dulcie got her to explain that Lloyd had been taken from his apartment by the Cambridge Police. What the distraught undergrad had been doing there she hadn't said.

'It's Lloyd,' Dulcie said as soon as she'd gotten off the phone. Polly blinked once, which Dulcie took as recognition. 'He's been arrested.' Suddenly, she realized that she didn't know the charges. Could there be some sensible explanation? A bad check or disgruntled landlord? So much had happened recently that she had automatically assumed the worst…

'That makes sense.' Polly's calm declaration interrupted the whirl of her thoughts, and as if that had settled everything, she turned to walk back into the kitchen.

'Why? What do you mean?' Dulcie followed Polly and watched as she calmly began washing the mugs, fighting the urge to grab the thin blonde and shake her. 'Do you know what's going on?'

'I believe so.' Polly put the mugs upside down on the rack and began on the teapot. 'And I have to say, it isn't unexpected after Professor Bullock's complaint.' She seemed so calm, so matter-of-fact that Dulcie found herself paradoxically panicked, as if Polly's calm presaged the worst.

'What?' Dulcie couldn't stop herself. She reached for Polly's arm. 'Polly, please. I've known Lloyd for years. You have, too.'

'Well, I shouldn't talk out of school.' Polly paused and Dulcie forced herself to wait. Lloyd certainly had reason to complain about the professor's treatment of him. Had he said something? Done something? It took all her will not to tighten her grip on Polly's thin arm. But in that moment, Polly had reached a decision. 'Professor Bullock has noticed certain items have gone missing.' She reached for a dish towel, pulling away from Dulcie.

'What do you mean, Polly?' None of this was making sense.

'Valuable items.' Polly dried her hands and turned to face her. 'A Montblanc fountain pen, things like that. Professor Bullock is a good man and for the longest time he didn't want to do anything. But, really, this time Lloyd has gone too far.'

'How does he know it's Lloyd?' Dulcie refused to believe it.

Polly shrugged. 'He had access and everyone knows he's just scraping by. I don't know why now. Maybe a little ghost said something.'

The ghost reference was probably a joke. After all, Polly knew as well as anyone about Dulcie's area of specialization. But Dulcie was in no mood to laugh. Instead, she just stood there, staring at the wall, trying to make sense of the idea. Lloyd a thief? No, it didn't seem possible. But she couldn't stop thinking of the package on his desk. A wrapped book, much like the rare and beautiful ones from Gosham's, and just that night, Professor Bullock had reported a book stolen.

FORTY-ONE

No. Everyone knew that the theft report had been retracted. At least, that's what the scuttlebutt in the department had been—once Lloyd had mentioned it. Could Lloyd have spread that rumor to cover his own tracks?

Dulcie shook her head. This was her colleague they were talking about. She needed to help him. Excusing herself, she turned away from Polly and punched in a number.

'Suze? Glad I got you.' As quickly as she could, and knowing full well that Polly was right behind her, Dulcie explained the situation. The answer was not what she wanted.

'No way, Dulcie.' Suze sounded friendly, but firm. 'For starters, I'm still a student, too, remember? And the legal clinic doesn't take on criminal cases. Besides, Dulce, how do you know he's innocent? I mean, Lloyd's name has been coming up an awful lot recently.'

'That's because he's in the department.' Dulcie fought to keep her voice level. 'And he's entitled to some kind of defense.'

'Which he'll get,' Suze continued. 'I'm sure.'

'I'm not.' Dulcie tried to recall if Lloyd had ever mentioned any family. 'Hey, Suze, can I call you back?'

'Sure.' Suze sounded warmer now. 'Or you can just come home. Really, Dulcie, this sounds like a minor matter. They probably won't even hold him.'

Dulcie wasn't so sure, and the idea of her gentle officemate stuck in a holding cell on a Saturday night wasn't fun. She tried to think. Lloyd might not have family, but he clearly had one well-to-do friend. Scrolling back through her calls, she found Raleigh's number. The call went direct to voicemail—she must be on the phone—but Dulcie left a message.

'Raleigh, it's Dulcie again. Dulcie Schwartz.' She paused, not sure how to ask. 'Since you seem to know Lloyd so well, would you have a contact for his family? Or, well, would you know anybody who could bail him out?'

'Bail?' She heard the voice behind her and turned. Polly was staring. 'Do you think they'd give him bail?'

Dulcie snapped the phone shut, Raleigh forgotten. 'Why wouldn't they, Polly? It's just theft—a property crime, right?' Dulcie was no expert, but all those years living with Suze must have taught her something.

Polly only shrugged. 'For starters,' she said, her voice maddeningly calm. 'But from what the professor was saying, I think they may also want to talk to him about Cameron's…about the incident.'

Incident? The word hit Dulcie like a punch in the stomach. 'They suspect Lloyd of murder?'

Polly shrugged her thin shoulders again, and Dulcie wondered again just who this woman was.

'That's just not possible.'

'Who knows what men are capable of?' Polly turned, as if to go back to the kitchen. 'Do you think I should make more tea?'

MUTTERING SOMETHING SHE hoped was coherent and not too rude, Dulcie grabbed her coat and headed for the door. Something was definitely off at Professor Bullock's, but Lloyd was more likely the victim than the culprit. And if Polly was having personal problems, she added as she jogged down the stairs, they weren't Roger Gosham's fault.

She headed back toward the Square with one thought in mind: Chris. No matter what was going on with their relationship, he'd listen. And Dulcie needed someone to do that now—someone who didn't think strictly in terms of law and liability. Suze's response had shocked her. Her roommate was undoubtedly being sensible, and trying to look out for Dulcie, too. But the legalistic nature of it had been a little cold, a little harsh. Maybe, thought Dulcie, it was just as well she wasn't going to

Thanksgiving at Suze's this year. Was this distance the natural outcome of them each having different specializations, a gradual shift that was only now settling them into different world views? Or was it simply that they hadn't spent that much time together recently, both of them so caught up in their studies—and with their new boyfriends—that neither knew what the other found important? That thought stopped her, and Dulcie paused halfway across the bare Common. Were she and her old friend drifting apart? Would she and Suze ever be as close as they had been, all those single, lonely years before? A pang went through Dulcie, matched by a gust of frigid air. Night had dropped Cambridge into a frosty chill, but the stinging in her eyes wasn't all from the wind.

'No pizza?' To his credit, after his initial disappointment Chris looked happy to see her. And as soon as she started to explain what had just happened he even waved off a tired-looking student to tune in.

'Five minutes, Sal. Check your coding.' He'd glanced around. 'Hey, let's surface, Dulcie. I can take five.'

She followed gratefully as he led the way up to the Science Center café, hanging back only when two more students way-laid him. They were worried that he was leaving, basically, and once he calmed them down he and Dulcie were able to retreat, snagging a corner table for bad coffee and warm chocolate chip cookies, still so hot the chips were molten.

'So, Lloyd is in jail?' Chris had helped Dulcie deal with a situation the previous summer, and they both had some experience with the law. 'Or is he just being questioned?'

'I don't know.' Dulcie bit her lip. 'I should have asked Raleigh. She just said he'd been arrested and I assumed the worst. But maybe the cops just picked him up to talk to him. Hang on.' She tried Lloyd's apartment and then his cell, getting voicemail in both places. Another call to Raleigh had the same result. 'All this communications technology, and we still can't simply talk.'

'I'm wondering.' Chris pushed the plate toward her; a large chunk remained. 'You thought the cops were looking at Professor Bullock for Cameron's murder, right?'

'Yeah.' Dulcie thought back, and ate the cookie. 'But he couldn't have done that—I mean, I was there.'

'Well do you think he ended up talking to them about something else? About the thefts?' Chris used one long finger to nail a crumb, under the guise of making a point. 'I mean, maybe he set some kind of trap.'

'I don't know.' Strangely, Dulcie wasn't finding it unbelievable that her thesis adviser might want to sabotage a student. 'I just don't know if he could be that organized.'

Chris looked at her, and she shrugged. 'He's just sort of the absentminded professor these days. I mean, he keeps losing things.' She paused. 'Unless someone really has been stealing from him.'

'Could it have been Lloyd? I mean, not the murder...'

But Dulcie shook her head. 'No, no way. I've never had any qualms about leaving my bag in our office, or anything like that.'

'But you're another student, as broke as he is. And the professor has this big, fancy house up on Tory Row. Plus, from everything you've said, Lloyd has reason to resent Bullock. Maybe, this was a little revenge.'

'No, no way.' Dulcie stared at the table, looking for the answer in the patterned linoleum. When she looked up at Chris, her voice was firm. 'What you're saying makes sense, but that just isn't Lloyd. I mean, I'm not Lucy, but I do have a sense about people.'

Chris smiled and reached for her hand. 'Yes, you do. But if the cops don't have any evidence, why would he be under arrest?'

'You're so rational.' Dulcie squeezed her boyfriend's hand. 'But you forgot one option. Maybe it's simply that whatever implicated Lloyd could apply to someone else, as well.'

'Maybe.' Chris stared off at the space above Dulcie's head,

and she wondered for a moment if he was thinking of getting another cookie. 'But there's something amiss here. I mean, there's been a pretty brutal murder.' Dulcie knew what he meant, even if it was close to a tautology, and didn't interrupt. 'And the police are arresting someone for a property crime?'

'Well, life goes on.' Dulcie turned it over in her head. 'And if the professor complained…'

'Yeah, but why? One of his prize students is dead, and he's bringing charges against another of his protégés for, what? For pocketing a pen or something? I'm wondering if there's something else going on here. Like, maybe it's because Lloyd is the only one who didn't drink the Kool-Aid.' Chris looked at her. 'I mean, besides you.'

'What do you mean?'

'Well, I don't know the man, but from everything you say, he's a self-important jerk who hasn't done any real work in thirty years. And yet, he's revered like he's some kind of genius.'

'Twenty years, and he is a tenured professor,' said Dulcie, as if that explained everything. 'And English is a little different from Applied Math. But, hey, what did you mean about the professor bringing charges?'

'Why else would Lloyd have been arrested? At least, if he really was arrested for theft.'

Dulcie had nothing more to say to that and slumped back in her seat. When Chris got up a few moments later, she raised her face for a kiss, but kept sitting there, long after her boyfriend had gone. The café stayed open all night, and as she sat, Dulcie was dimly aware of comings and goings, computer-pale faces and the enticing aroma of those cookies. But all she could think about was her officemate and her professor. Something was going on, and she had no idea how to get at the truth.

FORTY-TWO

HER DREAMS DIDN'T HELP. This time, she was desperately searching a mountain-top castle, the high Alpine winds whistling outside as she tried to find the keys to the dungeon. She kept turning corners, sure she'd find them on a hook inside the next door. She could picture them, oversized antiques on a big, iron ring. But they were never where they should be.

'Misplaced or stolen?' A familiar voice cut through the wind. 'And who would know?'

In her dream, glowing green eyes stared out of a shadowy corner, but when she looked closer, they were gone. 'Mr Grey? What do you mean?'

The wind must have found a crack because suddenly a tuft of ash and smoke blew up from the fireplace, stinging her eyes. She stepped back and felt something brush against her legs. Something soft and strangely warm. 'Think about it, Dulcie. Who would care?'

It was no use. She woke in the dark to find the new kitten ricocheting off the walls. 'Kitten!' she called and the little cat stopped in her tracks, stared at Dulcie, and bulleted off down the hall. 'Wonderful.' Dulcie knew she wasn't being fair. Odds were, her disrupted sleep was what was causing the young animal to tear off like that. But she couldn't help feeling somehow misled. There was only one cat she wanted, and he was gone. No matter what anyone said about kitten behavior, she couldn't imagine Mr Grey had ever acted so crazed. And now, even in her dreams, he had grown frustratingly remote, his questions elliptical and evasive.

She drifted off, only to find herself in a different part of the same castle. This time, she could hear someone in the basement, rattling a door, and she felt the pressure to act—and act swiftly. But no matter how many stairs she raced down, how many heavy oak doors she pushed open, she couldn't find the keys. Only the sight—the merest glimpse—of a grey tail, somewhere ahead, kept her going, and she woke again, more tired than she'd been, with the same questions ringing in her mind. 'Whoever was being stolen from, that's who would care.' She punched her pillow into place. 'And we already know that Professor Bullock thinks Lloyd is to blame.'

Do we? She sat up. This time, she'd heard the voice while awake. 'Mr Grey?'

'Dulcie, Dulcie.' She felt, as much as heard, a soft padding, as if her late pet were settling in at the foot of her bed. 'Sometimes, you are such a kitten.' She was about to ask about that when she heard a crash and a muffled mew. Sleep would have to wait.

'I DON'T KNOW WHAT TO DO with this animal.' Dulcie was on her knees by the broken geranium pot when Suze came down the stairs, tying her robe. Beside the shattered clay pot, just visible in the first light of dawn, the tiny kitten was licking dirt off a white bootie.

'She's just a kitten, Dulcie.' Suze yawned. 'She probably wanted to play.' Behind her, Ariano appeared, his black curly hair sticking up like a fright wig.

'Everything OK down here?'

'Yeah. Sorry to wake you guys up.' Dulcie finished brushing the dirt into the dustpan and looked around for a place to put it. Suze fetched the kitchen garbage.

'Here. I think that plant might be history.'

Dulcie examined the broken stem. It had still been blooming, too. 'Kitten. What are we going to do with you?'

'Oh, she's a cutie.' Ariano reached for the kitten, her tiny body dwarfed by his broad hands. He stroked the flat black fur between her ears and soon her eyes were closed, a loud purr filling the room. 'She's been trying to get your attention, see?'

He handed the sleepy kitten over to Dulcie, and she held the small animal up to her cheek. So warm, so soft, and so small. Just a baby, really, and here she was expecting her to assume the duties of a full-grown cat. A particulariy wise cat. The purr was hypnotic and Dulcie realized her eyes were closing.

'Good night, Dulcie.' She looked up to see Suze smiling back at her, before she followed a yawning Ariano back upstairs.

'Back to bed, little one?' Dulcie nuzzled the sleeping kitten, who woke and stared at her, eyes as big and green as those in her dream. What was it about those eyes? Dulcie found her thoughts drifting as she followed her roommate and her boyfriend up the stairs. 'Cool as emeralds,' yes, but something else. The purring was softer now, the kitten once again beginning to doze in her arms. There was something else, something she was forgetting. She stumbled into bed and pulled the blanket over them both, the kitten now a warm weight against her neck. 'Sleep, little one. Time for all of this in the morning.'

'Was that you, kitten? Are you the little one?' Dulcie murmured, her face against the powder soft fur. 'Or am I?' But the kitten was fast asleep.

FORTY-THREE

SHE WOKE WITH A START, the pain sharp and sudden. 'What?'

There was the kitten, batting at her exposed foot, the needle-sharp claws just piercing her skin. 'Kitten!'

With a startled look, the kitten bounced off the bed and bounded out of the room. But the damage was done. Dulcie was awake and, despite her troubled night, more sleep didn't seem likely. Sun was streaming in around her curtains and she sat up, rubbing her sore foot. She was going to have to do something about that kitten, when it hit her.

The missing connection: Bullock's letter opener, with its decorative hilt and emerald 'eye.' It, too, looked sharp, for such a tiny thing. Sharp enough to be a murder weapon. When she'd told Suze about it, her roommate had wondered out loud about the possibility, and Dulcie had dismissed the idea, unable to believe such a pretty thing could have inflicted those horrible wounds. But that was before she'd seen Polly pocketing it.

In some ways, Suze's theory now made sense. Polly seemed to be quite dependent on the professor. If he had killed Cameron, she would want to dispose of the murder weapon. She was certainly acting oddly enough. Perhaps they had planned the act together, and she was only now getting rid of the evidence…

No, that didn't work. She reached for a pair of socks, determined to protect her toes from further damage. Bullock had been meeting with her when Cameron had been attacked. And unless Polly was a very skilled actress, she had truly been shocked by the discovery of the body.

Of course, the older woman could be a good faker. Dulcie pulled on her sweats and considered this possibility. In fact, she realized, she was only beginning to discover Polly's depths.

The kitten careened into the room and Dulcie reached for her, unable to resist. 'Could Polly have done it, little one? Could she and the professor have been in cahoots? Are they framing Lloyd?'

The kitten squirmed and Dulcie put her down. 'No, you're right.' She sat back on the bed with a thud. This wasn't a parlor game. She had seen Cameron. Seen what had become of all his spark and vigor. Even now, the shock of it made her head spin. Polly couldn't have been faking it. And besides, if the other woman had been involved, wouldn't she have had enough sense to get rid of the murder weapon before now?

Maybe it wasn't the murder weapon, and maybe her dreams had nothing to do with the crime. Between her thesis and this rambunctious kitten, she had plenty of other things to disrupt her sleep.

'You awake, Dulcie?' Suze's voice reached her with the scent of melting butter. 'Pancakes?'

'Yes, please!' Dulcie shouted back and reached for her robe. More likely her original thought had been correct, and Polly had just been doing some housecleaning, picking up after her scatterbrained boss.

Unless… She stopped on the landing, struck by a thought. Polly had said that things were being stolen. Dulcie herself had seen the professor upset, first about a missing pen and then about that letter opener. But what if Polly were the thief, and she had framed Lloyd? Maybe there was some kind of rivalry, a competition for the professor's favors, that Dulcie didn't know about.

Except that if Polly was stealing, why was the pretty little sword still in the professor's house? And what about that book, the one wrapped up like a rare piece from Gosham's, that Raleigh had left on Lloyd's desk?

'On the table!' Suze yelled, and Dulcie shelved her queries until further notice.

FORTIFIED BY BREAKFAST, Dulcie claimed the sofa and spread out her notes around her, determined to finish the anthology and see if any more unpleasant surprises awaited. If she couldn't figure out the rest of her life, she could at least work on the mystery of the dubious authorship. But between the kitten's rampages and the sounds of Suze cleaning up, and accompanying herself with her off-key singing, she found she forgot each page as she read it. Maybe it was the subject—those essays were uneven at best—but she just couldn't focus.

When she complained to Suze, coming in for yet another cup of coffee, her roommate was no help. 'You could come for a run. Ariano's heading out for work, so I thought I'd do a few miles along the river.'

Dulcie looked at her, not even sure how to answer.

Suze saw the look on her face and, to her credit, cracked up. 'Come on, Dulce. It wouldn't hurt to try. You might even like it.'

That laugh broke the ice. She didn't dare call Chris yet; with his schedule he'd be asleep till at least one. But Suze had come through for her before. Plus, her roommate had a pretty complete knowledge of the law, if not actually a license to practice yet. 'Actually, Suze, can I ask you about some legal stuff?'

'Uh-huh.' Suze sounded doubtful as she refilled both their mugs and took a seat at the table. Suze clearly expected Dulcie to go on about Lloyd, but she became thoughtful when Dulcie told her about her strange visit with Polly. By the time she was through, Suze had made even more coffee.

'Well, there's a lot going on here. More than you should necessarily be involved with.' She shot her roommate a look as she topped off her mug.

'Thanks, Mom.' Dulcie couldn't take it too seriously. Besides, it felt nice to have someone looking out for her on a non-astral plane.

'Seriously, Dulce. You know I had my doubts about this Lloyd from the start. Wait!' She held up a hand to stop the response she knew was coming. 'I'm just saying that I was thinking about the stealing. There really might be more there than you know. More than just need, anyway. Remember that criminal psych course I took last spring? Kleptomania is something you see developing in depressed or frustrated people as they near their thirties. Some people want it treated as a disease—'

'Suze!' Dulcie slammed her mug so hard on the table that coffee sloshed over the side. 'This is a colleague we're talking about. Someone I've known for years.'

'I know, Dulce. But think about it. He's overworked. OK, that's no different from any of us. But you've already said he's become erratic. And now this hot new student appears out of nowhere?'

'The way you're talking, you'd have him under suspicion for murder, too.'

Suze shrugged. 'I'd rather not think that way. But if I were the police, I might.'

FORTY-FOUR

SUZE WAS LACING UP HER sneakers as Dulcie hit the phone. There was still no answer from Lloyd, but Suze had explained that even for a minor charge, he'd probably have been held over till Monday, when he could be arraigned, before being released. Raleigh was either out of town or not returning her calls. Finally, she mustered her nerve and dialed the professor's residence. If Polly answered, well, she'd deal with it then.

To her relief, the gruff voice that greeted her was Professor Bullock's and it wasn't a recording. When she said she was hoping to speak with him, though, he sounded less than pleased.

'Dulcie, can't this wait? If you call back tomorrow, you can set up an appointment with Polly or come to my regular office hours.'

'It's...well, it's important, sir.' Dulcie swallowed. She'd never insisted on anything with the professor before. It felt odd. 'It's about my officemate, Lloyd.'

Silence greeted her, and for a moment she was afraid she'd offended. After all, he was Professor William Alfred Bullock, Cyrus Professor of Eighteenth Century Literature, and she was little Dulcie Schwartz. But she hung on and finally a loud sigh announced that the professor was still on the line.

'Very well.' He sounded resigned, as if to something highly unpleasant. 'I knew word would get out. Hang on a moment.'

In the pause that followed, Dulcie felt her resolve drain away. She was a grad student. He was a tenured professor. What right did she have to question him? Should she apologize for disturbing him on a Sunday? After all, they had never settled the issue of her progress report, and her academic future depended on his continued good will. She wouldn't ask. She couldn't. She would simply express her concern over Lloyd's absence and let the professor spin whatever story he chose. She would accept it, thank him, and hang up, after apologizing for being a nuisance.

'Dulcie!' The voice, sounding just to her left, made her stop and a sharp pain—like the nip of an annoyed feline—caused her to turn. No, there was no grey cat in the room. But the bite did make her sit up just as the professor came back on the line.

'So, how may I help you today?' She could imagine the professor, settling in on that library settee. He wasn't going to make this easy.

'I was trying to reach my officemate, Lloyd Pruitt, yesterday.' She paused. Silence. 'Your assistant?' After a moment's hesitation, she heard a grunt of acknowledgment. 'And I heard that he was taken down to the Cambridge Police Department.' That seemed a noncommittal and yet accurate way of describing what she knew. The professor remained silent. 'And, well, I believe I'd heard that you were talking with the police, too. And I was wondering if you could tell me what is going on with Lloyd?'

'Yes, well.' She heard a rustling and wondered if he'd been listening to anything she'd said. She could easily picture him reading the *Sunday Times* as she'd gone on. But after another pause, he spoke. 'I've been talking with the officials quite a lot,' he said. 'About the unfortunate incident last week, you know.'

'Yes.' Dulcie swallowed and forced herself to say the words. 'The murder.'

'Yes, of course. You were there, weren't you?' She nodded, unable to speak, but he didn't seem to care. 'They seem to believe that the attack was personal. That it wasn't just some random street thug who happened to wash up on my stoop.'

Dulcie waited, wondering where this was heading.

'And they seem to believe there were some unsavory aspects to young Cameron's life.' Dulcie wanted to interrupt—not that she was sure what to say—but the professor kept on. 'Not that I know anything about that, of course. But from where I sit, I do have rather a bird's-eye view. I had some insights that I thought they would be interested in.'

'Was it Raleigh? Was he involved with an undergrad?' She hadn't meant to speak, hadn't wanted to break his train of thought or to offer a theory. The words had just spilled out. 'Or Polly?'

The pause made her wonder if she'd gone too far. But he must have been simply weighing the possibilities. 'I wasn't aware of any involvement with anyone,' he said, finally, the heavy emphasis slowing his gravelly cadence more than usual. 'Certainly not Polly Heinhold. Polly is a scholar. Esteemed. And much too old for him.'

Curiouser and curiouser. Dulcie waited for the professor to continue. Could the rumors be true about a more intimate connection between the professor and his faithful assistant? If so, where did Roger Gosham fit in? Or Cameron for that matter? And what did any of this have to do with Lloyd?

'I'm sorry, Professor. I didn't mean anything.' Another silence. She'd have to prompt him. 'You were telling me about Lloyd?'

'Was I?' Bullock's voice took on a new sternness, and Dulcie felt a retraction on her lips. Before it could form, however, he continued. 'Yes, Lloyd Pruitt. He was another promising scholar. A bit too forward, perhaps. And so when the detective in charge asked me about those in our circle, well, I could do no less than be honest.'

He'd framed Lloyd. The realization made Dulcie gasp. 'Murder? You told the police that Lloyd could have murdered Cameron?'

'Why, yes.' He sounded puzzled. 'Whatever else did you think was going on?'

'Theft. Robbery.' Dulcie was aghast. 'I thought that someone was stealing. That things were going missing.'

'Pah!' He dismissed the notion. 'Nonsense. I can tell you where every book in my library is at any given time. That's how I made my reputation, you know. A mind for details. Now, if you'll excuse me, young lady, I really should be getting back to work. And you…' He paused, and she could imagine his piercing glare. 'You should be working hard, too. Don't forget, I expect you to be able to show me significant progress on your thesis. Significant.'

'But, Professor, I thought that with everything that's been going on—'

'A scholar doesn't let anything interfere. I take deadlines seriously, young lady, and I expect my students to do so, as well. In fact, I'd like to see something by the end of the day, Thursday. Something concrete.' And with that, he hung up.

FORTY-FIVE

'HE'S LYING, I KNOW HE IS.' After getting off the phone, Dulcie had gone over to Chris's. She found him just stirring. 'There's something fishy going on, I'm telling you.'

'You're thinking because Mr Grey—'

'Chris!' She cut him off just as his roommate, Jerry, walked in.

'Everything OK?' Jerry's red hair stuck out at all angles. Clearly, neither resident of the tiny Central Square apartment had gotten to bed till late. 'Is that coffee?'

'Everything's fine.' Dulcie poured him a cup and topped off her own. 'Except for the fact that my thesis adviser expects me to keep working as if nothing has happened. When, in truth, there was just a murder in my department, and I'm pretty sure my thesis adviser was involved.'

Jerry nodded and sipped at the coffee. 'From what Trista tells me about your department, I'm not totally surprised. Talk about Gothic!'

'I'm serious, Jerry. And I think he might be trying to frame my friend Lloyd.' Both men looked at her, and she found herself reaching for something more to add. 'And there's a chance I might have found the murder weapon—a letter opener.'

'Dulcie, isn't it possible…?' Chris started to say something—probably about her emotional reaction to the new deadline—but, seeing her face, reached for the Cheerios instead.

Jerry, ignoring the tension, scratched his head and looked at her. 'Shouldn't you be telling the cops this?'

'Yeah, I guess.' Dulcie paused. 'Only, to be honest, it's more of a hunch than anything else.'

'A hunch that came about after your friend was arrested.' Chris waved his spoon to make his point, a habit Dulcie usually found endearing.

'Chris, it was before that.' Today she felt hamstrung. How could she talk about Mr Grey with Jerry there? 'And it was Suze's idea originally.'

'OK, folks, I'm outta here.' Jerry put his empty mug in the sink. 'Something's going on and I don't want to be in the middle of it.'

'It's not—' Dulcie started, just as Chris said, 'Thanks, Jer.' With a wave, the red-haired roommate took off.

'Chris, you know what I'm talking about—and you know that I can't exactly explain it to the police.' More out of frustration than hunger, Dulcie poured herself a bowl of cereal.

Chris looked at her. 'I know that you've been under a lot of pressure, and that I haven't been much help. And I'm sorry about that. Really, I am Dulcie.'

Dulcie blinked. For a second, all her fears—the upcoming holiday, his absence, Suze's strange distance—came rushing back.

'But honestly, Dulce. What do you have? Besides a spectral nip on the ankle and a recurring dream, which really might just be about something else.'

'Chris, I saw Cam—I saw the body.' She paused to swallow the annoying lump in her throat. 'I saw what had happened. He was cut with something sharp and small, just like that letter opener.'

'Or like that steak knife,' he nodded over to the counter. Neither roommate was great about getting all their dishes into the sink. But the mention of such a homey object used to do harm made Dulcie shiver. Chris was immediately by her side. 'Oh, sweetie, I'm sorry. I know it's been a shock.'

She relaxed into his arms, grateful for the solid warmth of him. Whatever anyone else thought, she knew Mr Grey was back in her life. But as much as she valued his feline wisdom, sometimes one needed a warm, living body to hold.

'Nobody wants to think they've shared an office with a murderer.'

Dulcie sat up straight, pulling back. 'Nobody wants to think she has.' When she was angry, the words just came out. 'And Lloyd's not a murderer. I don't care what Professor Bullock says.'

'Please, Dulcie.' Chris didn't try to hold her again, but his tone pleaded with her. 'Let the police handle this. You've got enough on your plate.'

She eyed her cereal bowl and sighed. On top of everything, she'd eaten too much.

'Speaking of, what's going on with your thesis? When you talked to Bullock, was he able to tell you anything about that essay?'

'I haven't even thought about it,' said Dulcie. And with a slight shock, she realized that was true.

FORTY-SIX

LLOYD WAS STILL not answering, and now his voicemail was full. Raleigh wasn't, either, but at least Dulcie was able to leave her yet another message. Then, because what she'd said to Chris shocked her as much as anything else that morning, she headed into the Square to do some work.

At first, the idea of going to her office was disconcerting. Lloyd was always quiet and truly the neater of the two. But something about his absence made the silence seem obtrusive, as if the dust bunnies were all ganging up on her. Dulcie intended to just drop by, pick up the latest ramblings from her seminar students, and head over to Widener to see what she could uncover about that essay—or its author. But once she had unlocked the tiny space, another thought hit her. Maybe the hint from Mr Grey covered more than Professor Bullock's home. Dulcie was a scholar—a trained researcher. Maybe, she thought as she dumped her bag on to her desk and slumped into the chair behind it, she should be doing a little researching into her officemate's life. Lloyd wasn't a murderer, of that she was certain. But something strange was going on with her plump colleague. Something strange enough so that someone else wanted to frame him for murder.

Looking over at Lloyd's desk, which had already begun to fuzz with dust, Dulcie felt a little guilty. Especially with such a small space to share, they'd both been very careful to respect each other's privacy. But if she could find something that would help Lloyd, that would be a good thing, right? Fighting down the niggling suspicion that it was her own curiosity talking, she pushed her own chair back and walked around her desk to his. She should at least clean up a bit, shouldn't she? After all, they

both had to work here. She pushed some of the papers around.
'Structure in the Puritan Sermon.' Poor Lloyd, he must have a
section of English 10, too. Elizabethan Prose: 1560—1575. And
Bullock still had him researching that book. Was it possible? No,
she shuffled around a few more papers. Neither Bullock's prized
discovery nor the mysterious wrapped package were anywhere
here. Nor, with a twinge of guilt, were they in any of the drawers, though Dulcie did find a cache of Altoids.

She stole one and sat back, thinking. Everything here seemed
innocent. Which made sense. There was no room for anything
else in their shared space. Lloyd's desk wasn't that far from hers;
that would have been impossible in their nutshell of an office.
But after one too many rounds of giggles, they'd pulled the two
institutional metal monsters apart, so they were no longer facing
each other. Instead, while hers faced the side wall with its poster
of an Edward Gorey cat, his now looked toward the front door
and, to the left, an overstuffed bookshelf. The books she could
see were largely Lloyd's—*Origins of the Essay,* Sterne's *Short
Fiction,* and a collection of early-nineteenth-century prose—
and Dulcie thought briefly of re-arranging her own view. Maybe
if she constantly looked at her sources, she'd be a little more
productive. Of course, with the doorway in her line of sight,
she'd probably spend most of her time staring down the hallway, hoping for someone interesting to show up.

A shock as sharp as if Mr Grey had swatted her with his
claws made her catch her breath. She'd been assuming that Lloyd
had been dragged into this for no reason. But even if he was innocent, he could have gotten accidentally involved. Had he seen
something—someone—that had gotten him in trouble? The hallway was empty now, but she tried to remember who else used
those offices. Trista had a desk two doors down, but she was
rarely there. Sarah and another medievalist had the office at the
end. Who had the last office, the one with the window? With
a gasp, it all came back. Cameron Dessay had taken over that
last office, and as far as she knew he had somehow claimed it
all for himself. Had Lloyd seen something he shouldn't? With-

out warning, Raleigh's face flashed before her. If Cameron and Raleigh had been involved, Lloyd might have witnessed something. The pretty senior was certainly up to her neck in all this. Dulcie reached for her phone. She had to reach the girl and find out exactly what she knew.

Reception in the basement office space was iffy at best, and when Dulcie surfaced she was surprised to see a message waiting. More surprised to hear Raleigh's voice, breathless and clearly on the run.

'Dulcie! Thanks for all your calls. I had to fly back to New York to speak to my dad.' The next bit was obscured by traffic noise, but Dulcie was ready to smack the little metal device when Raleigh's voice came back. '…will arrange bail as soon as the arraignment goes through tomorrow.'

FORTY-SEVEN

IF ONLY MONDAY MORNINGS weren't so crazy. First there was the English 10 lecture. Some of her friends skipped it, and as Trista often pointed out, 'If I don't know what that blowhard is going to say by this point, I truly am a sinner in the hands of an angry God.' But Dulcie's section followed hard on it. That meant her students—primarily confused freshman—had enough time to stew about whatever Cranshaw had said, but not enough time to settle in and really think about it. Which usually translated into a headache for Dulcie.

Or, another headache, she mentally added, as she raced from the lecture hall to the Union common room where her students met. Normally, she'd walk like a normal person, letting the eager beavers catch up with her and air some of their confusion before the section started. Today, she just wanted to get it all over with, and had scooped up her notes and made a break for it. She hadn't really had a good night's sleep since finding Cameron's body, one week before. Last night had not been an exception.

Partly, it was the dream again. Locked, like Hermetria, in some windswept castle, she was seeking a key—a jeweled key—but everything she picked up proved to be the wrong size or not metal at all. 'False' was the word that came to mind, and when she woke, she couldn't help but think of her thesis topic, and *The Ravages of Umbria.* Yes, she had other matters to distract her—she never had made it over to the library the day before—but in her heart Dulcie knew that she was avoiding the bigger question for fear of what the answer would be.

Partly, it was the kitten. The little creature had been catapulting around her room on such a rampage that she'd finally locked her out. But then the kitten had scratched and pleaded at the door with such heartrending cries that even a mad monk would have felt something. Dulcie had, for sure, and when she let the kitten in, she thought all would be settled. The tiny beast had settled her body on the bed, her smooth black back warm against Dulcie's arm. But the little cat snored; there was no other word for it. And her dreams seemed to echo Dulcie's as she kicked and twitched throughout the night.

Now the grey sky and bracing air seemed like a rebuke for all those quiet hours wasted. But Dulcie took another slug from her rapidly cooling travel mug and continued to race walk toward the Union. 'Please don't let them be too stupid today,' she whispered her prayer to the glowering clouds. 'Please let them have gotten over midterms and not be overly worried about their final papers, just for today.'

'Dulcie.' The voice caught her up short and she stopped so quickly that a couple almost ran into her. 'Hello!' the girl snapped snarkily, but Dulcie was too preoccupied to care.

'Mr Grey?' She looked around, but all she saw were busy students, many looking as sleep-deprived as she felt. The bells in Memorial Church chimed eleven. 'Oh, hell.'

She picked up her pace, but her mind raced. What was Mr Grey telling her? What should she have been doing or looking for? If only she didn't have these stupid undergrads.

This time, it didn't take a spectral voice to stop her. Although she could easily imagine the glaring eyes, the lashing tail, she knew that she deserved the reproach. Hadn't she, Dulcie Schwartz, been just such a student once? New to the city—new to higher learning—nervous and eager, demanding attention just like a kitten? Hadn't she pestered her section leaders, anxious to sop up every bit of learning? Wasn't she still like that, at least a little?

'I'm sorry, Mr Grey,' she breathed into the cool air. 'You're right.' Suddenly, the clouds parted and a shaft of light shone down, illuminating the path before her. Dulcie laughed; not even Suze would believe this was coincidence. But just then a pant-

ing freshman caught up with her, and her moment of reflec
tion was gone.

Ninety minutes later, Dulcie was ready for either lunch or a
nap. Her section hadn't been frantic; maybe some of her own
renewed good spirits had rubbed off on them. But they had
been exhausting, wanting her to go over Cranshaw's theory of
the Europeanized American and how it related to Mark Twain.
Every few minutes, Dulcie caught herself about to say some
thing sharp—she was still sleep deprived. But like a trick of the
light, she'd catch a flicking tail in a far corner, and then she'd
modulate her tone and go once more over the literary conven
tions that the professor so adored.

What with the lecture, her section, and the four students
who had hung around after, wanting some kind of reassur
ance about their final paper, Dulcie hadn't even had a chance
to call Raleigh. When would Lloyd get out? Was there anything
she, broke as she was, could do to help? As she made her way
down to the basement office, she thought about what her gentle
officemate must have gone through. A weekend in jail. Had he
gotten to go on his big date?

The door was open as she walked down the hall, the light
spilling into the hallway. The sight caught her up short. She'd
run across too many surprises recently. But a peal of laughter
dispersed the worst of her fears and lured her further. Lloyd
didn't laugh like that.

But the officemate who looked up as she came in the door
was certainly smiling more broadly than she'd ever seen. Yes,
he looked tired, his light eyes deeply shadowed in his pale face,
but still he was beaming as he pushed back his desk chair and
settled his feet on an opened drawer. And his smile was aimed
at Raleigh, who had settled into Dulcie's chair.

'Oh! I'm sorry!' As soon as Lloyd looked up at Dulcie,
Raleigh had swung around—and then jumped to her feet. 'We
were just so thrilled.'

'Uh-huh?' Dulcie didn't know what to make of this, but she

did know it was good. 'Wow, I wasn't sure what was going to happen today, but when I got Raleigh's message—'

'It was my dad.' Raleigh now stood, shifting from one foot to another, as Dulcie dropped her bag on the desk and reclaimed her chair. 'He's a partner in a big-deal firm, so really all I had to do was call him, and he handled everything.'

'And believe me, I am grateful.' Lloyd took his feet down and sat up, his moment of celebration over. 'I'll call him later today.'

'He just sent an associate.' Raleigh seemed embarrassed, and Dulcie studied her face.

'He saved my butt.' Lloyd picked up a pen. 'But, you know, I should get to work now.'

'Yeah, of course.' Raleigh made for the door.

Dulcie called out. 'Wait, Raleigh?' The girl turned, her uncertainty splashed all over her face. 'I'm sorry. I just wanted to tell you that I've finally caught up with your thesis notes. You've done some great work here.' Raleigh flashed a smile that reminded Dulcie of the laugh she'd heard only moments before. 'And thanks.'

For the next few minutes after the senior had left, Lloyd appeared to busy himself with papers, scribbling notes and shuffling through the layers that Dulcie had examined only the day before.

'Lloyd?' Dulcie finally interrupted him. 'May I interrupt?'

He looked up, the fatigue more apparent now. 'Uh, yeah, sure, Dulcie. But I'm really kind of behind.'

'What happened, Lloyd?' There was so much she wanted to know, but this seemed the simplest way to start.

He didn't seem to think so, and sighed heavily as he put down his pen. 'You mean on Saturday?' Dulcie nodded. He wasn't getting off that easy. He took a deep breath and Dulcie watched as he let it out, wondering how much he was preparing to tell. Finally, he started talking. 'The police came over to my place around five. I let them in without thinking about it. I figured they had some questions about the professor. There, well, there have been some things going on.'

Dulcie nodded again. She'd get the details later.

'They asked me to come down to the station, and I thought they might want me to look at some things. But it very quickly became apparent that they didn't want me as a witness. They wanted me out of the way so they could search my apartment. As the two detectives were escorting me to their car, another team was on its way in.' He looked pained at the memory and Dulcie felt for him. Lloyd was so private, so meticulous.

'Were they looking for objects…?' She wasn't sure how to phrase it. 'Things that you shouldn't have had?' She tried to keep her voice gentle.

'What? No.' Lloyd's face wrinkled up and for a moment she was afraid he would cry. 'They were looking for a murder weapon.'

THERE HAD BEEN SILENCE for a few moments after that, while Lloyd remembered—and Dulcie tried to piece together all she had heard.

'I didn't know,' she started, and then tried again. 'Polly had said something about things going missing.' She stopped and thought of the wrapped package, so clearly a book. 'There was that book, the one Professor Bullock was so keen on and then reported missing…'

She left the sentence unfinished and looked at him. But Lloyd only shook his head. 'There was no book, Dulcie.'

'No book?' His face was set and he only shook his head slowly. 'But, Lloyd, Raleigh had left something for you while you were out. I thought…'

He continued shaking his head. 'That wasn't anything.' He sounded sad. 'Certainly not a rare book.'

'Oh.' Dulcie wasn't sure what to make of that, but kept talking. 'When we heard you were arrested, well, I was hoping it was that. That maybe the professor had accused you of…well…' No book? 'Something.'

'Better a thief than a murderer, right?' Lloyd's voice had some life back in it. Either the time spent in their office or the talking seemed to be bringing him back. 'No, when Bullock makes his case, he goes all the way.'

'Professor Bullock? He was the one who had you arrested.'

Lloyd nodded grimly. 'So much for the years of loyal service, huh?'

Dulcie shook her head, not understanding. 'But why? He can't really think you did it.'

Lloyd tilted his head and smiled. It was not a happy smile. 'Good old Bill Bullock has some issues with me, and he's not one to cross, Dulcie. I've found that out the hard way.'

FORTY-EIGHT

DULCIE WASN'T GOING to let such a tantalizing statement go without questioning it. But just then Lindsay, from her junior tutorial, showed up at the open door and, without knocking, slumped down in the one visitor chair the two officemates shared.

'So, I was thinking about what you were saying the other day in class.' Without so much as a greeting, the lanky junior seemed to be off and running. 'And I was wondering, you know, what you meant by a fake or falsified or somehow "untrue" book. I mean, there are so many options here, and, really, the way you posed the question contained just too many ambivalent features. I mean, when you say "book," what do you mean? Were you talking about the book as an object or the text, which, after all, is really what the book is about?' She stopped here to make quote marks with her finger. 'I mean, what is the book as we know it in an epistemological sense?'

To her right, Dulcie could hear Lloyd snort. At least he was amused.

'I mean the text, Lindsay.' She glanced over at Lloyd, in part to resist deconstructing her student's use of air quotes and in part to keep her from seeing that she was rolling her eyes. He met her gaze, but turned away quickly to start shoving books into his bag.

'Lloyd?' She really needed to talk to him.

'Later,' he said, shooting a glance at Lindsay. Then he stood and closed the bag. 'Of course, you're presuming a structuralist approach.' He had assumed a more authoritative voice, one that Dulcie recognized as borrowing from Professor Bullock. 'An approach in which some kind of absolute, some standard, exists.' He walked to the door and paused. 'Not only is that ultimately an anti-humanist approach, it's impractical. Books are written by people, for other people, which means you may want to consider the uncertainty principle, too.'

With that, he hiked his bag on to his shoulder and left, leaving Lindsay with her mouth hanging open and Dulcie stifling a giggle. This was a side of her chubby officemate she'd never seen. But as she sat there, listening to his soft steps echo down the empty hallway, she realized she couldn't let him go, not like this.

'Hang on a minute.' Dulcie ran out into the hallway. 'Lloyd?'

He turned, and even at this distance she could see the strain in his face. 'Not now, Dulcie. Please.' She started to protest, but he held up one hand. 'I'll explain, I promise. But right now I've got to do what I can to defend myself.' And with that, he was gone, leaving Dulcie to return to her student.

'You were saying?' Letting Lindsay rattle on gave Dulcie time for thought. As enigmatic, and troubling, as his farewell had been, something about Lloyd's earlier brief but effective speech had sparked an idea. At first, Dulcie thought it was simply its usefulness. She'd never been a literary theorist, but she would go back to her Foucault and Derrida if it helped keep her students in line. No, it was something else, the Heisenberg reference. But Lindsay had taken her silence as censure, and had shifted into a pleading mode. Something about her final paper, about losing her research through a power surge, and Dulcie, distracted, let her ramble on. Maybe she just needed to act more assured, she thought, even as she longed for simpler days, when hungry dogs were blamed. Maybe it wasn't what one knew, but how one presented everything. With that thought circling her brain, Dulcie finally got her tutee to leave, hinting at the possibility of an extension. Chris's classes ran longer than hers, anyway, so they wouldn't be leaving for his mother's till nearly Christmas. A moment of doubt clutched at her: Chris hadn't mentioned the invitation recently, not since he'd started disappearing into work… No, she decided, she wouldn't go there.

Still, it was a relief, when she finally locked up the office and walked out, to find that Chris had called. She reached him on the first ring, but any hope she had for some real-time company was quickly dashed.

'Sorry, sweetie, I should've been at work fifteen minutes ago.' He paused, as if he could hear her thoughts. 'Another tutorial. But, hey, think we could grab some dinner? And they're showing the Olivier *Rebecca* at Dunster House tonight. I know you like that one.'

'Maybe.' It was a peace offering, she could see that. She did love the old movie, with its mystery and murder and blackmail, all set in a much more romantic location than her own. But she wasn't crazy about going to the undergraduate houses for movies. Too much chance of being cornered by an anxious student. Some of her reluctance, she knew, was irrational. 'I'm sorry, Chris. I'm just feeling…' She stopped to think. Ignored? Inconsequential? 'Lonely,' she said at last. She was standing outside the Union at this point, students rushing every which way around her. 'That sounds silly, right? I mean, I've got a great roommate and you're there.' Except that Suze now had Ariano, and Chris had, well, he seemed to be working an awful lot. 'And the new kitten, of course.'

'Course, Dulcie.' That wasn't the reassurance she wanted, but she could hear the distraction in his voice as he hurried off. 'Speaking of the kitten. I was talking to Jerry and, you know, he wouldn't mind taking care of it—her, I mean—if something came up.'

'You mean, like the winter break? But I thought we could take her. I mean, we'll be taking the bus, right?'

'Yeah, that's fine. My mom loves cats. I just mean, well, if something else comes up.'

Dulcie bristled. 'Look, I know you and Suze don't think I'm being fair to the kitten. But, it's been difficult for me to get over Mr Grey. Especially since…' She paused, afraid of who might overhear. 'Since he's not really gone. But I've taken on the responsibility of caring for this animal, and I'm not about to give her up.'

Chris, to her surprise, was laughing. 'I didn't mean you had to give her up! It was just an offer. That's all!'

'Good.' Because as the heat of her anger subsided, Dulcie found herself thinking of the little furball and how she had cuddled up against her just that morning. This kitten would never replace Mr Grey, but she was a good little creature, in her way.

SETTING OFF TO GET A LONELY lunch, Dulcie tried to figure out what was bothering her. Lloyd's departure, dramatic as it was, had left too many questions. While she was grateful for the way he had shut down her student's more pompous ramblings, she kept thinking about uncertainty. 'I wish I had some uncertainty,' she muttered as she slid on to a stool at Lala's. Her problem was that she was becoming all too sure that *The Ravages* was faked, in every sense. But there was something else. An image of Mrs Danvers, the crazed villain behind all of the fictional Rebecca's problems, came to mind. Was there someone like that lurking in the background? No, she thought as she browsed the menu, knowing in advance what she was going to order. The only madwoman in her life was Lucy, and she was a good witch.

'I should call her,' Dulcie said to the waitress. 'And I'll have the three-bean burger, extra hot sauce, please.' The waitress moved on without blinking. In Harvard Square, she got all types. But what was it about Mrs Danvers—or about Lloyd? Suddenly, Dulcie remembered what Lloyd had said about Bullock, moments before they'd been interrupted. Lloyd seemed to feel that the arrest was personal, that their professor had it out for him. And Lloyd certainly knew the professor better than anyone, except maybe Polly. What had he meant about protecting himself? From the back of her mind another memory surfaced, something about research, about stealing students' work…

Could Lloyd be blackmailing Professor Bullock?

FORTY-NINE

THE POSSIBILITY CONSUMED the rest of Dulcie's day, interrupting her reading and making her short with the freshman who cornered her on the Widener stairs. Didn't they see she had other things on her mind beside their final papers? But remembering her earlier resolve, she bit back her planned retort and listened, the wind whipping across the Yard, as the freshman, an anemic-looking brunette, started spinning a story about an untenable roommate situation and the general difficulties of dorm life.

'It can be trying.' Dulcie smiled at her, thinking how lucky she was to have met Suze in freshman year. 'But can't you always go work in one of the libraries?'

'But they're so…' The girl paused, looking past Dulcie, up the steps to the university's main library. 'So anonymous. It's creepy.'

Dulcie raised her eyebrows, unsure of how to respond. 'They're the greatest resource you have as a student here.' She paused. 'Maybe I should talk to the professors about incorporating a research project into the curriculum.'

The look on the freshman's face stopped her short. She hadn't meant it as a punishment, but the query was enough to send the student on her way. Not that it mattered. Even when Dulcie had settled into her carrel down in the depths of the library, her focus eluded her. Partly, she admitted to herself, that was because she didn't want to find out more. The book of essays was still on her desk at home, waiting for her to re-read it—to confirm her initial impression that it repeated phrases she knew well from *The Ravages of Umbria*. Before she did anything else, she should check into the source of that essay. Perhaps the phrase—that line about emeralds—had been a literary convention. A cliché, even.

It was no use. Dulcie had read enough from the era to recognize the standard phrasings, to smile, even at the hackneyed phrases of the day. The 'shadow'd peaks' and 'loves forlorn.' That was why she had loved *The Ravages*. It had seemed so fresh. So unlikely. So...fake.

She gave up and closed her eyes. At least down here she was probably safe from undergrads. But as she sat there, feet up on the carrel, drifting toward sleep, another thought shook her. Undergrads. Raleigh. First the young woman worked with Cameron, then she bailed out Lloyd. Could she have been involved with her former tutor, or with his murder? And, if so, what did that mean for poor Lloyd?

By the time Dulcie emerged, she was completely confused. And a phone call from Suze didn't help.

'I don't know if I'm up to socializing tonight, Suze.' She'd only half listened as her roommate said something about a special at the People's Republik. 'And, I mean, I spend enough time at that bar as it is.'

'That's not what Trista was telling me.' Suze had her lawyer voice on. 'And besides, they're inaugurating their new grill. Burgers, panini, all that stuff—but the special is tonight only.'

'It'll be a mad house.' Dulcie already knew Chris would want to go—and that she should release him from his promise of a romantic movie. Her boyfriend packed away food like one of the crazed squirrels in the Yard.

'It'll be a lot healthier than some of the other houses you've been hanging in.' The way Suze spoke, Dulcie knew better than to argue. Besides, she had missed Suze. The bar might not be the best place for an intimate conversation, but she'd be able to air some of her thoughts, and get the kind of solid advice she'd come to rely on.

'I'll tell Chris.' She ceded victory. So much for Rebecca.

'He already knows,' said her roommate. 'Your buddy Trista called me. It was her guy Jerry who got the coupons.'

THREE HOURS LATER, she was grateful for the shove. Happily full from a ham and provolone panini, she pushed the rest of her chips over to Chris. He'd been less thrilled about his entree, a fruit, sausage, and cheese concoction that he'd dubbed 'interesting' (but finished, anyway), and accepted Dulcie's leftovers with a smile. Across the table, Jerry and Trista were sharing a slice of cheesecake. 'Frozen,' pronounced Trista, relinquishing it to her skinny boyfriend. He shrugged and dug in. Suze had indeed brought Ariano, but he was fitting in well with the university crowd, discussing the Patriots quarterback situation with Jerry and Trollope with Trista.

'He reads.' Dulcie noted with surprise, leaning over toward her roommate, her voice low. 'For fun!'

'One of us has to.' Suze sounded tired, and Dulcie looked up at her. Almost daily runs kept the color in Suze's cheeks, but the final, punishing year of law school showed in her drawn expression and the blue-black shadows that ringed her eyes. No wonder her roommate had been absent from her life.

'At least you're staying with the exercise.'

'It keeps me sane.' Suze shrugged. 'Speaking of sane, what's up with that crazy thesis adviser of yours?'

'Oh, man.' It was the opening she'd hoped for. An invitation to air. But in such company, after such a meal, Dulcie really wanted to leave the outside world alone.

No such luck. 'And, what's up with Lloyd? I thought I saw him in the Yard.'

'You did,' Dulcie confirmed, and then proceeded to tell the table about her strange encounter, leaving out only Lloyd's enigmatic final words and her own suspicions.

'She's got to be involved.' Trista had a taste for conspiracies. 'It's guilt. That's why she bailed him out.'

'Her father did,' Jerry corrected her. 'And he's some big-deal lawyer, right? I don't trust any of them. Present company excepted, of course.'

Suze nodded, accepting the charge. 'Well, he sounds corporate. With that kind of money goes power, so it's quite conceivable that he's paying to clean up some mess that his darling little girl got into.'

Dulcie almost interrupted. As much as she was predisposed to dislike a rich girl, and a beautiful one at that, she didn't see Raleigh as a spoiled brat who would run to her father to be bailed out. She was about to say something about this—something about how maybe it was personal, that despite her denial Raleigh had been involved with Cameron—when Ariano chimed in.

'Listen to you.' He was smiling, his broad grin showing white teeth in his black beard. 'Looking for murderers in the attic! Why not assume the simple solution. Lloyd has found himself a wealthy girlfriend, and she's helping him out. I don't know the guy, but I say more power to him!'

There was silence as five members of the university community absorbed his words. Then everyone started talking at once.

'Impossible.' 'Breach of ethics.' 'Ariano, love, you just don't understand.' This last was from Suze, and she held up her hand for silence from the rest. 'Lloyd is a graduate student. Raleigh is an undergrad in the same department. That's as off limits as it gets.'

'Oh, come on.' Ariano was still smiling, and he reached out to put his hand on Suze's knee. 'You're going to tell me that it never happens? The handsome young professor and the beautiful student?'

'A professor, maybe, if he was tenured.' Dulcie jumped in. 'But you don't know Lloyd. He lives for his work, but he's nowhere near anything like a tenure-track position. Not yet. If he were to get involved with someone like Raleigh, it would be the end of everything.' She paused, her own suspicions breaking through. 'I have to say, though, I wouldn't have put something like that past Cameron. He was an arrogant son of a gun.'

'And handsome, too,' said Trista in such a voice that Jerry turned to stare. 'I'm only saying,' she responded. 'Plus, he wasn't like Lloyd. I had the feeling he always had an eye for the outside opportunity. He wasn't going to end up Bullock's boy, no way.'

'Hey, isn't that Roger Gosham?' Dulcie wanted to hear more, but the appearance of the craggy bookbinder had thrown her. 'What's he doing here?'

'The rare books guy?' Trista strained her neck to see. 'I'm betting the same thing we are.'

Dulcie turned to watch as Gosham—it was definitely him—made his way to the bar. 'Is Polly with him?'

'No, why?' Only Chris and Suze had heard the full story, and so Dulcie briefly explained. 'So I think they're a couple.'

'I don't see it.' Trista gave the bookbinder one last look and then turned back to the table. 'Last time I saw them together, they weren't getting along too well.'

Dulcie turned toward her, as Chris signaled the waitress for another pitcher. 'Tell.'

'It was...hell, it was the day Cameron was killed. Polly was coming out of Gosham's building, and he came after her.'

Dulcie leaned in, intrigued. She'd known that Polly had come from Gosham's, but this sounded like more than business.

'He was angry,' Trista continued. 'He grabbed her arm, and she pulled away and went running.'

Dulcie mulled that one over. 'Could it have been a lovers' quarrel? Maybe over Cameron? And maybe he...' She left the thought hanging.

'And so he ran off and killed his rival?' Trista grimaced. 'I don't see it. He wouldn't have known that Cameron would be there—or that Polly wouldn't have gone straight to Bullock's. Besides, I can't see Cameron with Polly. I mean, she isn't—wasn't—in Cameron's league.'

'But Gosham does seem to be kind of a rough type,' offered Dulcie.

'He's a wannabe,' Trista countered. 'He completely fawns over Bullock.'

'Those aren't contradictory traits,' Suze broke in. 'In fact, you could say he epitomizes the town-gown struggle. As a rare book dealer, he's completely dependent on the university, and on the professors' patronage. But on his time off…'

'Maybe he just likes to have a pint,' Ariano finished for her. The pitcher had arrived, and he poured them each a round.

'Maybe.' Dulcie still wasn't convinced. In fact, the Bullock connection seemed another link between the bookbinder and the bookish assistant. But when no Polly surfaced, she gave it up. Soon conversation had moved on. It always amazed Dulcie how current her friends could stay on television shows. She barely had time to get her work done. But while Jerry and Ariano got into a heated debate about 'American Idol,' she left her seat and sidled over to Trista.

'Tris, what you were saying—about Cameron?' She left it open, but her friend looked up at her, waiting. 'Do you, well, was there something going on with him?' she finally asked.

She shrugged. 'He did like the ladies.'

'Tris?'

'Nothing happened.' The pixielike blonde looked over at her boyfriend, but he was still engaged in a heated debate about Paula Abdul. 'It was during one of Jerry's more Sox-obsessed weeks last spring, and Cameron had that way of tuning out the world, just focusing on you and your life. I've got to admit, I was tempted.'

Dulcie cringed. Would she ever be able to think of their handsome colleague without seeing him as she had last, so bloody and so still? Trista saw her reaction—and misinterpreted it.

'He wasn't that bad.' She kept her voice low, but there was something insistent in it. 'I mean, he liked nice things, but, hey, don't we all?'

'Depends if you're the "nice thing," or not.' Somehow, Dulcie was having a hard time seeing her friend with Cameron. Trista made a face. 'I'm sorry, I didn't mean it like that.'

'No, no, you're right.' Trista raised her hands in surrender. 'But you know, maybe that's your connection. Raleigh's a rich girl—maybe that made her worth the risk.'

'Maybe.' Dulcie leaned back in her chair, trying to put the

pieces together. 'But where does Lloyd fit into this? I mean, what's up with him?'

Trista shrugged. 'Maybe Ariano's right and he's seeing Raleigh?'

Dulcie shook her head. 'I just don't see it. I mean, on top of everything else, look at him.'

Trista craned around and Dulcie had to grab her arm. 'Sorry, I didn't mean literally. But I can't help thinking about what he said—about needing to protect himself.'

'What?'

Dulcie kicked herself. She hadn't meant to tell anyone of her suspicions, but Trista was a friend. Not wanting to be overheard, she motioned her friend over to the bar and, in a whisper, shared Lloyd's last words.

'So, I'm wondering,' she concluded. 'Do you think he could be involved somehow? Maybe he knows something. Maybe he's trying a little blackmail?'

'I don't know, Dulce.' Trista looked over her friend's shoulder and then quickly down. 'But I think we ought to go back to the table. Roger Gosham is staring at you, and he's giving me the creeps.'

FIFTY

TUESDAY MORNING DAWNED bright and clear, a fact Dulcie witnessed when her kitten landed on her head at a quarter after six. The little creature looked as surprised as Dulcie, round eyes huge in her bi-color face, and for all that she could have used the sleep, Dulcie found herself laughing.

'You really are a handful, little girl.' She lifted the kitten off the pillow, where she had slid, and placed her on the bed. Almost immediately, the kitten began washing, licking herself with a loud, sloppy sound that pretty much precluded Dulcie's return to sleep. 'Are you trying to tell me something?'

The kitten paused and turned toward her, blinking, before resuming her morning toilette. And so Dulcie, taking the only hint offered, got up to start her own day. The kitten followed her into the bathroom, staring curiously at the water and jumping the moment Dulcie turned it to the shower setting.

'So you're not psychic.' Dulcie fought back a twinge of disappointment. Mr Grey hadn't spoken to her when he was alive, either. But had he ever been such a clown? As she lathered her hair, she wondered what her old favorite had been like as a kitten. Maybe she could ask him, next time they talked.

What she should be doing in the meantime, she realized as she got dressed, was asking Lloyd some more questions. While she didn't share Suze's suspicions, something was definitely going on with the quiet scholar. What did he mean about having to protect himself, anyway?

'Ouch.' As if in response to her thoughts, the kitten had pounced, sinking her sharp teeth into Dulcie's bare foot. 'No! Bad!' But the kitten had bounded away. If only Lloyd's prob-

lems were so simple, but something—and it wasn't Lucy's in
tuition—made her think that more was at stake.

Speaking of Lucy, Dulcie realized she owed her mother a
call. Her voicemail had been beeping as she left the bar. And the
message, when she retrieved it, made her a little worried about
her mother's sanity.

'Never mind about the squash, dear,' Lucy had said. Her
mother had a tendency to pick up conversations wherever they
had been left off—even if the other party wasn't aware of them.
'I've got it figured out. But do be careful about the book. The
weirdness? There's something about research there. Maybe
you're doing too much research, dear? Anyway, it's not about
love, I know that. I'll tell you more when you call.'

'It's not about love?' Well, if Lucy's dreams were still focusing on *The Ravages of Umbria,* they had a point. In addition
to the romantic themes, the book did touch on women's self-
reliance as well as the interaction between the physical and
spectral planes. Dulcie had been excited to explore this as a
metaphor for the mental and emotional components of our lives,
back when she was still enthusiastic about her thesis. But knowing Lucy, Dulcie suspected a more spiritual interpretation was
in the offing. Listening to the message again, as she waited for
the coffee to brew, she checked the clock. No, with the time difference, she should wait until at least noon to call her mother.
Maybe she'd have something to report by then.

The walk into the Square was a pleasure, the day so brisk and
clear it was hard to remember that she'd stumbled on a murder
just over a week before. But that thought, once launched, skid-
ded like a dark cloud over her day, and suddenly Dulcie didn't
want to be alone. Yes, she should get to work, in the library ideally. But first, she'd drop by the departmental office. Might as
well refill her travel mug for free, she told herself, knowing full
well that she craved the company as well as the coffee.

'Dulcie!' Nancy, the departmental secretary, hailed her as she
came in. 'Glad you came in. There've been some calls for you.'

'Oh?'

'Well, about you, actually.' Nancy gestured for her to come closer. 'The police were saying it was routine, but...' She shrugged her disbelief.

'Did they ask about anyone else?' Dulcie didn't want to think about Lloyd, but she couldn't help seeing his face.

'No.' Nancy leaned toward her. 'Should they?'

'No, no reason.' Dulcie turned toward the mailboxes. Nothing but fliers.

'You'll probably see Lloyd Pruitt, won't you?'

Dulcie almost jumped at the name, but managed to turn and nod.

'Would you give him this?' The plump secretary handed a pink message slip to Dulcie, who automatically looked down at it.

Couldn't reach you on your cell. Please call a.s.a.p. Urgent. The last word was underlined three times and when she looked up, the question in her eyes, Nancy nodded. Dulcie glanced back down. The number was from out of town. The signature: A. Browning, Antiquarian Books.

FIFTY-ONE

DULCIE WASN'T SURE what to think, but she took the message slip and headed out. She'd go to their office, she decided as she descended the stairs. Ideally, Lloyd would be there. If not, she could leave it on his desk. Unless… But, no, she realized. For all that they were close study buddies, she wasn't exactly sure where Lloyd lived. Somewhere in Cambridgeport. An image of a cramped apartment in one of those old triple-deckers came to mind from a party the year before. Uneven floors. Bookshelves that had to be braced. Bookshelves full of stolen books? No, it couldn't be. But the idea of rare books seemed even less likely.

Maybe he was on an errand. Dulcie neared the Yard, the walk and the bright day improving her mood. Maybe he'd been tasked with finding something for Bullock, something Gosham didn't have or couldn't get. Dulcie pictured the craggy bookbinder. He wouldn't like losing the professor as a client. But really, what could he do?

That thought made her shiver, despite the sun. No. Nobody turned violent simply because of losing a customer. Though Dulcie wouldn't be surprised if that was why Bullock had handed the errand to Lloyd. What had Lloyd said about the professor using his students? Making them do his dirty work? But if that was the case, why had Bullock turned on Lloyd and had him arrested? And what had Lloyd meant when he'd said that he had to defend himself? The force of her curiosity as well as rising wind propelled her down Broadway and in through the gate. Dulcie needed answers.

But as she was about to descend to the warren of offices, her phone rang. She recognized the number—the community center back home. With a deep sigh, she settled down on one of the stone steps and answered.

'Lucy, what's up?'

'Dulcie, thank the goddess I've reached you!' As always, her mother sounded breathless.

'I got your message about the squash.' Dulcie had long ago learned not to react to her mother's emotional state. 'How is the group harvest going?'

'Dulcinea Schwartz! Are you listening to me?' Lucy sounded honestly exasperated, so her daughter assured her that, yes, indeed, she was. 'This is serious. You haven't gotten rid of that fake book yet. I can tell.'

'Mom, I'm on it!' Dulcie didn't realize how much she'd picked up her mother's mood until she heard her own voice. 'It's not like I can just abandon my thesis. I've been working for years, well, months on it. But I really am trying to get some definitive proof—'

'You don't need proof.' Lucy cut her off. 'That book is at the heart of everything, like a particularly nasty grub eating away at all that's wholesome.' The gardening question must have sparked Lucy's imagination, Dulcie realized. Still, it was a vivid image.

'Well, it won't be for long, Lucy.' Dulcie shifted to the side of the steps as a group of undergrads came clattering by. 'I've got to give my adviser a progress report by the end of the week. So I've got to tell him then.' With a sinking feeling, Dulcie realized what this would mean. The end of *The Ravages of Umbria.* The end of her thesis. Maybe the end of her graduate studies, unless she could find another topic—and fast. At least her mother would be at peace.

'Tell him?' But Lucy hadn't seemed to get the message. Instead, her voice went up a notch. 'Tell him?'

'Lucy, what is it?' Dulcie turned toward the wall and placed her hand over her other ear. Too many people were coming out of the building now, the big lecture hall upstairs must have just emptied—right as her mother seemed to be having some kind of crisis.

'You don't have to tell him, dear.' For a moment, Dulcie felt herself relaxing. But, no, it was her own research, not her mother's vision, that had made her doubt *The Ravages*. 'You probably shouldn't be talking to that man at all.' Lucy had kept on talking. 'He knows full well that book isn't right. Or, at least, sometimes he does.'

'Lucy?' Dulcie leaned into the wall, trying for privacy. 'Are you and Nirvana hitting the peyote again?' Most students didn't have to monitor their mother's drug use, Dulcie knew. But really, this was getting ridiculous. 'Is there something you want to tell me?'

'Dulcie! I'm completely holistic, you know that.' Dulcie nodded. She'd heard it before. 'I'm sorry I can't be more clear. It's not that clear to me, either.' The line went silent, and Dulcie contemplated signing off. 'Wait, Dulcie.' Maybe her mother really was psychic. 'Do you still have your spirit guide? Your cat?'

Dulcie sighed. 'Yes, Lucy, I do.' At times like this, she wished she had never told her mother about Mr Grey's visits.

'Well, what does he say?'

'He hasn't said much lately.' The truth of it hit her and she had to swallow. Hard. 'Not about this, anyway.'

'Well, since I can't be there, you should listen to him, Dulcie. He sounds like a wise spirit. He'll take care of you.'

'Thanks, Lucy.' Talking to her mother could be exhausting. 'I promise, whenever Mr Grey talks to me, I'll listen.'

With that she finally did get to hang up and finish her descent down the stairs. The after-class crowd had cleared out, and her footsteps echoed in the empty hallway. A sliver of light shone from her partially open door, cheering Dulcie considerably. If she could talk to Lloyd, she could finally clear everything up. He probably hadn't meant to be cryptic, and had simply not wanted to spill too much in front of a student.

But as she got up to the door of the tiny office, Dulcie paused. Something was wrong. The wood around the latch was splintered, the brass plate hanging loose from the catch.

'Lloyd?' She heard the question in her voice as she touched the door. 'Is that you?'

The door swung open, and Dulcie gasped. Every book on the shelves had been torn out and tossed on the floor. Several—with dismay she recognized an anthology from Widener—had been pulled apart, their covers ripped from their pages. Both desks had been similarly defiled, shelves open and papers dumped everywhere. And worst of all, Dulcie realized as she stepped back into the hallway, she'd been given no warning. Someone had broken into her office—had violated her work space. And Mr Grey hadn't said anything about it.

FIFTY-TWO

THE CAMPUS POLICE didn't seem appropriately upset. As the aging patrolman had pointed out, it wasn't like anything of value had been taken.

'And I'm sure if you submit the report, the library system won't hold you responsible for the damage.' His partner, a young black woman, was already filling out the necessary paperwork. 'This is unfortunate, but vandalism does happen.'

'You think that's what this was?' Dulcie was sitting in the hallway. The senior cop had pulled her chair out of the wreck of her office, but its placement—outside, looking in—made her feel like a dunce. Like she was missing something.

The older cop nodded. 'We try not to publicize it, but there are tensions with the community, you know.'

'But why here? Why me?' The cops had seen the broken lock, she knew that.

'Maybe the other offices were occupied?' He shrugged. 'Or maybe this one looked easier?'

'Are you asking for a particular reason, Ms Schwartz?' The younger cop had finished with the form. 'Are you thinking this could be personal? One of your students, perhaps?'

Dulcie shook her head. She didn't know what she was thinking. 'It's just, there's been so much going on.' She looked up at the young cop. 'You know about Cameron Dessay?' The two police exchanged a look. 'I found him.'

'You've had a hell of a couple of weeks, then.' The older cop looked down at her. 'Would you like a ride home?'

Dulcie shook her head. 'If you're done, I think I should start cleaning up. And I should try to reach my office partner.'

'Lloyd Pruitt, right?' The younger cop said the name like she knew it. Dulcie nodded. She'd hoped to keep his name out of this, but of course, there it was: on the door, as well as on half the papers that now lay scattered on the floor. 'We've got a call in to him, as well, Ms Schwartz. I wouldn't worry about him.'

TWO HOURS LATER, they were gone and a university maintenance worker was busy screwing a new brass plate on to the door. Dulcie hadn't made much headway in cleaning up. The dust that had been raised was incredible, but at least she'd reshelved most of the books. None of hers were missing, she was pleased to see. And only two—the anthology and another beautiful old text, a leatherbound Ann Radcliffe lettered in gold leaf—had been damaged. The others just needed to be brushed off, and she'd enjoyed doing that, rediscovering some old favorites even as the airborne grime made her eyes water and her nose run.

After taking a break to wash her hands—and to breathe—she'd come back to find the locksmith finishing up. She'd pocketed the new keys and closed the door, for privacy as much as anything else. She'd tried to make herself work on the papers, then, telling herself that Lloyd would prefer to reshelf his own books. She had no idea what order he'd had them in. But curiosity had gotten the better of her and she'd decided to at least get them off the floor. Novels, essays, a few texts—including the latest edition of Bullock's, with a new introduction by someone from Oxford—and some collections of critical works, all focusing on his specialty: eighteenth-century criticism. But nothing that looked any more valuable than what was on her shelves. Certainly nothing that would have interested Gosham, or any other antiquarian bookseller. And nothing Elizabethan, either. She leaned back against her desk and surveyed the papers below her and the shelves in front of her. If the intruder had taken anything, she couldn't see what.

'There is no book,' Lloyd had said. What had he meant by that? Clearly, there had been a book. A valuable book. Rare and beautiful.

'Like your own, Dulcie?' The voice came up behind her, nearly startling her off her seat. 'Like your professor's?'

'Mr Grey?' In the corner, where the slanting light from their one small window was captured in the slowly settling dust, she could just see the outline of a large cat. 'What do you mean?'

The image in the dust motes glowed and shimmered slightly, as if Mr Grey were purring, his wide paws kneading the paper he stood on.

'My book—*The Ravages*—is a real book. I'm just not sure if it is what it claims to be.' She shook her head, not understanding. 'And Professor Bullock's book was real, too. Or I think so, anyway.' She tried comparing them. 'They're different eras. Different types of works. I don't see the connection. Is it something in their lineage? Their history or origins?' The purring seemed to increase. 'Mr Grey?'

But just then the door opened, letting in a blast of air and scattering the dust into a disorganized swirl.

'Dulcie!' Lloyd came in, wide eyed at the mess. 'What the hell happened?' He looked around, taking it all in. 'I swear, if that bastard Bullock is behind this, I'll kill him.'

'Lloyd?' Dulcie could barely say his name. This was not the mild-mannered academic she was used to sharing an office with.

'I'm sorry, Dulcie.' He stepped in and closed the door behind him, surveying the damage. 'I didn't mean that. I shouldn't have said that. Not after what you've been through.' He smiled at her, looking for a moment like his normal self. 'It's just, well, to say that he and I are fighting would be an understatement.'

'But he's your boss. He's—'

'A full professor. Yes.' Lloyd's face grew grim. 'The Cyrus University Professor of Eighteenth Century Literature. At least until further notice. But, no, he wouldn't stoop to this. He wouldn't have to, really. He can just discredit me.'

'The arrest?'

He nodded. 'I think so. I've been calling him on some things. And so when I walked in and saw this…'

'It was a break in. The university police said it was probably just vandalism.'

'Ah, that explains it. I got a message to call them, but to be honest, I just figured they were doing the city cops' dirty work.' Lloyd was looking over his books, blowing the dust off the back of a volume of Richardson. 'I mean, why make their job easier?'

It was time. 'Lloyd, you've got to tell me what's going on. I saw that book on your desk. Raleigh dropped it off. And then we hear that a rare book has been stolen—and then you say there wasn't any book, but you're arrested, anyway?' She remembered the phone message. 'And Nancy asked me to give you this.' She held out the pink slip.

He took it and read it, and then started laughing. 'You thought I was stealing from Bullock? And selling his books?'

She nodded.

'Without a provenance?' Ever practical, Lloyd hit on the same line of thought that Dulcie had. 'No, Dulcie, I'm not a thief.'

'But I saw the package on your desk, Lloyd.'

'You saw something wrapped in brown paper.' His voice was calm, soothing, but Dulcie felt he wasn't telling her the whole story.

'Lloyd, I can't leave it at that. Not after all this.' She gestured at the mess around them.

'Please, Dulcie. You don't understand what's going on—but it affects you, too.' He paused to look around, blinking in the dust. 'I'm sorry if this is because of me, because of anything I've done. But people's reputations are at stake. And that means I've got to sort it out by myself. Without the police.'

FIFTY-THREE

'I DON'T LIKE IT.' Suze was shaking her head, looking as grave as one can while stirring tomato sauce. 'Lloyd Pruitt is involved and he's gotten you involved, and now your safety has been threatened.'

'I'm perfectly safe, Suze.' Dulcie worked the cork loose. After the day of cleaning, she'd splurged on a Bulgarian red. 'I mean, the office was a mess, but all I got was a stuffy nose and a few paper cuts.'

'This time.' Suze turned to stare at her roommate. 'But what if you had been there?'

'Then whoever it was probably wouldn't have broken in.' Dulcie poured herself a taste and grimaced. 'This needs to breathe.'

'Pour me a glass?' Dulcie did. 'I don't know if CPR will help.' Suze winced. 'Ah, that's brisk. But seriously, Dulcie, how do you know what the intention was?'

'Whoever it was must have been looking for something.' Suze kept stirring. 'Right?'

'You said nothing was taken.' Suze checked the water. It was boiling, and she opened a box of pasta. 'From your books, anyway. Now, maybe Lloyd was lying when he said nothing was missing from his. Or—' she turned to look her roommate in the face '—whoever broke in wasn't a thief. Whoever it was wanted to do some damage. Maybe he wanted to scare you.'

'I'M SORRY, DULCIE, I'm with Suze on this one.' Despite Dulcie's best efforts to keep the conversation away from Lloyd, once Chris had shown up Suze managed to make her objections heard. 'I know you like him. He's an OK guy. But, well, there's something fishy going on and he's dragged you into it now.' He refilled Dulcie's glass, but she pushed it away.

'You're both treating me like I'm a child.' She turned from her boyfriend to her roommate. 'I'm not a fool. The campus police are looking into the break in.'

Chris and Suze exchanged a look. 'They don't know about the book. They don't know that something is up between Lloyd and Professor Bullock.' Suze's voice was calm, and Dulcie could hear the lawyer she'd soon be in it. 'They can't be expected to reach a reasonable conclusion without all the facts.'

'OK, then.' Dulcie looked from one to the other. 'What do you want me to do?'

'Simple.' Suze spoke first. 'I want you to call the cops. The Cambridge cops.'

BY THE TIME THE BOTTLE was empty, Dulcie had given up arguing. Suze might be more involved with the legalities of the situation, but Chris, she knew, was seriously worried about her. He even offered to escort her down to the police station the next morning, once he got off work.

'No, you don't have to.' She had walked him down to the front door. 'You should just crash when you get off. I'll call them in the morning.'

He looked at her without speaking.

'I will, I promise. First thing.' She looked up at his sweet face. 'I don't know if I could make sense of it all right now, anyway.'

He smiled at that. 'Well, then, I'll leave you with the dishes, then. Sorry to eat and run.'

'Get out of here.' She pushed him away, playfully, but then let him pull her close for a kiss. 'I miss you, you know.' She hadn't meant to say that. It was the wine.

'I know, Dulce.' He stroked her cheek. 'This is just temporary. I love you, too.'

And with that, he was gone. And Dulcie looked up just in time to see the black and white kitten careening down the stairs.

'Whoa, kitty. Come here.' She reached for the little cat, who mewed and batted at her. 'Are you going to get on my case now, too?' Lifting the small beast to her face, Dulcie looked into unblinking eyes. 'Or is there something else going on here?'

The crash of pots from the floor above obscured another soft mew, and Dulcie climbed back up the stairs. From the sound of splashing and the clattering of cutlery, she knew things weren't going smoothly.

'You're pissed.' The bad red buzzed in Dulcie's head, leaving her no patience for her roommate's mood.

Suze's shoulders heaved in a dramatic sigh.

'Suze?'

Her roommate turned. 'I just don't know about you, Dulcie. I know you're an academic. You love this stuff. I get it. But life is not all as depicted in your books.'

Dulcie stepped back, stung. 'Suze, I know that. I'm not completely naive about life, you know.' Suze grunted and splashed. 'And what's wrong with being an academic? At one point, you liked it well enough.'

Suze was running the water full blast and Dulcie couldn't tell if she'd heard. Still, she kept talking. 'Even if now you have made it patently obvious that you're ready to move on.'

'What do you mean?' Suze put down the sponge.

Dulcie swallowed, but in for a penny, in for a pound. Besides, what she'd said was true. 'You don't care about student life anymore. You barely ever hang out with us. All you care about is getting through this last year.' She was trying to do what Suze always did, list her facts in a reasonable and orderly fashion. But she felt herself getting choked up. That last glass of wine had been a mistake. 'I mean, I hardly ever see you anymore.'

'Hey, that's not fair.' Suze sounded hurt, and Dulcie kicked herself. 'You spend as much time with Chris as I do with Ariano.'

'Not anymore.' The tears welled up. 'Not recently.'

'Oh, kiddo, I'm sorry.' Suze stepped toward her, but stopped just short of a hug. Instead, she looked in Dulcie's face. 'Are you two fighting?'

Dulcie shook her head. 'No, he's just, I don't know. Absent.'

'I'm going to make some peppermint tea.' Suze put the water on. Dulcie watched her. It was a peace gesture. She should have felt better. But all she could think about was what she couldn't say. That no matter how she denied it, her friend was moving on. And for the last six years, she'd spent Thanksgiving with Suze at her parents' house. This year, Suze hadn't even mentioned the upcoming holiday once.

FIFTY-FOUR

THE FIRST THING she noticed was the smell of smoke. Faint, just a trace in the air, it tickled her nose like cat fur. Half asleep, she reached up to brush the kitten away. All that wine…she didn't want to wake up just yet.

But the smell grew stronger. Ashy. Unmistakable. And Dulcie woke fully with a start—to find herself not in her sunny third-floor bedroom but in a book-lined study, sealed with heavy drapes.

'What? Where am I?' Dulcie stood up, and realized she'd been lying on the floor in the kind of heavy brocade gown that would have made uncomfortable nightwear in any era. Indeed, the voluminous skirts made standing difficult, though as she swayed she realized that a throbbing headache contributed to her lack of balance. 'Hello? Anybody?'

Dulcie looked around. The smell of smoke was stronger now, but in the dim light—those heavy drapes—she could see no sparks, no fire. A tall brick fireplace in the corner was empty and dull. The shelves, their books reaching up into the gloom, equally dark. The ceiling, barely visible in the half light, looked impossibly high, though she could make out carvings in the dark wood. The fumes, though, were growing thicker. She had to shake off her languor, and fast.

Dulcie's skirts rustled as she ran over to the drapes, her head clearing with every step. But when she pushed them back, her heart sank. Tiny panes, leaded, looked out over nothing. A barren mountainscape, open air falling down to rock. Looking down, Dulcie could have sworn she saw a hawk making lazy circles, far below. It was hopeless, and Dulcie sank into the windowseat, ignoring the puff of dust that rose from the ancient velvet upholstery.

But there—wait! Over in the corner, obscured by shadow, was an exit. Leaping up, Dulcie ran over to the carved wooden door, desperate to wrench it open and, cailing out an alarm, run to safety. But the moment she grabbed the ornate doorknob, she jumped back in pain, falling to the carpet as she tripped over those annoying skirts. Hot as a frying pan, the metal knob had burned her hands. From her vantage place on the floor, she looked up. No, it wasn't glowing, though it might as well have been. And from down here she could clearly see the stream of smoke seeping over the threshold. Soon it would be filling her mouth, her nose. Her lungs.

Dulcie sneezed—and looked up into the round green eyes of her kitten. Blinking once, the kitten jumped back, and Dulcie realized that the tickle of smoke on her lips had indeed been cat hair. At some point, the kitten had laid down on her face.

'Kitty!' Too late. All she saw was the bouncing tail as it darted into the hall and down the stairs. Still, yawning in the early morning sun, Dulcie couldn't be too angry. That nightmare had been horribly real, the sense of danger and helplessness visceral. Too visceral to let her get back to sleep, she decided, even if the clock only said seven. Another stretch and she realized she couldn't lay all the blame on the kitten. Her own aching head was due as much to last night's cheap red as to the phantom flames. The pressures were getting to her, if she had drunk that much. Either that or she really had to upgrade her splurges.

But as she brushed her teeth, tiptoeing down the hall so as not to wake Suze, Dulcie realized something else was bothering her, too. Yes, she had promised Suze and Chris that she would talk to the Cambridge police. She didn't know how much the university cops shared with the city, and it did make sense to make sure that everyone was on the same page. But Lloyd was her friend, too. Thinking back to how trapped she had felt in that dream, she knew she couldn't do the same thing to him. She'd talk to him first. Come clean about her—or her friends'—suspicions, and give him a chance to accompany her to the Central Square station. Or, at least, to get his story straight.

And so, after scooping the kitten's litter ('good cat!'), she tip toed down the front steps, tied on her sneakers, and let herself out into the brisk morning air, full of good resolve and without a clue where she was going.

FIFTY-FIVE

NOBODY WAS ANSWERING the departmental phone. Even the efficient Nancy didn't get in this early. But Dulcie wasn't a researcher for nothing. And as she made her way toward the corner coffeehouse, she had formulated a plan.

'Latte, double shot.' This early, she was able to grab a table, and once the barista had taken her order, she pulled her laptop out of her bag. Thanks to Chris's attentions, the little computer was supercharged—and primed to pick up on any wireless connection. His additions had made it a little slow to start up, however, and while she waited, Dulcie surveyed the café. Central Square, only blocks away from the university, might as well have been a separate world. The thin man in the black turtleneck could also be a student, and Dulcie would have put money that the couple huddled in the corner, arguing over opened notebooks, went to the tech school down the road. But the bulk of the clientele at this hour were commuters, popping in to fill their travel mugs and pick up a croissant for the road. Even the buff guy in the painter's pants probably had a job. The speed with which he was throwing back a steaming chai spoke of places to go and deadlines to meet. Above the counter, well back from the steaming machines, a small bowl held a bright red Siamese fighting fish, Nemo. He swam placidly back and forth, his flaglike dorsal fin down, surveying his domain.

'Milky twofer.' A pint glass thumped down on the table, startling Dulcie from her reverie. But as she had waited, her computer had gone into gear, and as she sipped the comforting brew she began punching in various searches, hoping to catch Lloyd Pruitt in the worldwide web.

Ten minutes later, she had what she wanted. An address

that seemed current for an apartment down in Cambridgeport. For this kind of chat, she'd already decided, face to face would be best. But as she saved the listing, Dulcie felt the tickle of curiosity. When she'd plugged Lloyd's name in, more than a dozen items had popped up. Most were pretty obvious. She knew he'd won the Bulgar Prize two years ago. She'd even read the *Harvard Gazette* article that was linked to the university press release. But when she saw Lloyd's name highlighted on an antiquarian book site, she had to pause. Was this electronic eavesdropping? Conversely, was it anything she really wanted to know?

Dulcie looked up at Nemo. The little fish looked back, or at least it seemed that he did, his tiny red mouth opening and closing in her direction as first one eye, and then another pivoted toward her. But if he had an answer, he wasn't talking. Dulcie stared at the screen and hesitated, taking another sip of her coffee. Whatever it was, it was public, right?

'Mr Grey, what would you do?' She tried to summon the spirit of her pet, but in the noise and bustle of the café nothing spectral was forthcoming. Instead, the room seemed to be getting louder. Late commuters, she figured, rushing in panicked and looking for a caffeine fix. Another sip and—crash!— a short-haired man in a suit had knocked into a table, knocking someone's backpack and coffee mug to the floor with a dramatic bang. A round of good-natured applause went up and the man bowed. Dulcie smiled. Just last night the kitten had tried to get into her bag, sending it—and her own round form—tumbling to the floor.

That was it. Curiosity went with cats. She clicked on the link and waited for the image to resolve. What she saw was more elaborate than she'd expected. An auction site, hosted by an international firm, had listed its recent sales. A first-edition of Dickens had gone for a record amount, and Dulcie imagined Trista there, thumbing through *Little Dorrit* and making wisecracks about its condition. A few signed letters from various dignitaries had been lumped together in one lot. And there, under 'arcana,' she found it. One of the pricier offerings had been an early, annotated edition of *Humphrey Clinker,* complete with notes made by its author, Tobias Smollett, shortly before his death. The book was listed as selling to the collection of a Wm. A. Bullock, no title or university affiliation given. But the listing noted that the purchase had been made by one Lloyd Pruitt.

NEMO WAS WATCHING AS Dulcie finished her coffee and headed for the door. He could have told her that she was too distracted. That the idea that her friend might in fact be a thief was blinding her to other possibilities. He could have told her that a moment after she left, the door opened again as another slipped out, much more quietly, from the busy café. But he was a fish, and he didn't.

FIFTY-SIX

WALKING THROUGH CENTRAL Square as the morning commute died down, Dulcie began to have second thoughts. The main Cambridge Police Station was only a block away, and she had promised both her roommate and her boyfriend that she'd tell them all she knew. As she got the walk signal to cross Massachusetts Avenue, she almost veered off to the right. It would be the work of a few minutes, and then she'd be done. It wasn't like she was ratting out Lloyd. Rather, she was just sharing information, important information that could be connected to a brutal crime.

She turned—and was smacked.

'Sorry! Sorry!' A young man yelled and waved as he bustled past, a briefcase in one hand and a cell phone up to his ear. As he lowered the hand holding the briefcase, he nearly caught a bicyclist on the back. The cyclist responded with a stream of truly inventive invective that left Dulcie feeling both impressed and vindicated.

And, if she were being honest with herself, filled with second thoughts. One of the things she loved about the academic world, and the little city on this side of the Charles River, was its sense of community. People watched out for each other here, and the oblivious ones—like that cell phone guy—were still in the minority. She turned and surveyed the crowd. So many of these people were probably just like her. Maybe not academics, but dreamers, looking for a way to make things work. In fact, she almost felt like she recognized faces in the crowd. It wasn't that big a city after all. And with that thought, her mind was made up. Turning back toward the river, she bypassed the police station. She'd talk to the cops, but only after she had told Lloyd her intentions.

When she got to Lloyd's building, a looming old brick thing, she stepped into a tiny alcove and was relieved to see PRUITT spelled out on the bell. Suze might run almost every day, but the twenty-minute walk had tired Dulcie. Her first ring went unanswered, however, and she began to doubt the wisdom of marching down here without warning. What if, after all this, Lloyd was right now in their shared, convenient office? She rang again.

'Hello?' Even with the electrical pop and hiss, the voice was clearly Lloyd's.

'Lloyd, it's Dulcie.' She paused, and heard only silence. 'Dulcie Schwartz? I need to talk to you.'

More silence, and for a moment Dulcie wondered if the ancient wiring had cut out.

'Dulcie.' Lloyd came back with a hiss and a crackle. 'Hang on. I'll be right down.' The line went dead for real.

Dulcie looked around the small alcove. The tile floor was littered with takeout menus; the wood paneling above the mail-boxes showed the wear of generations of renters. Not the best place for a heart-to-heart. She stepped back outside and down the three cement stairs. Was there a park near here? Any kind of shared yard? A bare tree took up the space to the right of the stoop, its grey bark nearly matching the color of the steps. To the left, a sickly shrub seemed to extend around the building.

'Raleigh?' No, it couldn't be. As she'd been looking around, she thought she had seen the pretty undergrad rushing, head down, from behind Lloyd's building to the nearly identical one next door. She'd caught a glimpse of long chestnut hair and longer legs. But young women were far from rare in Cambridge, and when the dark-haired girl didn't look up, Dulcie shrugged. She was seeing familiar faces everywhere this morning. And right behind her, she heard a voice.

'Dulcie?' It was Lloyd. 'You wanted to talk?'

She jumped. 'Oh, yes!' Suddenly, she felt flustered. 'Sorry to show up unannounced. But, well, is there some place we could sit?'

He looked at her, concern on his pale, round face. 'What is it, Dulcie?'

'I need to go to the police, Lloyd.' She hadn't wanted it to be like this, standing on the sidewalk in the middle of Cambridge-port. But every moment she waited just made the burden worse. He had asked, and it just came out. 'I need to tell them what I know.'

'Dulcie.' He looked exasperated, rather than angry, and Dulcie took heart. 'What do you know?'

'About the book, Lloyd. About the wrapped package I saw on your desk. And that Professor Bullock had reported a book missing, and now you're saying that this book supposedly didn't exist.' She took a breath. 'And I know that you've been buying books in his name, Lloyd. I don't know what any of it means, but something's going on. I know it is, and I think the police should know, too. But, well, we're friends. Officemates, anyway. And so I wanted to come and tell you that I was going to do it.' Saying that gave her courage. 'I mean, you could come to the police with me.'

'Yeah, maybe I should.'

That startled her. 'You will?'

He nodded. 'I just needed some more info first.' He motioned to the stoop and Dulcie followed him. The concrete was cold, but it felt more congenial to be sitting side by side, even if they were only facing a sagging triple-decker. 'I called that dealer back. The message you took for me? And he's confirmed it. There's something wrong with that book Bullock was so excited about.'

'What do you mean? How could a book be "wrong"?'

Lloyd shook his head. 'I don't know yet. I'm working on it.' Dulcie looked at him, and he sighed. 'Dulcie, things have been weird for a while now.'

'Yes?' Dulcie could hear the trepidation in her own voice.

Whatever was going on, Lloyd was involved. Now that he was about to tell her, she wasn't entirely sure she wanted to know.

'You know I work pretty closely with Bullock, right?' She nodded. 'Well, it started out just as research. But recently, my duties, such as they are, have been growing. For instance, he's been having me check the provenance of any book he was interested in, having me do the paperwork. Handle the actual purchase for him.'

The auction report. Dulcie nodded.

'Now, with Gosham, that's never been a problem. He's used to working with Bullock. He's been selling to him for years. Every now and then, Bullock gives him something back to sell. Like, when he got that first-edition Sterne?' Dulcie didn't know about that, but she nodded, anyway. 'It was in better shape than the one he had, so he got Gosham to fix it up, list it online. Got a good price for it, too. But over the last few months, he's been getting a little crazy.'

'Roger Gosham?' Dulcie remembered the bookbinder's outbursts, both at Polly and herself. But Lloyd was shaking his head. 'No, Bullock. He's been in a sort of frenzy, selling stuff that I know he cares about—and then buying books without really thinking about them. Books he already has copies of, books that, well, have dubious origins. A few times, I had to step in when he was going to make purchases without checking out the wares first. That's what gave me my first clue. I've learned that I've got to be careful. In some ways, I've become his protector.'

A city bus drove by with a cloud of exhaust and the two jumped up, coughing. 'Lloyd? What are you talking about? What do you mean by protector? I mean, you took his book—and now you're saying there's something wrong with it?'

'It is a fake, Dulcie. A forgery. Very well done, but not the real thing.' Lloyd stared after the bus, his round face grown sad. 'Browning Antiquarian is the top Elizabethan expert in the country. I told Bullock I suspected as much. That's why he got so angry at me.'

'But why? I mean, it's not your fault, unless you—' She paused, the central question coming back to her. 'You didn't buy it for him, did you?' Lloyd shook his head. 'Then how did Bullock get it?'

Lloyd was still staring after the bus. 'I don't know, Dulcie. I don't know how that book got into his collection. I think, maybe, things have finally progressed too far for me to control.'

'For you to—' Dulcie reached out to Lloyd and he turned to her. 'Lloyd, I don't understand, but first things first. What are you going to tell him? And what did you mean when you said the book didn't exist?'

'It may as well never have.' He shrugged, a small smile on his face. 'You see, Bullock hasn't seen that book for over a week now. He's probably forgotten that it ever existed.'

FIFTY-SEVEN

In retrospect, it all made perfect sense, and as Lloyd explained, Dulcie found herself plugging in the details. Everyone knew that Professor Bullock was slipping. Hadn't the department made moves to push him toward retirement? But nobody knew the extent of his decline.

'At first, I thought he was just tired or something. Then, I just felt bad for him. I don't know if it's Alzheimer's or what,' Lloyd was saying. 'Some days, he's still as sharp as a tack. But on his bad days…' Lloyd shook his head. 'The problem is partly that he knows, at some level, what's going on. And he hates it—and hates anyone who knows it. So, on one hand, he's taken me into his confidence. He trusts me to look out for him. But then sometimes he lashes out. In fact, when I first heard about Cameron, I was afraid…' He looked at Dulcie for confirmation, but she shook her head.

'No way. I was with him. Unless you think he could have planned it?'

'He's not capable.' Lloyd grimaced. 'I mean, I don't think he could be organized enough anymore. The most he can do is get angry and react.'

'The arrest?'

'Yeah.' Lloyd looked grim. 'He was really unhappy with me that day.'

'So, the pen and the letter opener probably weren't stolen.' Dulcie found herself piecing things together. 'Probably nothing was, no matter what Polly said.'

Lloyd shrugged. 'Polly.' His voice was noncommittal, but it didn't convey respect.

'She doesn't know?' Dulcie found that hard to believe.

'I don't know what she knows.' Lloyd paused and then looked at Dulcie. 'Or what she wants to believe. She's got some issues, and he's like her god, you know?'

Dulcie nodded. 'Yeah, I believe it. I wonder what she'll do?'

'He'll need someone to look after him. I don't think he has any family.'

With that word, something occurred to Dulcie. A wave of relief flooded over her, and she felt her troubles washed away. 'What did you say?'

'That Bullock has no family?'

'No, but I do.' As quickly as she could, Dulcie explained Lucy's vision to Lloyd. 'So here I've been terrified that *The Ravages of Umbria* is an elaborate forgery. But maybe that's not what she was talking about. Except…' The other shoe dropped. 'Oh, hell.' She sunk her face in her hands. The anthology. The phrase. It wasn't all in Lucy's head.

'What?' Lloyd bent down to look into her face. 'Come on, it can't be that bad.'

'Yes, it can.' She turned to face her friend. 'And now neither of us has a competent senior faculty member to help us out.'

SICK AT HEART, DULCIE didn't feel like talking about it. Besides, they had been sitting at the side of the road for more than a half-hour by then. They both had sections at ten, and so Dulcie took Lloyd's hand and let him pull her to her feet.

'We should tell the cops, you know.' The concept was collegial now, not threatening.

'Yeah, we should.' Lloyd still didn't look happy about the idea. 'Especially now that I've heard from Browning.'

'Are you worried?' After all, Dulcie wasn't the only one who had hitched her wagon to Bullock. Lloyd was not only further along on his doctorate, he also counted on the professor for employment. When news of Bullock's increasing incapacity broke, he would end up looking bad, the scapegoat for the delayed cover-up. Plus, everything he had written or published under Bullock's auspices would be suspect.

'It's not fair,' said Dulcie, once Lloyd had pointed this out. 'I mean, if anything, it should be the opposite way around. You should be getting more credit. You've been doing his work for ages.'

Lloyd smiled at her. 'Thanks. In truth, he hasn't done much. And he's good on automatic pilot. I've just been doing my own research and trying to keep him out of trouble at book auctions. But what are you going to do?'

'I don't know.' Dulcie shook her head. In some ways, she'd be like Raleigh, launched on a thesis and suddenly without an adviser. The thought of the pretty undergrad brought to mind the figure she had seen, flitting between the buildings. 'Hey, Lloyd. Does Raleigh live around here?'

'No. I mean, I don't think so.' He looked flustered. 'Why do you ask?'

'Nothing.' It had been a full morning, and the two were now back in Central Square. 'So, you want to go talk to the cops?'

Lloyd looked at his watch. 'Not if I want to keep one of my jobs. I've got a tutorial in ten minutes.' Dulcie raised her eyebrows. 'But I will, Dulcie. I promise. This afternoon.'

DULCIE FELT LIKE SHE WAS sleepwalking for the rest of the day. For one section, she just let her students argue. ('Well, that imagery doesn't seem very metaphysical to me!' It wasn't worth clarifying.) Even her junior tutorial floated by.

'Dulcie? Miss Schwartz?' Lindsay, her most annoying student, actually looked worried.

'Sorry.' She'd smiled in response. 'Thesis worries.'

'In this economy, I'm not surprised,' her student had sat back, pleased with having gotten a response. 'My mother says that anybody who goes for an advanced degree in the humanities these days should be independently wealthy. Or certified.' Her expression was smug, challenging, but Dulcie refused to rise to the bait.

By the middle of the afternoon, she realized that she just didn't have the energy to go to the police. Yes, she had promised Suze and Chris, as well, but so much had happened since last night. And now she was about to be cast adrift, a grad student without a thesis adviser. Without, possibly, a thesis. In response, she found herself heading over to Widener. She could completely understand Lloyd's reluctance to say anything. As long as the problem wasn't public, they could pretend it didn't exist. Maybe they could wait until she just had something on paper.

With a start, she remembered that she was supposed to be meeting with Bullock the next day. And she was supposed to be able to report on her progress. Poor Professor Bullock! The thought came to her unbidden. No wonder he wanted her to show some tangible results. He was fighting for his position—for his sanity, really. Well, it wouldn't hurt her to give it one more day—and maybe in the long run, having some paper filed in some office saying that she'd made significant progress on her thesis would do them both good, the student and the teacher.

Of course, that would all disappear if Lloyd had already talked to the cops. As she made her way across the Yard, she dialed his number. 'Lloyd, I was thinking,' she said to his voicemail. For all she knew, he was already in the Central Square police station, telling all. 'If, well, if you haven't spoken to the police yet, maybe we could wait? I've got a meeting with Bullock tomorrow.' She paused. He would understand, wouldn't he? 'Well, maybe you're already there. Let me know, will you?' And with that, she snapped the phone shut and ascended the stairs to her last refuge, the wide grey library that held so many of her dreams.

FIFTY-EIGHT

'ONE MORE DAY...' Dulcie couldn't block that thought from her mind, as she pulled reference works and piled them in front of her on the carrel. 'One more day,' she muttered as she stared at their covers, unsure whether even to open them. How could she focus on a thesis that already seemed to be unraveling—for an adviser who also seemed to be unraveling? For the first time in ages, the quiet hum of the library felt ominous. A spirit waiting for her to falter, waiting for her to fail. 'One. More. Day.'

'That's ridiculous.'

The voice caused her to spin around, knocking the books off the carrel top.

'Oh, please!' The vision of Mr Grey wincing, as cats will at loud noises, flashed in her mind, and Dulcie found herself apologizing.

'Mr Grey! I'm so sorry. It's just that, well, everything is falling apart.' Somewhere, a set of large grey ears flicked, and Dulcie found herself getting a little peeved. 'Seriously, Mr Grey. This is important to me.'

'I'm not dismissing your emotions, Dulcie.' The deep, calm voice sounded a little condescending to Dulcie. 'I'm simply questioning the validity of your concerns.'

'That's because you're a cat.' Dulcie heard the nasty tone creeping into her voice. 'Or, you were a cat.' Silence. 'Mr Grey?' She tried to picture her late pet, how his tail would lash and those velvety ears would turn back and flatten. In the hum of the ventilation system, Dulcie thought she heard something more threatening. A growl, perhaps? And suddenly the enormity of her thoughtless reaction hit her. 'Mr Grey, I'm sorry! Please don't leave me.' Her eyes filled up with tears.

'Now, now, kitten. Why would I leave you?'

Dulcie sobbed with relief, but dashed the few escaping tears from her face with the back of her hand. 'It's just been such a difficult time.' She swallowed the lump in her throat. If she lost Mr Grey, she didn't know what she'd do.

'You know, you do have others in your life now. New friends to lean on.'

His voice was warm, but his words pushed her near to tears once again. 'It's not the same, Mr Grey. I mean, I'm not even sure what's going on with Chris. And Suze is…' She couldn't think of how to explain what was happening with Suze. 'I don't really know if I have anybody, Mr Grey. Nobody like you.'

'Trust goes both ways, Dulcie.' Dulcie sniffed. Yes, he was right. She was going to have to talk to Suze—and to Chris, too. 'And there are others in your life, too. Some whom you haven't even named.'

'Lloyd? Yeah, I do trust him, Mr Grey. And Helene, too.' The thought of her stolid and businesslike neighbor gone all goofy over her kittens was cheering, and Dulcie felt her equilibrium returning. 'I guess everything has just been getting to me. My thesis and, well, what happened with Cameron…'

'Hmmm…' The sound was akin to a purr. 'Be careful what you take on, kitten. And keep in mind, sometimes when we get bitten, it's because we've been chasing our own tail.' Mr Grey's voice was fading, and Dulcie sat up and strained to hear.

'Do you mean I'm looking for trouble?' Deep in her heart, Dulcie wanted to believe that was true. That *The Ravages of Umbria* was really all she'd hoped it was and that all her fears were based on her misinterpretation of Lucy's dream. 'But there was that quote, and if you look at the dates—'

'Character counts, Dulcie. Character can be motive.' The voice was getting softer. 'Remember, the key is in the book.'

'Mr Grey?' It was no use. Something in the air—the humming of the ventilation system, or the far-off footsteps of another researcher in the stacks—told her that Mr Grey was gone.

Still, his visit had been heartening. 'Maybe I *was* looking for trouble,' Dulcie muttered to herself. 'And anyway, I still have that meeting tomorrow.' And so, blocking out all thoughts of who that meeting was with—a barely functional professor who was likely soon to lose his university position—she hunkered down and got to work.

A shade then, more mystical than wild... Before long, Dulcie was caught up again in the magic. Did it matter, really, when the book had been written, or by whom? What mattered was the magic of the words. The story. The characters.

Dulcie thought back to what Mr Grey had said. So she didn't trust people? Couldn't judge character? Who could blame her, when a nasty Demetria might be lurking. No, she shook her head. Suze was a good and faithful friend. It's just that she had moved on. Just like Mr Grey had moved on, leaving her with only the kitten. The klutzy, mute kitten.

Something tickled at Dulcie's consciousness, but she was too distracted to make it out. Time for a break, she decided, looking at her watch. And nearly time for dinner.

'Chris? It's me. Just wanted to know if you wanted to grab something to eat.' Dulcie's heart sank as she left the message. He'd been so eager for her to go to the police, but he hadn't even touched base to ask how it had gone. Of course, she had to admit as she trotted down the wide library steps, she hadn't actually spoken to the police. But did he know that?

'Dulcie...' Dulcie whipped around, sure she'd heard Mr Grey's voice. But the only people on the steps were a group of Japanese tourists, all listening as the guide spoke loudly from the top. It didn't matter; she knew she was being silly.

'I'm sorry, Mr Grey.' She whispered as she trotted the rest of the way down. 'I'll try to be a little more fair to everyone. If I get through tomorrow, anyway.'

'Dulcie?'

'Sorry.' She looked around at the grey clouds scudding across the sky. Already the shadows were lengthening, the day growing frigid. 'As soon as I get through tomorrow. That's what I meant.'

A dry oak leaf, caught in a gust, slapped against her face, its pointed edges momentarily scraping against her cheek before flying off. 'Point taken, Mr Grey.'

GIVEN HER LACK OF ACTION, Dulcie was a little relieved to find Suze gone and a note about a late showing of *Casablanca* on the fridge. She had too much on her mind to focus on an old film, no matter how great, but at least she wouldn't have to explain the day to her roommate. By the time she'd heated up some dubious leftover pizza—when had this been from?—Chris called back. She bit into the pizza, glad for the company, even if remote. But he sounded distant, apologizing for the noise as he ran through the Square from a teaching section to the Science Center.

'So, did you talk to the cops?' From the sudden quiet, Dulcie guessed that he'd reached his second job of the day.

'It's a long story, Chris.' She took another bite. She was famished. But she also, she admitted to herself, wanted to stall.

He made a noise that didn't sound happy and in her fatigued state, Dulcie almost snapped at him. But, remembering her encounter with Mr Grey, she opted for the diplomatic approach. After swallowing, she made sure to keep her voice even. 'It would be easier to tell you about it in person, Chris.'

'Yeah, I know.' That wasn't the answer she expected and she nibbled on a piece of pepperoni. Did he sound particularly tired, or was that something else in his voice? 'We've got to talk, anyway, Dulcie.' It was fatigue. It had to be. 'About a lot of things.'

Dulcie coughed out the cold sausage as her boyfriend said something about dinner the next day. Mouth dry, she could barely respond. 'We should talk.' She didn't need to be a semiotics major to know what that meant. Was she going to lose her thesis, her adviser, and her boyfriend all in the same week? Somehow she choked out a response, agreeing to meet after her powwow with Bullock, and they hung up. Suddenly the remaining pizza looked disgusting to her, congealed and stiff. She sat there, stunned, staring at it until a certain small feline scrambled on to the table, knocked over the salt cellar, and mewed as loudly as a cat twice her size.

'Kitten, I don't...' Dulcie swallowed the lump in her throat. 'I can't play right now.' But the kitten pounced, wrestling Dulcie's hand to the table, and she was forced to pick up the small beast.

'Oh, kitten.' She held the little cat up to her cheek. Even as the tears fell, she could feel the kitten start to purr. This wasn't Mr Grey, far from it, but there was something comforting about the tiny animal's warmth and the rhythmic rise and fall of soft fur.

FIFTY-NINE

THE DREAM CAME AGAIN, full of choking smoke and sparks. This time, Dulcie was more aware in it. She knew, right away, what was happening—and that the large, carved door in the corner was not an option. She couldn't keep herself from glancing out the window once again, but those leaded panes only looked out over a terrifying drop. The rocky slope below was too steep and too far away for it to provide an escape. For a moment, she leaned against the window, the glass still cool against her palms. But she could hear the flames now, the snap and hiss as sparks caught. Already the edge of the carpet glowed, as embers caught in the ancient wool. Time was running out.

That left only the shelves of books, and in the dream Dulcie started pulling at them. Against all reason, she grabbed at them, indiscriminately. Some she opened, most she simply knocked to the floor. Behind her, the pages of one bound volume had already taken a spark, the pages turning red—then black—as the fine old rag paper was eaten by the flame. Still, she kept pulling at books, desperate now, in a panicked attempt to find something. But what? *Look in the book, Dulcie.* Even in her dream, the ghostly voice called to her. *The key is in the book.* But the smoke was rising, and Dulcie tripped over her long skirts to tumble to the ground.

ROUND GREEN EYES STARED into hers and blinked once. It was the kitten, and Dulcie was awake—on the floor.

'Kitten! Are you okay?' Dulcie raised herself on one elbow, trying to figure out how she'd gotten so tangled up in the sheet. In response, the kitten scampered off, leaving Dulcie to shake off the remnants of the nightmare and begin her day.

'Well, you're under deadline so that could be a "burning" issue.' Suze had put down the paper when Dulcie came downstairs. Her take on the nightmare was more psychological than psychic. 'And all that about the books, well, it does make sense.'

'But what was I looking for?' Try as she might, Dulcie couldn't dismiss the idea that the dream was more than symbolism. 'What was the key?'

'Does it have to be that literal?' Suze stopped, mouth open. But Dulcie knew her well enough.

'You think I'm turning into Lucy, don't you?' The recurrence of the dream had made her wonder.

'I think you were raised in an environment where psychic phenomena—magic—is taken seriously.' Suze was choosing her words carefully. Too carefully for Dulcie.

'And my mom is a nut.' She poured herself more coffee and then refilled Suze's mug, too. It wasn't her roommate's fault if she was rational. 'But there is something odd about this dream.'

'Why should your dream be any different from the rest of your life?' Suze smiled as she said that and Dulcie had to agree. Why indeed?

Despite the disturbing dream, Dulcie felt strangely calm as she got dressed and headed into the Square that morning, deciding at the last moment to splurge and take the T. Perhaps, she told herself, this is what condemned prisoners go through. Some strange mix of resignation and denial. After all, it wasn't like she had any choice. She'd go teach her section. Then she'd gather up what notes she had and make her case to Professor Bullock. Maybe he'd see what she had done and sign on for another half-year of grants. Maybe, she thought, with Lloyd in mind, he wouldn't understand what she was talking about, but for his own reasons—to hide his disability—he'd sign off on her grants, anyway. Or maybe he wouldn't. Nothing she could do about it now.

Dulcie checked her cell phone before she descended into the T. Chris had called to wish her luck, in the tired and distracted voice she'd almost gotten used to, and to stress that they needed to talk. Great. But she hadn't heard from Lloyd yet, so she was hoping that the fourth option—that Bullock would already be either in custody or on his way out of the department—was off the table. By dinner time that night, she'd know one way or another.

Maybe it was that certainty. Maybe it was the way Suze had slipped out while she was in the shower, but Dulcie felt a need to settle things. Waiting for the rush of air that presaged the arrival of the train, Dulcie thought back on the morning—and her own attempt to set her life straight. Suze had been dismissive of her dream, but not hostile. After all, to a legal mind, proof was something physical and everything else was speculation. But Dulcie had other concerns besides that strange recurring nightmare. Before heading up to the bathroom, Dulcie had tried to feel her roommate out about the upcoming holiday—and about the new distance that seemed to have grown between the two old friends. A few pointed comments had been met with non-committal grunts. And her one outright question, asking about Ariano's Thanksgiving plans, had been countered with an observation on the time. Suze was certainly honing her lawyerly skills, and Dulcie had given up, partly because the clock had shown the morning getting on. Chris, however, should be somewhat easier to tackle.

'Hey, Chris. It's me.' Dulcie heard her grammar slipping and hoped her boyfriend would find it vulnerable and endearing, rather than sloppy. 'I'm glad we're going to get together. I have some things to talk about, too.' She swallowed. 'About Thanksgiving.' She hung up. For good or ill, the message had been left. Of course, that just meant her imagination could run wild. Maybe he was planning on breaking up with her. But wasn't it just as likely that he'd been working so hard that the approach of the holiday had eluded him? He was a computer geek, after all. She paused on the T platform. Or maybe he'd found someone else during those long nights in the Science Center. Someone more rational and law abiding. Someone slim and pretty, like Raleigh. They were both tall and graceful, and Dulcie could picture them, heads together and laughing, at the Krullworth Awards banquet, while she toiled away at her new career as a waitress...

That distracting vision evaporated as she found herself slammed into the wall of the stairway. 'Watch it!' A large woman gave her a dirty look as she pushed past. 'This is a T stop, you know.'

Before she could come up with a cutting remark, Dulcie found herself carried along to the top of the stairs and deposited out on the street. But the body block had done her some good. There was no point in moping, she decided, as she swung her bag back on to her shoulder and queued up to cross Massachusetts Avenue.

Just as the light changed, her cell rang. She ignored it until she'd reached the opposite curb. Let him wait! When she pulled it out of her bag, however, her heart sank. Lloyd—but he'd left no message. He'd probably already talked to the cops. Her fate might already be sealed. Maybe that was a good thing, Dulcie told herself, looking up at the wrought-iron gates of the Yard. Between Lloyd and Bullock, Chris and Suze, maybe she was getting a message. Maybe karma had other plans for her. She'd always been a bit of an interloper here, anyway: Dulcie Schwartz, the hippie's kid. Maybe the leap from a cooperative yurt to the ivy-covered halls of academe was just too steep. Maybe...

SOMEHOW, DULCIE HAD GOTTEN through her section, the odd looks she'd gotten from her students and the long silences before she thought to ask another question only confirming in her mind her unfitness for life as an academic. But even the most awkward classes end eventually, and as the church clock rang out the hour, Dulcie searched out a quiet place where she could sit and think.

This was harder than it looked. Neither the library nor her office seemed very welcoming at the moment, and undergrads flooded the other Yard buildings, darting back and forth like crazed birds, preparing for their big migration. But, at a few minutes past the hour, things had quieted down, only the occasional stray wandering along the bare paths. Dulcie took a seat on the cold steps of an administration building and tried to make sense of her day.

'Mr Grey, where are you?' She found herself staring at a fat grey squirrel. But although its black eyes looked up as she spoke, she heard no answering voice. No touch of fur. 'I could really use a friend right now.' She was sinking into self-pity, she knew. And really, what reason did she have? Suze had a lot going on in her own life. Lloyd was probably doing the right thing, legally and morally. And Chris, well, she'd hear what Chris had to say later. Maybe it wasn't that bad.

Almost before she realized what she was doing, Dulcie found herself calling the community center's number back in Oregon. 'Lucy Schwartz, please?'

'Karma!' She heard someone calling and could only hope that her mother had not taken it on herself to change her name.

'Dulcie, dear, what's wrong?' Whatever she was calling herself, Lucy had come to the phone immediately. And at that unfamiliar motherly prompt, Dulcie broke down. Chris, Lloyd, Suze, Bullock…everything from that awful moment when she had found Cameron lying there came tumbling out. Even Mr Grey's relative silence was thrown on to the bonfire of her life. Tears streaming down her face, Dulcie hiccuped. This was what she needed. To talk to a sympathetic person. To talk to her mother.

'And so I thought, well, maybe it was time for me to come home.' She hadn't realized how much she craved the comfort of the commune with all its silly rituals and self-affirming warmth, until she said it. But once it was out, she realized just how right a move that would be. 'I don't belong here, Mom.' She paused. 'I mean, Lucy. I think it's time for me to go back to the land.'

But Lucy's response was not what she'd expected. 'Absolutely not! And give up on all the dreams you've had? All the work you've done?' Her mother sputtered. 'Your father may have dropped everything to go off and meditate. But you're a Sellenbock as well as a Schwartz, young lady! You are not a quitter; that's not how I raised you! You're going to get your degree!'

Dulcie hiccuped and sat up. Was this really Lucy Schwartz on the phone?

'But, Lucy—'

'You're having a rough time, dear. I understand that and, frankly, I'm not surprised. Mercury is retrograde and your sign, as I recall, has Venus in the ascendent. Very tricky right now. But you can't lose hope, Dulcie. I'll see you soon enough.'

'But—'

'Dulcie!' Lucy's voice had taken on a tone that Dulcie had never heard before. It sounded, just a little, like her grandmother, Lucy's mother. Despite herself, she smiled. 'You just stay with it, dear. Keep on searching. I'm sure you'll find the key.'

For the first time ever that Dulcie could remember, it was her mother who ended the call. But for a good ten minutes, she continued to sit on the cold stone steps, pondering her mother's newfound determination and the strange phrases she had used. What did Lucy mean when she said she'd see her soon enough? And why, for the second time that day, had she been told to keep on searching for a key?

SHE MIGHT HAVE SAT THERE till she was numb, if her reverie hadn't been broken by another buzz. A message, probably delivered while she'd been talking to Lucy, had just made its way to her voicemail. Well, the morning couldn't get any worse, she reasoned as she poked in the access code. As soon as she heard Lloyd's voice, though, she remembered her earlier fears and regretted her bare-bones optimism.

'Hey, Dulcie. It's Lloyd again. Bother, I wish I'd caught you.' Should she hang up? No, she decided. Let's get the worst over with.

But despite her first concerns, her friend and officemate hadn't been calling to tell her that he'd reported Bullock's bizarre behavior to the police. Nor was he calling to say he'd told the departmental powers-that-be about the tenured professor's decline. What he was saying was garbled and a bit frantic, causing Dulcie to hit 'replay' and listen again. Yes, Lloyd had gotten Dulcie's message; he had not told anyone anything. Now, however, he was regretting his lack of action. Because at some point this morning, after he had gone out, someone had broken into his apartment. As far as he could tell, nothing had been stolen ('I don't have much to take, anyway, Dulcie.'). But his bookshelves had been emptied on to the floor, and the covers of several larger volumes torn off.

'My place looks like a cyclone hit it.' He'd paused then, but Dulcie could hear a tremor in his voice. 'It looks like our office. And, Dulcie, I'm scared.'

SIXTY

'LLOYD?' SHE'D CALLED HER friend back, the fear in his voice pushing her own concerns aside. 'Are you OK?'

'Yeah, I'm fine. I mean, I'm glad I wasn't here when it happened.' She heard a thud. 'Sorry! I didn't realize the chair was leaning so far over. I'm at home now, trying to clean up.'

'Shouldn't you call the cops?'

'They've come and gone. Unfortunately, they don't seem to think it's a big deal.' Another thud and a small grunt. 'Oh, man, my desk drawers have all been emptied out.'

'How can that not be a big deal!? Do they know about our office?'

'I told them. Asked them to check with the university police.' Another grunt, but this time it sounded like Lloyd was sitting down. 'But they gave me a whole spiel about crime in the neighborhood. About how I should have had window locks on the fire escape. They seem to think it was random.'

'That's impossible.' Dulcie realized she was gesturing when she smacked a bystander. 'Sorry!' The office workers were beginning their lunchtime exodus, and Dulcie retreated off the stairs to talk. 'It sounds like the same person, doesn't it?'

'To me, sure.' Lloyd sounded tired, his voice flat. 'But the city cop who took my report was just going on about how the neighborhood is changing, how there's new money right up next to the older buildings.' Dulcie was surprised to hear a soft chuckle. 'When he heard I was a grad student, I think he thought I was part of the "new money."'

'Yeah, I get that sometimes.' Dulcie had to smile. 'With the new Harvard Square and all. But you said nothing was missing?'

'Nothing much to steal. I have to finish going through my books, though.'

Books. Something sparked in the back of Dulcie's mind, something about books and the Square. 'Hey, did you hear that Gosham's is expanding? Trista said something. I guess there must be some money in used and rare books. You think someone's looking for something to sell to him?'

Another grunt. 'Considering that his main clientele are academics, it would be pretty stupid to steal from one of us to sell to another, don't you think? Besides, I don't have anything worth anything.'

'Still...' Dulcie couldn't quite dismiss the idea. 'Maybe I'll ask Gosham next time I see him. Or see if I can get Polly to.'

Lloyd laughed out loud at that. 'I'd love to see that. Gosham terrified of losing Bullock's patronage. Polly fluttering about. I don't know, Dulcie. Maybe the cops were right.'

'Maybe.' But Dulcie didn't believe it. 'Hey, Lloyd, could Bullock have done this? Could he have forgotten what you found out about that book of his, and maybe been searching for it?'

Lloyd seemed to consider this, but after a moment he responded. 'No, I don't think so.' Another pause. 'He was too embarrassed. Humiliated, really. Besides, he's never been violent. His way of lashing out was to sic the police on me. And also, to be honest, I don't know if he could get it together enough to come here and do this. I mean, find my address, come over here, climb up the fire escape, and break in and all? It's just not likely.'

Dulcie nodded, a little relieved. 'Hey, do you need any help cleaning up?'

'No, thanks.' Lloyd sounded better now, too. The shock had passed. 'I've got a friend coming over. And speaking of Professor Great Books, don't you have a meeting with Bullock today?'

'Oh, hell!' Dulcie looked at her watch. 'I'm going to be late.'

'Don't worry about it, Dulcie. He probably won't even remember.'

It wasn't until they'd hung up and Dulcie was trotting across the Yard that she thought of another possible suspect. Unless her eyes were fooling her, she'd seen Raleigh slipping away from Lloyd's building the day before. From all she knew, the pretty undergrad didn't need money, but she was an unsettled young woman. And both physically and mentally capable of climbing up the building's fire escape. Could she have been scoping out Lloyd's apartment for some reason? Could Raleigh Hall have broken in and trashed the place?

DULCIE'S PHONE RANG again as she dashed across the Common. It was Lucy. Probably felt bad about being so hard on her only child. Well, she'd call her mother back later. Maybe she'd have reason to come home soon. But as she closed the phone unanswered, letting the call go through to voicemail, Dulcie felt a strange pang. Guilt? It was true that she'd just unloaded on her mother, and now she was avoiding her. But Lucy had wanted her to get on with her life, hadn't she?

Or could it be something other than guilt, that strange momentary flush? For a moment, Dulcie paused. Was she that afraid of what would happen? Over on Garden Street, a bus went by. In its wake, the breeze picked up, tossing a handful of leaves into a short-lived flurry. She watched them dance and smiled. They were free, and she…she was being silly. So she might have to find a new adviser; that didn't mean the end of the world. For that matter, even if she had to change her thesis, she still had time—and if she ended up exposing *The Ravages of Umbria* as a nineteenth-century cheat, a Gothic pastiche, so what? Whatever its origins, the work she had come to know and love was still a wonderful book, a piece of literature that spoke to her on so many levels. That alone made it worth her time. Dulcie took a deep breath and let it out slowly. She was tired of being afraid. What was it Mr Grey had told her? She had to have faith. The key was in the book.

SIXTY-ONE

POLLY OPENED THE DOOR looking like she'd seen a ghost. Pale, vaguely sweaty, Polly might have been ill, were it not for the red-rimmed eyes.

'Polly, are you all right?' Dulcie stepped into the foyer and reached for the other woman. But Polly stepped back, almost wincing, and Dulcie dropped her hands. 'Polly?'

'I'll tell the professor you're here.' Polly turned away, wiping her hand under her nose. But Dulcie wasn't about to let her go.

'Polly, please. Is someone… Has someone hurt you?' She stepped forward to see into Polly's face, but the older woman ducked her head, all the while shaking it in denial. Dulcie remembered that other visit, when Gosham had turned on her. 'Was it Roger Gosham, Polly?' She tried to keep her voice gentle, but she wasn't going to let a case of abuse go unquestioned.

In response, she got a mumble.

'I'm sorry, Polly, I couldn't hear you. Was he here?'

'I didn't let him in.' She sniffed again, but Dulcie relaxed. This seemed more a matter of the heart than of physical violence. 'But I'll have to.'

Dulcie straightened up. Had she heard that correctly? 'Polly, you don't have to let anyone do anything.'

'He knows.' Polly sniffled, her already soft voice muffled as she stared at the threadbare rug. Dulcie thought she made out one more word: 'Cameron.'

'I'm sorry, Polly. I wasn't thinking.' So much had happened, Dulcie was surprised how little she had thought about her late colleague recently. But if Polly had been involved with him, as sounded likely, then their discovery just the week before would have been especially traumatic. She kicked herself for being insensitive and reached again to embrace the older woman, her voice gentle and soft. 'You must miss him.'

'Miss him?' Polly reared back, her voice a hiss. 'Cameron? I hated him!' And with that she turned on her heel and stormed out the front door without her coat, leaving Dulcie standing in the hallway, shocked into silence.

'Ah, Miss Schwartz.' Before she could recover her wits, Professor Bullock had stuck his head out of his office. 'Come in, come in.'

Her mind still reeling from Polly's sudden outburst, Dulcie followed her professor into his office. At least here everything seemed solid. No matter what else was about to happen, she could look around here and see life unchanged. The overflowing ashtrays, the shelves of books; the professor's own great work prominently displayed. With a sigh, Dulcie sank into the desk chair—and immediately jumped up again. She'd sat on a book. *Elizabethan Short Prose.* Taking it in her hand, she sat again and looked it over. In front of her, Bullock had settled in behind his desk and was hard at work lighting his pipe.

'Professor...' Disparate ideas were beginning to come together. She opened the book in her hand. It seemed more like a bound catalogue, listing sources and brief biographies for sixteenth-century writers. 'That book you had. The one that you reported stolen?' Someone—Lloyd maybe—had used this book, the one in her hand, to begin to uncover the truth. It was here that the questions were first asked, the questions that seemed to have been solved when Lloyd sent the supposedly rare text off to an antiquarian in Texas.

'Oh, that. Nothing much. Mistake all around.' The professor was making a much bigger fuss over his pipe than Dulcie thought necessary. She looked from the reference work to her adviser. Under his bushy eyebrows, his eyes looked clear, but he wouldn't meet her gaze and instead started examining his pipe. Reaching into his top desk drawer, he pulled out a small scraper and began cleaning out its bowl. The light of his desk lamp cast deep shadows on his face, concealing his expression even as it illuminated the hand-carved bowl and the professor's gnarled hands. He muttered something, and tapped the pipe against the ashtray again, clearly hoping to draw out the procedure.

He was, Dulcie realized, embarrassed. And for a moment, all her own worries faded away. Yes, she might be facing a setback, but for Professor Bullock, everything was at stake. 'Maybe I should refile this.' She stood up and walked over to the bookshelf, intending to give him a moment to recover. Give them both an opportunity to change the subject.

And that's when she saw it. Over on the shelf, next to Bullock's magnum opus, almost obscured in the shadows. The letter opener. The one she'd seen Polly pocket only a few days before.

Dulcie turned toward her mentor. He'd been so upset. Did he know it had resurfaced? The best approach, she decided, was the direct one. 'Professor,' she said, lifting the miniature sword. 'You found it!' She turned the little sword in her hands, noting again how heavy it was for its size. Catching the dappled light that came through the ivy-covered window, its jeweled hilt glinted and glowed.

'What?' The professor looked up, glancing from Dulcie to the letter opener. But although his eyes seemed clear and focused, there was no recognition in his face.

'Your letter opener.' Dulcie held the item out to him. 'The one from your gift set?'

He reached out to take it, the pipe momentarily forgotten. Turning it over in the light of the desk lamp, she could see him admiring the workmanship, the emerald-green stone that glowed like a living thing. 'Charming,' he said. 'A little Excalibur, isn't it? Pretty little thing.'

Dulcie caught her breath. Of course. He was forgetful. He couldn't even remember missing it. Unless it hadn't been the letter opener that had gotten him so upset. But what… Suddenly, an odd thought popped into Dulcie's head. Could this be the emerald, the one she'd been dreaming of? But why? What did it mean? For the first time she started thinking back toward her own sources of information. Could it be?

'You weren't given this letter opener?' She kept her voice level, posing a theory to be tested. 'It wasn't a gift after you spoke at McGill?'

He shook his head. 'No.' His voice was calm and sure. 'I've never seen this object before in my life.'

'Professor Bullock?' She eased into her chair, unsure of how to continue. 'That book, the one that Lloyd took care of for you? You didn't buy it, did you?'

He looked up and quickly back down again. 'Must have.' He turned the sword over in his hands and made a small parry with it, as if it were indeed a full-sized weapon. 'It was in my library, wasn't it?'

'Not necessarily.' Something he had said—something about the miniature sword being a 'pretty thing'—had triggered a memory. Someone else had spoken about liking pretty things. The same someone who had told her that the professor was being robbed. 'In fact, I'm wondering if there are other things in your house that you didn't buy. That, in fact, nobody bought.'

He looked up and although his confusion was clear on his face, Dulcie felt he was following her every word.

'Wait a moment, please, Professor Bullock.' Pushing back her chair, Dulcie went toward the door. Where had she seen that paperweight? The ornate blown-glass one that she had so admired in the Harvard Square boutique. That she and Polly had both been admiring. 'I'll be right back.'

She ran down the hall, the realization of it all making her head spin. Lloyd hadn't been stealing; Polly had. Only, not from Professor Bullock. Instead, she'd been shoplifting in the Square—and bringing her treasures to his house, her haven. The letter opener, the paperweight. And maybe even the troublesome book. The professor might be sinking into dementia, but he hadn't purchased a forged Elizabethan work. He had enough sense left to rely on Lloyd, and Lloyd was neither a thief nor a charlatan. But once that supposed rarity was in his house, in his library, Bullock must have assumed it belonged—and that in his decline he'd overlooked a treasure that might rebuild his reputation. No wonder he'd been frantic, and then horrified by the truth.

Dulcie closed her eyes for a moment to think all of this through. When the store clerk had been so rude, she'd felt bad for Polly, rather than herself. Polly, after all, was not much more than a shadow, a woman whose life had passed her by. Could that be why she stole, why she pocketed the 'pretty things' she could not afford? Was it because she felt so helpless in other aspects of life? Or did it all have to do with the professor's decline? Perhaps she was paying tribute to him. Bringing him treasures to brighten his declining years.

Whatever it was, it had to stop. And right now Dulcie believed the professor would grasp the problem. Maybe as a last act, he could get help for his troubled assistant. At the very least, Dulcie knew, she had to reveal Polly's secret. She'd get the paperweight and explain its history. Professor Bullock would understand.

Feeling the necessity of seizing the moment, Dulcie searched through the library. She could clearly envision the paperweight, the heavy globe with its swirl of blue. It had been opposite the door, hadn't it? But when it didn't show, she kept looking, climbing up on the dusty settee to check the highest level of the built-in bookcase. Finally, she was down to the last shelves, behind the opened door. Clearly, these were little used: the row of alumni reports on the bottom was coated with dust while the oversize books on top—Swinburne and the *Neo-Gothic Roots of Romanticism*—were positively fuzzy. It was no use, she realized. Polly must have a dozen hiding places in the big, old house, and Dulcie had no desire to root around further. In an ideal world, Professor Bullock would deal with his longtime assistant in private and, Dulcie hoped, with mercy.

As she pulled herself to her feet, however, she realized that the confrontation might come sooner than expected. The sound of a door opening and then shutting came from down the hall.

Polly had slammed out only minutes before. But perhaps she'd already come back, her fit of temper cooled off by the November wind. Dulcie hesitated. If Polly had gone into Professor Bullock's office, she really didn't want to intrude. Still, she herself had run off without explanation. The professor seemed to be alert and interested in what she was saying. And besides, once again, Dulcie had left her bag in the professor's office.

Then she heard the shouting.

SIXTY-TWO

'No, Professor!' The voice was male, gruff but pitched high with strain. 'I'd never!'

Dulcie ran back to Bullock's office to see the professor facing off against Roger Gosham. Although the bookbinder was younger and significantly more muscular, he was the one cowering as the elderly Bullock advanced on him. 'I wouldn't!'

'This man broke in.' Bullock spoke without turning, his eyes on the frightened bookbinder. 'I stepped into the kitchen for a moment and came back to find him here, looking through my shelves.'

Dulcie glanced at the bookbinder and back at Bullock. Could this be his dementia in action? 'This is Roger Gosham, sir. The book restorer.' She tried to hold her voice steady, but the bizarre nature of Bullock's anger scared her.

'I know that!' Bullock snapped at her. 'But he came into my office!'

'I'm sorry!' Gosham had his hands raised, as if in surrender, and started inching around the wall. 'Nobody answered and the door was open.'

Bullock glowered, and Dulcie chimed in. 'Polly sort of ran out, Professor Bullock. And, well, this is an old building...'

Either her tone or her explanation must have mollified the old academic. With a grunt, he dismissed Gosham and walked over to his desk. To Dulcie, it looked even messier than it had when she'd stepped out. Whatever the professor had been hoping to find in the kitchen, perhaps he'd sought it among his papers first. As he sat, something caught his eye and he reached under a journal.

'So, how may I be of service?' His voice was faintly mocking, and Gosham seemed taken aback. He stood there silent as the professor removed a tennis-ball-sized object from under an open *Times Literary Supplement* and wrapped his long fingers around it. 'Well?'

'I was looking for one of my projects.' Gosham stepped closer to Bullock's desk, but his eyes were on the shelves. 'A piece that wasn't finished. Shouldn't have left my studio, really.'

'Do you mean a particular volume?' Bullock passed the object from hand to hand. Even in the dim light, Dulcie caught a glimpse of blue. 'An Elizabethan romance, perhaps?'

Gosham winced. 'There was a mistake. I just need it back.'

For a moment, Dulcie felt for the man. He looked pained, as pale as his dark skin could get. But Bullock was a man enraged. 'You! You were trying to make a fool of me. You thought I was past it. That I wouldn't know.' The professor was practically spitting. 'It was you who sold me that…that…false book!' He shook the object in his hand, and Dulcie could see that it was indeed the glass paperweight. As Bullock shook his fist, it caught the light, the swirl inside sparking like a blue flame.

'No, he didn't.' Dulcie stared at the paperweight, pulling it all together in her mind. 'He wouldn't. He needs you too much for his name, his reputation.' She looked up at Gosham and saw surprised recognition in his eyes. 'It was Polly, wasn't it? She must have seen it and admired it. She stole it and brought it here.'

Both men turned to stare at her. 'That's what you had over her, wasn't it, Mr Gosham?' Dulcie stared at the wolflike man. 'But she figured out that it was a forgery—a counterfeit—and then she had a hold over you, as well.'

Gosham opened his mouth, but before he could say anything, Bullock jumped in with a roar. 'You used me!' He was shouting now, shaking the paperweight in the other man's face. 'My name. My reputation. Your shoddy, little workshop—'

Before Dulcie could do anything, Gosham was on him, his hands around the older man's neck. The heavy paperweight fell to the floor with a thud. 'Roger! Mr Gosham!' Dulcie pulled at the big man's arm, but he simply swatted her back and she tripped over the desk to sprawl on the carpet.

'For God's sake, man. It isn't worth it.' Bullock's voice was hoarse. He gasped, and Dulcie saw the small, sharp blade Gosham held. She immediately thought of the letter opener. Would that ornate toy really serve as a weapon? 'It's just a book,' Bullock gasped.

'No, it isn't.' Dulcie caught her breath and slowly, carefully stood up. 'It's his new business. It's how he's succeeding, despite the economy. Despite the rising rents. Despite…well, everything.'

Gosham glanced over at her, but kept the menacing blade up to the professor's throat. From this angle, Dulcie could see that it wasn't the pretty toy. No, what she saw was steel. One of the honed tools from Gosham's workbench. With such a slender blade, it wouldn't be hard to jimmy the lock, not on this old house. Is that what he had done? What he had tried to do at her office—or at Lloyd's? Is that what he'd been intending to do the day Cameron was killed?

'You were here that day.' She heard the rasp in her own voice. He didn't ask which day she meant. 'She'd taken it. I knew she had. Knew she had light fingers, the little minx.' His hand moved a bit as he talked and Dulcie saw the professor jerk back slightly. Gosham wrapped his big hand around the back of the professor's head and kept talking. 'I thought I could catch her. Maybe sneak in and get it. There would have been no harm done.'

'She went out shopping, I bet. Windowshopping to cheer herself up after you'd threatened her. But Cameron saw you.' She looked for a spark of recognition. 'Cameron knew, didn't he?' The pieces were falling into place. The eyes—those watching eyes. Emerald eyes. Hadn't Lucy said something about a watcher, about someone who sees? Yes, Mr Grey had been watching out for her—but Cameron had green eyes, too, and he'd been watching them all. Looking for any weakness, for any opportunity. Asking questions. 'Cameron saw you. Cameron figured out your secret, just like he knew Polly's.' A small gurgle from the professor. 'And Professor Bullock's, too. He was blackmailing them—and he figured he could add you to his list.'

Gosham acted fast. He threw the professor back toward the wall, toppling his chair. The older man hit the shelf with a bang and tumbled to the floor. With a cry, Dulcie darted toward him—stopping only when she saw that wicked blade in Gosham's hand.

'Oh, no, you don't. I've worked too hard for this. For all of this. And nobody—not you, not the professor here, not some smartass grad student who never had to work a day in his life— is going to take it away.'

From the floor behind the desk, Dulcie heard a groan. Gosham did, too. 'Good. A fall would look suspicious. But with all he smokes—' He was backing toward the door, one hand extended, holding the knife, the other fishing in his pocket. 'Nobody will look for one missing treasure when this is over.'

He stepped back further, lowering the knife as he reached to gather something from the floor. Dulcie ran over to the professor, who was moaning softly. She took his head in her lap and looked up at Gosham, who was still fussing with the shelves. Pulling out books and dropping them. 'The book is gone. It's not here. Lloyd...' She stopped. Did she really want to send this madman after her friend? But he was shaking his head.

'No, I searched his apartment. It's here. But not for long.' And with that, he slipped out the door and slammed it.

'What a jerk.' For a moment, Dulcie felt relief. 'Good riddance.' She lowered the professor to the floor. 'Hang on, Professor. I'll call 911.' She stood and looked over the desk. No, it wasn't just a computer that was missing here. In all his antediluvian splendor, the professor wouldn't have anything as annoying as a telephone on his desk. And, yes, that was her bag Gosham had taken, either by mistake or pure malice. Well, the kitchen would have a phone. With a quick glance at the professor, she reached for the door.

And found the brass knob wouldn't turn. It was locked. She started pulling at the door. Kicking it. Banging on it. But the thick old wood stood firm, muffling the sound of her fist pounding on its dark, stained panels. And that's when she smelled the smoke.

SIXTY-THREE

'DULCIE?' THE PROFESSOR'S voice was weak and he was still on the floor, though now propped up by the bookshelf behind him. But he cleared his throat again. 'Dulcie?' he said, and pointed. Dulcie followed his gaze and saw what he did: the fringe on the ancient carpet was smoldering, its faded pattern embellished by a glowing red edge that was slowly spreading.

'Oh, hell!' Gosham's madness momentarily forgotten, Dulcie ran over to the carpet's edge and stamped on it, grinding her heel into the thin edges. The immediate crisis consumed her as she looked around for water—a vase, an old coffee cup, anything— to pour on the glowing embers, just to make sure. And saw that two other small fires had been set, one at another corner of the carpet and the other in a pile of old journals and papers, which Gosham must have tented for maximum air flow. Grabbing her coat, Dulcie ran to smother that fire first; the paper had already started curling and open flames began to shoot up as she approached it. To add insult to injury, she recognized the pages piled on top. 'A new interpretation of *The Ravages of Umbria,*' she read the title aloud. This had been an early draft, presenting her thesis idea to her mentor. Briefly, Dulcie wondered if the placement of those pages, her name clearly visible in the top right, had been intentional. Then she spread her heavy coat over the flames, stomping on them. Lifting the coat, she saw a spark fly out, and so she quickly re-covered the area, pressing down on it with both hands, hoping to smother the flame.

'Dulcie?' The professor still hadn't moved, but his voice was louder now and she saw why. The other fire, in the fringe, had spread, bright sparks crawling like living things. From the edge of the carpet they had traveled to the frayed stuffing of a chair. Already, the stray threads were curling in the heat. Dulcie found herself staring, mesmerized, as one long fiber twisted back and forth, fighting off its invisible attacker before it blackened and fell to the floor. Another took its place, executing a slow and final dance before breaking off.

'Dulcie!' The professor's voice, as much as the loud crack of a spark, called her back to reality. She raced over to the chair and knocked it on its side, tearing at the upholstery and pulling the loose, smoldering stuffing out. A thin stream of smoke eked out from under her jacket, and she jumped over to stomp on that, as well.

'Professor? Do you have a fire extinguisher anywhere?' She turned from the smoldering chair, but he just stared at her. 'You know, like with foam or something?' She mimicked holding a canister and spraying, but his face was blank now—either the injury or his illness taking hold. 'What am I thinking?' She knew she was talking to herself now, but the sound of her voice was keeping her calm. The professor needed medical attention. And she needed to get out—either to the kitchen, to get a pot of water, or to call the fire department. The little fires seemed under control, but they made her nervous, tangible evidence of Gosham's ill will, not to mention his craziness.

But even though the small fires in the professor's office seemed to be more or less out, once Dulcie paused to catch her breath, she realized that the air was getting thicker, not clearer. In fact, her eyes were watering more now than they had been when she'd been pulling the stuffing out of the chair. Could there have been something toxic in the old upholstery?

'Enough.' Dulcie reached for the letter opener. She needed to open the door and get them both out of here. How hard could it be to pick a lock, anyway, especially one as old as this house? But when she knelt in front of the brass plate, Dulcie felt her head spinning. Maybe the activity had driven the smoke into her lungs. Maybe there had been something funky in that old chair. 'Hang in there, Professor,' she called out as she stared at the keyhole, wondering how to begin. 'This can't take too long.'

She inserted the letter opener and jiggled it a bit. The smoke was definitely getting thicker, and she coughed just as something seemed to give. Had she jimmied it? Would the door open? Choking, her eyes streaming, Dulcie reached for the knob. And jumped back, knocking the letter opener to the floor. The heavy brass was hot to the touch, hot enough almost to sear her skin. The pain did clear her head, however, and now she saw it: through the keyhole and under the door jam, smoke was pouring in.

'OK, then.' Wiping her eyes, Dulcie stood up. Speech made the coughing worse, but Dulcie felt the need to talk. To keep calm. To stay organized. 'Mr Grey,' she said aloud, not caring that the professor was right behind his desk. 'Now would be as good a time as any to help me out!'

Nothing. Nothing, that is, except for a low hiss and a crackle from outside the door. Dulcie took a step toward it, tempted to peek out the keyhole and survey the situation. But she stopped herself. Now was not the time to observe and reflect. Instead, she trotted toward the window. Unlatching the old-fashioned catch, she braced herself under the wooden rail and pushed. Nothing. She moved on to the narrow sill for better leverage, knocking over a full ashtray. The ashes floated down, flaky and cold, but Dulcie ignored them. Instead, pressing her palms up under the rail, she braced herself and shoved. Nothing. 'Professor, can you lend me a hand?'

He looked up at her, but she couldn't even tell if he recognized her anymore. The smoke was getting thicker, and Dulcie no longer bothered to wipe her streaming eyes and nose.

'OK, then. I'm sorry I've got to do this, Professor.' And with that, she grabbed the guest chair and hefted it up. 'Whoa!' Between the smoke and the unaccustomed weight of the big, wooden chair, Dulcie nearly toppled over backward, coughing. For a moment, she was tempted to give up. This was crazy. Someone had to have seen the smoke by now. Someone would come to save them. A fit of coughing bent her double, the dizziness driving her down to the floor.

Someone would come.

'Dulcinea Schwartz!' To her surprise, it was Lucy's voice, not Mr Grey's that she heard in her head. 'That's not how I raised you!' But it had the same effect. Coughing and gasping, Dulcie struggled to her feet and swung the chair. The window cracked and she jabbed at it with the chair legs, the weight nothing to her anymore. Finally, one of the small panes shattered and fell out, the fresh air flowing in.

'Oh, thank God.' She pressed her face to the open pane, gulping in air, until a loud snap broke her reverie. The rug was smoldering again; the room filling with smoke despite the missing pane. 'Enough of this.'

She turned and quickly searched for a suitable tool. The paperweight was heavy, and at that moment she didn't care about broken glass. Instead, she began smashing pane after pane, letting the glorious air in, finally smashing through two of the wooden crossbars to reach the iron grill.

'Oh, come on!' This was ridiculous. Oblivious to the broken glass, she started pushing on the grill, rattling it. Desperately looking for a way to push it out or up, she saw a catch. An old, blackened latch held tight by a padlock.

'Professor! Professor Bullock.' She turned toward the blank-eyed man. 'How do you open this? What should I do?' He blinked at her. 'Help! Help us!' she called through the broken window. But there was no way of telling whether her voice carried far enough beyond the dark ivy to be heard. 'Help!'

She screamed herself hoarse, settling back on to the sill. This was crazy, she realized. Although they had fresh air, they had no escape from the flames that even now were licking under the door, blackening the old wood and making the aged floorboards warp. They were on the first floor of a house in the middle of the city. The window was open, and yet they were trapped.

'It's not like we're stuck on a mountaintop somewhere,' she said. And suddenly her own words brought it back. Her dream—the nightmare of the fire. In that dream, she'd been trapped, too. But Mr Grey had spoken in it. What had he said?

The key is in the book.

'Mr Grey, I don't need metaphors right now!' She yelled, causing the professor to look up at her. 'Mr Grey?'

What if it hadn't been a metaphor? What if he'd been preparing her? She did, after all, need the key. 'Professor.' She knelt by the stricken man, holding him by his shoulders. 'Is there a key to the window grill? Is it hidden somewhere?' He looked at her. She resisted the urge to shake him. 'A key?'

His lips moved, but nothing came out. 'Professor?' Behind her, another loud crack and a new smell, acrid, as something else caught on fire. 'Please?'

'In…' His voice was faint, more breath than sound. Dulcie waited. 'The.' She nodded. 'Book.'

'Which book, Professor? Which book?' But he only stared at her. Another snap and Dulcie noticed that the smoke was changing color. Thick, black and oily, it was curling, gaining ground on the fresh air that came through the broken panes. Easing the professor back against the shelf, Dulcie stood and started pulling books from the shelves above them. One after another, she grabbed at spines, hardcover, paperback, and rifled through them. As the heat grew, she worked faster, tossing them to the ground. Half a bookshelf lay by her feet when she stopped herself. She had to think. There were too many books here not to. She had to have a plan. The key would likely be somewhere where the professor could get at it. Where it wouldn't be forgotten and lost. It had to be near his desk somewhere. It had to be…

Unlocking the Great Books.

Nearly tripping over the professor's extended legs, she grabbed her mentor's great work. There, taped inside the front cover, was a key. Choking again despite the opened window, she climbed up on the sill and, with shaking hands, slid the key into the lock. It fit. It turned. The lock unlatched and Dulcie tossed it to the ground, swinging the grate wide open. Oblivious to the shards of flying glass, she grabbed another book and smashed out the rest of the window and then, taking a huge gulp of air, she turned back to her aging mentor.

'Professor Bullock! Can you stand? We have to get out of here.' She crouched by his side and took his arm. It hung loose, like so much dead weight, and she swung it over her own shoulder, wrapping her other arm around his waist. 'Come on, Professor. Help me here.'

He was muttering something and she leaned in, his beard soft against her ear. But all she could hear was a calm, low voice from another time. 'You know what makes a heroine, Dulcie. Trust yourself.'

And with that, she dragged the inert man over to the window, climbed up on the sill, and pulled him toward her so that they both toppled through the ivy and into the damp, leaf-strewn yard beyond.

SIXTY-FOUR

'So GOSHAM KILLED CAMERON?' Suze had been the first to get to the hospital, although Dulcie had called Chris as soon as she was allowed to use a phone.

'Uh-huh. Think so.' Talking hurt from all the smoke that had belatedly settled into her throat and lungs. 'Blackmail.'

'He was blackmailing Gosham. Polly, too?' Dulcie nodded and gestured with her left hand. Her right was still sore from its many cuts and the stitches, despite the painkillers that made everything seem rather muddy. 'And the professor?' Suze sounded skeptical and Dulcie shrugged. To her it made sense: Cameron had focused his extensive research skills on his colleagues and, sure enough, plenty of them had something to hide. It would explain her late colleague's wealth. And, maybe, his death.

'So Gosham was stalking him?'

Dulcie shook her head. It was getting harder to focus, but this she was pretty sure about. 'He'd come looking. The book.' Her eyes started to close, but as they did, she saw Cameron's body once again. Cold, still, and unnaturally white. 'Polly had stolen it. But he'd seen her. He'd yelled and she ran. He figured she'd go back to Bullock's. But I think she was too upset.' The image began to fade, and with it her consciousness. 'She went out looking. Pretty things…' For a moment, she could see them. Gosham showing up at the house. Maybe he'd waited for Polly. Maybe he'd tried to jimmy the door right away, determined to get the incriminating fake away from his patron's house. Cameron must have surprised him there. Dulcie could picture them, the older man, a little frantic, bent over the lock with his blade. He would have figured he'd been hidden from the street, at least from a

casual observer, by the overgrown holly. But Cameron hadn't
been a casual observer. He'd made a career out of watching
people, out of manipulating their frailties. He'd misjudged the
bookbinder, however. Maybe he hadn't registered his level of
desperation, or else he hadn't seen the blade the older man held
in his hand. Had they argued, Cameron taunting Gosham with
the loss of everything he'd so painstakingly acquired? Or had
Gosham merely lashed out in surprise or fear or anger? No
wonder Gosham had seemed haunted to Dulcie. He'd killed a
man, and he still hadn't recovered the fraudulent book. Yes, he'd
been behind the break-ins and, now, the fire. Dulcie recalled one
of the police talking about 'attempted murder.' That was after
the fire trucks had shown up and she was being carried away,
an oxygen mask over her face. She'd been in no shape to ask
any questions then.

'Bullock?' She sat up with a start, the pain in her hands
slapping her back to full consciousness as she did.

'He's going to be fine.' It was Chris. He was sitting up close
by the bed and he was smiling broadly. 'I mean, he was konked
on the head and he's homeless. But other than that...' To Dulcie's surprise, it looked like he was blinking back tears. 'Thanks
to you, I gather. You're a heroine.'

She heard a throat clear. 'I'll leave you two to talk.' She saw
Suze stand up and started to protest. 'Don't worry, Dulcie,' her
roommate said. 'I'll take care of the kitten until you get out of
here.'

With that, Suze left and Dulcie collapsed back into the pillows. Suze had missed her point. Despite everything that had
happened, Dulcie hadn't forgotten Chris's last message. She
might be a heroine now, but that didn't mean he wanted to be
with her. She knew as well as anyone what 'we should talk'
meant.

She closed her eyes for a moment, trying to summon Mr Grey
for comfort. But all she felt were the clawlike pinpricks of her
cuts. 'Go on. Say it.' She didn't even open her eyes.

'What are you talking about?' Chris's voice was soft, but she wasn't fooled.

'Just say it.' The drugs must be wearing off. She felt a thousand little claws digging into her and she pulled herself up, the pain making her impatient. 'Look, Chris. I've had what you'd call a bad day. So why don't you just break up with me and leave? Then I can go back to sleep.'

'But…' He sputtered. 'I…'

For a moment, Dulcie felt a bit smug. He might be about to dump her, but at least she'd taken the wind out of his sails first. But when she looked up at his sweet face, all wide-eyed and bewildered, she was flooded with sadness—and confusion. Had she gotten it wrong?

'You're not…?' Her throat closed up even more. She couldn't even say it.

'No!' He reached for her but, seeing her bandaged arms, settled on patting her shoulder gingerly. 'Of course not. Whatever made you think that?'

'You're never around anymore.' She choked down a lump. 'You're always busy. You're always "working."' She heard the peevish accent she put on the last word. She couldn't help it. Finally, she broke down. 'And Thanksgiving is coming up and you haven't even asked me if I want to spend it with you or anything!' She started crying in earnest, the tears stinging what must be fresh cuts on her cheeks and lips. She reached awkwardly for a tissue from the bedside box, but her bandaged hands couldn't quite manage.

'Here.' Chris pulled a bunch out and held them up to her nose. 'Blow.' She did, and he then wiped her face with a fresh one. He was smiling now, his broad grin splitting his thin face despite a few stray tears of his own.

'Oh, Dulcie, I didn't know.' She looked up at him in wonder. 'I was so intent on keeping everything a secret, I had no idea you'd misinterpret.' He cradled her cheek in one hand. It hurt, a little, but at that moment, she didn't care.

'It was supposed to be a surprise. In fact, I'm amazed that

Lucy didn't spoil it already.' She shook her head, not under
standing. 'I've bought us plane tickets. We're going to you
mom's for the holiday. I figured you're going to meet my family
over the semester break and I wanted to meet Lucy and see
where you grew up. Besides, she makes such a big deal about
the harvest and I knew we'd missed Samhain, so I thought this
would be the next best thing. She's been calling me constantly
to ask me about food for some kind of feast.'

'My mom's really into her squashes,' she said softly. 'No,
really. They're like the one thing she can grow and so she's
really proud of them.'

'Well, she can be proud of her daughter, too.' He bent to kiss
her, and it didn't hurt at all.

It was afternoon the next day before the doctors let her go. And
while it was awkward to be wheeled to the hospital entrance,
the crew assembled outside greeted her with such a round of
applause that Dulcie blushed with happiness.

'The avenging angel of the English Department!' Lloyd came
up as Chris helped her out of the chair. She seemed to have done
something to her ankle, but together they got her to the car as
Ariano jumped out from behind the driver's seat to open the
door.

'Oh, come on. I'm not that bad off,' she protested. And looked
up to see Raleigh coming up the drive from the parking lot.
'Um, I don't think we're all going to fit.'

'Not to worry.' Lloyd smiled. 'Raleigh's got her car. Suze
said we could all come over. That is, if you're up for it?'

'You kidding? I could use a party.'

In truth, Dulcie still felt exhausted and dozed against Chris's
shoulder as Ariano drove them home. Suze, in the front seat,
was going on about the kitten. 'I guess she really missed you.
She was bouncing off the walls. Clawing at the windows. At one
point, she even threw herself against the door of your room. I
thought she was going to injure herself!'

'I wonder if she knew…' Dulcie had a hint of an idea, but it faded. And then they were home.

'Surprise!' Trista and Jerry were waiting in the living room, and someone had ordered what looked like the entire Lala's menu.

'I don't know if I'm up for any more surprises at this point.' She looked at Chris and smiled. 'But thank you.' Jerry had come back from the kitchen with a bottle of something that bubbled, and after the toasts, the serious eating commenced.

Lloyd had grabbed the seat next to her, and in a lull in the feasting, Dulcie nudged him. 'So, you and Raleigh?' She glanced over at the pretty undergrad.

Lloyd blushed and nodded. 'She was taking time off when we met. And, well, she graduates in just a few months.'

'Assuming she finishes her thesis.' Dulcie smiled, and he recognized her teasing for what it was. In the overall scheme of things, Lloyd's transgression seemed fairly minor.

'So that was the famous fake she dropped off, right?' Dulcie asked Lloyd once his color had returned to normal.

Lloyd nodded. 'I'd already arranged to send it to Browning's for appraisal. But, um, I'd left it at her place.' His blush returned. 'But when I told all that to the cops, they didn't even seem interested. I guess the professor never followed through with the charges. He was just angry, but he knew he had as much to lose as I did. More.' He took another bite of felafel. 'I did pass through the Square this morning. Gosham's is closed up. I don't know if they've arrested him or he's fled, but I don't think Professor Bullock will be buying any more books there, real or counterfeit.'

'Well, that's a good thing.' Dulcie paused, the stray edge of a thought sticking in her mind. 'Hey, Lloyd? What was the forged book, anyway? I mean, what was it called?'

Lloyd snorted, a dismissive sound. 'That's just it, Dulcie. If Bullock had been in his right mind, he'd have known it was totally wrong.'

'Why?' Dulcie held her breath, a feeling like cat's claws pricking at the back of her neck.

'The Purloin'd Sword, or The Jewel of the Night.'

Dulcie burst out laughing, so hard that Lloyd looked nervous. 'No, no.' She waved off his concern. 'It's not you or even the professor…' Catching her breath, she explained the dream, the recurring image—and the small, stolen trinket that had finally clued her in.

'It should have been obvious,' said Lloyd, finally. 'And then, maybe…'

'Yeah.' Dulcie, quiet at last, nodded. They both paused a moment, thinking of the odd relationship: the declining professor and the artisan-tradesman who must have hated his dependent position.

'So, what's going to happen to Bullock?' Dulcie's voice was soft. This felt private, between the two of them.

Lloyd shook his head. 'I know they're keeping him in the hospital, at least for a few more days. They said it was because of his more intensive injuries, but I think they're doing other tests, too. Neurological tests.' He glanced over at Trista and Dulcie shook her head. She hadn't had time to tell anyone else about the professor's dementia.

'It's my guess that the professor will take some kind of personal leave,' Lloyd continued. 'I mean, his house was just destroyed by a fire. And then, maybe he'll just quietly retire. Which I guess leaves us both without thesis advisers.' He made a face.

'At least you have a thesis.' Dulcie shifted in her seat. She was going to need more pain pills soon, champagne or not.

'Yeah, you'd said something about that earlier, but I never followed up. What did you mean?'

Promising herself a Percocet and another drink as soon as she got through it, Dulcie told him the whole tiring tale. How she'd been tracking down unusual phrases from *The Ravages of Umbria,* hoping to get a clue to the author's identity. 'I guess if I'd been more alert, I'd have noticed something more about the emerald.' She thought of the phrase from the book—and from her dream. Maybe she should have put it together with the letter opener; maybe she could have uncovered the truth about Polly's kleptomania earlier and saved them all some trouble. 'But the crushing blow was when I found that essay.' She described that day in the library. The way her stomach had sank as she read the passage and realized what it meant. 'I mean, Lloyd, that's impossible. That essay was from forty years later. It could only mean one thing.' She swallowed hard, felafel dry in her throat. '*The Ravages of Umbria* must really be a later book. A pastiche. Another fake.'

She couldn't understand why Lloyd was laughing. 'Oh, Dulcie! Is that what you were worried about? And you were trying to keep it from Bullock while you sorted it out?' He was actually wiping tears from his eyes. 'I wish you'd told me earlier. Dulcie, this is what I do. Eighteenth-century non-fiction. Biographies. Critical essays. I could have told you that Gunning isn't a reliable source for dates! Bullock could've told you, too, if he still had it together. Hugely popular up through the late Victorian period, but his books are compendiums, collections of essays that have been previously published. The Gunnings were talented amateurs, collecting old journals and chapbooks that would otherwise have been lost. That's why we still use them. But the sourcing? The dates for the original material itself? I'm sorry, Dulcie. I thought you knew.'

He paused. 'Actually, you may have made an important find. I don't know if anyone has ever put those two together. I think you're on your way to prove that the author of *The Ravages* was indeed someone who thought about these issues, one of those early feminist essayists. You might not have her name, but you have found her signature, and that... Well, Dulcie Schwartz, that might be the key to the text!'

BY THE TIME EVERYONE LEFT, Dulcie was fading. Although her mood couldn't have been higher, Chris kept looking at her bandages and so when he'd urged her to take another pain pill, she agreed. 'You just want to keep me from working,' she said drowsily as he helped her upstairs. 'But I'm on to something with *The Ravages,* Chris. I really am.'

'I believe you, sweetie.' He tucked her in and kissed her gently. 'But I think it will wait. And I have one more overnight shift. Ken covered for me last night, so I owe him.'

'G'night.' Her eyes were closing as he left, but she heard the soft thud as the kitten jumped up on her bed. 'Kitten!' She reached out to feel the downy soft fur and was rewarded by a heavy purr. 'I hear you were with me, at least in spirit.' A damp nose touched her cheek. 'Mr Grey was, too. Did you know him?' The kitten kneaded the pillow by her head, and Dulcie imagined the two felines meeting. 'Mr Grey, this is Kitten. No, that won't do.'

She forced her eyes open and looked over at the little cat. Green eyes. Black and white fur. Whiskers white and wider even than her huge ears. She was going to be a big cat. But right now, she was still a kitten. A little jewel...

'Esmeralda,' she said. It was Spanish, not Italian, but it had a ring to it. 'That sounds about right. Esmeralda the cat. I can call you Esmé.' The kitten blinked. 'Does that sound OK to you, Esmé?'

'Finally!' The voice, young and strong, seemed to come from nowhere and Dulcie jerked back, startling the cat, who sat up and stared, green eyes wide. 'But none of this nickname stuff. It's Esmeralda, please. Principessa Esmeralda. I am royalty, you know.' And with that she grabbed Dulcie's hand for a tussle.

'Now, now, little one. Settle down.' The voice was deep and gentle, this time. The voice of Mr Grey. 'It's been a big day for everyone, and it's time to sleep. We've a lot to learn, all of us, but I believe we're making progress.'

* * * * *

W9-BZB-748

BY RITA LAKIN

Getting Old Can Kill You

Getting Old Is Très Dangereux

Getting Old Is a Disaster

Getting Old Is To Die For

Getting Old Is Criminal

Getting Old Is the Best Revenge

Getting Old Is Murder

Getting Old
Can Kill You

A MYSTERY

Rita Lakin

DELL

NEW YORK

A Dell Mass Market Original

Published in the United States by Dell Books, an imprint of The Random House Publishing Group, a division of Random House, Inc., New York.

DELL is a registered trademark of Random House, Inc., and the colophon is a trademark of Random House, Inc.

ISBN 978-0-440-24560-5

Cover design: Marietta Anastassatos
Cover illustration: Hiro Kimura

Printed in the United States of America

www.bantamdell.com

9 8 7 6 5 4 3 2 1

Dell mass market edition: July 2011

This book is dedicated to Judy.
My sister. My friend.

"What is the secret of your life?" asked Mrs. Browning. . . . "Tell me, that I may make mine beautiful, too."

He replied: "I had a friend."

—JAMES RUSSELL LOWELL

Introduction to Our Characters

GLADDY AND HER GLADIATORS

Gladys (Gladdy) Gold, 75 Our heroine and her funny, adorable, sometimes impossible partners:

Evelyn (Evvie) Markowitz, 73 Gladdy's sister. Logical, a regular Sherlock Holmes. Now remarried to Joe

Ida Franz, 71 Stubborn, mean, great for an in-your-face confrontation

Bella Fox, 83 The "shadow." She's so forgettable, she's perfect for surveillance but smarter than you think

Sophie Meyerbeer, 80 Master of disguises, she lives for color coordination

YENTAS, KIBITZERS, SUFFERERS: THE INHABITANTS OF PHASE TWO

Hy Binder, 88 A man of a thousand jokes, all of them tasteless

Lola Binder, 78 His wife, who hasn't a thought in her head that he hasn't put there

Enya Slovak, 84 Survivor of "the camps" but never survived

Tessie Spankowitz, 56 Chubby, newly married to Sol

Millie Weiss, 85 Suffering with Alzheimer's

Irving Weiss, 86 Suffering because she's suffering

Mary Mueller, 60 Neighbor whose husband left her; nurse

Joe Markowitz, 75 Evvie's ex-husband, now remarried to her

ODDBALLS AND FRUITCAKES

Sol Spankowitz, 79 Now married to Tessie

THE COP AND THE COP'S POP

Morgan (Morrie) Langford, 35 Tall, lanky, sweet, and
  smart
Jack Langford, 75 Handsome and romantic, Gladdy's
  new husband

OTHER TENANTS

Arlene Simon, 80
Merrill Grant, 77

BEST FRIENDS

Lauderdale Lakes, 1955

Arlene Steiner feels giddy as she enters the foyer of her tiny third-floor apartment and takes a deep breath. It's Wednesday, 11 A.M., and here she is getting off early on a weekday—for the first time!

Thank you, Woolworth's, for having a busted water pipe and giving all us employees the rest of the day off. *The apartment is so wonderfully quiet, and it's nice to be home all by herself. Feeling daring, she tosses her purse down onto the green Formica and chrome kitchen table. She never does this when her husband's at home. Edward's motto is: A place for everything and everything in its place. Not that she minds him being so opinionated about everything. He's right. They have a small space and clutter would only make it smaller. For a moment she reflects fondly on growing up, how her room was always a mess, but her mom never seemed to mind. Besides, she never had a problem finding her things when she needed them.*

She opens her Kelvinator fridge and pours herself a glass of milk. What shall she do with all these extra hours? Well, there's always the laundry. But that's a Saturday job. It can wait. She doesn't want to waste this gift of free time.

She could do something special for her darling Edward.

She smiles at the thought, remembering how he insisted on their first date that she call him Edward. Not Eddie, not Ed, not even Ned. How did she ever land such a drop-dead-handsome guy? Six feet tall, wavy brown hair, sexy blue bedroom eyes, a physique like an athlete. He could have been a movie star.

If Mamma were only alive, she thinks. It was every Jewish mother's dream. Her daughter married a doctor—a plastic surgeon, even. Though Arlene never even finished high school, it didn't matter. Even if once in a while Ed—she corrects herself—Edward, makes her feel, well, not so smart as he is.

Still sipping her milk, she walks into the living room and glances at herself in the wide gilt mirror hanging over the hi-fi cabinet that Edward picked out. She examines herself critically. Five feet small, petite, fashionably slim. Long blond hair in a page-

boy style. Light blue eyes. She wears very high heels to seem taller. Pretty is as pretty does, Mamma used to tell her.

She switches on the hi-fi and places the needle into the groove of her favorite record. Her body sways to Frank Sinatra singing "Young at Heart." She hugs herself and dances, singing along. "Fairy tales can come true. It can happen to you . . ." The song and the way Sinatra sings it bring her to tears; she doesn't know why, but it makes her feel restless and lonely.

She's never been good at making friends, except for Joyce, her very best and only friend since childhood, living on the second floor in the apartment directly below theirs. Joyce was such a good friend that she'd moved in right after the wedding, just to be near Arlene. Arlene doesn't know what she'd do without Joyce, who is more like a sister than just a friend.

Joyce is Arlene's opposite—dark, very curly hair; velvety brown eyes. Kind of a cuddly body. It was fun when they used to go out together. Guys would be attracted to either "the skinny blonde" or "the buxom brunette." Arlene was sure Joyce would be the one to get married first, but Arlene turned out to be the lucky one.

Arlene suddenly gets a great idea. She'll call Joyce at work and maybe they can have lunch together. They've never been able to do that. The telephone company where Joyce works is too far away from Woolworth's—especially since she is only allowed a half hour off. What a treat this could be! But then she remembers that Joyce has a dentist's appointment at lunchtime today. Oh, well.

Arlene pouts for a moment. It hasn't been easy for the friends to get together. Early on she invited Arlene up for dinners but Edward has never made her feel comfortable and Joyce says she won't go places where she isn't welcome. Maybe when Joyce gets married, it will be different. They'll be two couples, then, and Edward would have another man to talk to while the women gabbed. Won't that be fun?

She sits down on the couch and picks up the book that she left on the kidney-shaped coffee table—Marjorie Morningstar, a new bestseller. She can really identify with the story of a young Jewish girl who falls in love with a handsome, talented guy. She settles back against the cushions and tries to read, but once she realizes she's read the same two lines over again, she gives up, unable to concentrate.

What to do? What to do? How about making Edward's favorite dessert tonight? A romantic evening. That's what they need. He's been distracted recently—working late hours. Candles and wine and his favorite key lime pie after a hearty dinner, that's the ticket. Their fifth anniversary is coming up, and Edward promised they could have a belated honeymoon since he couldn't get away while he was in med school. Now that he has his own practice, maybe he can squeeze it in. Arlene has always wanted to go to Niagara Falls. But he said maybe twice. Not a good sign.

Tonight she's determined to change his mind. She'll wear the nightgown she bought and hid for a special occasion. She giggles. They better travel soon. Because her next big wish is for a baby. Twenty-five years old is getting kind of late for a baby, and once that happens, no more trips, that's for sure.

She's getting excited. Lots to do to get ready.

In the kitchen she happily checks her supplies. She has enough limes. And plenty of graham crackers to make the pie crust. She's got the condensed milk and the eggs. Oh, no, she's out of vanilla. Not a problem. She knows Joyce will have some.

But wait. She'd better make sure Edward won't be late tonight and spoil all her dinner plans. He's made her promise never to interrupt him at his office or at the hospital, but surely he won't mind when she just needs to ask him this one little thing. It will only take a minute. His nurse can get the answer for her if he's busy.

She dials his office and the answering service picks up. Darn it, it must be his lunch break. She asks the operator what time he'll be back. The operator primly informs her that Dr. Steiner isn't in today. His office is closed on Wednesdays.

It takes Arlene a few moments to realize she is still clutching the phone after the operator has disconnected. She puts it down. How could that be?

Suddenly a series of photos come to mind. An article—was it in Life *magazine? Doctors playing golf on Wednesdays. Edward plays golf, that must be it. But she's certain he plays only on Sundays. He always goes to work on Wednesday. There must be a logical explanation.*

Something's not right.

Don't think about it now. Discuss it tonight. Plan the dinner. Keep busy.

She ties on the apron that she bought at an Avon house party a few weeks earlier. Suddenly she's a whirlwind of activity. Pulls out the pots she needs. Lays out the ingredients, all in a row. Removes the steak from the freezer to defrost. Takes the peeler out for the potatoes.

Suddenly she remembers the vanilla. She grabs her set of keys off the foyer shelf and heads out the door. Useful that she and Joyce have keys to each other's apartments in case of an emergency.

Arlene unlocks Joyce's door and walks into a bad movie. A trail of garments lies on the floor. Red satin high-heel shoes seem to lead the way through the foyer. Followed by silk stockings. A garter belt points toward the living room, where she finds a matching red satin dress with a low-cut bodice casually thrown across an armchair. Dangling garnet earrings tossed on a side table right outside the bedroom door.

For a brief hopeful moment Arlene thinks that perhaps she's in the wrong apartment. Joyce doesn't own sexy stuff like that. Joyce is very neat. She hangs up her clothes.

She hears sounds from the bedroom. She giggles, quickly putting a hand to her mouth to stifle the sound. Maybe Joyce brought her dentist home with her. Wouldn't that be nice?

But as Arlene turns to leave she recognizes her husband's brown woven Thom McAn Oxford shoes off to one side of the living room. And there are his argyle socks. And his Fruit of the Loom boxer shorts.

"Is somebody there?" Joyce's voice calls out.

For one hysterical second, Arlene is tempted to shout out the comedy line "Nobody here but us chickens," but it sticks in her throat.

Then her husband's voice says, "You're imagining things," and he lets out a seductive chuckle that his wife has never heard before.

"I am not. I could swear I heard a key in the lock."

Run, Arlene, run. But she's rooted to the spot.

Joyce appears in the living room doorway. And sees Arlene. "Oh, shit! What the hell are you doing here?"

Time slows down. Arlene takes in the fact that her friend is naked. She hasn't seen her that way since high school gym class. When did her body get so perfect? Joyce's been to the beauty parlor and hennaed her hair. And she smells heavily of Shalimar.

Arlene manages to squeeze out the now-foolish words. "I came to borrow vanilla."

Edward appears wearing a T-shirt and a towel wrapped around his waist. There are lipstick stains on his sleeve.

Why is she bothering with these details? Isn't her life ending right at this time and in this place? Can't she see that?

Edward, frozen, can only reiterate, "Oh, shit!"

Joyce turns on Edward. "I warned you to break it to her. This wouldn't be happening."

"I told you I'd tell her in my own way and my own time."

"Yeah, well, your time just ran out."

"What is she doing here?"

"Damned if I know. She says she came to borrow vanilla."

They are behaving as if Arlene isn't in the room.

Finally she finds her voice and confronts Edward. It's an edgy voice. She points at Edward's shoes and socks. "A place for everything. Everything in its place?"

He looks at her as if she's gone mad. Maybe she has.

Her voice grows stronger. "You think I liked all those years I spent in Woolworth's Ladies Foundations Department so I could send you through medical school?"

She turns to Joyce. "And you, my best friend! We know each other from kindergarten!"

Joyce shrugs. "Hey, hon, I always did like the guys who liked you."

With that Arlene lurches at Joyce and grabs at her hair. "I'm gonna tear every phony red hair out of your head! You do this behind my back? Since when did my close friend and my husband get so cozy? I thought you hated each other!"

Joyce howls, trying to pry her off. "Stop it!"

Edward stands watching in hideous fascination.

Arlene pulls Joyce's hair harder. "Suddenly you're a floozy wearing low-cut dresses with your boobies hanging out? Where is your loyalty?"

Joyce shouts at her lover, "Ed! Do something!"

Arlene is astonished. Ed? She gets to call him Ed? It is indeed a day of wonders.

Ed shrugs, helpless.

"Crazy—you're crazy!" Joyce screams. "Why are you only picking on me?"

Arlene grins at her but it's not a pretty sight. "I intend to curse him every day of his miserable life. Not only every day, but especially Wednesdays when doctors get to play golf!"

Edward winces.

"Ouch!" Joyce screeches as Arlene tears the necklace from around her neck. "My Chai! Give me back my lucky Chai."

"You mean the present I bought you for your eighteenth birthday?" Arlene shrieks. "Lucky eighteen. Well, your luck just ran out!"

Joyce wrenches away, falling backward into a chair, arms and legs splayed.

Arlene knows how superstitious her friend is. She twirls the necklace in front of Joyce's face as she taunts, "You're doomed. Jewish mysticism can't help you now. You'll never have a happy day as long as you live. When you die, you'll die a horrible death!" She throws the necklace back at her.

For a moment they are a silent tableau: she and Joyce gasping for breath, Edward staring at his wife in horror.

He laughs nervously. "Darling," he croons to Arlene, "you're young yet. You have your whole life ahead of you. You'll find someone else. I never meant to hurt you."

Joyce lifts her arms as if in supplication. "We just fell in love. It happens."

Arlene turns and walks into the kitchen. "Where's the vanilla? Where's the damn vanilla?" She pulls the butcher knife out of its wooden holder on the counter, shouting, "I should kill you both now!"

They follow her carefully into the kitchen and stare at her brandishing the knife.

"No, better yet, maybe I'll cut your faces up. Hey, Ed, I know a good plastic surgeon who might be able to put your nasty scheming faces back together!"

They gape at her, terrified.

With that Arlene drops the knife and flees past them out the front door.

She races upstairs. Her fingers shake as she opens her door. She barely makes it inside before she collapses in tears, sobbing onto the foyer floor.

Now she'll never get to Niagara Falls!

1

THE HONEYMOONERS

"Fantastic," Joe says to his new bride. "What a great idea. You gals choosing Niagara Falls."

"Again," my sister, Evvie, says cheerfully. She reaches out to touch Joe's arm, ignoring the clinging wetness of his souvenir poncho. "What about the fact that you and I came here for our first honeymoon?"

Standing next to Evvie and Joe, my brand-new husband, Jack, and I are huddled together on the deck of the *Maid of the Mist,* the blue tour boat that takes visitors alongside the massive, amazing waterfalls located on the border between New York and Canada—as close as it's possible to get. The dark blue ponchos that came with the admission price barely keep us from getting drenched by the spray. But that's supposed to be part of the fun.

My sister and I had an unforgettable double wedding and now we are sharing a honeymoon. And what a wedding it was. Not only did we walk down the aisle but so did a gorgeous French lady who still had a crush on Jack, albeit only because she was being chased by a killer who was determined to murder her. I'm sure our neighbors are still talking about it back home in our condo community, Lanai Gardens.

What a long way we've come. Joe and Evvie's rocky marriage ended in divorce—then half a century later Joe shows up again, needing, wanting to be with Evvie in the last days of his life.

And what about me? Widowed young and never imagining another man could take my first husband's place—and yet, here I am. Seventy-five and starting out again, my wonderful Jack at my side. I feel so lucky.

Joe leans to kiss Evvie's wet face. "I'm having a better time this trip."

Evvie can't resist a little dig. "And whose fault was that? Did it have to take you fifty years to grow up?"

Joe laughs. "All right, I'm a slow learner."

Jack says, "I have a confession. Fay and I had our honeymoon here, too."

I glance at my darling, surprised. "Why didn't you say so? We could have gone somewhere else."

Jack shakes his head. "I didn't want to spoil it.

You were excited about coming here. And I'm sure my late wife would approve."

"My first honeymoon was at a small hotel in the Catskills," I say. "But I've always wanted to see this remarkable place. Thank you for allowing me this pleasure."

"The pleasure is all mine," Jack says, smiling lovingly at me.

I look around at the couples kissing and hugging. I snuggle closer to my man.

Evvie and I exchange meaningful glances. Since we've been able to read each other's minds all our lives, I'm aware of what she's thinking. He's in remission, but we don't know how long Joe has before the cancer kicks back in. She wants to make every precious moment count.

Evvie remarks, "Isn't Niagara Falls considered kind of corny these days? I'm surprised newlyweds still come here."

I remind her how hard it was to get reservations. "The New York side of the falls is just as busy as the Canadian side. It's still a perfect place for romance."

Joe reads from the brochure. "Where we are it's 170 feet deep. The water travels down to the Niagara River to Lake Ontario, then to the St. Lawrence Seaway, and lets out into the Atlantic."

Evvie shivers. "Very interesting, but anyone up for going inside the cabin for a while? I'm soaked."

"I think that's the idea," Joe says, leering at her. "You get wet, go back to the hotel or motel, take a hot shower, have some champagne, and end up happily in the sack."

"Nothing wrong with that plan," Jack says.

We hurry inside the boat's cabin. We're lucky to find seats together. Evvie digs into her tote and brings out our thermoses of hot chocolate and packages of chocolate chip cookies. As we munch, she says, "Let's play."

Our guys look puzzled, so Evvie explains it to Joe and Jack. "It's our travel game. We look at people and try to guess who and what they are."

Practical Jack asks, "But how will we know whether we're right or wrong?"

"We won't," I answer him. "It doesn't matter."

We hunker down, moving closer to one another, keeping our voices low.

Joe comments, "We won't know much from their clothes, since everyone's hair and bodies are covered by the ponchos."

Evvie indicates the couples all around us. "Well, we know one thing for sure. Most everyone in here has to be a newlywed."

"Including the couple with the crying baby?" Joe asks.

The wife has the baby strapped to her chest over her rain gear, and the baby is draped in a second poncho. The wife and hubby are holding hands. They are quite young. Evvie makes a guess. "Teenagers. Shotgun wedding. Baby gets to go along."

Jack adds, "Family wouldn't baby-sit. Won't forgive their being careless about sex."

Evvie continues the thread, grinning. "Baby has colic. They won't get much sleep tonight. For the wrong reason."

I lean against Jack. I'm already so wet, his poncho can't make it any worse. "Now you guys are getting the idea."

Joe elbows Evvie. "Glance over across from us. Count four couples down to the left. Looks like they could be in their thirties."

She asks, "What about them?"

He answers, "They're sound asleep. What does that tell us?"

She smiles knowingly. "Easy. No sleep for them, either. For all the right reasons."

"As opposed to the guy and gal over there on the other side." I indicate as unobtrusively as I can a couple directly across from us. They are not sitting close and their backs are toward each other. "Too much space between them."

Joe suggests, "Maybe they're too wet."

Jack shakes his head. "No, look at their faces. He's scowling and she's staring down at her hands, tightly clenched."

I jump in. "And her lips, she's biting down on them. Her eyes are hooded."

Evvie, part optimist, part realist, says, "They'll make up later. After they decide who gets to be the boss in the family."

We get a chuckle out of that.

I say abruptly, "Oh, boy . . . more trouble ahead.

Look to your right. At the very far end seat near the exit door. Tell me what you see."

Evvie asks, "You mean the young woman holding a folded yellow umbrella?"

"Yes, that's the one."

Joe is puzzled. "What about her? She looks like everyone else. Soggy."

I suggest, "Yes, but what makes her different?"

Jack leans forward to get a better view. "She's alone."

Joe quickly says, "So?"

Evvie is getting it. "Yes, she's not sitting with anyone."

Jack continues, "Everyone around us is obviously a couple, except for the few families with children. Glance at her body language. She's leaning over, her head is down."

I comment, "My guess is she arrived here with her new husband, but he's not with her. Something's gone very wrong."

Joe sits at the edge of his seat to get a better look.

With sadness, I add, "I doubt anybody would take this trip alone."

Jack says, "She's been deserted."

Joe is confused. "Then why is she on the boat? Why isn't she at her motel on shore? Why hasn't she gone home?"

Jack says thoughtfully, "Maybe he didn't show up at the dock at the last minute and either for spite or in her unhappy confusion, she just got on."

Evvie points in her direction discreetly. "Now

she's rocking her body back and forth. As if she's keening."

I say, "She's crying into her collar so it won't be noticed. Poor woman."

Evvie sighs. "I feel so sorry for her, surrounded by happy lovers."

I add, "This trip must seem endless for her. How much longer until we dock?"

Jack looks at his watch. "Maybe ten minutes more."

We continue to stare at her, feeling her pain.

Evvie says, "I wish we could say something comforting to her. Like it isn't the end of the world."

Joe smiles at her lovingly. "I don't think she'll hear any of the platitudes. Too soon. I hope she'll be heading back to her family."

Excitedly, I cry out, "Something's changed."

Indeed the expression on her face is different.

Jack gets it. "She's stopped crying."

I add, "She seems almost resigned. Maybe that's a good sign. She's snapping out of it."

"No." Jack sounds alarmed. "Pay attention to the lift of her chin. She's getting angry."

"Who could blame her?" Evvie says.

"She's getting up," I say nervously. "She's looking toward the door to the deck."

Joe comments, "Maybe she needs some air."

Jack jumps up, and I can tell it's the instincts from his years as a cop kicking in. "She's moving too fast. She's doesn't want air."

They watch as the woman pushes open the heavy door and rushes out.

I leap up, too. "She's left her purse on the seat. Not a good sign!"

Jack and I race for the door as it slams shut. I grab her purse on my way out. Jack is ahead of me.

He yells, "She's going to jump!"

He fights the wind to get the door open and I'm right behind him.

The deck is still crowded. Wall-to-wall people.

I look around. "Where is she?" I shout to Jack over the roar of the falls. "How can she disappear that fast?"

"She couldn't have gone far." I see him plow through the nearest group.

Oh, God. I hope she hasn't made it to the railing. The railing is low, I remember with a shudder.

"Over here!" Jack yells. He raises his hand above the crowd so I can locate him. I can also tell by the muttering and movement of people being pushed out of his way.

By the time I reach Jack, he's found her.

It's as if everything seems to move in slow motion. The bereft woman has reached the railing.

The group nearest to her has no idea of what's happening. Jack moves slowly but carefully toward the young woman. I go to her other side. I can see her face. She seems as if she's in a trance.

Jack speaks very quietly to her. "Miss, you forgot your purse."

I hold it out to her. She reacts in confusion. We've

redirected her movements. She reaches for her purse. I quietly hand it to her.

We both lean into her and gently take each of her arms.

"You don't want to do this," Jack whispers. She looks into Jack's kind eyes. Sobbing, she buries her head in his chest. I hug her from the back.

Through her cries, almost hiccuping, she spills out her pain. "He said our marriage was a mistake. He's going home to annul it."

The people nearest us finally realize what's happening. They reach out to hug her also. Many of the women are near tears. The group parts, giving us a path, as we lead the distraught lady away from disaster.

Hours later, we make our way down into the hotel dining room. Much to our surprise, word has already gone around, and tourists and townspeople come by to congratulate us for saving the woman. Jack and I are embarrassed at the attention. Joe and Evvie beam.

Evvie and Joe toast us. "Here's to the hero and the heroine."

Joe says, "Well done. You two make a good team."

Evvie agrees. "Jack!" As she nods her head, I see her face light up, wide and shining. "You must join our detective agency! I nominate you right now."

I could kiss Evvie. What a great idea.

But Jack demurs. "I thought you gals were strictly a female business. Besides I don't know of any husband-and-wife PIs."

"You obviously don't read much crime fiction," Evvie says. "What about Nick and Nora Charles? Mr. and Mrs. North? Lord Peter Wimsey and Harriet Vane? Tommy and Tuppence? I could go on and on."

I agree. "Honey, your years as a cop would be a great asset."

Joe says, "Yeah, sure, but what'll Ida, Bella, and Sophie feel about a man poking his nose in?"

Evvie and I exchange knowing glances. I can just see their faces. The surprise will turn to dismay. They're going to hate it. They'll absolutely despise it!

2

MEANWHILE BACK AT THE CONDOS

"Come on, get the lead out." Ida snaps her fingers at her two malingering friends. "We'll be late to mah-jongg."

Irritated, she shakes her head, her coiled gray knot immovable as usual. Her toothpick-thin body's posture is ramrod, as if it is her way of holding herself together.

She stares at the two women who have become family in lieu of her real one so far away, both literally and emotionally. So utterly different. They copy each other in the clothes they wear—today, jumpsuits: Sophie in flamboyant red and Bella, as usual, in pale colors, currently lavender.

If the two of them had their druthers, they'd sit on a bench and not move all day. "We're going to be late. I don't know why I bother waiting for you."

Bella pleads, "But I need a short rest. And we're only two minutes away."

Ida sighs as they slowly get up and start inching along their path to the recreation room a bit faster.

Sophie asks, "Who put you in charge anyway?"

"Yeah," mimics Bella. "Anyway."

Ida mutters under her breath, "You Bobbsey twins are a pain in the neck."

"I heard that," Sophie says.

"When are the newlyweds coming back?" Bella asks.

Ida places her hands on her hips in annoyance. "I told you yesterday, the day after tomorrow."

Bella says, "I forgot. So what day is that?"

Ida says, "Figure it out. What's today?"

Bella appeals to Sophie. "I forgot that, too. Help me out."

Sophie, who has idly been gathering flowers en route, throws a daisy at Ida. Naturally it falls short. "Why do you always pick on her?" To Bella, she says, "Wednesday, they're coming home in the evening."

Bella smiles sweetly. "I hope they're having a happy honeymoon."

Ida moves ahead of them. "Grrrr. Hopeless."

Bella stops abruptly. And plops onto the next nearest bench.

"Now what?" Ida asks.

"I've got a pebble in my shoe." She slowly bends over, not an easy task with arthritis. •

Sophie sits down beside her. "If you sit, I could sit, too."

Ida stands over them, disgusted.

Sophie leans her arms over the back of the bench, ready to wait awhile. "You know, I've been having thoughts . . . Wanna hear?"

"I want to," Bella says eagerly. "Is it about what we should eat tonight? The deli has a special on knockwurst and baked beans. Maybe someone will drive us."

Sophie says, "No, this is important. It's about when Gladdy and Evvie come back as married ladies."

Ida perks up. "I've been thinking along the same lines. It was one thing when the men were just hanging around. Maybe they might have left eventually. But this is permanent. They're here to stay. Nothing is going to be the same."

Bella sings, off key, "Sadie, Sadie, married lady." She grins. "That's Barbra Streisand's song."

Ida has been doing leg bends, knowing they'll do anything to stall any kind of movement. They'll be here awhile.

She stops to put her hand over Bella's mouth. "Don't sing."

Bella pouts.

Ida continues. "Having husbands in the picture will get in our way."

Bella takes one of Sophie's daisies and starts peeling the petals off one by one. "He loves me, he loves me not . . . Do you think we'll ever get married again?"

Ida growls, "Don't be ridiculous. At our age? And besides, who'd be dumb enough to want to wait on some old grouchy male?"

"Hah," Sophie says. "What guy would want a grouchy female like someone whose name I wouldn't mention but is standing right here?"

Ida shoots her a dirty look.

Bella works on another daisy. She brightens at her thought. "Yeah, who'd want to wash some old guy's underwear anyway?"

Sophie grabs her daisy away from her. "Since when are you on her side?" She points an accusing finger at Ida.

Bella lifts all four feet nine of her off the bench and puffs out her chest. "I'm on the side of what's right. I'm proud to be an independent thinker."

"Hello," someone calls out to them. They turn to see their neighbor from Phase Three, Arlene Simon, coming toward them. Ida is always amazed by Arlene. Even though she's pushing eighty, she still wears skirts and dresses and high heels and continues to wear makeup and dye her hair golden blond. She's always put together perfectly. She wonders why Arlene does it. Most everyone accepts his or her shades of gray and white. Why all that bother to change hair color? And nobody in Lanai Gardens wears a heel over one inch. She has to admit Arlene is still a good-looking woman.

But what's this? She looks upset.

Arlene is out of breath. "I've been looking all over for you."

Ida steps up to the plate. "Are you in some kind of trouble?"

Arlene glances back and Ida notes she's looking at a small moving van unloading a king-size bed in front of her Phase Three building. "When is Gladdy coming home?"

Bella perks up. She knows this answer. "Wednesday. In the evening."

Arlene sighs. "I was hoping she'd be home sooner."

Ida says, "Can we help you?"

She shakes her head. "Thank you, but I don't think so. I'd like to talk to Gladdy. Would you please have her call me when they return?"

With that, Arlene leaves them. Ida watches their neighbor cautiously heading toward the back entrance of her apartment building.

"Hmmph." Sophie shows her annoyance. "What are we, chopped liver?"

"You see what I mean?" Defeated, Ida sits down on an adjoining bench. "It's starting already. Here's the potential for a new case. Did Arlene confide in us? No. She'll hire Gladdy. And without a thought about us, Gladdy won't want to hurt her new husband's feelings, so Jack will tag along. He'll always be right there at her side."

Depression sinks over them like a thundercloud. Sophie says, "No more five mouseketeers."

"That's musketeers," Ida corrects.

"Whatever. No more running in and out of their apartments any old time."

Bella takes up the chorus. "No more eating chocolate cake together in the middle of the night."

Sophie says, "Remember how Jack hated early bird dinners? Gone."

Bella sighs. "No more shopping till we drop. Gone."

Sophie groans. "Gladdy and Evvie won't go to bingo anymore. Or flea markets or even garage sales. Gone."

They have a long list of what will be gone forever.

Bella looks confused. "That's everything. So what *will* they be doing?"

Sophie gives her a pinch on the cheek. "Trust me, they won't be bored."

"That's it," Ida says. "We're toast. We're has-beens. Down with the Fab Five and up with the Double Dynamo. Gladdy Gold and Associates—finished."

Bella shudders. "What are we going to do? Once we've tasted blood, how can we be happy with bingo?"

Ida stands up, hands on hips. "I have a solution. I've been thinking about this ever since the newly-weds left."

Bella and Sophie look up at Ida warily. She has a dangerous expression on her face. That can only mean trouble for them.

Ida continues. "Why wait until we're dumped? I say we take action."

The girls are all ears. Ida's voice is stronger now. "I say we go into business for ourselves. We enroll in a detective school. Once we graduate, we're off on our own."

The girls perk up. Sophie announces, "Now you're talking."

Bella looks confused. "Now *you're* on her side?"

Sophie smiles knowingly. "Like in politics, you gotta go with the winners. Where do we find a detective school?"

"Not to worry. I already picked one out of the yellow pages. The guy had the biggest ad, so I bet he's the best. Think about it. A two-week class and we'll be up to speed in the PI biz."

Sophie worries. "Wait a minute. We don't have a car. How will we get to class?"

Ida says, "Not to worry. We can always take the bus."

The girls are revved up. Bella grins. "Let's sign up right away."

Sophie rises, ready to move back again. "They can't dump us. We'll dump them first."

The three march along, arms wrapped around one another. Late to mah-jongg and no longer even interested in attending.

Ida announces, "When they come back, we'll tell them we've got to talk."

3

THE RETURN

Such a flurry of excitement. It seems everyone in our Phase Two section has been hanging around awaiting our arrival. Moments after we get out of our taxi, Enya hugs us and tells us she's made a pot roast for us so we don't need to cook tonight. Tessie and Sol, happily addicted to rich foods, present us with brownies for dessert. Lola leans over her second-story balcony and offers freshly baked bread while her hubby, Hy, being Hy, presents us with his smart mouth. "So how was Viagra Falls, guys? Get it? *Viagra* Falls."

Joe calls up to him, not bothering to hide his sarcasm, "Got it, Hy, you're a riot."

Hy chortles, waves, then goes back inside his apartment.

After more welcome-home gifts and flowers and

neighbors asking about our travels, the group disperses. We lift our suitcases and, happily tired, head for our apartments. Such a balmy, beautiful night, South Florida at its best. But something's missing.

Conspicuously missing are the girls.

I glance up at Bella's second-floor apartment, next door to Evvie's. I see a curtain flutter for just one moment. What's this? Trouble in paradise?

I languidly watch Jack unpack our suitcases as I lie on our bed, shoes kicked off, and my hands behind my head. It feels so good to be home. He tells me he intends to spoil me rotten. He's already separated the dirty laundry. The pot roast is heating up. The table is set for dinner.

"Feel any different?" Jack asks. "Now that the ring is on your finger and around my neck."

I look at him in surprise. "Oh, really? Trapped, are you?"

"Kidding. That's a Hy kind of comment. It's catching."

"Least I can do is make you a drink." I climb off the bed. "What's your pleasure?"

"A beer will do. And some of those crinkly chips left over from our farewell party if they aren't stale."

I start for the kitchen.

Jack calls after me, "So what do you think is going on with the girls?"

I stop. "So you noticed, too."

"How could I not? From them I was expecting balloons and confetti; at least a brass band. But not the cold shoulder."

I return with a beer for him and lemonade for me.

"So you also think they're unhappy about something?"

"My guess is reality has set in. Jack and Joe are here to stay."

"Maybe so, but not to make an appearance? That isn't like them." I wind my arms around my wondrous new husband. I hug him and he hugs back. "I can understand that they might be concerned about things changing, but no greeting at all?"

The phone rings. I walk over to the phone on the bedside table. "Maybe that's one of them now. Hello?" I listen then turn to Jack. "It's Evvie." I listen some more. "We were just talking about that very thing." I report to Jack, "Evvie says there was a tiny knock at her door. By the time she answered, Bella had left a plate of cookies and then disappeared back into her apartment."

Jack shrugs. "I guess we'll find out what's bothering them soon enough."

"If you figure it out," I say to Evvie, "let me know. We'll talk tomorrow." I hang up.

I sit down on the edge of the bed and turn to Jack. "All I can think of is something must have happened while we were away. But what?"

The phone rings again. I reach for it. "It must be one of them this time." I answer and listen and shake my head at Jack. "Yes, of course we can."

"Who is it this time?" he asks.

"It was our neighbor Arlene Simon from Phase Three."

"Which one is she? Don't believe I've seen her."

"You would if I described her. Blond, dresses beautifully, the only one around who doesn't have gray or white hair."

He nods. "Now I do. She's still quite a looker."

"She has a problem and wants to meet with me. Now I think we have a problem of our own."

Jack is puzzled. "What's that?"

"That's probably what she said to the girls when she asked them when we'd be back. She asked for me. She didn't confide in them, my partners." I sip my drink, lost for a few moments in my thoughts.

"You know what I think? Knowing the girls as well as I do, logic tells me they've made some sort of decision and can't face us until they're ready to inform us. Bella leaving a little gift tells me Bella is nervous about it and doesn't want our feelings hurt."

Jack smiles. "Well, logic tells *me* it's too soon to ask us to get divorced—"

Suddenly I jump up, interrupting him. "Oh, my God, that's it. Because of what Arlene didn't say to them. They're going to divorce themselves from us!"

Jack is speechless. I am horrified.

4

BILL OF DIVORCEMENT

I leave my beloved sleeping, quickly drink my usual cup of coffee and grab a piece of toast, and out I go. It's time for our usual morning exercise.

Jack and I were in all last evening expecting one of the girls to call. But not a peep out of any of them. My plan for today is to pretend nothing is unusual and see who can't stand the suspense and says something. I'm betting on dear Bella. She won't be able to take the silence.

I'm sure Jack's plan for much of his day will be catching up with all the email he missed while we were away. Yes, I have to admit it, ready or not, Jack brought the twenty-first century with him when he moved in with me. We now have the ubiquitous computer with all its inner bells and whistles—email, Google, IM, Facebook, Twitter, and all that jazz. He's talking about getting something called Skype. Being actually seen by whoever calls? I don't know if I'm ready for that.

He likes to stay in touch with all our kids and grandkids in New York that way. Nice, but I still prefer talking to them by phone. I even had to give up my much adored rotary phone. Every time Jack walked into the kitchen, the sight of that old thing had him in stitches.

We also now have a modern TV set. First thing Jack dumped was my little table model, circa 1985, and we have one of those humongous, forty-two-inch practically-takes-up-the-whole-wall plasma TVs, whatever that means. Out with my old VCR and the tapes I used to mangle. Now it's DVD (until that gets obsolete) and TiVo.

Now, of course, everyone has been coming to our apartment to watch television. Are the girls willing to give up that luxury?

The girls are already grouped around our meeting place, the palm tree next to one of the small ponds. They are whispering like the little conspirators they are. Probably wondering if I'll show up.

I pop out of the stairwell and here I am bright-eyed and bushy-tailed, as the expression goes. I start my warm-up. "Hi, everyone. Isn't it a glorious day?"

Each of them faces a different direction. Sophie is suddenly busy tightening her shoelaces. Ida does leg bends. Bella doesn't do anything. She takes a quick peep at me, then turns away.

No takers yet. I try another gambit. "Did you have fun last night?"

Bella does fold first. She turns toward me, curious. "Fun? What was I doing that I was having fun? I don't remember."

Sophie turns. The next domino to fall. "Did I miss something?"

"Well," I say, "since nobody was around when we got home, I assumed you were out somewhere having a good time, I hope." Sometimes I can be such a meanie.

Bella blurts, "We were here. Didn't Evvie tell you I sent over cookies?"

Ida shoots her an angry look as if to say *traitor*.

I can see Evvie making her brisk way toward us.

"You could ask her," Bella adds.

Ida turns stiffly with a tone daring me not to believe her. "I had dusty curtains to wash and iron. That was my big fun evening."

"Hi, everyone." Evvie is equally cheery. "Missed you last night when we got back."

Well, that speeds things up. The subject is out in the open.

Sophie decides to move that topic along past any reference to their not showing up. "Did you have a good honeymoon?"

"Just great," Evvie answers. "The scenery was gorgeous. We rode in a boat that was very close to the falls. We got soaking wet but it was worth it. Really exciting."

They're still quiet, but they're beginning to look interested. Except for Ida, who pretends to be bored.

Evvie baits the hook. "We even had an adventure."

Sophie and Bella, loving a story, sit down on our bench. Yet again, any excuse not to exercise. Ida leans against our tree, arms folded. She still hasn't made eye contact with me.

Evvie tells the story. "There was a young woman on the boat who was going to commit suicide and Jack and Gladdy rescued her."

Bella's eyes widen as she says, "Wow! That's really exciting. Why was she going to kill herself?"

Evvie answers, "Because her new husband didn't show up on the boat. He told her he changed his mind about being married."

Bella is thrilled. "Just like watching *Days of Our Lives* on TV."

Sophie is equally fascinated. "What happened next?"

I continue the account. "But the husband changed his mind and was rushing to the boat to tell her. Because of his haste, he had an accident on the way and cracked up his car and landed in the hospital."

"Wow," Sophie says.

Evvie adds, "They were reunited at the hospital. Both of them sorry for everything that happened. He'd just had cold feet and she overreacted. A horrible tragedy was averted. They made up and were in tears."

I wrap up the story. "After the boat captain and the police and a mental health person released her, the couple promised to go home and go into joint therapy. All's well that ends well."

Evvie smiles. "Almost like Romeo and Juliet. They might have both died thinking the other one died."

Bella breaks out into a big smile. She always likes a happy ending.

Ida, the cynic, finally deigns to speak. "They were already fighting on their honeymoon. What makes you think those two will live happily ever after?"

I sigh. "We can only hope, Ida."

Evvie starts to move. "Are we walking, or not?"

Bella and Sophie slowly get up. Ida gets going.

As we pass the badminton court, I say casually, "By the way, I'm going to meet with Arlene Simon. I hear she spoke to you."

"Well," says Ida, now that it's out, "she only wanted to talk to *you*. So I guess you'll be taking her case."

Evvie and I exchange glances. Here it comes.

"There is no case," I say. "She just wants some personal advice."

Sophie is startled. "We thought it was a case."

Bella adds, "Just for you and Jack, not us."

"Since when would I leave you out?" I say. "And besides, Jack isn't one of our associates."

Evvie decides to bring it up. "Only if you'd like to vote him in."

Bella and Sophie quickly look toward Ida. I have a feeling they want her to get them out of what she probably got them into.

Ida takes a deep breath. "We've been thinking. Maybe it's time for us to regroup. Now that the two of you are married, we thought you'd like to be in business with them."

Them? It's as if she can't bring herself to mention the guys' names.

Sophie, realizing where she's going, breaks in. "But if Arlene isn't a case . . . we don't have to—"

Ida interrupts her. "We're committed to going into the private eye business for ourselves."

Bella and Sophie look dismayed.

Evvie shows her surprise. "You mean you want to leave Gladdy Gold and Associates?"

"It might be better that way," Ida answers.

"How do you mean, committed?" I ask.

"We're signed up to take a course and when we're done, we get a certificate and then we become Ida Franz and Associates."

Sophie glares at her. "We haven't decided on names yet."

Bella adds, in a panic, "We haven't signed up, either."

Ida announces, "I have. For all of us."

I shake my head in consternation. Ida, Ida, what are you doing? Why do you always have to be the rotten apple in the barrel?

Evvie tries to help. "Well, maybe you can still change your mind."

Nice try, Evvie. But that won't work. When Ida gets herself into a hole, she needs to dig herself in deeper.

Ida's shoulders shoot up. "As a matter of fact, we have to cut this short. We're due at class and we need to shower and dress." Without looking at us, she walks off, back toward our building.

Sophie and Bella are flummoxed. They don't know what to say or do. With last agonized glances at us, they hurry after Ida.

Evvie blows out her breath. "Whew, that didn't go too well. What do we do now?"

"Nothing. We just have to let them play it out and hope they don't end up in too much of a mess."

We continue our walk.

"By the by," Evvie says. "Joe and I made a decision last night."

I smile. "I don't know how many more decisions I can take in one morning."

Evvie puts her arm around my waist as we keep going.

Uh-oh, this must be serious. "Break it to me gently."

"Joe and I had a long talk. The honeymoon trip brought up a lot of memories of our earlier years when we were still happy. Joe admitted he was homesick and wanted to see our daughter and the grandkids."

I know where this is going and I hold my breath.

"We're going back up north. He wants to spend some time with our family."

She doesn't have to tell me why. "Do you have any plan for how long?"

"We're thinking maybe a month's visit, but if Joe wants to stay . . ." She hesitates. "Then, only God knows when we'll be back."

We turn and hug each other. I feel myself start to tear up. I attempt to make a joke of it. "So all the rats are leaving the sinking ship."

"Not all, dear sister. You still have Jack, and the two of you can build a better mousetrap!"

We giggle through our tears.

5

ARLENE TELLS GLADDY

"I hope you don't mind our meeting in your apartment." Arlene has repeated this three times since she walked over from Phase Three to visit with me. She may be having a problem, but she walks with regal posture. She's as impeccably dressed as always. Her blond pageboy is perfect, not a hair out of place. She wears a peach-colored skirt and top that look as sparkling new as if she'd just bought them. Of course her high heels match.

I am in my usual variation of beige slacks and white T-shirt and sneakers.

We're sitting at my tiny kitchen table having tea while she works up to telling me what's wrong. We've already discussed my honeymoon and events going on at Lanai Gardens. And small bits of information about the new European patisserie that just opened. I wait patiently.

Jack sent himself off on an errand. Even though she said she wouldn't mind his being there, we both thought she'd be more comfortable just the two of us. Women talk, he assumed.

She takes a deep breath and I think she's ready. She speaks softly.

"Did you ever have a nightmare over and over again and it finally happens in real life?" She doesn't wait for me to answer. "Well, I did and I'm living my nightmare right now. You may have heard me mention my late husband, Robby Simon, and our two children."

I nod at that. "Yes, I do."

"Well, Robby wasn't my first husband. I was married before to a man named Edward. He was a doctor. We were married for five years and he dumped me for my very best friend, Joyce." She laughs and the sound is brittle. "I guess I'm not too good at picking men. Robby cheated on me as well, but his mistress wasn't a woman. He turned out to be a gambler and pretty much wiped us out financially. He died shooting craps in his hotel room in Vegas."

I didn't mention that I'd heard about that from the girls when they were involved with that phony guru and his Dead Husbands Club last month, when Arlene's husband's "spirit" supposedly visited her.

I refill her empty tea cup and she continues.

"He was a rebound marriage. My true love was Edward. When I caught Edward in bed with Joyce, I behaved very badly. I'm ashamed to say I even picked up a knife to threaten them."

She bows her head not wanting to face me with those embarrassing words. "In all these years, I never even told my children of my shame. Bobby and Nicky would be horrified."

It's hard to believe this elegant, soft-spoken lady had ever felt such rage. The Arlene we've seen is a self-sufficient loner. A situation like that could make any woman lose control. Anger is a powerful emotion.

She continues. "Last week while you were away, I was aware of a moving van unloading. I almost fainted when I saw who was moving into my very own building. Joyce Steiner. Herself. My God, the last time I saw her was over fifty-five years ago! I almost didn't recognize her. I had to look more carefully. But it's her. I recognized those eyes. The way she tosses that red hair. The way she carries herself. I knew. That's why I needed to talk to someone and I thought about you."

She leans back in her chair. It's finally out.

"Arlene, dear, what is it you want from me?"

"I can't believe the strength of my feelings. I don't want any part of her in my life again and I don't know how to handle this."

She turns to me and I can see the sadness in her eyes. "I need your wisdom, Gladdy. I need you to help me sort out what to do."

I sip at my tea. "Did she see you?"

"I don't think so. The minute I was sure it was Joyce, I ran away until I saw the empty van leave. Then I rushed up to my apartment. I've been avoiding her since then."

"I'm sorry that you're so troubled."

"I can't seem to help it. I snuck downstairs and saw which apartment she moved into. You want to hear irony? When we lived in the same apartment building back then, I lived on the third floor and she, right under me, on the second. And it's the same now. As if history were repeating itself."

This puzzles me. I didn't know of anyone moving out of that Phase Three building.

I ask, "Do you know who had been living there before?"

"I don't know, but I learned it's a sublet and she pays the money to one of the neighbors, Leah Andrews, who lives across the way."

How strange. Leah's brother, Seymour, lives in an apartment on that floor. Can it be? Not likely. Seymour never goes anywhere. He's painfully shy; he barely leaves his apartment. Leah even does all his food shopping and cooking for him. But if Leah is collecting money . . . ?

Arlene breaks into my thoughts. "I don't know what to do. I can't keep creeping around like a spy to make sure I don't run into her."

"You never had any contact with Joyce throughout all these years?"

"No, why would I? She destroyed my marriage

and changed my life forever. But I did read in the obituaries that Edward died six years ago. Apparently he became quite famous and I suppose very rich."

"First I need to ask you, what do you think you should do? What would make you comfortable?"

Arlene twists the handkerchief she has in her hands. "How can I continue to live in Lanai Gardens if she's here?" She tears up. "I know it sounds ridiculous after fifty-plus years, but the minute I saw her, I knew I still haven't forgiven her for what she did to me."

"Try a worst-case scenario. What if you do meet up with each other? What do you think will happen?"

Arlene fairly stutters, "I don't know. I could hope that Joyce won't even recognize me, but she will, I know it. I don't want to speak to her."

I reach out and take Arlene's hands in mine. "Sometimes it might be a good thing to be forced to face a problem head-on. You've been living with this unhappiness so long; maybe this is an opportunity to get over it. I'm not a psychologist and perhaps you might want to make an appointment with one—"

She interrupts me. "No, please. Just help me and I'll take your advice."

I nod, thinking. "I have an idea. Tomorrow, Friday night, is our monthly get-together party in the rec room. You know how we always do this with newcomers. I think she'll be invited. Test it out.

Maybe you'll be surprised at how you'll feel. Half a century is a very long time."

"What do I do if she comes up to me?"

"Undoubtedly, Joyce will be introduced to our neighbors. She will be quite civilized, I'm sure. Maybe you'll be surprised and seeing her will be anticlimactic. We're all much older by now. What was important years ago might seem different to you when you face her once again."

"You'll stand next to me all evening?"

"I promise."

There's a polite knocking at the door. I go to answer it. It's Jack. He's carrying a bag and something in it smells wonderful. "Just wanted to know if it was okay to come back. Otherwise I'll leave these goodies and take a powder again."

Arlene appears in the doorway. "No, please stay. I was about to leave."

He walks in and lifts a tempting chocolate éclair out of his package. "Not until you've sampled one of these."

I'm already taking plates out of the cupboard. "Yes, Arlene, why not?"

She smiles. "Is that from the new European patisserie?"

"It sure is." He passes the package to me and heads for the teapot, ready to heat it up again.

I nod to Arlene to sit back down.

She shrugs. "You talked me into it. How can I resist?"

We three settle down to indulge. Jack is already charming her into smiling.

I'm not sure I gave her the right advice. I didn't know what else to say. She surprised me. She's not at all like the person one might think she is by her dress and her demeanor. She's quiet. She's gentle. And amazingly shy. I hope she won't get hurt again.

6

DETECTIVE SCHOOL

Sophie calls out to Ida, who is moving at a swift pace, "I don't like this street. It's creepy."

Bella clings to her arm. "Yeah, and I've got a stomachache. Who knew it would take riding in three different buses to get here? And besides, it's time for my nap."

Ida turns her head, but doesn't stop. "We're almost there, so stop kvetching."

She doesn't want to admit that she didn't expect the school to be located in such a bad area. Everything looks run-down. The gutters are filled with dirt and flying newspapers. The garbage cans smell as if they don't get picked up that often. She walks even faster to get them off the street as quickly as possible.

But she's not about to back off. She's the sergeant. They're her troops.

She looks at the piece of paper with the address on it once again. They're in the 900 block. One more street to go.

Sophie scratches at her arms. "I feel bugs around here. Why did you lie to Gladdy? We aren't registered yet. You said we'd come down just to look the place over."

Bella parrots Sophie. "I already looked. Let's go home."

Ida stops, her hands go to her hips, showing her annoyance. "I did a lot of research to pick this place and we're not going home until we see it."

Bella clutches Sophie harder. "But I'm scared. Everybody around here looks like they need a bath."

"Right," Ida says sarcastically. "Dirty people will hurt you."

Sophie adds, "I'm itchy, too."

"Just listen to me. Walk in the center of the street, not near any doorways and not next to the gutter. Then you'll be okay."

Bella asks, "What's that supposed to do?"

Ida says, "I read it somewhere. If you're in a dangerous place, if you stay in the center, they can't grab you out of a doorway or from a moving car."

The two squeeze even closer. "Thanks a lot," Sophie says, her turn to be cynical. "That really makes me feel better."

What is she going to do with them? They're impossible. Ida points. "There, I see the address."

The girls scurry to catch up to her. Ida stops in front of an old brick building with a scratched-up green-painted doorway and a small number over it. Ida senses it's seen better days, that's for sure.

Sophie sniffs her disappointment. "This is it? Where?"

Ida indicates a little note next to a bell. It says in handwritten scribbled letters, "Mike Gatkes. One flight up. Ring bell."

Sophie is disappointed. This building isn't what she expected. "It doesn't mention anything about a detective agency."

Bella cowers. "You said don't go near any doorways."

Ida ignores them and rings the bell as Sophie and Bella look alarmed.

"Who's down there?" a voice calls from the tinny speaker.

"Ida Franz, Sophie Meyerbeer, and Bella Fox," Ida announces. "We have an appointment."

A rasping buzzer rings. For a moment Ida hesitates, says a silent prayer, then pushes the door open.

The flight of stairs in the small, dark entry looks steep and poorly lit. A sign on the wall with an arrow pointing up says "Gatkes, one flight up."

Sophie says, "Where's the elevator?"

Ida looks. "I don't think there is one."

They climb up the steps slowly, all of them

clutching the banister with both hands to help pull themselves up. Bella, in the rear, is muttering under her breath.

Ida, annoyed, asks Sophie, "What's she mumbling about?"

Sophie says, "She hopes he won't kill us."

A rickety front door is open. A voice calls out to them, "Come on in, ladies. Be right with you."

The girls enter slowly, not knowing what to expect. They peer around the office in awe. To Ida, it looks like furniture she's seen in photos of the 1920s or '30s. There's an old beat-up desk. The faded gray sofa is probably filled with horsehair. She'd bet the muddy-colored rug hasn't been cleaned in years. Nor has the place been painted, either.

"He looks like an actor," Bella whispers, staring at a photo of a man she assumes is Mike Gatkes holding some kind of trophy.

Sophie comments, "An actor who plays serial killers."

Bella asks, "What does a serial killer look like?"

Sophie nods. "Him."

Ida whispers, "Shh, he's coming."

Mike Gatkes comes out of his kitchen with three bottles of water and hands them out to the exhausted girls. They drink greedily, gulping them down.

Ida's first glance at Mike is almost enough to

make her turn them around and run back down, but she knows the girls are breathing hard already and need to rest. Ida notes that he has a head of black spiky hair that looks as if he never combs it. He's short, very muscular, desperately needs a shave, and wears old odd-looking clothes and scuffed shoes. He does seem dangerous. Has she made a mistake?

"Knew those flights would be a killer. Sorry about that, ladies." He sounds friendly enough.

Bella says, "I think I counted thirty-nine steps."

"Like the movie," Mike comments, smiling, as if he were an old buddy reminiscing. "Remember that one with Robert Donat? There are only fifteen steps, but it probably felt like thirty-nine."

Bella is puzzled. "I don't remember an actor named donut."

Ida tries to make small talk as she finishes the water. "Your office looks like a movie set."

Mike beams. "Well detected. You're close. It's meant to be a replica of the movie office of San Francisco's famous author Dashiell Hammett. You know, *The Maltese Falcon.*"

"Really," says Ida to be polite. "How interesting." As if she would ever read books like that or even see the movie.

He proudly points out the oak armchair, the scarred desk, the brass ashtray. He grins. "Some say I even look a little like Humphrey Bogart, who played the lead in the movie."

Ida hmmphs to herself. What's he so proud of? Bogart was no beauty.

Sophie can't resist. "Gladdy should be here. She loves reading mysteries."

Ida doesn't want to let her talk about their former associates. "Well, Mr. Gatkes, shall we get down to business? Would you like to tell us a little about yourself?"

"Call me Mike. The photos on my wall tell my stories. Here I am with the mayor of Miami giving me a commendation." He points to the news photo of a man snarling as he's being arrested. "You heard of the famous Son of Sam case? Well, I captured Son of Sheldon. Scared the hell out of women in Boca."

He continues with other startling captures. "Remember the Fort Lauderdale Causeway terrorist? He snuck into his victims' houses via boat. I caught that big fish." He moves quickly from one action photo to another.

The girls are finally impressed. Ida still has reservations, but he seems to know what he's talking about.

Mike continues his tour. He takes them into the next room, which is a classroom with a chalkboard. "This is where I teach you the ropes. What a PI does. What kind of training you need. How to use firearms. How to handle evidence. Scene of the crime—what to look for. How to write reports. What clothing to wear."

He goes on and on.

"Once you're ready, your first assignment will be an actual case to solve. It will come from the list of clients I already have as a PI." He throws them a bone, so to speak. "Maybe you'll learn so much, you'll be able to even solve one of my cold cases." Not that Ida believes it.

She cuts to the chase. "What's your fee?"

He smiles. Ida notices his teeth are yellow and crooked. "First thing. You're entitled to your senior citizen discount."

At Ida's hesitation he winks and adds, "And for you ladies, a group price cut as well—a *threefer*."

That's more like it. She can make this work. She'll show Gladdy the real way to be a PI.

Mike is already moving to the next room. "Ready to try on trench coats, ladies?"

Bella and Sophie can hardly wait. Going shopping? He said the magic words.

Ida wonders, *Where are the other students?*

7

FRIDAY NIGHT
WELCOME PARTY

Evvie and Joe are the life of the party. I watch with tears in my eyes as everyone in the rec room is toasting their upcoming trip up north. Some know the truth about Joe. Others might guess. But all are laughing and being positive about the future.

Arlene clings to me like Saran Wrap. We stand off to one side. She visibly shakes each time the recreation room door opens.

Jack has brought us cookies and lemonade, but he's still keeping his distance. Arlene needs only me right now.

The girls haven't put in an appearance yet, but I'm sure they'll be here. They never miss a Friday night party.

Well, speak of the little devils. Here they come.

What's that expression? They look like the cat that swallowed the canary. Or should I say the *cats*. Very pleased with themselves, they are.

Hy stands with a group of the men. Undoubtedly he's telling one of his dirty jokes. I can tell by the leering looks on the guys' faces. The joke must be over because raucous laughter follows. The wives know to stay away. The jokes are mostly antifemale. Tessie, whose husband, Sol, is one of Hy's most loyal followers, has been threatening to smack him around one of these days. And with her weight and height advantage, she just might be able to do it.

"Maybe she isn't coming," Arlene says hopefully. "I think I should go home."

"Give it a little more time, Arlene. You're going to have to face her eventually. At least tonight you're among friends."

Here come Sophie and Bella fairly bouncing along. Ida has found some of her mah-jongg pals and stopped to chat with them. I can bet she intends to keep away from us tonight. The twosome, however, come over to say hello.

So I ask, "How was your PI class?"

Sophie says, "Really great. Our teacher is one tough-looking hombre. He looks like Humphrey Bogart and we're gonna learn a lot."

Bella giggles. "I already picked out a trench coat. Just like Sam Spade. Did you know those tough characters wore leather buckles on the sleeves?"

What can I say? Their insensitivity to the matter of having dumped our own partnership defies logic. "Very nice. I'm glad you're having a good time."

Suddenly Arlene touches my arm. "She's here."

Coming through the doorway is tall, hunched-over Leah Andrews escorting her brother's new tenant, whom she must have only met this morning. Leah always looks anxious, as if the world is out to get her, but tonight her face is more pinched than usual. She's obviously not comfortable having to tell everyone Seymour's away and here's an unexpected stranger who's taken over his condo. I'm sure the question everyone wants to ask is where on earth did Seymour go?

Bella points to Joyce Steiner. "She's here again?"

Surprised, I ask, "Who are you looking at?"

"The red-haired lady who came with Leah."

"Have you seen her before?"

"Yeah, she was wandering around about a month ago."

Before I can query her further, Sophie pulls on her. "Come on, let's move it. They just brought out more chocolate chip cookies."

Clueless about Arlene's tension, off they go. Sophie waves and calls back at me, "We'll keep you informed."

Arlene practically hides behind me, her head bent down. Leah is marching Joyce around to each group introducing her to the other neighbors.

Evvie comes over to join me. I've already filled

her in with what I know about the two women. She glances at the nervous Arlene, who looks very pale.

Arlene speaks in a low, tight voice. "It's her."

Evvie and I study the lady who gave Arlene so much pain. She and Arlene are the same age, but Joyce looks as if she had one face-lift too many. Her skin is sallow despite a layer of cosmetics. Her cheeks seem rigid and inflexible. Her red hair is very thin as well. Too many bleach jobs? Her clothes are expensive, no doubt about that. She had or still has a lot of money. She wears an elegant Chanel-style pantsuit. Where Arlene has aged gracefully, this woman seems as if she's been to hell and back.

Arlene whispers, "She's coming this way."

I watch Joyce, drink in hand as she greets the other residents. She's cool but friendly enough.

Arlene stiffens as Leah and Joyce reach us. "I'd like to introduce you to our new tenant," Leah announces, trying to hide any feelings she has about this strange turn of events. "Joyce Steiner, who's subletting Seymour's apartment. She asked me to introduce her to everyone."

There's a silence as Arlene doesn't dare look at Joyce. I watch this newcomer with a smile pasted on her face as if she's bored and going through the motions.

Evvie fills the void, but I don't take my eyes off the two women. "So we heard through the grapevine, Seymour's gone off on some trip?"

Leah says, "He's taken it upon himself to go on a

vacation or something. I walked in one morning to make his breakfast and there was a letter telling me he'd be back, maybe in six months, and he'd already sublet to Mrs. Steiner."

"How so unlike Seymour," Evvie comments.

"You're telling me? You could have blown me away with a feather." I sense Leah trying to hide her hurt feelings. With a pinch of anger, as well, for his ingratitude?

Suddenly Joyce Steiner shrieks, "Arlene? Is that you? Arlene!" She peers through her glasses to see better and moves closer for another look.

Arlene finally glances up. She shrivels up and says nothing.

Joyce rushes to Arlene and throws her arms around her, hugging and kissing her cheeks. Arlene is tugged away from my arm. "I can't believe it!" Joyce glows with happiness as she addresses the group of us. "This is my dear, dear friend Arlene. We haven't seen each other in a gazillion years!"

Arlene pulls away, out of Joyce's grasp.

As an animated Joyce turns and faces each of us, showing her delight, Arlene whispers, "Fifty-five years and three months to be exact."

I'm the only one who hears her.

Joyce shakes her head in wonder. "What a fantastic coincidence. I searched for you everywhere and I never could find you. And here you are! And look at you! You look gorgeous." She laughs. "Me, I look like an old hag, but you!"

Arlene stares at Joyce as Joyce twists her fingers

around a gold necklace. I recognize it as the Chai, a Jewish symbol of good luck. Arlene seems riveted by the sight of it.

Suddenly Arlene grimaces and clutches her stomach. She says, "Excuse me," and then runs off.

Joyce looks after her, eyes still shining. "This is the happiest day of my life. I found my best friend again."

I find it fascinating that she's oblivious to Arlene's response.

Leah leaves us, glad to deposit her new tenant with me. Evvie has gone to the bathroom to see if Arlene needs help. I'm curious to hear what Joyce will say or do now. She still seems to be on cloud nine.

"I'll bet she's in shock. I am, too. I just can't believe how lucky I am to find her."

I try for a reality check. "Arlene seems upset to see you again."

Joyce manages a rueful smile. "I suppose I can't blame her. I'm ashamed to say, I stole away her husband. But so many years have passed, I thought surely she got over our little breakup."

"Apparently not."

"Well, to tell the truth, I didn't get that great a deal. Ed was a rotten husband. These doctors have such God complexes. They're loyal only to themselves. Frankly, I did her a favor by taking him off her hands. She would have divorced him sooner or later."

I think it, but I don't say it: Maybe if he'd stayed with Arlene, the marriage might have worked. This woman has some ego.

Joyce continues to rave enthusiastically. "Over and over again, through the years, I've chastised myself. I should have taken my friend's side. We would have never broken up our friendship. Ours was the true relationship. I missed her so much and I looked for her everywhere, but of course she remarried and I didn't know her new name."

"May I ask you a personal question?"

Joyce preens. "Ask away."

"Why are you here in a sublet? Don't you have another place to live?"

Joyce sips at her lemonade for a moment organizing her thoughts. "Let me tell you; it's been so hectic. Even though I've lived in Florida all my life, my darling daughter, Stacy, has been nagging me to come live with her in California. She was so cute about it. Mama, she kept saying, you're getting old—but she meant that in a nice way. Come live with me, she said, and let me take care of you. She lives in that very fancy Marin County. I'm sure you've heard of Sausalito? Everyone has."

"Yes," I say, breaking in. Trying to slow down the barrage of words. "I hear it's a lovely place. Never been there."

Joyce rants on as if I never stopped her. "My Stacy married a doctor, too. But he's a foot specialist, so maybe they aren't such egomaniacs. We'll have so much fun together and I can see my adorable grandchildren every day. How can I refuse? So she says to me, sell your house and while I'm waiting to sell, she's going to add a cottage in her huge backyard. I guess they used to call them mother-in-law apartments. But I'm the mother."

I break in again. "That sounds lovely."

"Yes, very. Anyway, here's the funny part. Surprise! I sell my home right away and she's having contractor problems. You know how unreliable they are. So instead of moving into their big house and getting in everyone's way, I said I'd stay in Florida and sublet until she's ready. And now a miracle. Who should be living here? I find my dearest Arlene at last."

She says all that hardly taking a breath. Pleased with herself, Joyce opens her arms to indicate that she's finished her spiel.

Evvie returns just at that moment, thank goodness. The woman is exhausting. "Where's Arlene?" I ask, not seeing her with Evvie.

"She wasn't feeling well. I walked her back home."

I take Evvie by her arm. To Joyce, I say, "Nice talking to you. See you around." With that, I pull Evvie away.

"What?" she says when we're out of earshot. "Why the bum's rush?"

"I'll fill you in on our way back. What's that famous line from *Casablanca,* about all the gin joints?"

For Evvie, the movie maven, that's an easy one. "'Of all the gin joints in all the towns in all the world, she walks into mine.' What are you thinking?"

"I'm thinking, of all the condos in all of Florida, Joyce ends up in Lanai Gardens."

"Hell of a coincidence."

We see our spouses near the punch bowl waiting for us to rescue them. They both have lidded eyes and slouching shoulders, which indicate they've had enough partying. Time to go home.

Evvie shrugs. "I feel an earthquake about to erupt. This doesn't bode well."

"My sentiments exactly."

8

FRIENDSHIP

I sit in the snug chintz chaise in Evvie's bedroom watching her pack. She is having a hard time of it. The entire bed is filled with most of what was in her closet. Joe is at his doctor's appointment and I've offered to keep her company.

She holds up two skirts. "This is impossible! How can I decide what to take? I don't know how long I'll be visiting. I don't know how people dress up north anymore. I don't even have any winter clothes. This is madness."

"Westport, Connecticut, doesn't have any stores?" I smile at her. "Your daughter wouldn't lend you a sweater?"

She shakes her head the way a dog tosses off water. "I'm having a meltdown, aren't I?"

"Something like that."

"It has nothing to do with my clothes. Right?"

"Correct."

She plops down on the edge of her bed, shoving a small mountain of outfits out of her way. "I'm behaving like an idiot. Who cares what I wear anyway."

I shrug, pretending nonchalance. I'm just as distressed as she is, but we don't need both of us to go to pieces.

"And how will it be staying with Martha, Elliot, and the kids in that small house? Naturally my daughter insisted we stay with them and we have to, because we can't afford a motel for a few weeks or more. Everyone will be smiling too much and pretending we're here just for a short family visit. Joe's condition is on everyone's mind.

"I love my grandchildren, but twenty-four hours a day for how long, I'll go crazy."

Evvie stops herself and starts to smile. "You're just letting me blab on and on, Madamé Psychologist, on purpose."

"You got it." I offer her the box of candy I have on my lap and have been dipping into. "Come on, have another of Fannie May's indecently delicious chocolates. It works better than booze."

For a few happy moments we bite into the luscious dark confections, letting their sweetness linger on our tongues as we utter small contented sighs. Then take another.

I comment, "If I eat one more piece, I'll throw up."

Evvie pushes the now-empty box away. "Too bad we didn't think of that famous TV line from the Mary Tyler show way back. Remember when she held up the piece of chocolate and said, 'Why don't I just apply it directly to my hips?'"

"Too late."

We laugh.

Evvie starts again. "It's the big elephant in the room, isn't it? What I'm not talking about. Why I'm going back home. That's what it's really about. It's the thought that I might be coming back alone."

That does it. We both get up and hug and hold on tightly to each other, trying to keep back tears.

I say softly, "We do what we have to do."

"How am I going to manage without you?" Evvie says.

I try to reassure her. "We'll talk on the phone a lot. If you need me, I'll get on the next plane."

"I feel like I'm abandoning you. We haven't been separated in how long?"

I shrug. "I don't know exactly, but it's been a whole lot of years."

Evvie examines my face. "You seem calm about my going."

"That's because I'm such a good actress. One blubbering female is enough. Two is a puddle."

We hear Joe in the hallway. "Honey, I'm home," he mimics.

"In here," Evvie calls.

Joe arrives with a big grin on his face. He holds

up a white pastry box. "Guess what I brought home for my two favorite chocoholics for after dinner? A gooey, fattening chocolate cake with chocolate icing."

First, Jack and the chocolate éclairs, now Joe and his cake. What is it about us that makes our men ply us with chocolate? Maybe for Ogden Nash, candy is dandy, but liquor is quicker—for us it's the opposite.

Evvie and I look at each other and laugh again.

"Look," says Ida, "they're heading out now." The girls join her and stare out the window as Evvie, Joe, and Gladdy walk past Bella's door.

"I bet they're picking Jack up and going to the Continental for the Saturday night stuffed cabbage special," Sophie whines.

Bella looks stricken. "I want to go! All day long I've been thinking of hot pastrami with coleslaw and French dressing on rye."

Ida says, annoyed, "Well, stop. Think about eating whatever leftovers you have in the fridge. We can't go."

Sophie asks, "Why not?"

Ida is amazed. "I have to explain to you again that we're no longer part of Gladdy Gold and Associates? We made our bed and we have to lie in it."

Bella looks up, startled. "What's my bed got to do with pastrami?"

Sophie says, "I know all that. But it doesn't mean we aren't still friends."

Ida's hands go on her hips. "Did you hear the phone ring? They walked right past us. Did they knock on the door? They didn't invite us to go with them."

Bella sighs. "Maybe it's because we weren't nice to them."

Ida is annoyed. "Maybe it's really because they have husbands now and don't need us anymore."

Sophie is adamant. "What's one thing got to do with another?"

Ida moves away from the window. "It just does."

Bella is horrified. "You mean we're stuck here forever with no car? They have three! No early birds, no buying food at Publix? No window shopping? No movies?"

Ida answers, "We need to find a different way of getting into the city. Three buses to Gatkes is too much."

Sophie thinks hard. "What about that new lady who just moved in? She drives that fancy Jaguar. We can make friends with her. What's her name, Joyce?"

Bella perks up. "I met her. She's not too friendly, though."

Ida says, annoyed, "Don't be ridiculous. You can't have met her. Why do you always make things up?"

Bella sits up, puffs out her chest. "I'm not making

it up and if you don't believe me, then don't!" She gets up and heads for the door.

Sophie looks puzzled. "Where are you going?"

"Home," Bella says agitatedly.

Sophie goes to her and pulls her back. "You are home, silly. You live here."

Bella plops back down on the couch and reaches for the dish of Snickers bars. "What are we going to do? I miss our friends already."

9

THE MARRIED COUPLE

"I wonder what Evvie's doing." I sigh. I hand Jack the entertainment section. We trade and he gives me the front pages. This is one of our new shared pleasures of being married. Part of making our own traditions in our Florida room with its cheerful white wicker furniture. Sunday morning bulging newspaper. Bagels, cream cheese, lox, and coffee. The Bloody Marys are a plus. A sweet breeze comes through the louvres. Ah. Peace and serenity.

It's nice being in my apartment. Once Jack's building was reconstructed after the hurricane, we deliberated where to live. It made sense to stay here. Otherwise we'd have to replace all of his belongings that were lost when the building collapsed. So here we are.

Of course, the first new things he bought were to

replace all the tech stuff he lost—the TV, computer, etc. And another wardrobe.

"Evvie's gone exactly one week from last Sunday and you've already phoned her six times. Doesn't that help?"

I take a sip of my drink. "It's only been five. No. I miss her. She's not just my sister, she's my best friend."

He leans over from his chair and kisses my nose. "Can't I be your best friend?"

I kiss him back. "You are already, but she's my best girlfriend. It's not the same thing."

I try to focus on the news, but I'm not able to concentrate. I place the paper back onto the coffee table. "Speaking about how people are doing, I wonder how Arlene's been managing this whole week. It's been kind of quiet. Maybe too quiet."

Jack turns another page. "You might take it as a good sign."

"You know, discussing friendship makes me think of the situation with Arlene and her nemesis. The reason Arlene's unhappiness has lasted so long is because of Joyce's betrayal. It hurt her to the very depths of her being. It has to do with having a profound relationship with a very close woman friend."

"Are you saying women aren't able to feel that deeply about a husband?"

"Yes, of course they can, but, again, it's different somehow. These friends are the true soul mates. Usually ones you've had most of your life. They've seen you vulnerable and know your weaknesses and you are loved despite them. In fact, loved even more so for that very reason. It's about the person who will never judge you, or let you down. No matter what life throws at you, that one person is the ballast that you hold on to. If you're afraid, that person is willing to slay the dragons for you."

Jack reaches out for my hand. "That's quite a touching description."

I shrug. "I don't know how better to explain it."

"Are you saying that Arlene took losing Joyce harder than losing Dr. Ed?"

"I actually think so. For example, Evvie and I have been together all of our lives. There's only a two-year difference in our ages. I know just about everything there is to know concerning her. And vice versa. We have a solid history of trust and understanding. If I lost her, it would be unbearable."

I reach over and pinch his cheek playfully. "In simple terms, we're able to be our real selves, the selves nobody else can possibly see."

Jack tosses his papers aside and gets up. "I do understand what you mean. When I was growing up it was me, Charlie, and Dave who had our special friendships. We promised to be there for one another forever. I remember when we even took blood oaths on it. I can still see the expression on my mother's face when I came home with those bloodstains on my hand and shirt."

"What happened to those friendships?"

Jack shrugs. "I guess we just lost touch."

"The librarian in me studied the history of women over a long period of time. Men were the rulers, women their chattel. Men were dangerous. Women had only each another to depend on. They developed a secret code, a way to survive through friendship. It exists even today."

He reaches for my arms and lifts me up out of my slatted rocker. "Well," he says, "I can't make up for not having known you forever, but there's one advantage we husbands have that the best friends lack."

"And what's that, my darling?"

With that he kisses me lovingly and sweetly. And what a wonderful feeling it is.

"Makes up for it?" he asks, catching his breath.

"It certainly comes close." I move in for another of the same.

The doorbell rings.

"I knew it was too quiet. Maybe the girls are finally behaving as they did, BH."

"BH?"

"Before husband."

As I head for the door I suggest he make us another two Bloody Marys.

But it isn't the girls. It's Leah Andrews, in tears. "Are you still in the private eye business, Gladdy?" she says before she's even through the door.

"Yes, yes, I am."

"Then I want to hire you."

I call into the kitchen, "Honey, make that three Bloody Marys."

10

WHERE IS SEYMOUR?

We walk Leah back with us to the Florida room to continue to enjoy the breeze. Jack and I make small talk to try to help Leah get over her nervousness. Her hands are shaking. Isn't the weather fine? Nice party the other night, that kind of thing. I can tell the Bloody Mary is having an effect on her. She finally leans back against the couch pillows as Jack and I bend forward on our patio chairs.

"I've never hired a private eye person before," Leah says with trepidation.

I try to make it easy on her. "Just think of me as your neighbor who can also help people with their problems."

"Of course you realize it's about Seymour. I've

waited and waited to hear from him with no word at all, and now this."

She digs down into her small clutch purse on her lap and retrieves two postcards. And hands them to us. "Can you believe it? These came this week. Here's a picture of Seymour in Fiji. Another in Australia."

Indeed they are. In one, Seymour stands in a rain forest, wearing a T-shirt and shorts. *Fiji* is embossed on a baseball cap. The other Seymour photo is a variation, different T-shirt, and different shorts. The cap announces *Aussie*. He is posed in front of the Sydney Opera House. One says, "Wish you were here," the other, "I saw *Carmen* last night." In the second photo, Seymour seems to be getting a tan.

Now Leah can't hold back her tears. "How could this be? The man needed me to tie his shoelaces. Even at sixty, he is an innocent, clueless man-child."

For a moment she sobs. We wait until she's able to speak again.

"It was an accident. At school when he was eight years old. Children were pushing on the staircase. He fell down a whole flight . . . he was never the same again."

I hand her a tissue. "I'm so sorry . . . I didn't know."

"I've never told anyone. After my parents died, who else was there to take care of him? I did the best I could, but it was hard. He had a few jobs over the years. Simple things, like sweeping up a store.

"This was his life. All he ever did was take long walks or else he stayed in and watched all those silly reality shows on TV."

She becomes more agitated. "To just up and travel by himself? When did he ever get a passport? The few trips we took, and those were nearby, I had to pack his suitcase, because he couldn't manage it. And yet his suitcase is gone. And most of his clothes. He must have packed it. Somehow."

Leah stops, needs to take a break, then she continues.

"How could he plan? How did he know how to advertise for a sublet? Where did he get the money? He doesn't own a credit card. How did he manage to get to the end of the world?" She is beside herself. "How could he not tell me?"

We examine the postcards. They look authentic. The postmarked stamps are real. She hands us his original note. As she mentioned, all he says is he'll be back in about six months and he sublet to this Mrs. Joyce Steiner.

Jack comments, "Nothing about how he's traveling. Is he on a tour? A cruise? He doesn't mention hotels."

I ask, "Has he ever done anything like this in his whole life?"

Leah digs back in her mind. "Well, he did run away from the special school he was attending when he was thirteen. We found him at our local

Publix helping shoppers carry their bags home for small change. But that was because he was afraid of some bullies in his class."

Jack comments, "He looks quite happy and healthy in these photos."

"He's safe, from what we can tell. That's the important part," I add.

She uses the tissue to dab at her eyes. "I don't know what to think."

I put a caring hand on her shoulder. "So what is it you want us to do, Leah? You're not able to just wait until he contacts you directly at some point."

"I just need proof to know he's safe or to have him call me and tell me what's going on. I need to hear my dear brother's voice."

We look at our neighbor with compassion. She is truly suffering.

Jack says, "Well, there are a few things we'll be able to do once we get some facts. If he's on a ship or in a hotel, we can check where he might be. But without any real information, this could take a lot of time. By now, he's probably in a different country, so trying to track him in these two places wouldn't help."

I add, "We can talk to Joyce Steiner and learn how she found this sublet. Maybe he told her of his plans."

Leah gets up. "Anything you can do to find him, please, I beg you."

We walk her to the door.

"Anything."

In full sobs by now, she leaves us.

For a few moments we are silent, our minds on what Leah has told us.

I take a deep breath. "Without having anything specific, finding Seymour will be like looking for the proverbial needle in a haystack."

"Just about. But we can start with asking their neighbors if anyone ever saw Seymour leave. And how."

Jack starts to collect the Bloody Mary glasses. "Seymour is actually a missing person. But the cops won't take it seriously because there's no foul play. He hasn't been abducted. Is there really a case here?"

I gather up our breakfast dishes. "Here's something to think about. Maybe Seymour doesn't want to be found."

11

IDA FRANZ AND ASSOCIATES

"I think I see it. Here it comes." Ida waves her arms to indicate to the driver of the car that they are the people who are waiting to be picked up. They are standing at the front gate of Lanai Gardens. Far enough away so that their Phase Two neighbors won't know their business. Sophie and Bella have dressed prettily in twin outfits again for their first official detective class. Ida is in businesslike black.

The small lime green auto makes its way over to them.

Sophie frowns. "It's not much of a car. And look at that awful color."

Ida says, "It's better than three buses and costs a lot less than a taxi."

Sophie squints. "I don't see DWW printed on it."

Ida, annoyed, says, "They don't work that way. They're private drivers with their own cars who volunteer to take seniors around for a very cheap price."

Bella is nervous. "So how do we know it's them? It could be some robber or killer."

The car pulls up in front of them and stops. Ida says, "I called Drivers with Wheels and they said they'd send a car to this address in fifteen minutes and it's fifteen minutes now. Who else could it be?"

Sophie adds, "So ask for his credentials."

A young man jumps out of the front seat. Ida guesses he's about twenty. He's small and skinny, with curly black hair and dark eyes. He is all smiles, revealing one gold tooth. The Levi's he's wearing are torn at the knees, his scuffed once-white sneakers are untied, and he has on a T-shirt that says "Kiss me, I'm a hot Cubano."

The girls stare.

"*Buenos días,* ladies. Your driver is here at your service. These coming with you?"

Without waiting for an answer, he quickly lifts the three tote bags off each of their shoulders, raises the front compartment, and sets them in his tiny front trunk.

Bella's eyes grow wild. "What happened to your motor?"

The young man laughs. "It's in the back."

Bella is confused. "How can a car be backward?"

Sophie asks with trepidation, "Will we all fit in?"

The young man says, "Not to worry, my little

bug has a big heart." With that he opens the other three doors. "Hop right in."

Bella moves closer to Sophie. "What did he say about bugs?"

Ida practically shoves Bella into the backseat. "That's a Volkswagen. Move it."

Ida decides to sit up front with the driver. Sophie gets into the back next to Bella. It's a tight squeeze.

"Let me introduce myself. I'm Ricardo Leon, but please call me Rico. I aim to please. Me and my car—we may be small but we are mighty."

Ida glances at the thin tray between her and the driver. A half-eaten sandwich lies there, smelling of onions and garlic. Along with a half-empty beer can. She pulls far away from him until she's leaning against her door.

The driver turns so he can face all of them. "Seat belts. Seat belts. We are a safety-first automobile."

He sees Ida staring with horror at his lunch. He shrugs. "Not to worry. I was almost finished anyway." He takes what's left of the food and squashes it back into its bag and stuffs it into a small trash holder.

Ida asks with trepidation, "What do you mean, safety? That's a beer can! Have you been drinking?"

He shakes his head. "No, that is not real beer. Nonalcoholic. See, look at the label. Coors makes it. Not to worry." He turns to look at the two in back. "Do you like music?"

Sophie and Bella, sitting stiff as rods, manage a slight nod.

With that Rico hits a switch and music pours out from multiple speakers, loud enough to cause immediate deafness. Rico waves his hands with an imaginary baton. "You like?"

Ida pokes him in the shoulder. "No, no, too loud. Forget the music. Just drive."

Rico sadly complies. "You do not like the Buena Vista Social Club? Have you not heard of Rubén González?

Bella pipes up, "Maybe you have some Eddie Fisher? You know . . . 'Oh! My Papa'?"

Rico looks at her as if she's speaking another language. "No, *señora,* the Fisher's papa is not in my iTunes playlist."

"Are we there yet?" Bella asks in a small voice.

Sophie whispers, "We haven't even left."

Rico turns to them. *"No problema,"* he says and with that he takes off with screaming, smoking tires.

Bella whispers back, "We shoulda taken the buses."

Rico keeps turning his head when he talks to Sophie and Bella. Ida keeps pushing his face back so he can keep his eyes on the road. He is excited. "So you are lady detectives. This is so thrilling to me. I myself have dreams of going into the business of solving crimes. What was your best case?"

The girls by now are having a wonderful time. Sophie and Bella are enjoying the nonalcoholic beer that Rico is sharing with them. He has a cooler filled with cans that sits on the floor under Ida's feet. They are feeling quite cheerful, as if there really was liquor in the cans. Ida, of course, will drink only bottled water.

Rico has managed to charm them with his cuteness and enthusiasm. He wants to hear all about the cases they solved. They have been listing past successes, such as the Grandpa Bandit case. Romeo, the senior killer of elderly ladies. The eighty-five-year-old wife who was spying on her ninety-year-old husband, thinking he was cheating on her.

Sophie says, "My favorite was when we were in New York and we captured a thief who was stealing from the church poor box. We had to go underground to get him."

Ida corrects her. "That's undercover."

"Whatever," Sophie tosses back at her. She is feeling no pain.

Bella sits happily sucking on her nonbeer can, her eyes glazed.

Rico beams. "You are amazing ladies. So why do you need to be taking these lessons, since you are already experts?"

The girls look at one another. Ida decides to be the one who answers. "We want to learn more, so we can be better at our work."

Sophie and Bella nod their agreement.

"And," Ida adds with pride, "we are starting our very own company, Ida Franz and Associates."

Sophie hits her elbow against the back of the passenger seat, making Ida jump. "Stop saying that! It isn't decided yet!"

Stopping at a light frees Rico to grab hard-boiled eggs from his cooler. And a napkin for the shells. He hands them out. Ida refuses the offer. The others hungrily accept.

Ida shivers nervously every time he reaches under her feet and takes his eyes off the road.

The light changes. Rico takes off like a shot.

Rico is practically leaping out of his seat. "What about another partner? How about me? I am a man of many sides. I can do everything. I am like a man, invisible. You will never regret it. You learn upstairs with Señor Gatkes. I learn from you. We make a good team."

Ida holds up her hands. "Rico, you are going too fast for us, and I'm not just talking about your driving."

"*Está bien.* All right. We take one *bebé* step at a time. First, I am your number one driver. You call my private number." He reaches into a mess of papers and maps under his seat and retrieves a crumpled business card. "Day or night, you call, I am there."

He grins with his one gold tooth glittering at them. "Is a deal?"

He pulls up in front of Gatkes' building.

Ida says very quickly, "We teach you. You drive us free of charge."

Rico grins. "It's a deal."

12

THE POOL

Having finished with the Sunday papers and enjoyed our brunch, Jack and I head out for our morning dip in the pool. I'm not looking forward to it without Evvie and Joe here. And surprisingly, the girls are absent today. A neighbor already stopped us before we entered the pool gate and reported having spotted the three of them hurrying down the path toward the main gate, trying to look inconspicuous.

Inconspicuous? Not a chance. That's a joke at Lanai Gardens. Somehow, anywhere at any given hour, there will be a neighbor who is looking out the window or on a stroll, whose sharp eyes pick up any unusual behavior and immediately the condo jungle drums beat out the news.

And sure enough, some guy walking his dog

early this morning in Phase One was the tattler of unusual activity. The girls are sneaking out? Where are they going? Why aren't they swimming? Inquiring minds want to know. Which means everybody.

Sometimes I wonder why we don't swim at a different time or go to a pool in another Phase just so we can have some privacy. But then again, that news will also spread and feelings will be hurt. They should put up a sign, "Changes not welcome here."

One thing or another kept us from swimming all week, so Jack and I brace ourselves for the lunatic attack that awaits us from good old Hy Binder when we finally return to our daily routine. We turn the corner around the showers, reaching the pool and, sure enough, here's Hy. Like a tiger lying in wait, ready to spring.

"Well, look who's come to join us this morning. It's the honeymooners."

No one wants to pay attention to Hy, except for his parrot-wife, Lola, who adores every squawk out of his mouth. As does Sol, who is his best buddy. But Hy is too loud to ignore.

"Continued your honeymoon back here? Hiding away up in the *Chez* Gladdy bedroom?"

I poke Jack gently as he's about to take Hy on. I whisper, "Ignore him." After years of living through Hy's jokes and simplistic attacks, one stops paying attention. Jack, being a newcomer to our Phase, wants to take him on. Why bother? Why waste one's time and energy?

We make our way to our usual spots.

Hefty Tessie is swimming laps as usual. Hubby Sol sits at the edge, dangling his feet, watching his wife swim. This was not a marriage made in heaven. Tessie ran after him but he was too slow to get away.

Enya, our war survivor, sits in her corner, large straw sun hat blocking her face, eyes glued to a book, ignoring everyone as is her preference.

The snowbirds are devouring their usual Canadian newspapers.

Irving and Mary, still good friends, continue to visit Irving's wife, Millie, who remains in the Alzheimer's ward at a nearby facility. They visit her every day, even though she doesn't recognize either of them.

The two cousins, Barbi and Casey, who ran a computer information business, have moved back to San Francisco where they feel they will have more freedom to live the kind of life they prefer to lead. I suspect they weren't really cousins.

As we settle into our chaises, Hy starts in with another of his jokes. The Internet supplies him with these old saws by the hundreds. He practically dances up and down in his enthusiasm.

"Didja hear the one about the ninety-year-old guy sitting on a park bench crying? A cop comes over and asks what's the matter. Herby, that's his name, Herby says he just came home from his honeymoon with his gorgeous young wife. The cries become sobs. 'Well,' says the cop, 'good for you.

But why are you crying?' Herbie blows his nose and says, 'She's waiting for me in her negligee and I don't remember where we live.' "

There is a mild smattering of applause, mostly from Lola and Sol. I would guess that joke is as old as Hy.

Jack and I apply our sunblock. He does my back and I do his.

Hy wants to annoy us some more. He leans closer and pesters us about where the girls were going today and have we heard from Evvie. I say, "I don't know" and "yes." That's as much information as I'll give out to the likes of him. I lie down on my stomach, my back to Hy.

He'd try harder, but one look from Jack shuts him down. Off he goes to join Sol. They sit at his patio table and the two men start to play cards.

Peace and quiet at last. Jack is happily doing the Sunday crosswords and I am trying not to think of Evvie and Joe's two empty chairs next to me. I'll probably call my sister again today. I remember back to the days we all lived in the Bronx. We used to call each other three or four times a day, and laugh at ourselves. The second or third conversation always started with, By the way, I forgot to tell you, this or that . . .

And here we live in buildings directly across the way. We can even see each other in our windows and wave. Yet we still make the many calls. I smile.

Jack pokes me gently, pulling me out of my memories. "Company."

I turn over and glance to where he's indicating.

To my surprise, Arlene, in a bathing suit and coverall, is heading toward me, carrying her towel and swim tote. For a woman her age, her body is toned and agile.

I sit up. All eyes are on her. Hy lets out a wolf whistle and Lola gives him a small, playful smack.

Hy tells his wife, "Babe, I ain't dead yet. I can still look." He calls out, "Hey, Arlene. You get lost? Phase Three is thataway."

She doesn't hear him; she is focused only on reaching me.

Jack and I stand up to greet her.

"May I join you?" she asks with intensity. She whispers, "You know why."

I point to Evvie's empty lounge. "Of course. Take this chaise."

All eyes are on her. It's change. And attention is paid.

She adjusts the chair, sits down, and takes long breaths to calm herself.

I speak low as well. "Has anything happened?"

"I can't talk about it now. I just need to get away from there." She reaches for a magazine from her bag and attempts to read, but her hands are shaking.

I pick up my novel, but I'm not reading, either. I don't know how to help her. This is no solution. She'll have to run into Joyce one of these days.

The innocuous Muzak being piped in on the intercom starts to relax her. She places the towel across the front of her body, closes her eyes, and covers her face with her beach hat. I sense she might even sleep, she looks so tired.

Now I do start to read. Jack gets up, stretches, and walks over to the pool, ready to dive in.

But the peace and quiet is short-lived.

Suddenly I can sense something change in the atmosphere. The low buzz of chatter halts. I glance up to see what has caught everyone's attention.

Joyce has entered the pool area and is looking around. A peacock among the hens. I don't think any of us here have bought anything new or as colorful in at least five years. She is enveloped in a long loose muumuu-like outfit in strikingly bold and bright slashes of pink and green. Her matching sun hat is at a rakish angle. Her huge white-rimmed sunglasses almost cover her whole face. All of it is obviously expensive.

One can't help compare the two of them. Arlene is the real beauty and Joyce uses the cover of clothing to hide her unattractiveness.

Joyce spots me and starts to walk over, smiling as she does.

Hy has to butt in. "What's going on in Phase Three? What's with all these sudden visitors? An exodus? An epidemic? Somebody's grandkid pee in the pool?"

These things happen at once. Jack quickly comes back to me. I jump up, accidentally knocking into Evvie's chair, which startles Arlene.

As Joyce reaches me, Arlene leaps up off the chaise, her hat falling down onto the cement.

Both women gasp.

Joyce stops in her tracks.

Arlene turns to me, stricken. She whispers hoarsely, "What is she doing here? What?"

Even though Arlene speaks to me, Joyce answers her. "Our pool was so crowded, I thought I'd just come next door and see if there was room here."

Arlene grabs her towel and bag, forgetting her hat and her sandals, and begins to back away. She cries out, her voice shaky, "Please. Keep her away

Joyce, embarrassed, lifts her arms in supplication. "Wait, Arlene, don't go. I didn't know you were here. Honest. I'll leave, please, Arlene, come

But Arlene is running now. I'm hoping she doesn't fall. At our age, falling is a real danger.

Everyone watches this dramatic happening. News of this incident will spread fast and far.

I pick up the belongings Arlene left behind and hurry after her. I nod to Jack, who nods back, understanding that I need to try to help. No running for me, but I'm moving as quickly and as safely as of the Phase Three shower room, tears in her eyes. "I can't bear it."

I put my arms around her to comfort her. "Arlene, this is no good. You have to find a way to deal with this situation without getting yourself in such a state."

"I know, but you don't know what's going on. I can't tolerate the sight of her!"

"First, call your doctor and ask for a mild tranquilizer. You need to calm down." I'm hoping her doctor suggests she see a psychologist.

She nods her head. "I will. I promise."

We move toward her building. All the while Arlene glances behind her in case Joyce is following. "I have to do something. I'll have to move out!"

"That's not a solution. This is your home. You're happy here."

"Not anymore."

"But you have friends here."

Arlene stops and looks straight at me. Stronger now. "Do I? Do you ever see me with friends?"

I look at her, surprised at the unexpected comment. I try to recollect her being with people, other than at the few clubs she joins, but I'm not getting any picture of her hanging out with any of the club members. I remember she is considered a loner.

Arlene sighs. "I know what people say behind my back. How they see me. Why don't I conform? Everyone else has let their hair go natural. I still color mine. And go to the beauty salon every week. The 'uniform' here is to wear loose and plain clothes. I dress up every day. I still wear makeup. I go to the gym three times a week."

I try to defend her. "You can do whatever you want."

"Gladdy, really? Come on. Not so. As I mentioned, I was married twice. Each husband wanted a glamorous wife. So I dressed up for them and it became a habit. A habit I kept on following even though I'm single now. Can you understand what I mean?"

I comment, "Yes, as I was trained by my mother early on to always make my bed as soon as I woke up. And I still do that even though no one is watching."

"Exactly. When I came here, I thought I should change and be like everyone else. And then one day I said to myself, I'm not here to please them. I dress to please myself. What's wrong with that? The women here think it's necessary to be invisible because they're old. Society expects that. But we aren't obliged to look old. I'm not willing to look old."

I recall Hy whistling at her just moments ago. And Lola's response.

"So they think I'm a snob. And even a threat to the women. As if I'd want any of their husbands! Therefore, I keep to myself. I'm used to it and I prefer it." Her mood changes. Darkens. "And now I'm forced to deal with someone out of my past who is toxic to me."

She is getting disturbed again. "Listen. I'll go and

talk to Joyce. Let me find out how long she intends to stay."

Arlene looks up at me, unhappily. "I can always visit my son or daughter for a while until she's gone." She shudders. "It gives me the creeps knowing she's right underneath me. I can't go down for my mail. I can't shop for food. I feel trapped in my apartment. I only came out today because I thought I'd be safe where you are."

We reach her building. I suggest she go upstairs and lie down. She agrees. With a last look behind her she hurries into the elevator.

This is a mess. This woman I hardly know has touched me. How can I help her? I don't know what to do.

I return. Joyce has gone, but her memory lingers on.

Jack and I decide we've had enough of the pool today. We walk back to our condo. "What did I miss?" I ask him.

"A lot of staring and whispering. Joyce apologized for spoiling our swim time, shed some tears, and walked off in another direction."

Jack asks, "And what did I miss? You were with Arlene for quite a while."

"She's quite a woman. I had no idea. I'll tell you more over a cup of tea. I need to think about this situation."

Jack adds, "While you were with Arlene, I had an idea. Since we're on the Seymour case, it gives us an excuse to search his apartment. Hopefully, we can talk to Joyce at the same time and find some solution to Arlene's problem."

"Good thinking," I say.

"Not that I'm dodging my responsibilities, but as you pointed out to me, these are women's issues. You'd fare better talking to her alone."

I grin. "Aha . . . And what will you be up to, while I do all the work?" I give him a friendly nudge in his ribs.

"Maybe talk to Morrie and get some ideas on how to track Seymour."

"That's an idea." I smile, thinking of Ida renaming her PI group. "Soon you'll want to change our professional name."

Jack laughs. "Thanks for the suggestion. How about Jack Langford in big letters on our business cards, and in a corner, Gladdy Gold Langford, assistant, in tiny letters."

I punch him lightly on the arm. "We'll see about that."

13

SEYMOUR'S APARTMENT

Joyce is more than willing to let me come up to search Seymour's apartment. When I called her for an appointment, I had a feeling she wants to talk to me as much as I want to talk to her.

She opens the door to me dressed in a simple yet elegant jumpsuit. Her thinning red hair is tousled and half covered with a scarf.

As I enter, she tells me she's on the phone with her daughter in California, so I should just feel free to look around.

Joyce hurries back to the couch, picks up the phone, and continues speaking. "Yes, Stacy, honey, it's just one of the neighbors." I hear her sigh. "More delays? How hard is it to put in a Jacuzzi bathtub?"

I slowly look around, but I'm half listening. The

subject matter continues to be about the construction job on her new cottage in Sausalito.

To say Seymour's place is nondescript is putting it mildly. This man has lived here for twenty years and all he has are the basics. An ordinary wooden table with two chairs. A brownish five-foot couch and a black plastic recliner that's seen better days. And a small TV on a rickety stand. No pictures on the walls. A minuscule side table with a *TV Guide,* still open.

There's some kind of scrapbook leaning next to the recliner. I stop for a few moments to examine these two things. The *TV Guide* has a number of shows circled. I recognize them as reality shows. Then I look into the scrapbook. It's a shrine to these same kinds of shows. *The Amazing Race, Survivor, Big Brother, Fear Factor,* to name a few. Seymour is a big fan. Pages of information about the places, the people, the experiences. Interesting. This is the only object in this painfully plain apartment that shows an interest in life for Seymour. More like a passion, seeing how large this scrapbook is. I replace it where I found it.

In the bedroom, I'm surprised to see an expensive king-size bed along with a single-size bed pushed against a far wall and a simple chest of drawers. I open the drawers. Nothing in there. The closet has, I assume, what's left of Seymour's clothes after taking the rest on his trip. Joyce has hung up some of her things as far away in the closet as she can from his. The rest she seems to keep in her open suitcase near her bed.

In the bathroom, there's nothing in the medicine cabinet except for a half-used tube of toothpaste. Joyce keeps all her cosmetics out on the sink.

The kitchen has barely any cooking utensils. I open the fridge. Joyce has her groceries in there. Some yogurts, salad makings, juice, and coffee.

A few TV dinners are in the freezer, probably left over by Seymour.

My search takes five minutes. There isn't anything here. Seymour lived with practically nothing. Which makes sense now that Leah explained about his narrow existence. It seems to reflect Seymour's empty, sad life.

But the more important mystery: What is the obviously wealthy Joyce Steiner doing in a place like this? There's no doubt she comes from much better circumstances.

Joyce appears behind me, phone call completed. As if she reads my mind, "Dismal, isn't it? Amazing that anyone could live like this. As you might have noticed, I shipped my own bed here. I'm used to a lot more comfort, at least while I'm sleeping. I couldn't imagine myself sleeping in Seymour's bed. Would you like to join me in a cup of tea?"

"Yes, please."

Joyce boils the water in a small pot. There are literally only two cups. She brings over a package containing a selection of herb teas.

"Peppermint all right with you?" I nod. She pours hot water over our tea bags.

As we sit at the kitchen table, she asks, "Did you find anything? Nothing much here of Mr. Seymour Andrews, is there? I was quite amazed when I saw this place, to think that he's actually lived like this for years. At first I was appalled, and then I was not. I suddenly realized I craved what he had. Simplicity."

I wanted to ask questions, but I didn't need to. I let her ramble on. Heaven knows, I've already realized, she loves to talk about herself. She's doing all my investigative work for me.

"Most of my belongings have already been shipped to my daughter, since I thought I'd be going there as soon as I sold my place. When Stacy informed me there was a delay in construction, I panicked at first. But then I began to understand this odd situation was freeing me to do what I had to do. Deal with myself."

She grimaces, then reaches into her purse, which is at her side. It's large, and I'm curious as to what's in there.

Joyce takes out a pill bottle, spills two pills into her hand. She gets up and takes them with a glass of water. "Indigestion, acid reflux," she explains. "I'm ashamed. I don't even have a cookie to offer you. I've been dieting."

"Not a problem." She is painfully thin. Why do wealthy people need to look like skeletons? I'm happy that Jack talked me into a large lunch. She should stop dieting, but it's not my business to give her advice.

She continues. "At first I stayed at good hotels, but after a while I was bored with it. Too much temptation to drink and smoke and spend time with the kind of people I no longer enjoyed. I wanted to get back to who I once was a very long time ago, not this angry, rich wife, recently widowed. I realized I hated who I'd become."

Joyce chats on and on. About the mansion she had just sold that was on the Intracoastal Waterway. It's a throwaway remark, as if it was no big deal, but I know that area. Just about everyone does. Yet, few of us ever get to see it. The waterway covers three thousand miles of land touching the Atlantic and Gulf coasts. It runs nearly the entire length of the eastern seaboard. But what she's talking about is a section of Fort Lauderdale and Sunrise. Both towns contain incredible real estate. No way to visit them unless invited. Or if one takes the tourist boat trip that shows off these expensive homes, known for their astronomically high prices because of their privacy and exclusivity.

We are probably a twenty-minute drive from those homes, but they might as well be on the moon for how far they are from our reality.

Joyce regales me with tales of servants, country clubs, what she called in her words a useless life. The cash register in my head is tallying up real estate and memberships and Jaguars and yachts and I'm way up in the millions.

Joyce is still throwing pearls to the swine, so to speak. Seemingly so bored with her affluent life. "I gave up on hotels and looked for a sublet. And that's how I ended up here. And then to my utter amazement, I found Arlene. It was *beshert*. You know, fate."

She pauses. I guess she is finally giving me a turn to speak. Or cueing me on what should come next? Or skipping over details she doesn't want me to know? Gladdy, I chide myself, don't be so cynical.

I do ask the most obvious question. "However did you find this place?"

She smiles. "Well, that's a story in itself. You'll laugh. Purely by accident. I happened upon Seymour, who was walking in Lauderdale Park. I was walking, too, for exercise. We met one day and the next day we ran into each other again. We sat on a park bench to rest and then we started to talk. He was planning a trip but was worried about leaving his condo empty."

She suddenly looks at her watch. "Oh, dear. I forgot to tell Stacy something important. I must call her right back before she leaves the house and takes her children to the dentist."

She quickly moves me toward the door.

As I stand on the landing, she says, "You're a good listener, Mrs. Langford."

I startle for a moment. I'm not quite used to my new name.

I'm not about to leave until I say what I came up there to discuss. I face her directly. It's harsh, but I say it gently. "Arlene doesn't want you here. Do you think you can change her mind?"

Joyce shifts from one foot to another. She's in a hurry. She wants me out. I watch her face shift from irritation to bland.

She gives me an answer. "I thought so until that outburst at the pool. There is no forgiveness in her heart. I don't know how to reach her. I don't want to cause her pain all over again. What should I do?"

As much as I'd like to, I can't just tell her to leave. I try a different tack. "Arlene is talking about moving away."

Joyce hangs her head in shame. "Because of me? Then there's nothing else for me to do—I should be the one to leave. I'll start searching for another place to stay immediately."

I feel sorry for her. Everything she said made sense, so why do I feel so uncomfortable? She was like all angles and sharpness—too slick in the telling?

Then I realize she never fully answered my question about how she met Seymour. I don't know what to think.

14

SHOPPING SPREE

Ida won't admit she's as excited as Sophie and Bella about today's class. Today they get to the good stuff. She's been wondering if she made a mistake and they were wasting their time in this so-called private eye course. Gatkes seems all over the place. He talks about "good cop" and "bad cop" roles when dealing with prisoners. What's that got to do with being a PI? Then he sells them clothing. She thinks he's made all of it up. And besides, where are the other students? She expected a classroom filled with other enthusiastic students. The girls are clueless. They follow whatever Gatkes tells them. But she cannot admit defeat. So she has high hopes about what they'll learn today: how to defend themselves.

They eagerly follow Mike Gatkes as he leads

them to what might be a storage room far back down the hall from their usual classroom. This is a larger apartment than she thought.

He takes out a set of keys and unlocks half a dozen locks on this one door.

"Today you have your chance to buy your weapons of mass destruction." He laughs. "Kidding." Gatkes teases with a lilt in his voice. Ida is beginning to wonder, along with all the other things she questions, what's with the drama queen in their teacher?

He opens the door with a flourish and they enter, eyes growing wide with amazement at the huge quantity of killing equipment. Again, what's this? Do we kill a flea with an elephant gun?

Ida comments, "Would we really need stuff like this?"

He shrugs. "But a PI should always be prepared. Trust me. You'll find something useful in here."

Ida hates with a passion when anyone says trust me. The sign of a big liar.

The girls gaze at row after row of all sizes and shapes of scary-looking guns as Gatkes calls out his favorites. He likes a hefty handgun, especially the Glock. The Taurus revolver is a big seller, too. His KAC SR Enhanced Match Carbines are guaranteed accurate. "But let's not get too involved here. You girls don't want to carry."

Sophie and Bella shake their heads in horrified agreement. No, sir. They don't want to "carry."

Ida whistles, staring at the $1,075.99 price tag on something called a Long Range Sniper machine gun. "Who buys this stuff?"

Gatkes shrugs. "Your basic war fighters, law-enforcement and security guys, and law-abiding civilian shooters. Let me show you what you might need."

He waggles the next item through his fingers. "Here's a dandy pair of handcuffs. Always useful. The prices range from $88.99 down to a bargain at $13.99."

He passes a pair to the girls, who handle them as if they were diamond bracelets at Tiffany. They look to their leader, Ida, hopefully.

She says, "Okay on the cuffs, the ones at $13.99."

Sophie and Bella are gleeful.

Gatkes marks a list he is carrying.

He moves things along, continuing his comments. "You might not need these leg irons, but they're a sweet buy at $30.99. Or the expandable baton, a giveaway at $19.99."

Bella whispers to Sophie, "What would we use that for?"

Sophie shrugs. "For a band concert?"

Gatkes says, "What you would definitely need are night-vision glasses. Great for nighttime, low light, and poor weather conditions." He hands each girl a pair, then hits the switch and they are in darkness.

The girls ooh and aah. Even Ida is impressed by

how clearly she can see. The girls move around waving their arms, making silly faces, having fun with being able to see one another.

Ida commands, "Enough already."

The girls stop short. Gatkes turns the lights back on.

Sophie says, "But we gotta have these. They're cool."

"Good choice," Gatkes says encouragingly. "That's the top-of-the-line Cougar 492.5, at $99.99. An incredible buy."

"Whoa," says Ida. "Way too rich for our blood."

Her reticence doesn't faze Gatkes. "I respect your price range. I have a nice Bushnell Nightwatch. For you, $79.99."

Ida comments, "Gatkes, you sure do like that ninety-nine-cents thing. Why don't you just say a hundred bucks and be done with it?"

"Would you buy it at a hundred?"

"No."

"So $99.99 sounds better."

"I get your drift," Ida says. "But we're not buying even for $79.99. Flashlights will have to do."

The girls are disappointed, but Ida is in charge.

Ida smiles seeing how the girls are awed by her takeover personality. She's determined to talk them into having her name in the title of their new business.

Gatkes gets them to follow him down another aisle. "Here's our selection of excellent deterrents. The Tasers and Mace start at $49—"

Ida says it before he does. "—ninety-nine."

"They're scary," Bella says. "Don't they hurt?"

"Yeah," adds Sophie. "And what if we accidentally tased or maced ourselves?"

Gatkes agrees. "I see your point. May I suggest the less dangerous, but equally useful pepper spray?"

"What the heck is this?" Ida reads from a nearby tag. "'Counter Assault Bear Deterrent Spray with brush holster.'"

"Bears?" Bella asks, moving backward from Ida, looking every which way, terrified.

"Not for you, ladies." Gatkes winks conspiratorially. "No bears in our beloved Florida, though you might run into the occasional alligator. Kidding."

He walks them over to another shelf. "I think you'll like this handy-dandy little number. The Hot Lips lipstick. Looks like an ordinary lipstick for that element of surprise. You get an eight-second burst of pepper and an eight-to-ten-foot range. At a delightful price of $9—"

Now it's the chorus of three calling it out. "—ninety-nine."

The girls look eagerly toward their leader.

Ida says, "Sold."

The girls are delighted.

Gatkes smiles and reaches into another bin. "This last item will put the finishing touch on your basic equipment package. The Kevlar vest."

He holds one up, turning it around for them to appreciate.

Sophie and Bella, really getting into it, take turns trying on the various types of vests.

Ida shakes her head as she watches them modeling, turning, dipping, and preening as if on the runway of a Saks Fifth Avenue fashion show.

Gatkes moderates. "Here we have the antislash Covert Ladies' Hoodie made of aramid fiber, being modeled in pink by Mrs. Fox and in blue by Mrs. Meyerbeer."

Ida smiles contentedly as she reaches for her credit card. This may be costing them a fortune, but now she realizes Gladdy Gold and Associates was sooooo old-fashioned.

15

AT RICO'S PAD

Ida is nervous about going to Rico's home. Logically, it's a good idea. Since the girls don't dare invite Rico to Lanai Gardens, which would give away their secrets, he has opened up his home for their meeting place. Here they can discuss their new business and make future plans, as well as teach Rico what they learn.

It's a neighborhood far from where they live. She tries to pay attention as Rico drives, but nothing looks familiar. She has no idea where they are. Maybe a mostly Cuban area, from what Ida sees as they drive down his street. People are sitting on steps, chatting. She hears much laughter. And music. Children playing in a tiny pocket park. She considers how quickly they've accepted Rico. Enough to follow him without question.

A smile plays across Ida's face. She is pleased with herself. She has led the girls into what could be murky waters, but so far, all goes well. They are having an adventure. Which is more than what Gladdy Gold and Associates offers.

Rico actually lives in a small house. White clapboard. Neat. Painted. All good signs. Very much like all the rest of the homes.

Ida watches as the girls investigate all six hundred square feet of living space that is Rico's home. It's as neat inside as it was outside. The three of them practically fill up all the empty space. All the while Rico is delighted as he examines the stuff they've bought in Mike Gatkes' back room.

"Great choices," he says as he examines the Kevlar vests.

"Thanks," Ida says, taking credit.

Rico has graciously allowed them to store their new purchases here as well.

Every inch of this small space is in use. Rico is proud of the fact that he helps support his eight younger sisters and brothers, who live with their mother in Miami. He points to photos of his family on his one small dresser.

The girls are impressed. Not only does he volunteer with the senior driving project, but he holds down three jobs.

He informs the girls of his method. Indicating the computer equipment, he explains how he goes to garage sales and flea markets, buys things, then sells them on eBay. A bicycle takes up most of another wall. This is what he uses to deliver his morning newspapers. He has a steady route that he starts at 5 A.M.

At night he delivers pizzas.

The girls applaud him for his hard work. They are really getting to like this kid.

While they sip their nonalcoholic Mojitos, with their delicious strawberry daiquiri flavor, they admire Rico's posters of Cuba on the walls.

Rico congratulates them again on their great buys. He's sure they'll find good uses for everything they bought. They are ready for business.

"Ouch," Bella yelps suddenly. "That hurts!"

Ida and Rico turn to see what's going on. Sophie has put the cuffs on Bella.

Sophie looks chagrined. "I just wanted to see how tight they can get."

Bella pouts. "Well, now you know. Loosen me."

Sophie tries.

"No, you're going the wrong way! Ouch! Ouch!"

Rico comes to the rescue. He unlocks the cuffs and frees Bella.

Bella rubs her wrists to ease the pain. "Just don't try out the pepper spray on me," she warns.

"I'm sorry," Sophie says, meaning it.

Bella gratefully announces, "I think we should invite Rico to be a member of our new company. At least he knows how to safely handle our gear."

She glowers at Sophie, who hangs her head, feeling bad about hurting her friend. "I agree," Sophie adds.

They look toward Ida. Rico eyes her eagerly, holding his breath.

Ida puffs up. "Well, it's all right with me. But I don't know how he'll find the time to work with us."

Rico is thrilled. "You will love having me. I am so good at everything. Especially high-tech things," he says, holding the handcuffs up and laughing.

Ida has to make sure of their deal. "You still drive us, cheap."

"*Absotively posilutely,*" Rico says, purposely mangling the words.

They raise their Mojitos for a toast.

Ida says, "To Ida Franz and Associates!"

Bella and Sophie growl, but this time they don't argue.

16

LUNCH WITH MORRIE

"**S**o Ida led the rebellion. Ida now has her taste of power." Morrie laughs.

Jack replies, "And we all know how power corrupts." He laughs, too.

I add, "I'm sure Sophie and Bella want to come back into the fold, but they dare not cross her."

We're sitting in a favorite restaurant of ours. Greek food. Greek music. Yum, my favorite, moussaka. And that delicious lemon soup.

We're having lunch with Morrie, now officially my stepson. Usually, my new family cop hardly ever has time off during the day, so this is a treat. I always enjoy being with Jack's handsome son. I look at him and then at his equally good-looking dad and I know exactly how Morrie will look when he gets to Jack's age. Tall. Salt-and-pepper hair. Big and comfortable, like my teddy bear kind of guy. Lucky Morrie.

We are talking about friendship.

I add, "We hardly see much of the girls anymore. They're out very early and even when they're home, they aren't spending time with us. The most we've gotten out of them the few times we've actually seen them, Bella mentioned that they're with this Rico boy, who is driving them around since I was no longer their designated driver. Ida wasn't happy about her blurting out even that."

Morrie dips his pita bread into the hummus. "Well, whatever the girls are doing, I hope they're keeping out of trouble. I'd hate to have to arrest them for breaking and entering or something."

That gets another laugh.

"Do you want me to do some checking up on this guy? Find out his last name? Make sure he's legit?"

I answer, "Not yet. What's that old political expression? Let her swing in the wind for a while. If it sounds dangerous, I'll let you know. Bella will tell me."

"So how's your love life, Morrie?" Jack asks, changing the subject. He's not one for subtlety, when it comes to his son. "We haven't seen much of you lately."

Morrie actually blushes. He sighs. "All right, you twisted my arm. Yes, there is someone. She's smart. She's beautiful. She's funny. But I'm keeping her under wraps until I think she can handle good old Dad's friendly inquisitions."

Jack pretends to pout. "Bring her around. I promise to be on my best behavior."

"Actually, Dad. And Gladdy. We're very busy becoming good friends. Romance might come later."

"Good thinking," I say.

The waiter arrives with our lamb kabobs. We tuck in to enjoy them.

"My turn for quickly changing the subject," Morrie says, chomping away. "Speaking of friends. What's the latest with the Arlene and Joyce situation? Have they kissed and made up yet?"

Jack looks to me to fill him in.

"Actually, things are worse. Arlene is falling apart, having Joyce show up in her life. Joyce promised me she'd look around for another place to live. But I don't get the feeling she's looking too hard. I think she keeps hoping she can change Arlene's mind."

"And Seymour? Still no word?"

"Not a word," I say.

"Hmm, strange." Morrie passes the dolmas to me. "What's your take on the situation?"

Jack jumps in. "Frankly, that 'I'm looking for simplicity' line doesn't ring true. That woman is or was very rich. She could probably live anywhere she wants. I ask myself, Why Lanai Gardens?"

I agree. "She's a regular windup Chatty Cathy doll with me. She blabs and blabs, throwing out all kinds of unasked-for information. As if by dazzling us with her footwork we won't notice what's really going on. As Shakespeare once wrote, 'The lady doth protest too much, methinks.'

"Wait a minute! Just wait a minute." I wave my fork full of spanakopita in the air in excitement. "What about this? Which came first, the chicken or the egg?"

"Which means . . . ?" Morrie asks.

"She said it was fate that brought her to that apartment so she could meet Arlene again. What if . . . what if she knew all along that Arlene lived there and she made it her business to meet Seymour?"

The two men stop eating to listen.

Jack gets it. "So she could replay her past. Joyce needed to live in the apartment underneath Arlene!"

Morrie turns to me. "When did you come up with that?"

"Actually, right now. It just hit me. That would connect the dots. If she wanted to see her old friend that badly again, this rich lady was willing to pay an easily led old man enough money to get him out of his supersafe cocoon. She assumed, and rightly, Arlene still hated her and wouldn't see her if she tried to call her directly.

"She wanted the opportunity to win her back, so she went to all this trouble to 'accidentally' move into our condo."

Jack says, "Which, unfortunately, is not going too well. Arlene's anger runs too deep."

I add, "What if Joyce did all of it with him and for him? It would make sense considering Leah's description of her brother. Joyce must have taken him to get his passport, helped make the travel plans. That trip, whatever it is, cost a lot. Why else would she give this odd man that much money in order for her to live in that depressing apartment?"

"I think Gladdy's onto something," Jack says. "This makes more sense than thinking Seymour could do it all by himself."

Morrie says, pleased, "Not only does your idea sound feasible, it tells us something else we haven't yet thought of."

Now it's my turn to stare at Morrie.

He takes a sip of his retsina. "This means that Joyce knows very well where Seymour is. I'd bet money on it."

17

THE COOKING CLUB

As we drive up to Jack's appointed parking spot, I see two women waving their hands frantically at us. Jack pulls in. I recognize our neighbors Fatima Baener and Elaine DeKyser, from Phase Three, rushing toward us. They are avid members of the Red Hat Society and as usual they are wearing red and purple. A large group of Lanai Garden residents belong to that unusual women's club based on a poem written by Jenny Joseph, who wrote that when she got old, she would wear purple.

But why are they running toward us?

They can hardly wait until I get the door open.

Fatima says, "Thank goodness you're back. We've been looking everywhere for you!"

"What's wrong?" I ask.

Elaine reaches for my hand. "Plenty. All hell has broken loose in our cooking class."

Fatima talks at the same time. "Arlene's gone bonkers. I think she's trying to kill Joyce."

That's all it takes. Jack and I are running with the anxiety-ridden women. Elaine is pulling me along.

I'm puffing to keep up. "Tell us more. How did it start?"

Both women start talking, overlapping each other's words.

Fatima says, "We're practicing making key lime pies and Arlene is doing okay, even though she thought we were baking lemon meringue today. Then Joyce shows up."

Elaine says, "Joyce said that she read in our newsletter we were making key lime pies today, and since it's her favorite, she joined us. She didn't know Arlene would be there."

Fatima tells us Arlene is not happy to see Joyce.

Elaine adds that Joyce tries to be nice about it.

Fatima says, "Joyce starts to remind her of how, when they were young, they used to make pies together and had so much fun."

Elaine adds, "And Arlene reminds *her*, she was baking a key lime pie the day she caught that bitch—excuse the language, that's the word Arlene used—sleeping with her husband!"

"And she didn't say 'sleeping with,' either," Elaine adds. "It's a word I never, ever say."

"We snuck out when Arlene wasn't looking. We had to find you," Fatima says, relieved.

We reach the club room door and hear shouting inside.

What a sight before our eyes as we enter. Fatima and Elaine stay put at the doorway. They don't dare come in.

I recognize the two other members. Frances Tarvin and Sandra Litzman, both wearing aprons, stand clinging to each other at the far end of the kitchen, holding on to each other in fright.

The room is a shambles. Kitchen pots have been thrown about. A lemon-colored pie lies splattered all over the butcher block. Utensils are scattered. Other freshly baked pies sit on the stove. I'm aware of how good the room smells. How ironic—the scents of vanilla and fear.

Arlene stands at one side of the large chopping block in the center of the room. On the opposite side is Joyce, arms held up as if in submission, perhaps believing she'll need them to deflect a blow.

What's frightening is that Arlene is brandishing a huge, serrated bread-carving knife. My God, what's happened to her? It's a different Arlene. What's changed since we last talked? The perfectly put-together lady is a mess. Her clothes and apron are covered with custard and meringue. Her hair is flying about her face and her eyes are wild and unfocused. Dear God, she looks demented.

Arlene sees us. "Gladdy," she cries out shrilly, "tell her to leave me alone! Make her stop stalking me!"

Jack and I look at Joyce and I can read the pity

on her face. She shrugs. She says quietly, "I don't know what she's talking about."

Arlene screams, "Liar! Liar!" She slams the knife handle in her fist on the wooden block, sending pie crust bits into the air.

Jack walks slowly to her. Speaking softly. "It's all right. Everything will be all right." He reaches for the knife.

I hold my breath. Oh, Jack, don't . . . What if . . . what if . . . I can't bear to think it . . .

Arlene doesn't seem to recognize him.

Jack says, "I'm here. Gladdy is here. We'll help you."

The knife quivers in her hands.

Frances stifles a cry. Sandra closes her eyes, terrified of what might happen.

Arlene hands the knife over to him, as if surprised to see what she had been holding. He slides the knife into the butcher block drawer.

I join him. Together we put our arms around her and lead her out. Her whole body is shaking. She turns once more and glares at Joyce.

She sobs. "Die, damn you! Die. I wish you were dead!"

We start to walk Arlene along the path, heading toward our own apartment, but we don't get very far.

She suddenly pulls away. "You don't believe me, do you?"

Our worried eyes betray us.

Arlene reverses herself and heads back toward her own building. She starts to run. "Leave me alone! Just leave me alone!"

We stand still looking after her.

Moments later, we can see Joyce, head down, walking away from the club room by herself. She seems to be moving aimlessly.

Jack and I nod. Quickly, we both reach her and head her off.

"We should talk," Jack says to her.

She shakes her head. Distraught, she cries out, "Not now. Please. Later!"

And she runs from us, too.

18

A WAITING GAME

We have leftover pot roast for dinner. Usually a favorite dish. Especially when it's served the next day and the juices have saturated the meat and made the taste even better. But neither of us is hungry. I move my fork absently around my plate as I listen to Jack attempting to call Joyce for the third time this evening. He hangs up.

"Still no answer."

My turn. I attempt another call to Bella. Again no answer. I've left a number of messages on her machine to call me as soon as she gets in. But nothing.

"Frustrating," I say as I get up and look out the window across the silent parking area up to her second-floor window. Still no movement.

"No kidding. Here I've worked myself up to

playing bad cop tonight with Joyce and either she's not answering or maybe she's gone to some bar to forget that horrific scene this morning."

"She's got to come home sometime. Both of them do."

"I'm determined to make her admit to knowing where Seymour is so that we can get him back."

"And I'm just as determined to ask Bella to explain that remark she made at the newcomers party about having seen Joyce at an earlier time. I want to prove my theory that Joyce knew where Arlene lived."

I start to clear the dining room table. "I don't suppose you want dessert. Sandra gave me one of the key lime pies that she made this afternoon. She said she lost her appetite."

Jack gets up to help me. "Well, so have I."

"Poor Arlene. I just can't get over the change in her. I wonder what's going through her mind right now. Why is she so frightened? Why does she insist she's being stalked? What could turn her into the woman standing there with a knife in her hand? Clearly Joyce didn't know what she was talking about. This has all gotten out of control."

We stack the dishes in the dishwasher. I soak the big pot in the sink with suds to loosen the grease.

I turn to Jack. "While we're waiting, TV or gin rummy?"

"TV. I don't want to think. I need mindless entertainment."

"Ditto."

But first, I beckon Jack to follow me. I open the front door and we go out onto the walkway.

Across the way we can see the flicker of a few TVs. The sun is beginning to set. "Listen," I say.

"I don't hear anything."

I put my arm around his waist. "That's what I mean. It's too quiet. I feel like we're standing here waiting for the proverbial other shoe to drop."

19

THE CANDY MACHINE CASE

Ida rushes the girls up the steep stairs yet again. Mike Gatkes has phoned and told them to come back to his office. Something big is happening, he says. And they won't want to miss it.

She practically pushes Bella and Sophie from behind. They are huffing and puffing, almost hanging on to the banister, climbing on their knees, praying for the strength to make it.

Mike Gatkes paces in the hallway outside his office, waiting for them as they try to catch their breath. He glances importantly at his watch, which Ida notices has a Mickey Mouse face.

"About time. Just got a case hot off the griddle. Thought you'd like to be working along with me. We're going on a field trip."

He shoves his forties vintage fedora onto his head and starts skipping down the steps. "Follow me."

The girls can hardly move. Ida weakly calls down to him, "Mr. Gatkes, wait."

Sophie gasps, "Water."

Bella cries out, "A chair. I need a chair."

Gatkes looks up at them. "No time. We gotta hustle."

The girls hold on to the banister for dear life. Half walking, half sliding, they make their way back downstairs.

Bella mumbles, "Getting old can kill you."

"Useless, I tell you, the police are good for nothing." Ida watches the car wash owner, Harvey Fleigel, move agitatedly along the line of rolling cars as they get soaped, washed, waxed, and dried. Ida notices that his workers ignore him. She looks again, puzzled. They kind of, sort of look like Fleigel.

They're all talking loudly over the noise of the car wash mechanisms.

Harvey is all hands and waving arms and shrugging shoulders as he cries out his problem. "The cops come, they scribble on their little pads, and I never hear from them. And it happened again last night. Twelve dollars in quarters. All the coins, gone with the wind. Gatkes, I'm going crazy here."

Bella whispers, "I haven't seen that movie in

years. Is it playing around here?" She mimics dramatically, "Frankly, my dear, I don't give a damn."

Ida hisses at her, "Shh. Pay attention."

Ida hovers over Bella and Sophie, who are sitting on beat-up red and orange plastic customer chairs behind the low wall alongside the passing wet cars. They are fanning themselves with the Shiny Bright Car Wash brochures.

"Harvey, calm yourself," Mike Gatkes says. "I'm here and I brought my students along to learn. I will crack this case wide open. I promise."

Ida grimaces as he pretends to look sweetly at his students, who now resemble a bunch of wet rags. "Look around, ladies. Take notes. The car wash and parking lot are locked every single night. Harvey here closes off the chain-link fence himself. Examine the top. Barbed wire. If anyone climbed the fence, the alarm would go off. Not only that, the crook wouldn't be able to get back out. In fact, with all the barbed wire hitting his *touchas*, he wouldn't be able to sit down again for a week. Yet someone manages to sneak in every night and steal every quarter out of the candy machine."

Gatkes points and the girls attentively follow the line of his fingers. "Voilà, the candy machine."

Ida smirks. Suddenly Gatkes talks French?

Bella pokes Ida. "Is it all right if we ask for a candy bar? I'm getting hungry just looking at all that chocolate."

Sophie agrees. "Good idea. We can sample the evidence."

Ida ignores them.

"I read the printout. I know how many bars get sold, and no coins." Harvey is getting purple in the face from so much aggravation.

Gatkes tries to calm him. "But the thief doesn't take the bills."

"Hah! Three one-dollar bills. Big deal. Everybody uses coins."

Gatkes pulls Fleigel off to one side. He wiggles his thumb in the direction of his team of young workers and whispers, "You're sure they're clean?"

"Fugeddaboudit. They're relatives. I inherit all the lazy dropout nephews. Besides, the machine ain't been tampered with. There's no way to get the coins out without my keys."

"Ladies." Gatkes addresses the girls. "Comments? Ideas?"

Sophie pipes up, "Gladdy would call this a closed-room case."

Bella is confused. "How could that be? We're outside, on the street."

"Well, it is. There's no way anybody can get in or out." Sophie is proud of her detecting prowess.

Ida shushes her. "Never mind about Gladdy, this is our gig. So just be quiet."

Bella raises her hand. "I've got a question."

The two men turn to her.

Bella looks duly puzzled. "Why don't you empty the candy machine before you go home?"

Mike claps. "Good question. See, Harvey, I told you the old broads were sharp."

Harvey puffs out his chest and beer belly. "It's the principle of the thing. I wanna catch those guys in the act, those *momzers* who're stiffing me."

"Well," adds Ida, in a tone she uses for fools, "at least take most of the coins out, so you only get partially robbed."

"Nice detecting," Mike says, clueless of her sarcasm. "But, Harvey, don't do it yet. I got to work out a plan for how to trap them. I'll get back to you in a couple of days."

Rico arrives to pick them up from the bus stop bench where they sit waiting for him, exhausted and hungry for dinner. He parks and joins them on the bench with a small cooler he's brought.

He opens the cooler and offers the girls Cuban *pastelitos* as a snack. At first they don't want to touch them, always fearful of the unknown.

But Rico says, "Try it, you'll like it. My *mamacita* baked them." Hunger wins out, and they do. They happily lick the sweet top of the delicious coconut puff pastry as they fill him in.

Rico joins them in their snack. He comments between bites, "Impossible! No way could anyone climb over the fence. And besides, look at this street. It's crowded all the time. Probably wild stuff going on all night long. Someone would notice a break-in."

They glance around, taking in the street scene evolving around them.

Sophie comments, "It's more interesting than where we live. Like a circus."

Bella tugs at her. "Look, that guy even has a cotton candy machine."

Rico says, "How about those cute kids dancing to salsa?" Rico applauds them and drops a few coins into a baseball cap they have lying on the ground.

Sophie comments, "They even have an organ grinder with a monkey. Can we get bananas and feed him?"

Ida is impatient to leave. The crowds and smells are annoying her. "Eat up already. This place is giving me a headache."

"Well," sums up their sort-of new partner, "this calls for a stakeout."

Ida looks at him sharply. "I'm the boss. I make the decisions." She pauses, then announces, "It's time for a stakeout. Fast, before Gatkes comes up with his plan. Rico, how much for overtime driving?"

Rico grins. "Here's my deal for you. I come along. One stakeout. Round trip. Free ride. Nighttime snacks from *Mamacita*."

Ida makes a quick executive decision. "Done."

"Tonight. We'll hang out at my pad until it gets dark. Maybe around eight-thirty."

Bella shivers with excitement. "We never get to stay up that late."

"How about I make us pulled-pork sandwiches

and we have more of that fake beer for our dinner?"

The girls look a bit perturbed at the idea of a spicy pork dinner.

Then Sophie says, "Why not! We only live once!"

With that she grabs Bella's hands and they dance together to the Cuban music. Rico takes their hands and joins them. "We'll have a hot time in the old town tonight."

Sophie says, "I can't wait. This is gonna be such fun."

Ida shakes her head. Now she has three children to drive her crazy.

20

STAKEOUT

They stand in the dark back alley behind Rico's building, getting ready to pack up his car. Ida does the last-minute checkup of what's in their totes.

"Flashlights?"

Three sets of hands hold up their flashlights. Flick them to make sure the batteries are working. "Check," says Rico.

"Clothing?"

All are dressed completely in black. Sophie and Bella lift up their extra-large dark shirts to show their pink and blue hoodies underneath.

"Check," says Rico.

"Weapons."

The lipstick pepper sprays are held aloft. "Check."

"Sleeping items?"

"I got the blankies," Bella says.

Ida sees Bella hide her teddy bear. She's not about to admit she can't sleep anywhere without it.

"I have the pillows," Sophie remarks.

Rico grins. "Houston. We are ready for takeoff."

They climb into Rico's now totally stuffed little lime VW bug.

As planned, they arrive at the car wash five minutes before closing. Rico parks his car in the lot and takes a ticket from one of the indifferent nephews. He and the girls pretend to walk toward the exit. Instead, with a careful eye out so that Harvey won't spot them as he unwinds his chain-link fence, they race to the restrooms.

"Hide," Rico says, "and wait ten minutes."

Ida snarls. "I was just about to say that. I'm in charge here. Hide!"

"Yes, boss," Rico says.

In the bathroom they face a small problem. There are only two stalls. Ida grabs one and Sophie and Bella squeeze into the other. They whisper to one another.

Bella kvetches to Ida, "It's a tight fit."

Ida says, "Make it work."

Ida hears shuffling noises. "What's going on?"

Sophie says, "Never mind. I'm sitting on the closed seat. Bella is on my lap."

They talk to each other over the tops of the stalls.

Bella giggles. "This is so much more fun than mah-jongg."

Sophie asks, "Should we stand on the toilet seats so no one will see our feet?"

Ida says, "Brilliant idea, then they'll only see your head."

Sophie is puzzled. Was that sarcasm?

"I like the idea," Bella says. "But I don't know if I can climb up on it."

"Or we can sit on the seat with our feet up," Sophie suggests.

"With the lid open or shut?" Bella wants to know.

Ida closes her eyes, exasperated. "God, give me strength," she prays.

After a few minutes, Sophie whispers, "Isn't it ten minutes yet? I can't even breathe in here, it's so crowded."

Ida says, "Okay, I think we're safe. I doubt whether Harvey or his boys would walk into the ladies' room."

More noises from the other stall. Ida hears the flushing of the toilet. "Shh. Who did that?"

"Me," Bella confesses. "Might as well use the facilities."

All quiet at last. The girls and Rico walk around the enclosed car wash, making sure they're alone. It is a black, clouded, starless night and they need to use their flashlights. Sophie and Bella cling to each other as they cautiously head back to his car.

"I don't know," Ida says. "Sitting in that small car all night is going to be a hardship. Is there anyplace else we can hang out without being seen?"

Rico says, "There are three other parked cars. We can hide between them if we bend down, but that's not much better."

"Not with my arthritic knees," Sophie complains.

"Mine, either," Bella adds. "I'll never be able to get up again."

Ida shrugs. "Could we stay in the bathrooms until we hear something?"

"Not good—we won't be able to see or hear." Rico sighs. He walks around surveying their options. He looks down the empty car wash tunnel. "But we have time. If we've guessed right, it'll be the nephews who made copies of their uncle's keys. *Los stupido*s will probably wait till around midnight."

He grins, getting an idea. "Might as well give my bug a bath. It could use it." He adds, "And the price is right."

Ida looks askance at him. "Are you sure you should do this? What do you know about how a car wash works?"

"Piece of tortilla," says their new partner. "What's to know? You press a button and it washes."

He gets back into the bug and drives slowly. The girls follow him as he makes his way to the front of the car wash. He gets the car into the starting position, lining it up with the conveyor belt.

Sophie knocks on his window. "Could I ride along? I always wanted to be inside a car when it's getting washed."

"Me, too," Bella says happily.

He waves them in.

Sophie takes the front seat next to him, and Bella the back.

He rolls down his window and calls out to Ida, "Wanna come along for the ride?"

Ida, never the adventurous one, folds her arms. "No, thanks."

Rico tells the girls to stay put as he jumps back out the car and studies his wash options from a list on the wall. "Might as well get the extra wax job."

He turns to Ida. "Okay. First, I'm gonna look for the faucets to turn on the water. Ida, you can help. Go in that little room over there and flip open the switch to start the motor."

She gives him a dirty look, but rather than argue, she heads for the small room. With her searchlight, she stares at the wall filled with switches.

She sticks her head out the door and calls in a heavy whisper, "Which one? There's a lot of them."

He calls back to her, "How many are there?"

Ida dutifully goes back and counts. She calls out to him, "Twenty-four."

"Then switch them all on."

"Are you sure?"

"Yeah."

As she does so, all the lights in the entire car wash suddenly go on, illuminating the entire scene. Moments later, a deafening noise follows.

Ida races out of the storage room in a panic and confronts Rico, who is on his hands and knees still searching for a water spigot. "What was that sound?"

The expert shrugs. "Must be a hydraulic drive or a water pressure pump."

"Oh, swell, now we're all lit up and making enough noise to wake the dead."

A muffled scream comes from the girls as the conveyor belt starts to move the car along its rail. "Get on! Get on!" Sophie shouts.

"Hold your *caballos,* I'll be right there. I found the water." He quickly turns the water on. "Rightsy tightsy, lefty loosey," he recites as his reminder.

He rushes back to the wall facing the moving bug and starts pressing all the buttons. The car wash begins doing its thing.

He runs along the walkway as the bug passes him on the conveyer belt, shouting after them, "Sophie! Bella! Whatever you do, don't open the windows!"

They can't hear him above the noise. Sophie opens her window. She calls, "What did you say?" as a huge wave of water hits her.

"Close the windows. Close them!" Rico shouts.

Terrified, the now soaking wet Sophie does so.

Ida rushes down the walkway to reach Rico, who

is still following his precious bug. Ida sees the girls, their hands smacking at the closed windows, their faces twisted in horror. She sees them mouth "Help!"

Then they disappear under the flapping wings of the foamlike washing mechanism. The car is enveloped by globs of soapsuds.

Ida sneers at Rico. "Some terrific idea. Now everyone in the street can see and hear us!"

They turn to look at the cluster of people watching them. Bag ladies and drunks enjoying the free show. The audience members wave gleefully.

"Good show," one of them calls, waving his gin bottle.

Ida grabs tightly on to Rico's arm. "Now see what you've done. The police will be here any minute."

Rico removes her clutching arm, reassuring her and changing his earlier tune. "Not to worry. No way any of those weirdos out there have cellphones, and besides, even if they did no one around here ever calls cops. And cops never come around here at night. It's too dangerous."

"But the alarm. Won't it go off?"

"Only if you're climbing the fence."

"Well, you and your big idea about washing your stupid little car. The crooks won't come near us now with all this light and all this commotion."

They can hear the muffled sounds of Bella and Sophie screaming at them, begging to be let out.

Now the wax is spraying. The two girls look

distorted by the pattern of the zigzagging wax buildup.

Ida yells, "Rico, get into the car and stop them!"

"I can't," he says, "there's no way for me to jump on. It's too slippery."

"Then turn the damn thing off!"

Rico shouts to the girls as he runs alongside them. "I'm going to shut you down. Just, whatever you do, don't touch the steering wheel." He motions with his hands imitating the steering wheel and shaking his head from side to side.

The girls add their own signals. Sophie and Bella are both nodding their heads up and down and pointing to something somewhere behind Rico's head.

Suddenly Sophie turns the steering wheel toward him as hard as she can.

"No!" Rico yells, "Don't do that! I said *don't* touch the wheel!"

Too late. Rico's car jumps the tracks and everything comes to a grinding halt.

Rico groans. "We're stuck! I'll never be able to get my car out."

And Ida adds, "And we're gonna get caught here like rats in a trap. I can see the headlines now: 'Four Stupid Crooks Arrested for Breaking and Entering.'"

Rico sloshes his way over to his car and opens the door. The residual water inside splashes onto him.

He pulls the girls out and yells, "Why did you do that?"

They are wet and grinning. Sophie says, "We wanted to show you."

"What's so damn funny?"

The two girls pant and point again.

"Squirrel," Sophie says, almost incoherently through her laughter.

"Squirrel," Bella says, giggling and trying to squeeze the water out of her sweatshirt.

Rico and Ida look behind them to where the girls are waving.

And there's the candy machine with a squirrel squeezing its way out of the coin slot with quarters in its mouth.

Ida and Rico can hardly believe their eyes as the little varmint slides up a water pipe heading for the roof with its ill-gotten gains.

"Case solved," Sophie says gleefully.

21

END OF QUIET

I shake myself. I must have dozed off. Jack is snoring away at the other end of the couch. The movie we were watching is long over. There's another classic film on now. I touch his shoulder, trying to wake him gently.

He jumps up, startled.

I smile. Watching an old black-and-white movie is better than any sleeping pill. I check the time. It's a little past midnight.

We wander into the kitchen. I boil some water for tea to help us wake up.

Jack looks out the window. Still no light at Bella's. "We must have missed the girls coming home. She's probably asleep by now."

By now all of Lanai Gardens is out cold as well.

As we sip our tea, we try to decide what to do about Joyce.

Jack straightens up his shirt and runs his hands through his hair. "I'm going over to her place. I don't care if I do wake her. This madness has got to end. Maybe catching her half asleep, she'll let down her guard."

"Okay, but finish your tea. Do you want me to go with you?"

"No, I'm going to play the alpha male and I won't let her talk me into a stupor. Joyce needs a tougher approach." Jack grabs a sweater from the closet, kisses me on the cheek, and heads out.

I stand on the walkway watching Jack head for Phase Three. Just as I'm about to go back inside, my eyes are caught by a bilious green VW bug pulling up in front of our building.

To my immense surprise, out pop Ida, Bella, and Sophie, all of whom are in great spirits. They are laughing and saying loud good-nights to their driver.

My imagination is piqued. I hurry downstairs to catch them. By the time I get there, the driver has turned a corner.

The girls greet me happily.

"Hey, late birds, where have you been all day and half the night?" What's this? They look disheveled and Bella and Sophie look wet? Is that possible? Where would they get wet? And what are those strange things they're wearing? Sweatshirts with hoods?

Ida is haughty. "You wouldn't believe us if we told you."

Sophie chimes in, "We were on our first case."

Bella finishes, "And we solved it. We were good!"

The girls high-five each other.

Sophie says, laughing so hard she can hardly get the words out, "And we caught the thieves. Well, not really, but on Rico's phone camera. The squirrels did it!"

"Shh," I say, "you're waking the neighbors."

Bella hiccups.

I ask an obvious question. "Were you girls out drinking?"

Bella giggles. "We were celebrating. I love near beer."

"Where were you? And who's Rico?"

Ida looks smug as she answers me. "He's our chauffeur."

Bella adds, "And our new partner."

Before I can make any sense of what they're talking about, I am suddenly aware of Jack running toward me. He looks as if the devil himself were chasing after him.

"What?" I ask. "What's happened?"

Jack barely nods to the girls.

"I knocked on Joyce's door and as I did, it swung open. I called out to her. She didn't answer. All the lights were on. I didn't know what else to do, so I went inside. And I found Joyce.

"She'd dead, Gladdy. Joyce is dead!"

22

MORRIE ARRIVES

By now enough people have been awakened by the unusual nighttime activity that a sizable crowd in bathrobes is witness to these latest arrivals. A patrol car pulls up and I'm surprised to see Morrie step out of it along with a policeman. The paramedic unit arrives right behind them in their truck.

Morrie greets us. "I know you didn't expect to see a detective answer the 911 call, but when I saw the address and Dad's name as the one who called it in, I decided to come. What happened?"

Jack answers him. "It's Joyce Steiner. I went to see her"—he looks at his watch—"half an hour ago. I found her on her kitchen floor, dead."

Jack puts his arm around my shoulder. He leads Morrie and his team to Phase Three. A little parade follows. The girls are a little farther behind us. The straggling group of neighbors timidly continue the march. Word has seeped out about Joyce. Naturally, they are now wide-awake and fascinated by these goings-on.

Morrie talks quietly, so only Jack and I can hear. "Could you tell anything?"

Jack answers, "No, not much. From the hallway I could see her lying there. I carefully moved close enough to take her pulse. She was gone." And knowing what Morrie would say next, the ex-cop adds, "Except for the doorknob, I touched nothing else."

We arrive at Phase Three. Jack and I are the only ones who are allowed to go upstairs with Morrie, the cop, and the paramedics.

Jack and I stand in the little hallway, keeping our distance, as Morrie carefully enters the kitchen.

I try hard not to look at Joyce's dead body being checked out by the paramedics. They concur. The woman is definitely dead. They are about to cover her face and take her away, and I don't want to watch that. I turn and concentrate on what Morrie's saying instead.

Jack is aware of my feelings and he continues to hold me for moral and physical support. I think of Joyce this afternoon alive in the kitchen activity room fearfully standing there being threatened by a furious Arlene. I can still picture the look of pity on Joyce's face. And now, she's gone.

How will this affect Arlene?

"It looks as if she was in the middle of eating some pie when she collapsed," Morrie comments, and the cop takes notes of what he says.

I shudder seeing a half-eaten slice of key lime pie there on the table. With a fork on the plate. A crumpled napkin beside it. A bitter reminder of this afternoon. Along with two almost-empty glasses of what looks like water.

"She may have had company," Morrie continues, indicating the glasses. "Before, during, or after her demise."

He turns to us. He looks at the expression on my face. "You know something?"

I don't want to say anything. I fear it will make things bad for Arlene. But it's my nature. I can't hold back important information.

I fill Morrie in about Arlene's behavior at the cooking class this afternoon.

"So the pie may have come from that kitchen? It doesn't look like she baked anything here tonight. No wrappers to show she brought it from some store. Maybe it was carried up wrapped in that napkin next to the plate."

He turns to his father. "Why were you going up to see Mrs. Steiner this late at night?"

"We'd decided to finally face her with the fact that we no longer believe Joyce accidentally found her old friend. We believe she purposely talked Seymour into moving out and letting her in. I intended to ask her if that was the truth. And if so, where was Seymour?

"When there was no response to my knocking and I found the door open, I felt something was wrong and that was why I entered the apartment."

Morrie turns to one of the paramedics. "What does it look like, Dan? Her heart?"

"Maybe. Maybe not. You'll have to leave it for the ME to tell you."

Morrie addresses the cop who came with him. He points to what's on the kitchen table. "Phil, bag it all. Just in case."

I have to know. "Just in case what?"

He turns to us. No longer just chatting with his father and his new stepmother, all business now. "You report an angry incident this afternoon. You tell me you were going to see her, wanting important information late at night. You find her door open.

"I have to take into consideration as to whether any of these possibly suspicious events played a part in her death. Was Mrs. Steiner alone when she died? Why the two glasses? Why was her door left open? Was Mrs. Steiner so bereft she had a heart attack?" He pauses. "Enough to commit suicide?"

He hesitates. And I'm horrified, sensing what he'll say next.

"Or was it murder?"

I gasp. Oh, no, it couldn't be.

Morrie turns to Phil again. "Nothing is to be disturbed until I send in the team. We need the photographs, the fingerprints. Meanwhile, I want this door locked and no one is allowed to enter."

We exit the apartment and watch his cop assistant attach the all-too-familiar yellow crime tape on Seymour Andrews' apartment door.

Big trouble ahead.

23

THE PLOT THICKENS

Needless to say we didn't get much rest that night. Morrie questioned us some more. He wanted to know if Joyce had any relatives. I told him there was a daughter, Stacy, living in California, but I didn't know her last name. Morrie was sure he'd find it when they went through her belongings.

We got into bed, exhausted, but then couldn't fall asleep. There was so much to think about and discuss. One thing was for certain: too late now to get Joyce to tell us where Seymour was. Next there will be Leah to deal with. We decide not to mention our theory about Seymour being deceived by Joyce. It would upset her needlessly. We have to find a different way to locate Seymour.

And poor Arlene. How will she take this horrible

news? She couldn't have hurt Joyce. Yet I still have that picture in my head of her standing there with that knife. Could she? Please let that autopsy determine natural causes.

I make coffee waiting for Jack to get dressed and join me. My mind is reeling with things that must be done.

I wonder if the girls have heard the news already via the grapevine.

I have to call Evvie and tell her what's going on.

There's a knock on the door. Eight in the morning and it's already beginning. I open it to the girls standing there. Serious expressions on all three faces. They appear uncomfortable.

I invite them into the kitchen. They turn to Ida, waiting for her to speak for them all, and when she doesn't immediately, I start to pour them coffee. They sit down quickly, as if I might change my mind and chase them out. Guilt might have a lot to do with their behavior.

Ida stiffly, as is her fashion, says, "We came here to offer our services. We know we've separated our businesses, but for right now, we want to help."

Bella and Sophie nod their heads eagerly.

"Thank you," I say, just as formally. "Happy to have your help."

Guilt assuaged, they take their coffee and reach for the plate of buttered toast. Bella digs into the fridge to where she knows I keep the jam.

Ida asks, "What did Morrie tell you last night?"

I'm not willing to state too much yet. "He says we have to wait for the autopsy report."

Sophie says, "We already figured that."

I look to Bella, now enjoying her guilt-free breakfast. "I have a question for you. About Joyce. You mentioned something the other night at the get-together evening about having seen Joyce before she moved in."

Ida is about to interrupt and say something negative. I know her too well so I stop her by raising my hand. "Let Bella speak."

Bella puts down her toast and jam, wipes her hands delicately on a napkin, happily feeling important at the moment. "It was months ago. I'm not sure when, but it was raining a lot. I see this woman walking around looking confused. I ask her if she's lost. And I make a joke that everybody gets lost at first in Lanai Gardens."

Bella smiles at this well-known fact. "She wanted to know how to get to Phase Three. I have nothing better to do, so I take her there. I ask her who she's looking for since we know everybody who lives everywhere. She tells me she's looking for an old friend. She thanks me and stands still and I can tell she's waiting for me to leave. I figure it's none of my business so I skedaddle." Bella is pleased with her recitation.

I'm surprised. Is it possible she actually told Bella the truth, thinking it was safe to mention a friend? That this sweet, innocent-looking woman would forget about it? Shades of Agatha Christie! Assuming Bella was invisible.

Ida has to say it. "How can you be so sure it was her?"

Sophie shrugs. "Well, Joyce is quite dramatic. You couldn't mistake her for anyone else."

Bella pauses to take another bite of toast, chews, then comments, "I almost didn't recognize her because when she was wandering around, she was wearing plain dark clothes and a scarf that covered her hair. And an umbrella. But it was her. I know it."

"Well done," I tell Bella.

"But why is that important?" Sophie asks.

"Because we think it was Arlene she was looking for. Once Joyce found out where she lived, she'd then find out who resided in the apartment directly below. Apparently Joyce lived in the apartment underneath Arlene years ago when they were still friends."

Ida gets it. "So first she locates Arlene and then she finds out that Seymour lives in the apartment Joyce wants to use."

I report, "She actually told me she met Seymour in the park on one of his walks—"

Sophie interrupts. "Aha! She follows him and pretends to accidentally meet him on his daily walk and talks him into renting his apartment."

Bella is puzzled. "How weird. Why go to all that trouble? Why didn't she just call Arlene up and make a date?"

I comment, "Because she knew how much Arlene hated her. She had to find another way."

I put two more slices of whole-wheat bread into the toaster. "You ask what you can do to help? Somebody else must have seen Joyce lurking about. Somebody may have seen Seymour leave his apartment for his trip. I know he had a suitcase. Did he take a cab? We need to know how and when he left."

"Easy, peasy," Sophie says. "We'll cover all the Phases and ask around until we find out."

The girls are now relaxed. All's well once again in our little world. Time for me to do a little prying myself. "So tell me more about your teacher, Mr. Gatkes, and your PI class."

Bella blurts, as if she can hardly wait to impress me, "Wait till you hear about the guns! Rifles! Machine guns!"

Sophie adds excitedly, "Assault bear spray!"

Ida looks as if she'd like to clamp her hands over both their mouths, but she restrains herself. "I'm sure Gladdy wouldn't be interested." She turns to me. "We were just looking. Not buying guns."

Sophie jumps in. "Wait till we show you our lipstick!"

Good grief. What on earth are they talking about?

Sophie's about to go through her huge floppy purse, which of course matches her lime green jumpsuit, but just then Jack wanders in, buttoning up his shirt.

The girls clam up in the presence of all that skin and chest hair. My very tall, impressive, sexy alpha man has made his appearance.

They all jump up. Ida says, "Well, no time like the present. Let's get started canvassing right now."

Sophie and Bella echo her words. "Right now."

Hello, Jack. Goodbye, Jack. And they are gone.

Jack grins as he reaches for the coffeepot. "I sure know how to clear a room."

I fill his cup for him. "One of these days they'll get used to you. Maybe. Drink your coffee and let me tell you about assault bear spray and lipstick!"

I figure my sister is up and about by 9 A.M., so I call her in Connecticut. I fill her in on everything. Evvie has a lot of questions. It takes me about twenty minutes. Finally I say to her, "What do you say to all this?"

"What do I say? I say, my grandchildren are already bored with me. I'll ask Joe if he's ready to come back after a week of visiting. I'm going to make a reservation on the first flight out tomorrow morning to Fort Lauderdale. I say there's a lot of detecting to do and I want in. What do *you* say to that?"

The answer I hoped for. "Call and tell me your schedule. I'll be there to pick both of you up. With bells on."

I can hardly wait for her to get home.

Immediately after, it's the door again. Jack, being

closer, answers. When I reach the hallway I see the distraught figure of Leah. She's wearing a light cardigan over a thin dress. The buttons are done up wrong. I sense she just threw something on in a hurry. Next. We're playing revolving doors around here this morning.

She's hardly in the entry hall when she cries out, hysterically shrill, "Is it true? She's dead. Dead in my Seymour's apartment?"

Jack answers, "Yes, she died sometime last night."

"Of what? How? Why is that yellow tape on the door? I watch *CSI, Miami*. It means it's a crime scene? What's the crime? Did she do something to my Seymour?"

Jack takes her by the arm and helps her into a kitchen chair. Still warm from my last customers, no doubt.

Jack speaks. "We don't know much yet. We have to wait for the police to tell us."

"But I can't get into his apartment. I had a visit early this morning. Got woken up by a cop who wanted my key to his apartment!" She's biting her fingernails down to the nub. "When can I go back in?"

I answer her quietly, "Not yet. But soon."

"How could any of this happen? How could Seymour have rented to this woman?"

I say, vague at best, "Hopefully we'll have answers soon."

Leah shudders. "A dead person in that apartment. Is there blood? Seymour will never want to step foot in there again. He's very sensitive." She tears up. "That's if I ever see my brother again."

She reaches into her sweater pocket and pulls out and waves two postcards. "Here's some more come in my mail. This one, he's in Tahiti and he's beating on some creepy-looking drums. And then he's in Hawaii, wearing a lei around his neck." She practically throws the cards at me.

Now she's crying. Jack pats her gently on her back. I bring her a drink of water. But she can't sit still. She jumps up. "I have to go now." With that, she's out the door.

We both examine the cards. Jack shakes his head. Fiji, Australia, Tahiti, Hawaii. "What the hell kind of itinerary is that?"

"Maybe so, but look at the smile on his face. He's having the time of his life."

Jack shrugs. "They're not even in the same hemisphere."

Who's next?

Jack insists I eat a hearty breakfast before I tackle Arlene.

24

ARLENE REACTS

I knock on Arlene's door. It takes a while until she answers. It's nearly 11 A.M., and from the way she looks when she opens it a crack, she hasn't slept well. I've clearly awakened her.

She lets me in. I'd been here once before, a while ago, and I remembered her furnishings, all light and airy rattan with plush pillows in cool colors and cheerful patterns. This is the kind of furniture picked out by a happy person.

Now the apartment is dark. Every window curtain is drawn. Poor thing, she looks awful. The perfectly-put-together lady looks bedraggled and exhausted. She leads me into the living room and we sit down on her couch.

In the dimness, all seems gray. As gray as her life is now.

I ask, "You didn't sleep much last night?"

She shrugs. "On and off."

"Have you been eating?"

"A little. Not much."

Why am I stalling? Why don't I blurt it out and be done with it?

Arlene fluffs a couch pillow absently. "I'm so sorry for the way I behaved in the cooking class. I guess I just hit the wall."

What I'm doing is cruel. I'm actually interrogating her. "Have you ever been in Joyce's apartment?"

She screws up her face in distaste. "No, never."

She quickly turns her head away from me. Please don't be lying, I silently beg of her. I can't put this off any longer. "You didn't hear all the noise last night around one A.M.?"

She thinks a moment. "I guess I was asleep then."

"The police were here."

"Why?"

Oh, Gladdy, get on with it. I can't stand what I'm doing. I feel like I'm taking advantage of her. "They were in Seymour's apartment."

Her eyes open wide. "What . . . ?"

I take a deep breath. "Joyce's gone, Arlene. She died last night."

Her body stiffens. She stares at me. "What are you talking about? You saw her yesterday afternoon!"

"She's dead now."

In the silence, I imagine her trying to absorb this incredible news. What must she be feeling?

Arlene starts to giggle. "I'm glad. I'm so glad. I'm free of her at last!"

I don't know what I expected, but not that.

She sees the expression of shock on my face.

"Oh, God, what am I saying? I'm so ashamed."

She reaches out and grabs my hands. "Is it possible? Can a person wish with all her might for something and then it happens? I wished her dead. And now she is."

I answer her quietly. "I don't think so. Whatever killed Joyce, it's real."

She gets up again and nervously paces the room. She absently reaches for a painting and straightens it. She wrings her hands. "Dead, she's really dead?"

I nod.

She starts for the door and I know I have to follow. She looks at me and says, "I honestly don't know how I feel."

She opens the front door for me.

"Forgive me," she says. "I need to be alone now."

25

EVVIE COMES HOME

The next day I drive Evvie home from the airport. She tells me Joe changed his mind at the last minute and decided to stay.

"Was he feeling ill?"

"No, just a little tired. Those grandkids keep him on his toes. But he loves every minute of it."

"You feel all right about leaving him back there?"

"He insisted I go. I told him I'd be back in about a week. Since it's just a short plane trip away, if needed I'd be right back. Besides, my darling knew I was restless. There's where he needs to be, and right now I'm where I want to be."

We're silent for a few minutes. It's what's left unsaid. There's no way to know the inescapable future. We could be talking about months, maybe sooner or later.

"Joe and I have had a lot of really deep talks lately," she says, breaking the silence. "We examined our earlier married days and what went wrong. It's hard to believe how angry we were with each other. And for what? He was insecure about his future. I was worried about how we would manage. The job he had was taking him nowhere. He had his dream of what he wanted to do, but I got pregnant too soon and that was more pressure for us. We were just too young."

"I know." I remember those terrible days. "You were so in love, but he was so angry."

"He took his anger out on me. It was safe to hurt me when he was really angry at the whole world and the way his life was turning out. We look back on how we behaved and could kick ourselves for wasting all those years. If only we had more confidence in ourselves and each other. If only we could have talked it out with each other. Woulda, coulda, shoulda.

"Well, that's the good part of getting older. What's that book title? Don't sweat the small stuff? Trouble is, it didn't seem small back then."

Evvie shrugs. "Enough about me. I can't get over the terrible news about Joyce. I'll bet Lanai Gardens is in an uproar. What's the latest on her demise?"

"We'll be hearing about the autopsy report very shortly. So strange. Joyce must have gone to a lot of trouble to move in close to her old friend again.

She's only been here a very short time and now, suddenly, unexpectedly, it's all over."

"Do you think Arlene would have relented eventually and forgiven her?"

"Doesn't seem like it. She was truly relieved that Joyce had died."

"What do you think happened? She just keeled over?"

I give her Morrie's three possibilities.

"Murder? Impossible."

"Let's hope you're right."

Evvie shakes her head. "Wow. It's all so sad. Well, we all know about holding a grudge for years, don't we? I'm so lucky that this time around Joe and I had the chance to forgive and forget."

"Poor Arlene," I say.

"Poor Joyce," Evvie adds.

26

MORRIE BRINGS BAD NEWS

Morrie shows up at our door. He told us on the phone he had the results of the autopsy and he wanted to report to us in person.

The look on his face tells me the news is not good.

I offer to feed him some lunch. He agrees gratefully, saying he hadn't had time to grab a bite of breakfast or lunch anywhere.

"Not even a doughnut?" I say, trying to lighten things up with the old joke about how cops are famous for eating doughnuts. No response. He's too serious.

We sit at the dining room table. I bring out already-made egg salad with rye bread and a pitcher of iced tea. Morrie goes for it eagerly. Jack joins in. My throat is so choked up, I can't swallow.

I sip at my tea. I'm nervous. And it turns out rightly so. The news is bad. How can they eat?

Morrie states simply, "Joyce died of a drug overdose. The slice of pie on her table was laced with Valium . . ."

He stops and looks up at me as I gasp at the name. My body stiffens from fear.

"We've been through the apartment again. There is no sign whatever of the container that held any Valium. We went through the trash. Nothing there."

"She could have dumped the bottle anywhere and just kept the pills. I mean I've done that before. When a few pills are left I put them in a cute little pill holder." I'm grasping at straws—I don't want to tell him what I know. I hope there is the possibility of Joyce having the same prescription drug Arlene had. But what are the odds? "Can't we locate her doctor and find out?"

"There were pills in Joyce's purse."

I jump in at that. "I saw her take those pills. She said it was for indigestion, an acid reflux problem. Maybe she didn't want me to know it was Valium."

Morrie stares at me for a moment. I get the feeling he has worse news. I brace myself.

Morrie says it. "Her medication in her purse was morphine. For severe pain."

"What? Not Valium? Oh, no."

Jack comments, "Morphine? That's a pretty serious drug for her to be taking."

Morrie continues. "We had another big surprise come out of the autopsy. Besides the poison, Joyce's body was riddled with cancer. Lung cancer. We called her physician, whose name was on her medication. Joyce had chemo, as her doctor explained, with no good results. She stopped the chemo, knowing it was hopeless."

I shudder at the realization. Now it makes sense. Her thin hair growing back from baldness! Covering her head with scarves! Her almost emaciated body. Not dieting. Dying!

Jack shows his astonishment, too. "She was close to dying of cancer? In severe pain. Then surely that's a reason why she didn't want to live."

I touch Jack's hand for comfort. "That would explain her wanting to find Arlene. To make amends before she died. Arlene refused her plea for friendship. So Joyce gave up hoping. Doesn't that make sense?"

Jack pats my hand. I am trying to hide my agitation. "If only she'd told Arlene, maybe this would never have happened. Maybe Arlene would have forgiven her."

Morrie shakes his head. "What's puzzling is if she wanted to commit suicide, why didn't she take the morphine? She had plenty of pills left. She had to know how dangerous they were. It would have taken much more Valium to do the job than if she used the morphine. So why did she use Valium and where did the Valium come from?"

Morrie looks at my expression. He knows I'm

hiding something. I never did have a good poker face. "What?" he asks.

I sigh. "Arlene takes Valium. It was my idea. She was so stressed out I suggested she get something from her doctor to relax her. Couldn't it be a coincidence?"

"It's not likely."

Morrie frowns at me as if to say I should know better about coincidences. I do know better.

"I'm sorry, Gladdy. I have to consider Arlene a person of interest. She hated Joyce. She threatened Joyce in front of witnesses, with a knife. She is quoted as saying she wanted her dead."

"But perhaps she didn't mean it. People say foolish things in anger."

"I need to search Arlene's apartment. Will you come with me? With you at my side, she might agree to let me in. Otherwise I'll have to get a warrant. Which I will do."

I have no choice but to do his bidding. I feel awful. He's going to look for her pill bottle.

Morrie gets up from the table. His plate is empty. As is his glass. Jack did almost as well with his meal. I haven't touched a bite.

"Shall we go?" he asks me.

I get up, start to clear the table, then at Jack's knowing look, I stop stalling and head for the door.

As we go out onto the walkway, Morrie says, "Thank you for the lovely lunch, Stepmom."

I smile grimly. I feel like a traitor.

27

MORRIE AND ARLENE

Morrie looks me straight in the eye. "Please don't inform her of anything I told you earlier."

Of course I know that and he knows I do. But he wants my assurance. I nod my head in agreement.

Again I knock at Arlene's door. I'm not happy having to do this. She looks better this time, showered, dressed, made up, and hair combed. That's a relief. She smiles seeing me, but the smile fades quickly when she sees Morrie.

And two other policemen who've been waiting outside the door.

Morrie turns to Arlene. "Mrs. Simon, I'm Detective Morgan Langford and I'd like permission to search your apartment."

She looks at me, defeated. "Because I said those terrible things to Joyce?"

"Something like that," he answers.

"But why? The woman had a heart attack—"

He interrupts. "No, it wasn't a heart attack."

"I don't understand why you want to search my apartment. I didn't do anything."

She looks to me for guidance. I say hopefully, "Then they won't find anything that could hurt you."

She looks up defiantly at Morrie. "Go ahead. I have nothing to hide."

"Thank you," Morrie says.

"Just try not to make a mess," she says sweetly.

I walk out the door with Arlene. Morrie beckons and the two policemen enter. Jack is allowed to stay behind.

Arlene is shaking and I have my fingers crossed.

We wait at Evvie's apartment. Strangely, now I'm hungry, but it's nervous hunger, and I snack on the cheese and crackers she's brought out for us.

Of course Arlene can't eat a thing. She's frightened and angry at the same time.

She says, "Because I hate her they assume, what? That I would kill her? That's preposterous!"

I am so anxious that I'm not allowed to mention the cancer. I can barely stay still. The word sticks gluelike in my mouth.

Evvie keeps glancing at me. She knows I know something but I can't tell her in front of Arlene.

We sit silently for a few minutes. Arlene begins to cry. "I have to tell you what has been going on since Joyce found me."

Evvie and I exchange glances. She can see that something is worrying me. Later, we signal each other.

Arlene paces. "All you ever saw of me was my shouting at her and telling her I hated her and wished she was dead. But you didn't know what she was doing to me. I meant it in the kitchen class when I said she was stalking me."

Evvie says, "Arlene, dear. Joyce's coming into your life has been very upsetting for you. Are you sure you weren't distorting things?"

Arlene smiles grimly. "In front of you she played the poor misunderstood friend who only wanted forgiveness, but late at night that woman would creep into my apartment and wake me up. Every night. Very, very late to make sure nobody saw her come in. Eventually I couldn't fall asleep at all knowing she'd come in."

Evvie asks, "How could she do that?"

"She had a key. I don't know how she got it. I swear to you I'm not imagining any of this."

I ask, "What did she want?"

"I don't know!"

Evvie continues to go along with this, even though I can see the disbelief in her eyes. "What did she say to you?"

"Horrible things. Vicious things. It was so strange. She hated me even more than I hated her. She blamed me for her marriage to Edward being a failure. She was blaming me for everything that went wrong in her life. She would sit on my bed and torment me about her sex life with Edward. She called me filthy names. If I got out of the bed, she followed me. She terrified me."

"Why didn't you tell anyone about this sooner?" I ask.

She stares up at the both of us, sadly. "Because I felt threatened. She said she would hurt me if I told anybody anything. And I believed her." She pauses. "I think she was crazy."

Oh, poor Arlene. She will be the one they think is mad if she tells this story to the police. It will be her word against Joyce's. If it seems unbelievable to us, how will strangers react?

Evvie says, "Even if we believe now that Joyce didn't accidentally move here. That she found you and then trailed Seymour in order to get his apartment; why do you think she would do this?"

"Not to ask my forgiveness. To torture me, that's what."

So much for my guess that Joyce wanted to make up with her before she died.

I think of her body being consumed with cancer, deciding to find Arlene and then doing what Arlene says she did. Could the cancer have affected her brain? Could that, plus the morphine, literally make Joyce insane? Otherwise, her tormenting an old friend doesn't make sense.

There is a knock on the door. Morrie and Jack enter, leaving the two cops outside.

Evvie and I look up with trepidation. They are not smiling.

Arlene sits down, holding on to the arms of the chair. Her body goes rigid at the sight of their serious faces.

Morrie holds up a small plastic medicine container in a glassine evidence bag. "Are these your pills?" he asks Arlene.

She peers at them closely. "Yes. Valium. I took them for my nerves. Gladdy suggested I should get some. I did."

I hang my head. How much guilt can a person stand?

Morrie waves the bag. "Then can you explain why the bottle is empty?" He upends the bag to indicate it is indeed empty.

Arlene looks surprised. "That's odd. But I only used a few. I really don't like to overuse pills like that."

I look at Jack and he shakes his head.

Morrie then takes out another evidence bag. "Is this yours?" He holds out the Chai necklace we've seen before.

Arlene says, "Yes, it is—" Then she suddenly reaches up to her neck and feels for her own necklace. It's there. She looks confused. "I don't understand . . ."

Morrie says, "I suspect this one belongs to Mrs. Steiner. I believe she's the only one around here that has the exact same necklace as yours. We found it in one of your dresser drawers covered in a scarf. A necklace and scarf that belonged to Mrs. Steiner."

Arlene is horrified. "Then she put it there. I didn't!"

"How could she do that?"

"She had a key to my apartment." She looks at me to help. But I know I mustn't interrupt.

"The only keys we found in Mrs. Steiner's apartment belonged to Mrs. Steiner."

"You have to believe me . . ."

It's obvious he doesn't.

Morrie continues. "Have you ever been in Joyce's apartment?"

"No, never . . ."

I hold my breath. She's going to be caught in a lie.

"Then if we take your fingerprints, they won't show up on a glass of water you drank in her kitchen. Right next to the slice of pie that you brought for her to eat—filled with your pills all ground up."

Arlene jumps up, sobbing. "All right. I went there that night because she said she was leaving. She found another place, and wanted to apologize and say goodbye. I was so desperate to believe it, I went downstairs."

Morrie comments, "She gave you a glass of water."

"Yes, I only sipped it. I couldn't wait to get out of

there. She lied again. She had no intention of leaving."

She stands up, unable to sit a moment longer. She cries out, "I didn't bring any pie. I didn't put any pills in the pie. I didn't kill her!"

There is silence for a few moments as she stands there shaking.

Surprisingly Morrie turns to me. There's a funny expression on his face. I'm trying to read it, but I can't. It's as if he's warning me about something.

I look closely at Morrie. His eyes are sad.

He turns back to Arlene.

"You knew, didn't you, about her having cancer?"

He waits and I shudder. He was asking me to understand that sometimes a cop has to be cruel. I can't bear to watch him.

Arlene staggers, holding on to the arm of the couch. "What are you talking about?"

Morrie says in a low voice, "You knew she was going to die very soon. Couldn't you have waited?"

Arlene looks terrified, like someone trapped in a nightmare.

I tremble when Morrie says, "Arlene Simon, you are under arrest for the murder of Joyce Steiner . . ."

As he starts to recite the Miranda, Arlene faints.

28

THE ROAR OF THE CROWD

Why am I surprised? There is a huge crowd waiting outside Evvie's building. The word has spread like wildfire. Joyce is dead and they're bringing Arlene down to take her off to jail. Thank goodness Morrie listened to me when I begged him not to put the handcuffs on. Arlene is in enough pain. And he was so kind about letting her rest awhile after she recovered from fainting.

I walk out of the apartment with Jack and Evvie. We stand aside on the third-floor landing to let them get past us. Morrie and his cop assistant leave with Arlene being held by the arm by Morrie.

I look below and recognize the crowd. Most of Phase Two and Three are there. Of course the girls are in the group, their faces reflecting their feeling very sorry for poor Arlene. My eye is caught by

Leah, standing on the fringe. She looks like she's in shock as she watches what is going on.

When they reach the ground floor there's a collective groan among the watchers. Then silence. Everyone stares. Poor Arlene. She looks totally defeated. The fight is gone out of her. She glances back up to where we're standing and I see such sadness there. Then her head bows down. She doesn't want to look at anyone else.

It's like a bad scene out of any of the many cop shows on TV with Morrie making sure her head won't hit the police car roof. It's chilling to see Arlene behind the locked security screen, already looking like she's behind bars.

They drive off.

Then everyone talks at once.

By the time the three of us get downstairs, there's a ruckus going on.

They've almost separated into two camps, or so it seems. One group, the women minus one from the kitchen class. And Leah. With others from Phase Three behind them.

Our side, Sophie, Bella and Ida, and many Phase Two regulars: Tessie and Sol, Irving and Mary, Lola and Hy. Lola clutches her husband's arm.

And the body language is easy to read.

Fatima, our red-hatter, is angry. Arms folded. "We were there. We heard her threaten Joyce."

Elaine, her friend, adds, hands on hips, "Standing there with a knife, ready to kill her there and then."

Hy is a sight to be seen as he stands legs spread,

fists raised, reminding me of a bantam cock fighter. "Who are you to judge? That's what we have courts for."

"Yeah," adds Lola. "And juries of her peers."

Elaine says, "You've all seen her. At the pool. At our kitchen class. Just getting weirder and weirder. She's a nutcase."

Tessie pipes up, "She didn't get nutty until Joyce showed up."

Another voice in the crowd: "Oh, please. She's the ice maiden. With her nose stuck up in the air."

One of the male Canadian guests says, "That's not true. Arlene was always a lady. A very nice lady."

First time I've ever seen any of our snowbirds get involved in our affairs. Bless them.

"Oh, really?" someone else shouts out. "She was very snooty. With her fancy clothes and fancy high heels. She thought she was better than us. Who did she think she was anyway?"

Tessie snarls, "You're just jealous, you old hags! You only wish you could look as good as she does at her age!"

Hy raises himself up to his full five feet. "I don't care what you think about her or what you saw or think you know; this is still a free country!"

Sol gets into the act. He places himself right behind Hy. "Damn straight!"

Fatima shouts, "Yeah, and I'm free to be a witness at her trial. I know what I saw and what I heard!"

Frances Tarvin, a tough-looking woman from the kitchen group, steps forward, invading Hy's space. He doesn't move an inch. "She's a murderer and she ain't gonna get away with it!"

Hy is not one to be pushed around, especially by a woman. He reaches over and gently pushes her face away from his. Frances sends a fast fist out to punch him. He ducks. She hits Sol instead.

Sol says, "Ouch."

His wife, Tessie, that plus-size dynamo, elbows pointed out in weapon mode, goes head to head with the aggressive Frances for revenge.

A couple of the other Phase Three residents drag their belligerent neighbor away amid cheering and booing. Depending on which side they're on.

The Phase Two group pulls on Tessie.

Hy is on a roll. He shouts above the hubbub, "In this fine country we live in, You. Are. Innocent. Until proven guilty!"

Lola hugs him. "My hero."

Hy always manages to surprise us. I forgive him for all the bad jokes.

People leave. Much mumbling and grumbling. Dinners are waiting. The drama is over. For now.

It will boil down to what I've been afraid of. It will be Joyce's word against Arlene's. Wait until the news leaks out about Joyce dying of cancer. All sympathy will shift to her. Being dead trumps being alive. We've got to do something to prove Arlene's innocence, and fast.

29

OUR MEETING WITH MORRIE

Morrie sits behind his desk. Jack and I sit in the two halfway comfortable low chairs in front of him. Though Morrie and Jack are equally tall, Morrie's desk chair is a lot more comfortable than the one Jack is in.

Forget that we're family. This is police headquarters and we are here on serious business. We report on that frightening crowd scene that took place after Morrie carried Arlene away. "And it's been like that for days now. That's all everyone talks about and thinks about. And has opinions about."

Jack comments, too. "And our opinion is that knowing Arlene, we still find it hard to believe she could commit murder."

I reach over and take his hand.

"All right," Morrie says to us, being sympathetic.

"I appreciate that you like the woman. But I have to deal with the facts in this situation. At this time everything points to Arlene as having killed Joyce Steiner."

I have to ask, "But aren't you even going to try to find out if anyone else could have killed her?"

Morrie is sorry. "We believe we already have the right person."

I try another tack. "But what about Seymour? How does he fit in?"

Jack concurs. "We were hired by Leah to find her brother and she still expects us to do the job. We're sure that Joyce knew where he was."

Morrie says, "Look, there's nothing wrong with citizen help. Especially from the two of you. In fact, I can easily make Dad a consultant due to his having been a police detective. Which means he gets to sit in on all meetings."

"Fine with me," Jack says, crossing and uncrossing his long legs trying to get comfortable in his chair.

Morrie says, "You and your group of lady PIs can continue to investigate. As long as you share whatever you find." He smiles. "Just don't make me look like a dope if you solve the case before I do."

We smile. Feeling more relaxed now.

I add, "As long as you share with us."

"Dad is free to divulge whatever comes up in my meetings unless I inform him that there is a very good reason not to. Fair enough?"

"Yes."

"One way you both can help your case and mine is to find out anything else you can about Joyce. Her purse revealed nothing. She had a cellphone with no contact list on it. Surely she had a lawyer to handle her affairs or maybe someone as executor of a will. Interesting, though, we couldn't even find her driver's license. Or any kind of papers in her car."

"That's another thing," I say. "Doesn't that show that someone is getting ready to kill themselves, by cleaning the slate, so to speak?"

"Maybe so, but there's too much evidence that confirms it was murder."

Jack tries again. "Maybe she got rid of everything so you wouldn't be able to learn the truth about her."

"But what truth?" Morrie asks.

"We're definitely going to find out," Jack promises.

I ask hopefully, "Is there any chance Arlene would be allowed out on bail?"

He shrugs. "Depends on the judge. Most judges would not set bail on a murder case. And besides, the fact that she has relatives living in New York and Chicago, he might see her as a flight risk and could set any bail at an impossible amount."

Not good. Not good at all. I can't imagine how to help her with that. I watch Jack get up to walk around a bit to relax his cramped leg muscles.

"Can I pace with you?" I ask him.

"Sure, why not."

Morrie says, "Arlene still hasn't picked a lawyer. She keeps interviewing and turning them away. She needs to do it as soon as possible."

Jack says, "We'll talk to her and see if we can help."

Morrie gets up and walks toward the door. "Take a five-minute break. I need to see someone down the hall for a moment."

We stretch when he leaves.

I look at Jack in despair. "But if she isn't allowed to go home! How long can they keep her there? That's awful."

"I know, but let's keep calm and take things one at a time. Everything will work out."

"Yes, but how will it end for poor Arlene?"

He puts his arms around me and hugs me. "We will do all we can. Besides, we're an unbeatable team. Right?"

"Right." We kiss.

Morrie walks in on us. He grins. "We'll have none of that around here. I might have to arrest you for indecent behavior." He goes back to his chair.

We return to our seats, smiling.

"Where were we?" Jack asks.

"Next," Morrie says, "I just heard this morning from the Sausalito police that they went to the home of Joyce's daughter, Stacy, last name, Wilson, in order to inform her of her mother's death. They learned from their live-in help that Mr. and Mrs.

Wilson and children have been traveling around Europe for a month. She expected them home soon, but she didn't know when and she didn't know how to reach them. So I left your phone number and an urgent message to call when they return. I'm sure it would be easier on her hearing from compassionate people like you rather than a tough, cold cop."

Jack says, "All right with us." He looks at me and I nod my agreement.

Morrie gets up. "That's it for now."

We get up also. Jack stretches his back, trying to straighten it out.

Morrie walks us to the door. "Keep in touch."

I say, "Don't worry, we will."

Morrie says, "May the best man, and/or woman, win." He winks at Jack. "Is it all right for me to kiss my new stepmother?"

Jack shrugs. "Be my guest."

I take my parting shot at Morrie. "Just remember all the fairy tales you read as a kid. The stepmother was always the meanie. So look out."

With that he gives me a big kiss on my cheek, while laughing.

I sure do love both my men. I know Morrie is doing his job, but this is hard to bear.

30

THE DREAM TEAM

The sign we tacked up on the door of the rec room announces a closed meeting—with a title: "For the defense of Arlene Simon. Anyone with information contact Gladdy Gold."

In typical fashion for any get-together of Gladdy Gold and Associates, there is food. Always food. Corned beef and pastrami deli sandwiches, pickles, coleslaw and potato salad, and always a favorite, Dr. Brown sodas.

Also a new acting member. My Jack. The girls are very impressed that Jack, named as consultant, gets to sit in on police meetings. That's a big leg up.

And another new interested party, Rico Leon. Ida lets us know that although our businesses are now two separate entities, we are united for this cause. Rico has been invited to join us. Sophie and Bella add that they are considering Rico to be their new partner for the still contested name Ida Franz and Associates. Their team insists Rico is invaluable and definitely on our side and can be trusted. He is their hero since the success of solving the car wash mystery. Squirrels, indeed.

After debating over these two newcomers, then officially welcoming both, we start the business at hand. Arlene's case.

The girls, between bites of sandwiches, are still reeling over the fact of Joyce having cancer. They agree, it's bad news for our team. The sympathy will all be for Joyce, seen as the poor dying friend wanting to make up, and cruel Arlene rejecting her with venom. It's an uphill battle.

"Okay," I say. "We all agree on flyers. We will divvy them up and put them on bulletin boards in every Phase of Lanai Gardens."

Evvie, as secretary, takes notes. She reads back what we've decided so far to put in the flyers. " 'Any information concerning Arlene Simon, Joyce Steiner, and/or Seymour Andrews, please get to us. This rec room will have someone in attendance here every afternoon from two to five. We need your help.' "

Sophie interjects, "The mah-jongg group was very gracious about giving up their weekly game here and are temporarily meeting in Phase Four."

Bella claps.

Evvie nods and continues reading the flyer. " 'We

are looking for anyone who has information about Seymour Andrews leaving Lanai Gardens sometime around three weeks ago. He would have been carrying a suitcase. We are guessing he left late at night and might have been picked up by a cab or car.'"

Sophie comments, "I just don't understand why the cops don't do all this."

Jack answers her. "Because as far as they're concerned, they have their killer. They have evidence. They have motive. Arlene has no alibi. It's up to us to prove they're wrong."

I take over. "Joyce managed to leave practically no information about herself, but we now know where she lived. With Jack's ability with a computer, he has located her former address on the waterways. We should canvass that area, talking to neighbors and getting any info on her there."

I look at my darling. "Jack, your report?"

Jack says, "Naturally, nobody lives in a vacuum, and we've found out the name of her business manager. Gladdy and I will get in touch with him. As it seems that Joyce was wealthy, it was highly probable someone managed her money. And hopefully, he'll lead us to the executor of her will, assuming she made one."

"What about the cooking class?" Evvie asks. "Granted we know three of the women who were in the ill-fated kitchen event are against Arlene, but there was one other, Sandra Litzman."

Bella raises her hand. She always does that to ask permission to speak. "Sophie and me know Sandra. We can talk to her."

Sophie agrees.

Evvie nods, says, "We need to know more about the key lime pie incident. Whose idea was it to make the pies? How come Joyce knew they were baking that particular pie that day? We now know how bad a memory that food evoked for Arlene. Why did she even go that day? Since Joyce wasn't a member, how did she find out what they were planning? Who cleaned up the room afterward? What happened to the rest of the pies?"

Ida, taking her own notes, looks up. "Got all of that. We'll find out."

Rico gets into the act. "I can't believe that nobody ever noticed Joyce going up to Arlene's apartment late at night. You tell us Arlene says it was every single night. Someone has to have seen them. We should be asking everyone on those two floors. In fact, we should talk to everyone in Phase Three."

Bella and Sophie smile at their protégé.

Rico has something else to say. The guy who loves cars brings up an interesting point. "What about the Jaguar? It's still in Joyce's parking spot."

"Good question. We have to find out what to do about that." This from Ida, proud of him. What magic spell has that cute young guy cast over our girls? But he does seem eager to help.

"Good idea," I say.

Ida adds, reaching for a Dr. Brown's Cel-Ray Tonic, "I can't believe how secretive that Joyce was. She talked and talked about herself, but told us nothing."

Evvie agrees. "What other family did she have? Who were her friends? Enemies? Somebody has to have wanted her dead. Who was it? If it was a stranger, was he ever seen on our premises? We don't know anything."

I say, "She was hiding behind all those words and we have to find out what really went on in her life. We still haven't been able to reach her daughter, Stacy. Funny, when I walked in on Joyce that day, she was talking to Stacy in California about the continued problems building her guest house.

"Then, when I started to ask her how she met Seymour and got his apartment, she suddenly cut me off by saying she had to call Stacy back right away because she was leaving to take her kids to the dentist. Yet according to her maid, Stacy and family were traveling in Europe at that time. She couldn't have been talking to her in California. Was she even talking to her at all, or was that an out-and-out lie?"

There's a knock on the door. Evvie goes to unlock it. Hy and Lola are there. Lola announces, "We have something to offer. Can we come in?"

They are made cautiously welcome. Hy immediately spots our raspberry *rugallahs* for dessert. Sophie says, "Help yourself."

While chewing, Hy announces that he has an ex-brother-in-law who is a criminal defense lawyer. "Never lost a case," he says with pride.

Ida asks, "Ex?"

Lola says, grinning, "He was married before me, if you can imagine."

"A major mistake," Hy admits. "Dumped her, but stayed friends with her brother."

Lola blushes. "I rescued him."

Hy gives her a quick peck on the cheek. "My soul mate."

Ida sneers. She cannot stand affection shown in front of her. "What's your point?"

Hy looks at her with disdain. "I am willing to go to him and ask for his help. Arlene needs a top lawyer." He smiles proudly. "If I ask David, he'll help."

Sophie asks, "Won't he be expensive?"

"He owes me. I once loaned him money in his early days in practice. We're talking pro bono here." He looks jeeringly at Ida. "That means free of charge, in case you didn't know."

Never at a loss for a snappy comeback, she says, "I watch the same lawyer shows you do, smarty-pants."

Before they come to verbal blows, Jack steps in. Always a calming influence. "That would be great, Hy, if you can manage it."

"Have another *rugallah*," Bella the peacemaker says.

Looks like a good time to stop. I announce the meeting is over. "Everyone, let's get the show on the road."

The girls pack up any leftover food and the fight to save Arlene is in full swing.

31

SURPRISE!

We have a busy day planned, Jack and I. We're going to visit Arlene in jail and then head for the address where Joyce lived before she entered all of our lives and caused chaos. Jack even has a meeting with one of Dr. Edward Steiner's old nurses who's willing to speak to us. We overslept a bit. A quick hit of coffee and toast and here we go, because we're getting a late start.

Once out on the walkway we are aware of an unusual noise for a Sunday morning. We look over our railing and what a sight meets our eyes!

The courtyard where everyone's cars are always parked has been emptied. Except for Jack's and my cars, conspicuously the only ones left and now surrounded. The area is strangely crowded with people. There is an air of a carnival with balloons flying from palm trees and lampposts. And music ringing out from somebody's boom box. It's not a holiday. What's going on? It reminds me of our midyear tailgate-garage sales. Tailgate, because we have no garages. But this isn't the right date.

Tables have been set up. Mostly card tables, some actual kitchen tables carried down for this event. People are lined up in front of them. There are signs but they are under our walkways, so I can't read what they say. Further staring shows me that the girls are gathered behind one table. Bella glances up, sees us, and pokes Sophie. The two of them wave happily to us. Ida is busy handing someone something. But what? One hand giving, the other hand taking?

Tessie and Sol are behind another table. Hy and Lola, another. My heavens, even the Canadians have a table! I recognize neighbors from many of the other Phases.

Jack and I stare at each other. Well, we have to go downstairs anyway, so we'll see what's going on. And even more important, how do we rescue one of our cars out of that mob scene?

All is revealed by the signs behind each of the participants: "Save Arlene." "Sign the petition telling the police they have the wrong person." "Donate money for her lawyer." That one, I note, is behind Hy and Lola's table.

We look at the booth nearest to us. Tessie is having a bake sale. She makes wonderful homemade breads and must have been up at dawn to have baked this many. And they are selling like hot-cakes. They smell divine.

Somebody is a beader and beaded crafts are another hot item. That's from Kim Chang from Phase Four.

The Canadians are selling Canadian objects. I'm curious and I check them out. I greet Nigel and Elizabeth, who vacation each winter in a flat, as they call it, on the first floor of our building. Elizabeth smiles when I ask where they got goods from Canada so quickly. She laughs. "Dearie," she says, "we've accumulated far too many 'odds 'n' socks' as is. Great excuse to clear out the bins."

There's Jack's old neighbor, Dora Dooley, from Phase Six, before he lost his apartment in the hurricane. She's serving pink lemonade and chocolate chip cookies.

Jack had disappeared from my side, but then I see him. He's chatting with someone selling rare books, as I can tell from a sign. I walk over to his table. The man doesn't look familiar. Jack tells me he's actually a dealer, with a shop on University Avenue. He heard about our plight from his aunt Lillian, who lives in Phase One and was happily donating sales to our cause. Jack has already bought something. A fairly rare copy of one of Horatio Alger's rags-to-riches novels.

By now, I'm near tears. I wish Arlene could see what's being done on her behalf. Jack, reading my mind, takes out his iPhone and snaps some photos. Yes, he even has one of those gadgets.

I finally reach the table where the girls are, assisted by the now ever-present Rico. All of them are wearing colorful aprons, including Rico.

"I'm amazed," I say. "How did you all put this together so fast?"

Ida says gleefully, "Actually this is Hy's doing. Why should you be so surprised? Let's see—we have six Phases. At least one yenta living in each one. The word spread like cream cheese on a bagel."

"So what are you selling?" I ask.

Bella proudly shows their wares. "Remember when we did crafts? We still have leftover pot holders and decorated kitchen towels and aprons." She indicates the ones they're modeling. "We're doing good."

A sign over another table catches my eye. It reads "We Take Care of Our Own." And behind it there's Sandra Litzman, who lives next door to Arlene. And was also at the kitchen debacle. She tells me she already gave Sophie and Bella a report of her view of what happened that morning. She has no idea who decided on the baking of key lime pie that day. She got a note to bring ingredients, which is what they usually do when someone has a preference, but she doesn't remember who sent it.

Interesting. I wonder if any of the women actually knew who sent that note. Must check on that. Again, coincidences always plant red flags in my mind.

I try another question. "Since you live next door

to Arlene, did you ever hear anything? Did you ever see Joyce go into Arlene's apartment?"

She shakes her head sadly. "No, never. I wish I had, but I'm such a sound sleeper, even the hurricane we went through didn't wake me."

There are tears in her eyes. "When I was sick, it was Arlene who took me to doctors and hospitals. And bought groceries when I couldn't get around. I don't know what I would have done without her. This terrible charge against her is a lie. She couldn't hurt anyone."

I am touched. I keep this in mind if Arlene ever goes to trial and needs character witnesses.

I thank her for her efforts and move along. I spot Evvie in front of a table manned by Irving and Mary. They have the petition asking to free Arlene. People are lined up to sign. I greet the two of them, thanking them. Mary, the nurse, has another sign-up sheet. She's offering consultations on using medications. How kind of her.

I pull Evvie off to one side.

I look at her in amazement. "You knew all about this and didn't tell me?"

"No, I swear, I'm as surprised as you are. I've been asking around. The word is Hy pulled all of this together. He's still so mad at those gals who fought with him the other day. We forget that before he retired he was a manager of a big furniture store. He knows how to organize."

"Amazing. All of this so fast. But why didn't he

tell us? Hey, we have enough junk in our storage closets to fill more than one table."

"No kidding, I don't know, but I can guess. Maybe he's intimidated by Jack. Not the least of which is Hy's size compared to your over six-footer. But also that he was a cop."

"Really," I say, smiling. "How delightful." I get a kick out of the idea of anyone intimidating Hy.

Jack comes over to me, pointing at his wrist-watch.

I tell Evvie we have to be on time for our visit with Arlene.

"Give her a hug for me. If you're allowed to."

"Will do."

"Spoke to Joe this morning."

"How is he?"

"Just great. He says he's gone into second child-hood with the grandkids. Misses me. Thinking he might come back next week."

"Sounds wonderful. What are you up to today?"

"I was going canvassing neighbors, but Hy just informed me he needs me."

"He gave you a job here, too?"

She smiles. "Hy put me in charge of collecting the money at the end of the sale and of making sure nobody changed their mind and is keeping their profits."

I laugh. "That's our Hy."

Just as we are about to rescue Jack's car, I hear someone calling my name. It's Leah, hurrying toward me. Jack and I exchange glances. He'll let me deal with her while he extricates our surrounded vehicle.

She reaches me, out of breath. "No more weekly postcards. They stopped coming! Nothing since last Monday," she says, almost choking. "Something terrible must have happened to my Seymour."

I put my arm around her. "Leah, dear, don't fret so. Maybe he's somewhere away from any mailbox. We will find him. I promise. We will not let you down."

Even as I'm consoling her, I think to myself, *The coincidences are piling up*. I feel we are getting close to something important. So the postcards stopped coming the day Joyce died. Did the postcards stop *because* Joyce is dead? There must be some connection.

Leah, tearfully, heads back home.

Jack waves. He's managed to free up the car. I hurry to join him.

32

VISITING HOURS

I've been to police headquarters many times for meetings in Morrie's office, but I never found myself in the separate jail section of the fairly new modern police headquarters on Oakland Park Boulevard.

Morrie has arranged for us to visit Arlene. I don't know what to expect other than what I've seen in many movies. I could picture myself leaning in and speaking to her through bars with an attached phone. Both of us whispering, looking tense and secretive. But I'm pleasantly surprised. We are directed to a large room not unlike our rec room at home.

There are many plain tables and chairs that could seat six, and that's about it in the way of decor. The walls aren't painted the bilious greens also seen in cop shows and movies. They're actually a peaceful beige.

Naturally a couple of police guards stand watching, but all in all, not an unpleasant place. Easy for me to say, but it must be unbearable for Arlene.

Many of the tables are taken during these visiting hours.

We see Arlene and she is talking to a man and a woman who look like they're in their late fifties or sixties. They resemble Arlene so I'm assuming her son and daughter have come to see her. It's been a long while since they've been down to visit, but I remember them as being a close and happy family.

Arlene looks perturbed, as if she's been having an argument with them.

"Maybe we should wait," I say to Jack.

But Arlene has spotted us and she waves us over. She looks all right, but I can tell from the dark circles under her eyes, she is not sleeping well. Even in jailhouse clothes, Arlene manages to still look stylish.

"My son and daughter," she says, introducing the people at her table. "You remember Bobby and Nicky." She indicates us. "These are the two wonderful people I've told you about. Jack and Gladdy Langford."

We all shake hands. Jack and I sit down next to them.

Nicky clutches her mother's hands. "I'm so sorry we haven't visited often enough, Mom, but with our jobs and the kids . . ."

"It's all right, you're here now. And look at the mess I've made."

Nicky says, "Don't say that, Mom. There's been a terrible mistake. You'll be free soon."

Bobby turns to us. "Please talk some sense into our mother. We want to help pay for all her expenses, whatever they are."

"I don't want your money," Arlene insists.

"We don't care. We will do whatever it takes to get you out of this jail. You're innocent."

Arlene looks sad. "The police don't think so. I may be going from jail to prison. For a long time. Not that I think I'd last that long in such a dreadful place."

She says these terrible words with a trace of irony.

"But you didn't do anything," Nicky says.

She manages a smile. "You're just biased."

Jack asks, "What happened in court? What about your lawyer?"

Arlene manages a small smile. "He's very good. And kind. Bless Hy for helping me like this. I could never have afforded him. And someday I hope to pay him back."

Nicky says ruefully, "Here's a woman who hurt my mother over fifty years ago, a woman we never met, and yet she was able to put our mother into this hellish situation."

"I did it to myself," Arlene says. "If only I had kept my cool, as the kids say, maybe none of this would have happened. I made a damn fool of myself in front of everybody."

Nicky says, "Tell Mr. and Mrs. Langford why we were quarreling. Let them be the judge. You haven't answered their question. Tell them what went down in court."

"My new lawyer tried to get me bail in spite of the odds against it."

Bobby comments, "He was great. The prosecution was arguing that because it was murder, she was too much of a flight risk. And the judge was agreeing."

Nicky adds, "But this David Rice was elegant and funny. He said a woman of eighty should not have to live in a jail cell, and besides, she can't run that fast. She didn't seem much like a flight risk to him. He got the judge to smile. But the judge would only agree if the bail was $100,000 . . ."

Arlene overrides him and says sadly, "It doesn't matter. Even the fifty thousand down payment is still out of the question."

Bobby appeals to us. "Talk some sense into her. We'll find a way."

Arlene is adamant. "I am not allowing you to mortgage your homes and take my grandchildren out of college. No. I won't let you do it."

This is when Jack takes out his camera phone and shows Arlene what's been going on today back home. She looks at one photo after another of her neighbors rallying to help her cause, then tearfully passes the phone over to Nicky and Bobby.

Arlene starts to sob. "Bless them. Bless them all. But they'll never be able to raise that much. It's hopeless."

A low bell rings, signaling visiting hour is over. The tables empty out. Arlene stands up and kisses both her kids. They hug for a few moments. And then she hugs us.

The inmates are herded out. Seeing the devastated look on Arlene's face as she turns away is heartbreaking. We leave with Bobby and Nicky. None of us speaking, lost in our own troubled thoughts about Arlene's fate.

33

THE RICH LADY

As we drive along, I can't stop thinking about that sweet woman in jail. It's not fair. I am convinced Arlene would never hurt anyone. Jack and I talked for a while with Nicky and Bobby outside, in the parking lot. All of us needed to get out of the police station and breathe fresh air.

They gave us the number of the hotel they are staying at, but they did have to get back home soon. They thanked us profusely for all we were doing, and we promised to keep them informed. I wish we were able to give them more hope.

I don't know what we expect to find, but I feel we need to see where Joyce lived.

We are making our way through a very exclusive area known as Sunrise Key on the Intracoastal Waterway. Breathtakingly beautiful homes with an incredible water view. Very private, very exclusive. Expensive cars in and out of garages and, ditto, yachts or sailboats on nearly every dock. I can just imagine how these mansions might look inside. Models for *Architectural Digest,* one and all.

Jack breaks into my reverie.

"Here we are. This is the Steiner house." We look at the famous architect's exquisite three-level designer house situated right at the water's edge. At first we hoped someone was living here and we'd try an excuse to be invited in. Maybe. But the house was empty. We tried calling a realtor hoping to find out who bought it. But since the deal was not yet closed, the information stayed private. Interesting, that fact. I wonder if the new owners will find out that the previous one was murdered.

But we did learn something. Houses around here start in the low millions. Dr. Edward picked the right specialty. Plastic surgery paid very well.

Besides, if we really needed to go inside, Morrie could arrange that. But I bet sneaky Joyce hadn't left anything inside that would reveal something we'd need to know.

We turn around as a tourist boat lumbers by. These houses are a must-see during the season. People on the deck wave to us, so we give them a cheap thrill and pretend we live here. We wave back.

"Yeah, sure," I say with tongue in cheek. "Joyce couldn't wait to leave her three-thousand-square-foot home and move into Seymour's pathetic apartment."

"Considering that we now know the state of her health, she knew she wasn't going to be there very long."

Sad but true. "Let's see if any of the well-to-dos are at home. Unless they're on the adjoining golf course or in the country club having cocktails."

"Do I hear some envy?" Jack asks, raising an eyebrow. "We live in our own country club. We have sports. Hey, bocce and badminton are very popular with the over-sixty crowd. Don't we have cocktails, too, for those of us who aren't on meds that say no booze?"

I give him a quick kiss. "Never mind. I can dream, can't I?"

"Besides, what would you do with three thousand square feet?"

"I was thinking along the lines of a bowling alley."

Jack smiles.

After snooping around as much as possible, but not seeing much since all the blinds are closed, we make our way back to the car. We drive over to the next and nearest McMansion. Dogs start barking. The sprinklers are on. Two cars are in the driveway. A brand-new BMW and an old battered Honda Civic.

Owner and maid? I make an educated guess. And indeed a maid answers the door.

We introduce ourselves to a small, round-faced

young woman who might be Cuban and ask to talk to anyone who's home. Concerning their neighbors, the Steiners, we inform her. She closes the door on us after telling us she'll be right back.

The maid returns with a tall, slender good-looking woman. Are rich women always thin? She's a kind of Lauren Bacall type. Long, lean, and leery. She's dressed in some white leisure swirling gauzy caftan outfit that probably cost as much as my entire wardrobe. She stands in the half-open doorway, hands on hips.

"Are you police?" she asks.

Jack says, "No, we're private investigators."

Before we can show ID or explain why we're there, she beats us to it.

"You want to discuss the Steiners? He was a letch and she was a witch. That's as much gossip as you'll pull out of me." With that she turns and walks back inside. All I get is a quick glimpse of the entry. Huge round marble table in the center with an enormous bouquet of flowers. I'm sure they're freshly real and not plastic. And a staircase that would have made Rhett Butler and Scarlett O'Hara proud.

We head back to our car on the pseudo-cobblestoned driveway. "That went well," I say. "A real no-nonsense type of rude person."

"Excuse me . . . ? *Por favor.*" Someone is calling after us.

We turn and the maid is following us. "You want

to know something? My sister, Consuela, worked for the Steiners. I am Lydia."

We introduce ourselves. "Anything you could tell us. We are working with the police. Mrs. Steiner just died."

The woman crosses herself. "*Madre mia . . .* My sister will be sad. At least for *la niña*. The daughter, Stacy. It was not a happy household. Much shouting."

"Can you tell us more?" I ask.

With a backward glance to make sure she's alone, she says, "There was a terrible night. My sister, she was getting ready for serving for a party. It was before the guests arrived. The doctor got so angry at the wife, he ran outside with her running after him, screaming and calling him names. He jumped in his boat, and he wasn't thinking good. He wrecked it on the dock. It was like that a lot of the time."

"Thank you," I say.

"*De nada,*" she says. "I must get back."

We shrug. Nothing really accomplished, but we are getting a picture of the late Mrs. Steiner. Very different from the act she put on with us.

Jack comments, "Someone famous once wrote about the rich being possessed by their money."

"Probably Shakespeare. He said everything worth remembering."

"I don't think that was his line. But anyway, enough of the idle rich. I don't believe we'll find out too much else. I'll drive you back and then I'll head for Dr. Steiner's former office nurse who said she'll talk to me."

"Good plan."

We get into his car and drive off.

I sigh. "If not a bowling alley, an indoor pool. The three thousand square feet."

Jack smiles.

A mile or so later, I say, "I can't believe we're making jokes."

Jack quotes again, " 'Laugh and the whole world laughs with you . . .' "

I recite along with him, " 'Cry and you cry alone.' "

"Also not Shakespeare," Jack says.

"Definitely not Shakespeare."

34

BACK TO THE KITCHEN

Jack drops me off at home. I'm looking forward to some iced tea and maybe a short nap. The outdoor flea market/garage sale is winding down. Most of the tables are gone. The balloons are still twisting in the breeze. I wave to a few people and keep going. That cool bedroom with just a sheet to cover is calling out to me. But that's not to be right away.

I run into Tessie, who is carrying her bread machine. She informs me that Evvie told her that if she saw me, she should tell me to meet them in the cooking-class room and hurry up. All of that without taking a breath.

Oh, well. No nap for the weary. I take the path to the building that holds our club rooms.

Not only Evvie, but the girls are there, too. As are

the four other original members of the ill-fated cooking class. Fatima, Elaine, Frances, and Sandra are looking perturbed. They have teacups in front of them. But no one seems to be drinking.

"What's going on?" I ask as I enter.

Evvie informs me they are at an impasse even though she found out something interesting. "The club works by someone deciding what they want to cook and sending the suggestion in advance in order for the others to bring ingredients."

Ida jumps in. "The cooking club members assumed they all got the same note to bring ingredients for key lime pie. But Arlene was confused. Her note said lemon meringue. And here's the thing. None of them is the writer of the note."

Sophie takes a turn. "And their notes are always handwritten. And usually signed. This was done on a computer. With no signature."

Fatima, who is leaning against the fridge, is still negative. "So Arlene could have used one of the computers in the tech club room."

Sandra makes a face. "Arlene was as dumclueless as we are about high tech."

Fatima crosses her arms, still not convinced.

Sandra continues, "And why would she have done that? She would never have come to class if she knew that was the recipe for the day."

Elaine adds, as she sips her tea and makes a face—the tea is cold—"So maybe Joyce sent it. She was still trying to get Arlene to talk to her. She figured maybe with us around . . ."

"That's ridiculous," says Evvie. "She had to know how much it would bother Arlene."

Elaine, taking Fatima's side, insists, "I'm sure she didn't think she'd get that frazzled, unless there is something very wrong with Arlene."

Ida says, getting huffy, "You don't know what you're talking about."

Before they erupt into something angrier, I step in. "Then what happened? Arlene had her outburst and then what? After I left."

There is a pause. I assume they are trying to recollect.

Evvie asks, "Did Arlene leave?"

Sandra says, "She left with Gladdy, but she came back a few minutes later, crying. Joyce had already left. Nobody said a word."

There is a silence. What are they leaving out? I say, "There's more. Keep talking."

Frances shrugs. "I went home next. I had enough."

Sandra says, "I tried to comfort Arlene, but she wouldn't let me."

Elaine says, "I looked around the kitchen in disgust. I was furious. I said who's gonna clean up this mess?"

Sandra says, "That's when Arlene spoke again. She apologized and volunteered, since she felt she was the cause of it."

Fatima puts down her teacup and heads for the door. "That's when the rest of us left. She ruined our class and I'm not about to forgive her. And I've had enough of her tantrums."

She exits and Frances and Elaine immediately follow.

Sandra, our only ally, shrugs. "I'm sorry. I didn't know what to do, so I mumbled something kind to Arlene and walked out, too."

"So Arlene was left alone in the room?" I ask.

Sandra says, "Yes."

Evvie asks the next logical question. "And did she clean it up?"

Sandra sighs. "Not really. When we checked later, we could tell she did a little bit. Some of the pies were gone. I assumed she dumped them down the garbage disposal. But I guess it was all too much for her. She didn't do a good job. And worst of all she left the kitchen door unlocked. We never do that. We have expensive stuff in here, like our Cuisinart and cappuccino machine."

We thank her and she leaves, wishing us well. At the door, she smiles. "And don't *you* forget to lock it when you leave."

For a moment our group is silent.

Finally Ida comments, "Another nail in Arlene's coffin."

Bella shudders. "Yuk. Couldn't you find a better way to say that?"

Evvie says, "But if the door was left open someone else could have come in."

Ida says, "Like who? Joyce? What for? She wouldn't want the pies."

Sophie says, "Maybe the one who murdered Joyce did."

Everyone heads for home. No one wants to talk any longer.

Everyone has left the kitchen even more confused than when we went in. On the way home, Evvie and I stop to pick up our mail. In my mailbox I find a note. It's from our ex-Marine Cane Fu instructor, Merrill Grant. Evvie reads over my shoulder. Merrill writes, "Saw your flyer. I did see Seymour leaving one night. He did have a suitcase with him. I was coming home from a late pinochle game and just as I was entering the Lanai Gardens front gate, I saw a Jaguar stop and pick him up. He didn't hesitate to get in. Seemed like he was waiting for this ride. A man was driving. Sorry I didn't get a good look at him because I wasn't paying attention. I hope this helps you. Call me if you need to talk."

A man? Evvie and I look perplexed.

This is a whole new thought. Did Joyce have an accomplice?

Evvie and I go up to my apartment just as Jack arrives. He reports that he didn't have too much time to speak to the nurse since she was only on a short break, but he thinks it was very illuminating.

I defrost a chicken casserole for dinner later as we listen to him.

Jack loosens his tie and takes off his jacket. He pours himself a glass of water. "The nurse hated working for Dr. Edward Steiner. She was a married woman and very religious. She felt Steiner was unethical and had the morals of an alley cat. He obviously was sleeping with some of his patients. Unable to stand it much longer, she called him on it and asked how he could betray his wife like that. His arrogant answer was that his wife had her own lover. So it evened out. Besides, he told her, they had an 'open' marriage. The nurse didn't believe him. She'd seen and heard many a screaming tantrum from the very jealous Mrs. Steiner, who dropped in many times, probably hoping to catch him dallying with his patients. They both knew she couldn't stay any longer. It was right after that she quit before he could fire her and got the job she now has."

"The plot is thickening," I say.

"More like sickening," Evvie comments.

Jack says, "I made another call. So tomorrow we have an appointment with Joyce's business manager, Kenneth Ryan. I told him Joyce was dead. He sounded shocked. He said we caught him just in time. He is flying off to Hong Kong on a business trip tomorrow, but he definitely needs to see us. She left a will and he's the executor."

"Bingo," says Evvie.

Jack adds, "I know Morrie will want to come with us."

I heat the oven for the chicken. "And I know what he'll say when we catch him up. Everything so far is circumstantial and won't stand up in court. I hope this guy has something we can use."

35

THE BUSINESS MANAGER

As we expected, Morrie listens patiently as Jack and I catch him up. We tell him what we know as we drive to the executor Kenneth Ryan's office. Morrie is interested in what we've learned so far about Joyce's background. But her fights with her hubby seem irrelevant since he died some time ago. So she had a temper, so what? Well, at least we know Seymour was picked up to begin his travels by someone he knew. At least he wasn't kidnapped. It was probably Joyce's Jaguar. But the driver was a man? It was dark. Too bad Merrill couldn't describe him.

Additionally we've helped prove that not only Arlene but Joyce also had access to the key lime pies in the empty kitchen. But that doesn't change

Morrie's mind about Arlene's guilt. We were right. Everything is still circumstantial.

"About the daughter, Stacy," Morrie says, "the Sausalito police tried again to reach her. This time the maid said she did hear from her and the family was due back in about a week. They left another message to call both them and you."

I tell him, "We've been phoning her house, since she hasn't tried to reach us, but this time we got the answering machine, so hopefully she's returned."

He can tell I'm distressed that there's a daughter out there who doesn't yet know her own mother has died, so he changes the subject. "What's the background on this guy we're meeting?" he asks.

Jack says he Googled him. "He's a business manager with a law degree and another in accounting. Pretty successful it seems. In a high-rent district of Boca Raton. Has some well-known wealthy clients."

We arrive at the affluent Congress Avenue address, so we're not surprised at the fancy digs. The office appears as if it was designed by a professional who knew how to stage an office. All of it is done ultra modern in shades of black and white. Even the photos of early Boca are black and white. Very dramatic.

Kenneth has a suite that includes the usual front receiving area, private office, and conference room.

Kenneth, a man in his fifties, looks deliberate as

well. The suit is expensive. As are the shoes. The haircut just right. To me he is on the downside of good looking. Probably considered handsome when younger. Maybe too much booze over the years, I'm guessing by the reddish veined nose. There is weariness to his demeanor.

He greets us himself. "I can't tell you how shocked I was at the news of Joyce's death."

Morrie says what he's had to say hundreds of times as a cop, "I'm sorry for your loss."

Kenneth shakes his head as if to indicate, Don't say any more. He can't take it.

Kenneth hands us his business card, and Morrie passes back his police identity card, Morrie explaining that "since these two people," indicating us, "are strangers to you, you might want a person of authority to be here."

We introduce ourselves, saying we knew Joyce, but for only a short while.

He beckons us to follow him. "Very thoughtful of you. I was wondering about who was coming to see me."

As we tour our way along his hallway, we express our admiration of his perfect decor. Kenneth thanks us. And remarks that Mrs. Steiner was his decorator. "That was her avocation, besides being a wonderful wife and hostess."

I think to myself, Joyce has at least one admirer. I guess he missed all the good fights. But I do find it interesting that Joyce had a lucrative career. And it may also be that he and Joyce knew each other for a very long time. What *was* their relationship?

We follow him into his office.

"I gave my secretary a few days off, since I'll be away, so I hope no one wants coffee."

I almost expect him to offer us liquor. He doesn't, but when he mentions coffee he instinctively looks to the elaborate wet bar where bottles of booze are in abundance. I read somewhere that's a sign of an alcoholic or someone on his way to it.

Morrie says smoothly, "We know you have a plane to catch today. We'll try not to take too much of your time. You're leaving tonight?"

"Yes, I am. Quite late. Have you ever been to Hong Kong?"

We all shake our heads no.

"Extraordinary place. Not to be missed. I heartily recommend the Peninsula Hotel if you do." He looks at me and smiles. "But the Star ferry to Kowloon calls for a very strong stomach."

Hmm, how did he know I get seasick? Maybe he assumes it because I'm a woman. Or he's just being condescending. Hong Kong is not in our budget.

Jack smiles wryly at me. Do we look like the kind of people who could afford such an expensive trip? Is Kenneth Ryan playing us?

Kenneth indicates we should sit down. We do. He takes his seat behind his white marble desk. Marble seems very popular around Boca. His desk chair is an Eames design in black. The office seems excessively neat. No papers anywhere, except for a blue folder on his desk that could be the will. What is this absence of things reminding me of? I'll have to think of it later. I need to concentrate on that will.

He expresses his concern. "I have to say, your news about my client was not unexpected. I knew Mrs. Steiner was very ill. It was only a matter of time. She was quite important to this office. I'm so surprised I hadn't already heard the news. What were the circumstances of her death?"

Morrie takes charge of the meeting. "Mrs. Steiner wasn't living at Sunrise Key at the time. She was residing at a one-bedroom apartment in Fort Lauderdale on Oakland Park Boulevard. A sublet as it were."

Kenneth lifts very bushy eyebrows, showing surprise. He knows that's a lower rent area. "How very peculiar."

Morrie says, "Then I assume you hadn't been in touch with her for a while."

"I did speak to her a few weeks ago to ask how she was feeling. She said she was doing as well as could be expected, as she put it."

"Did you talk with her on her home phone?"

He thinks for a moment. "I believe I did."

I keep watching this man very closely. From my angle I can see his legs under his desk. He is tapping one leg—a nervous tic? Well, he's busy and does have to catch a plane. He's probably hoping we won't stay much longer. Aha, another quick glance at the bar. Or is it that he can't wait to hit that bar the minute we walk out?

Morrie takes a breath. "I'm sorry to have to tell you this, I have shocking news. Mrs. Steiner did not die of cancer, she was murdered."

It's almost as if Kenneth turns pale. His face twists into a horrific grimace. "What? What are you saying? You can't be serious."

"Very serious," says Morrie.

"Who? What? Why?"

"We have a person of interest being held. I'm sorry I can't go into further details of the case." Morrie is being cautious. "It's a long story. However, as you can imagine, it is necessary for us to see the will."

Kenneth shudders. Then pulls himself together. "Of course. You must get in touch with me when the body will be released. I'll have to cut my trip short."

"It will be a while," Morrie assures him.

He starts to open up the blue-covered file, then stops, looking pained. "Sorry. I can't quite get my head around Joyce's death. You must give me a moment. You can understand."

"Of course."

We stay quiet. Jack and Morrie glance around the room. I can't take my eyes off him. His eye twitches.

He finally says, almost tearfully, but regaining his professional demeanor, "Knowing I was going to be traveling, I have provided the name and phone number for you of the estate lawyer who drew up the will. He can handle any questions you have for me. He can file the death certificate with the probate court. And of course, he can reach me if necessary."

"Very thoughtful of you," Morrie says.

He hands us each a copy of the will.

I want to leap up in shock, but I hold myself back. What? I can't believe what I'm reading. I have to reread it twice before it sinks in. Joyce Steiner left everything in the world she owns to Arlene Simon!

The three of us exchange amazed glances. The date of the will was a month ago.

Kenneth says, "I must explain. I've known all these years that Joyce was searching for a dear old friend. I was quite surprised when she came in and told me she'd found her at last and this was her wish. To make up to her for a mistake she made years ago. I asked her if she was sure she wanted to do this; she was originally intending to donate everything to her favorite charity. Her comment was that the charity is fine without her contribution. Giving to her dear old friend would make Joyce very happy. It seemed quite important to her."

Jack and I look at each other. Unbelievable!

Morrie continues reading slowly and carefully. He, too, is totally amazed.

Jack speaks. "There is a list of her holdings?"

"Yes, of course. The money accrued on the house

just sold in Sunrise Key. The money from the sale of her Jaguar, as well. The yacht. All her stocks and bonds. Her property investments. Her assets as an interior designer. She was a shrewd business-woman. Mrs. Simon will be a very wealthy lady." He smiles. "Won't that be a wonderful surprise for her?"

I can't stand it. I lose my cool. I have to know. "How much is all that worth?"

He studies another sheet on the desk. "My balance sheet totals Mrs. Steiner's assets to $11 million, to round it out."

Ohmigod!

Kenneth stands and starts moving us to the door. "I really must get cracking here. Lots of odds and ends to take care of." He shakes his head, still pondering the incredible. "Murdered. Poor dear Joyce."

We all three get up. Even Morrie is stunned. Who knows from that kind of money!

On the way home I keep hearing those numbers in my head. We're quiet for a while, dumbfounded. Then I cry out, "Somebody say something! I can't stand it!"

I turn to Morrie. I can't hold back my thoughts. "You know what he didn't say to you? What everybody always says—you'll find the killer, won't you?"

Jack asks Morrie, "Do we tell Arlene?"

"No."

Morrie has two things to say. "First I need to find out whether Arlene knew about the will. That she's the beneficiary. Talk about motive. Eleven million motives."

I can't bear to even think what the other is.

"And?" Jack asks. The suspense is excruciating.

Morrie states for me what he's sure Jack knows, "The law says, and I'm paraphrasing it, a convicted felon may not gain profit from his or her crime."

"The Lord giveth, and the Lord taketh away," Jack says softly.

36

WHERE THERE'S A WILL

Evvie and I wait in my car, which is in a shady spot in the jail parking lot. The day has the kind of heat that makes you want to never leave your air-conditioned home. But Arlene is expecting us and every visit is so important to her. The AC in the car will have to do. We're a little early and have to wait until it's the exact moment until they open the doors. We are killing time with the help of a thermos of iced tea and a couple of cookies.

Evvie is still reeling from the news about the will. "Eleven million. She could build her own city. She could give jobs to hundreds of people just on the interest alone. She could build a world-class hospital—"

I interrupt her. "Enough already with your list of

fantasies. I can't stand what we're doing here today."

Evvie comments, "I still think Morrie was some chicken, leaving it to us to draw it out of her."

"He chose us rather than him having to interrogate and intimidate her. He knew we'd be kind."

"It was bad enough to have to reveal the Valium. What if she did know about the will? I feel like a Judas already."

"To add to your Bible metaphor, if she did know it, it will be like handing him Arlene's head on a platter.

"I can't stand it that we'll be helping the prosecution."

Evvie, the movie critic says, "I'm trying to remember that picture we saw when the comic was being helped by friends and they just kept making things worse. He kept saying, 'Don't help me. Don't help me.' It was very funny."

"I don't remember and this isn't funny."

"I'm just trying to lighten the mood."

I feel bad about not having shared this incredible piece of news about the will with the girls, but we're not allowed to tell them. Morrie has instructed us not to give out that information and we keep our promise.

"You know they wouldn't be able to keep that a secret anyway," Evvie says, reading what's on my mind as usual. "It's just too big. It will ooze out of one of them some way. Even I can barely stop saying it. Eleven million. Eleven million."

"Please let it happen that Arlene does not know about the will."

The entrance line is starting to move. We close our thermoses and whisk the cookie crumbs off our skirts. The jail has a dress code. Very bland outfits only.

We brace ourselves as we climb out into the stifling humidity.

Of course Arlene is very happy to see us. She thanks Evvie for coming also. Unlike anyone else, Arlene has put on some makeup. To cheer herself up. Or, as she told me, a habit. A need not to give in to the depression around her. Evvie looks around the room, taking it all in the way I did the first time I came. Glancing at the other visitors. Feeling what it must be like to be a prisoner in this place. Seeing the desperation. The tears. One could almost smell the fear.

We exchange glances. Arlene doesn't belong here.

Arlene blurts out her news. "They were trying to set a court date for as soon as possible. But at the arraignment, Hy's lawyer friend got a continuance so he'll have more time to prepare."

Evvie comments, "Well, that's good."

Arlene isn't happy. "Maybe yes, maybe no. Sometimes it could take months. I don't know how much more I can stand living like this."

I feel bad for her. We're all a long way from being able to raise the bail money. She looks thinner. Her cheeks have become hollow. She probably isn't eating much.

Evvie says, changing the subject, "Sorry I didn't meet your kids. I guess they had to go home."

Arlene tears up. "It will be hard for them. Worrying from far away, not knowing what's really going on."

Arlene, also wanting not to stay on that topic, asks for some new gossip, so we cheer her up as best we can.

Evvie reports, "Since Hy put together the tailgate sales, everyone's been coming up to say good things to him. That swelled head of his will be ten times bigger by the time this is over—"

Evvie stops short at the expression on Arlene's face.

"That was insensitive of me. I meant by the time you get out of here. And I know you will."

But Arlene manages a smile. "It's all right, dear. I know things will turn out well because so many people are sending out prayers for me."

I'm very aware of the short time we have left before the buzzer rings us out. I have no choice. I grit my teeth and dive in.

"We had a meeting with Joyce's business manager. Joyce left a will."

Arlene shrugs. "Yes, oh, that. I remember in one of her wild raving night sessions she told me she left everything to me in her will. I laughed out loud. Sure. That'll be the day. But then right after it, that crazy woman said I'd never get to spend it."

Evvie gasps.

I sigh. She did know. God help her. But what about that last remark? "Did she say why you wouldn't get to spend it?"

"No, I ignored it, as I did every other mad thing she told me. As if I could believe she even had eleven million dollars."

I hear Evvie next to me groan.

Arlene knew about it and, unhappy spy that I am, I must report it to Morrie.

But Arlene continues. "In front of everyone she pretends she loves me. Then she comes to me at night and screams at me. What kind of madness is that? Another time she was blaming me for her marriage failing. How was I supposed to do that? And frankly, as far as I'm concerned, she and Edward deserved each other."

She stops to drink water from her plastic cup. I pity this poor woman with no one to talk to in this awful place.

"Another nutty thing she did. I was trying to clean up the mess I made in the kitchen that awful day and who should come in? The damn trouble-maker said she wanted some of the pie to eat. What nerve! I practically threw it at her. Joyce got me so distraught again. I never did finish cleaning up."

Evvie and I exchange glances. Joyce took the pie up to her apartment. Not Arlene.

I ask her another question. "Why did you go down to Joyce's apartment the night she died?"

Arlene reaches for a tissue in her pocket. She

clenches it, almost ripping it. "Because I was stupid. I knew better than to believe her, but she said she gave up. She was leaving. She'd found another apartment. She wanted to say goodbye in person because she would be gone by tomorrow."

How sinister. She knew she'd be dead by the next day.

"But of course it was another of her lies. I only stayed a few minutes."

And Joyce got her to conveniently leave her fingerprints on a glass of water.

The warning bell rings. Five minutes left. Arlene talks faster.

"I keep asking myself why. What's the point? You know, I sit in that cell for hours, what else is there to do but think and think. I look back and go over our friendship. In my mind, as I was growing up, I thought we both felt the same about each other, but it really wasn't that way at all.

"She always wanted what I had. If I ordered the chocolate milkshake and she the vanilla, she'd say she changed her mind and wanted my chocolate. And she did that with clothes, jewelry, anything I had. And I always gave in to her. It was the same with boyfriends.

"After she'd seduce the guy I was dating and take him away, she'd drop him. Then she'd always announce she never liked him anyway.

"Why was I so surprised when she went after Edward? I bet she tried before we were married and was annoyed she didn't succeed."

The room is empty. A guard is coming toward us. Arlene stands up and speaks faster.

"Even when we were very young her parents both worked, so she had the key to their apartment. We'd play in her room—fantasy games with our dolls. She always had to be the princess and I'd have to be her maid."

The guard reaches us. We are out of time. She takes turns hugging each of us, holding on tightly.

As the guard leads her away, she calls out one last question, "Why won't the police believe me?"

37

MORRIE LISTENS

Arlene's question had me in tears. Even though Evvie, Jack, and I have tried to convince Morrie, he still holds firm. Where's our proof? We are now determined, even desperate, to convince Morrie, and therefore the police, about the utter improbability that Arlene could have committed this crime.

I called him for an appointment as soon as we returned from the jail and begged him to make it soon. He agreed to meet us the next day when he could fit us in. In the very late afternoon. I was on pins and needles waiting. I gathered Evvie and all the girls together.

Morrie has agreed to hear us out one more time, which is kind of him. He's willing to listen to our thinking and feelings on the subject. He doesn't expect that he'll change his mind but out of respect, he's here. We are going to present this case from Arlene's point of view.

We meet in our living room armed with pizzas and drinks. The girls are on their best behavior. I'm now part of Morrie's family, but he is still a cop, after all. Even though the girls do know there's a will, they have accepted our instructions to not ask about it.

I feel strangely optimistic. I sense we are getting close, but to what I don't know.

Jack had suggested that I start it with the list of our pros. He'd jump in later.

I ask that everyone listen with the understanding that nobody interrupts until I finish. Then I stand up and begin.

"Yes, Seymour was picked up. Our witness says he saw a man driving a Jaguar. Coincidence? Joyce had a Jaguar. And where was he taking him? Who is the mystery man? We think Joyce had an accomplice. But an accomplice to do what?

"Yes, about the kitchen. Who wrote the note asking to make key lime pie? Who else could it be but Joyce? In order to get Arlene to lose her temper yet again in front of witnesses? Later, when Arlene was in the kitchen cleaning up, Joyce arrived. Arlene insists she did not take any pie. We believe Joyce took the pie. Why? To torment her even more? Or for something more insidious?

"Arlene swears she was visited by Joyce every

night. Saying terrible things to her. It's very possible that Joyce did have a key to her apartment."

I reiterate the many things Arlene knew because Joyce told them to her in a middle-of-the-night rage. "Joyce admitted she set all of this up—finding her, getting Seymour to leave, moving in right below her to re-create the living quarters they occupied when they were very young. She admitted planting her scarf and the necklace. And she could have easily gotten the Valium as well."

Morrie is keeping his word. He's actually taking notes.

"What kind of person would do all that? Can you really believe Arlene Simon could make this up? We've known her for years. There is no way she could suddenly invent this convoluted, bizarre story.

"Nor could she possibly kill someone no matter how troubled she was.

"Joyce was able to set up scenes where she knew Arlene would behave badly. At the welcome party. Pretending she had just discovered her long-lost friend when in fact she moved in knowing where Arlene lived.

"At the pool. Joyce just happened to think her pool was too crowded? No, she tracked Arlene to our pool.

"At the kitchen club. The strange notes, none of which were written by the women there. Joyce had to have sent them. Arlene getting the note that said lemon meringue pie because Joyce knew she wouldn't have shown up otherwise.

"It wasn't Arlene who forced these confrontations. It was Joyce every time who managed to show up where Arlene went. Even when she was hiding from Joyce. Arlene said she stalked her day and night. During the day, playing the sweet friend who only wanted to make up. Knowing how badly it would affect Arlene. At night, gaslighting her. Making her vulnerable during the day being sleep deprived.

"Yes, Arlene was told about the will in one of those middle-of-the-night rantings, but she thought it was a vicious joke. Why would Joyce tell her about the will?"

I glance over at Morrie. He is paying very careful attention.

"So that the police would think it was the motive. And then Joyce drops the hint that Arlene would never get that inheritance. Joyce knew very well that the law would prevent her from collecting. She made that will out as the final trap so that Arlene would be suspected of murdering her."

I have to stop. My mouth is dry. I down a full glass of water. I'm aware of how still the room is.

Ida can't stand it. She takes the opportunity to quickly toss in a question. "So who gets the money if Arlene doesn't?"

Jack answers her, "A favorite charity was named."

Ida is puzzled. "That doesn't make sense."

I continue my impassioned plea. "You're right, Ida, it doesn't. Because here was Joyce talking about her dear daughter in California where she was invited to live. And how happy they all would be. How come Stacy wasn't the one she left the money to? How come Stacy wasn't mentioned at all?

"I realize now Joyce lied to me. The day I went up to Seymour's apartment, she said she was on the phone talking to her daughter, Stacy, in California. But we've learned since that Stacy was traveling in Europe then and couldn't be talking about what was happening with the cottage, or taking her children to a dentist that day.

"Arlene saw a very different side of Joyce at night. A woman who might be certifiably mad."

I nod to Jack and let him continue. I'm emotionally exhausted. It's his turn to jump in.

"What about her business manager? There was something off about him. Is it possible Kenneth Ryan knew more? His response to being told that Joyce was living here didn't ring true. His client and very old friend, even the decorator of his office, just dumps everything to come to Lanai Gardens? She leaves a three-thousand-square-foot designer house and he is only mildly surprised that she's moved into Seymour's place? Perhaps he already knew that.

"How about the fact that her 'beloved' daughter, Stacy, was not in that will? He knew that, too. He knew where Joyce was and why."

Ida can't help it. She has to blurt out again, "I never believed her cockamamie story of wanting the simple life. In Seymour's ugly apartment? She could have gone to a spa, or a retreat, even a convent for goodness' sake . . ." She stops, remembering she wasn't supposed to break in. "Sorry."

I smile. "But again you're right. It's quite a stretch of the imagination. And something about Kenneth having to go on this sudden business trip feels like a red flag."

Jack continues. "And since when does a businessman go on a long-distance trip and tell his secretary to take the time off? Wouldn't he want her to stay and take care of the office?

"Why has Seymour stopped sending postcards? Is it connected to the date Joyce died? Has something bad happened to him?"

There is a pounding on the door. We glance around in surprise. We aren't expecting anyone else.

Evvie goes to answer, and almost as if on cue, there's Leah, like a whirling dervish, dashing into the living room, hair flying. She is waving a small package. She doesn't even acknowledge the other people or that she's intruding on something private. She looks only at Jack. And me. The people she hired.

"I found this," she says shrilly, "in Seymour's mailbox. It must be from him. I opened it and it's one of those tape thingies." She immediately hands it to Jack. "Maybe it'll tell us where my Seymour is."

Jack takes a handkerchief out of his pocket and takes the article out of the mailer with it. It's a DVD. There is no note. He immediately hands the wrapping in the handkerchief to Morrie. We three exchange glances. I notice that there are no stamps on it. No return address. We are thinking the same thing. It wasn't mailed. It was placed in the mailbox by someone who had a key.

Leah is hysterical. "I can't work Seymour's TV set. It's too complicated. You have that kind of equipment. Gladdy, you have to play that for me. Right now!"

We try to calm her by telling her there are people here and we're busy, but she's having no part of that.

I look at Morrie. "Morrie?" I don't know what he would want us to do.

He nods. "Go ahead, play it."

Jack is still teaching me how to deal with CDs and DVDs and TiVo and On Demand and cellphones that take photos. I haven't gotten it down yet. So I leave it up to my expert.

Everyone now marches into our Florida room, where the TV is. And it's plenty crowded what with all of us in this small space. Evvie settles Leah in my rocker. The girls squeeze onto my rattan couch. Evvie and I crawl into the small loveseat. The guys, being gentlemen, stand.

Jack inserts the DVD into its slot and does whatever it takes to change it from TV to DVD.

Everyone is holding his breath.

What we see immediately is Joyce's face filling the entire screen. Joyce speaks slowly and earnestly, looking directly into a camera.

Sophie gasps. Bella grabs her hand. Leah leans far forward, as if to climb into the TV set.

Joyce begins. "If you are watching this, then I'm already dead. I've been murdered."

With that, Morrie says quickly, "Dad, turn it off!"

He does so, fast.

A shock wave runs through the room. What is this?

Morrie turns to the startled group. "Ladies, I have to ask all of you to leave. This is obviously a police matter."

With a little grumbling, the girls climb out of their comfortable seats and head out. Ida sort of rounds them up. "Come on. We gotta go."

Bella is petulant. "We're gonna miss the best part." But she allows Ida to push her along, too.

Sophie grabs one of the pizza boxes. "This goes with us," she announces.

Leah looks totally puzzled. "Where's my Seymour? Isn't he on that thing? Why do I have to leave? What does it mean?"

Jack gently takes her by the arm and leads her out, soothing her as best he can. He hands her over to Evvie, knowing she'll take care of her.

Evvie exchanges glances with me. Translation: I'll be able to tell her about the recording later. She exits with the wailing Leah.

Jack and I are alone in the room. I ask Morrie, "Do you want me to leave also?"

"No, the two of you will watch with me."

Jack returns and we settle down to stare at what's in front of us.

He starts it up from the beginning and we hear again: "If you are watching this, then I'm already dead. I've been murdered."

38

YOU OUGHT TO BE
IN PICTURES

Needless to say, we are riveted to the screen. Forty-two inches of Joyce in HD reciting to us. High definition, as I've been taught.

"I am putting this on record because if I die tonight, you need to know the facts. I came to Lanai Gardens specifically because I wanted to see my dearest and oldest friend, Arlene Steiner Simon, before I died of the disease that was eating away at my body.

"I knew it wouldn't be easy, because I hurt her deeply. But I soon realized it was hopeless. When she pulled a knife on me in the kitchen class, it reminded me of when she did the exact same thing fifty-five years ago. She didn't kill me then, but I now knew she intended to finish the job this time.

"I could have told her I was dying in order to get

her sympathy, to save myself. I refused to buy her with pity."

She shifts her body slightly. Tears begin rolling down her face. The camera seems to tilt to another angle. "It's all right. I don't care anymore. I'm glad she's putting me out of my misery. I can't take any more of the pain. The morphine makes me feel awful. She's called to make a date with me late tonight, so no one will see her come down to my apartment. I know she took one of the pie slices with her. I know what's she going to do and I accept my fate. I deserve to die. I only hope in time she will forgive me and herself.

"Please don't punish her."

The recording ends with Joyce bowing her head. The screen fades to black.

Jack turns it off. We are silent for a few minutes.

Morrie shakes his head in despair. "Very bad for Arlene."

I sit stunned. Jack and Morrie look at me to get a response.

Finally I put my hands together. Slowly I clap. "She should get an Academy Award for that performance."

Morrie stays for dinner. Each of us drinks more wine than we eat food. We merely pick at a quick salad I threw together. We've discussed everything over and over.

I comment, "She moved her face when the phony

tears began to fall and the camera moved with her. She didn't intend to move. She wanted it to look like she set the camera on a table and let it photograph her. Someone was holding that camera and filming her, but who? I'm sure now there is an accomplice. And I bet we know who it is. Where did she find a place to get a blank DVD and film it so fast and find someone to photograph her so quickly on the day she died? Obviously, this was planned ahead."

Morrie paces around the dining room table, wineglass in his hand. "When the prosecution shows this to a jury, it's all over. I don't know which is worse, the recording or the will."

I take a few sips of my chardonnay. "Let's examine Joyce's very busy day. She goes to the kitchen class in the morning, knowing her letter worked. Knowing Arlene will have a fit when she sees what they are baking.

"And Arlene does blow up at the sight of her. Sleep deprived and angry. Joyce picked this day on purpose.

"So Joyce then races out to meet with her accomplice, who has all they need to photograph the very thing that will destroy Arlene. I wonder where they meet. It wouldn't be in Kenneth's office. Too risky.

"She rushes back home and puts it in Seymour's mailbox."

Jack jumps in. "Then she calls to invite Arlene to her apartment. Arlene would never have gone there. So she used the only excuse that would possibly tempt her. Joyce pretending to say she gives up and wants to say goodbye. Please come down for a few moments, says the spider to the fly. Even if Arlene had doubts, she still would have gone just to hear the words she'd been waiting for. She might have thought not to go alone, but whom could she call in the middle of the night?"

Morrie comments, "Joyce must have been tempted to leave the DVD on the table with the water glass and the poisoned pie. Joyce was smart enough to know we'd see it as too pat. All the evidence neatly lined up to be found alongside her dead body."

I say, "She knew Leah would open Seymour's mailbox as soon as she was gone."

Morrie paces. "My God," he says, "if all of this is true, it's diabolical."

Jack shakes his head. "It's premeditated murder. Only she's committed suicide and made it look like murder. Setting it up so Arlene would be destroyed."

I add, "And the ultimate slap. Joyce dangles the will she's set up to be used against Arlene in her trial. She knows the law, that Arlene would never be allowed to receive that money as a felon. The arrogance of that woman, admitting to Arlene that she'll never get the money."

We are silent for a long while. Morrie finally says, shaking his head, "And it's still all circumstantial."

I manage a small smile. "But at least you're on our side now."

We sip our wine, thinking our own thoughts. But, finally, I need to say this out loud. "What must it have been like for Joyce? Sitting at her table, having just gotten Arlene's fingerprints on the glass. Was part of her tempted to tell Arlene exactly what she was going to do? Maybe invite her to stay and watch her old friend die? But no, her need to ruin Arlene was too strong. What were her last thoughts as she ate the pie she had laced with Valium? Did she eat each bite slowly? Was she afraid? Did she regret anything? Who did she think about? What were her last thoughts? How did she feel about dying all alone?"

Unexpectedly, I begin to cry.

39

CHASING THE FACTS

The three of us talk well into the evening. Plotting how to undo the horrific damage Joyce Steiner has caused. Finally we have a plan.

The key is Kenneth Ryan.

Morrie says, "The first thing I'll do is find out exactly what flight he took to Hong Kong. We need to know just when he planned this business trip. We'll get his bank records, his phone records, find out how often he was in touch with Joyce during this period. Interview his secretary and find out why he didn't have her stay to run his office while he was away."

Jack eats what's left of the salad. "We could also get a photo of him and show it to Merrill Grant and see if he recognizes the man who picked Seymour up."

I stack the dishes, ready to take them into the kitchen. "Yes. And surely Stacy must be back by now. Joyce's daughter hasn't called, probably because she was busy after coming home from a long trip and perhaps didn't think it was important."

Jack comments, "But a call from the police concerning her mother? And she doesn't call?"

I start clearing the dishes. "And this fact really fascinates me. I can't wait to find out why Joyce didn't leave her estate to the daughter she loves."

Jack adds, "We may never find out the truth about that. We have to find Stacy. We have a lot of questions for her."

Morrie is about to put down his wineglass. "We have a busy day tomorrow. I better head out."

Jack teases, indicating his glass, "Are you sure you can drive? We wouldn't want you to be picked up by the cops for DUI."

I can't resist adding, "And have to walk that silly line in front of your peers. It would be so embarrassing."

"Ha-ha," Morrie says. "I've been nursing this one drink all evening, smart guys. I think I can manage to get home in one piece."

We smile and exchange hugs.

"Tomorrow we clear up this mess," he says, lifting the wineglass in a toast.

We do the same.

"Tomorrow," Jack says.

Amen.

40

TOMORROW

Things are moving very fast and furiously. With Morrie's police team doing the legwork, answers are coming in practically every hour on the hour. Morrie keeps us in the loop all day long. Every so often Evvie and the girls drop in to hear the latest news reports. Needless to say we're very excited.

Kenneth was definitely the key. He lied about everything. His phone records show he was in constant discussion with Joyce since she moved into Lanai Gardens. They were so sure of themselves, they didn't even bother to hide their tracks by using prepaid cellphones.

He wasn't going to Hong Kong. He never intended to. Based on the way this trip was ticketed, he bought it the night Joyce died. He knew she was dead before we notified him. He knew we'd discover that he was the person holding her will. So he needed only to wait for us to meet with him, spin his prepared story, and—poof!—he was gone.

Apparently Kenneth Ryan had the entire fortune. Joyce's house sale profits. And the Jaguar. And the yacht. All her properties. How did he manage to keep that information secret? It doesn't matter now. All the profits went away with him. All eleven million, and as he arrogantly told us, whatever more that would round it out. All gone. There was no money left in his or Joyce's bank account.

Our boy transferred all his funds to his next destination, his new home. Not Hong Kong. And where did he move to? Dubai, United Arab Emirates. And why there? It's all about extradition. The United States can't bring him back on any charges.

His secretary had a lot to say. Mr. Ryan had been acting oddly for a long time. He was constantly going to "meetings" but never told her where or when or with whom. Very unlike him. He used to have her keep detailed records of all his appointments, but that changed suddenly. She suspected he had a secret place where he went quite often. She had no idea where. We assume he was with Joyce.

Kenneth made a number of practically overnight

trips overseas for very short periods of time. His secretary didn't know where.

He also told her just before he left that he wouldn't be back for a long time. She was now looking for another job.

A new shocking piece of information: Morrie contacted the lawyer we were told would handle Joyce's affairs from now on, a man named Jeffrey Finch. Mr. Finch had a different will from the one we were given to read. Apparently Joyce came in and changed the earlier one, thereby canceling that one out. This new will stated that if Arlene Simon was disavowed because of criminal charges, it all went to Kenneth Ryan.

Apparently Mr. Ryan took a jump start on his inheritance.

We questioned the validity of such a document. Could Joyce's lawyer write up a will that makes him the beneficiary? No, legally he couldn't. But Kenneth and Joyce thought of everything. He didn't prepare this last will; this Jeffrey Finch, who did not know Kenneth Ryan, was the new executor of her estate.

The stunning news keeps coming in.

After an exhausting day of absorbing one shock after another, Jack and I collapse on our sofa, reeling from the information about this incredible plot that these two people concocted. Probably hadn't been difficult for Joyce to entice Kenneth into assisting her. He had those eleven million as his reward for helping Joyce destroy Arlene's life.

The phone rings and we don't want to answer any more calls. Too tired to explain to one more person what had been going on.

We let it ring and the answering machine clicks on. "Hello," we hear a woman's voice, "this is Stacy Wilson calling from California. You've been trying to reach me . . . ?"

Jack and I sprint for the phone. I am closer. I quickly press the speaker button, so we both can hear.

"Yes, hello," I say breathlessly. "My name is Gladys Gold. We live in Florida. My husband and I have been trying to reach you for some time now. Did you speak to the Sausalito police?"

"No," she answers. "I was more curious to find out why total strangers were also leaving messages for me."

Jack speaks. "Hello, Stacy. My name is Jack Langford. But didn't the police leave word that it concerned your mother?"

I hear a sound that makes me think she's lighting a cigarette. There's a rather long pause. We wait. Then she speaks again. "Yes, they did, but frankly I had no curiosity and wasn't the least bit interested in hearing anything pertaining to my mother."

Jack and I look at each other. What's this?

I say as gently as I can, "We called, sorry to be

the ones to inform you, to say your mother has died."

Another pause. I'm beginning to get a feeling about what is coming next.

Stacy laughs, causing herself to cough. Definitely a cigarette raspy cough. "Hell," she says, "I thought she died years ago!"

Now we're the ones needing to pause. What do we say next? But Stacy saves us the trouble.

"And more to the point, as far as I'm concerned, my mother has been dead to me since I was twenty-one, when I was finally able to break away from my parents. That's when I got married and moved to California, getting as far from them as I could."

I might as well go for it. "But before she died your mother said she was going to move to California and live with your family in a guest cottage you were building for her on your property."

The laughter this time gives her hiccups. "What guest house? There is no guest house. My looney-tune mother was not coming to Sausalito to live with me and my husband and children. Over *my* dead body before I'd let that happen. What had that witch been up to?"

Jack comments, "Frankly, we're stunned hearing this. We believed her story."

"That's not too hard to understand. My parents could turn on their devious, charming personalities when they wanted to get their way."

Her tone is sarcastic now. "Let me fill you in about my life with Mummy and Daddy. Doctor

Edward, as he liked to be called, was too busy. He was never home, and I learned to be grateful for any precious moments he bestowed upon me. Which were few and far between. Mom, on the other hand, was toxic. She was a horror. Luck of the draw. I had a sick mother who should have been institutionalized. She was the mother from hell. When she met my husband-to-be, the witch even tried to seduce *him*. That was the last straw.

"When I got married and moved out, I never looked back again. Frankly, it always amazed me that I turned out normal after those two misfits finished raising me. I was lucky I was able to choose a decent, caring, sane man and was able to love someone." Stacy laughs again. "I may have married a doctor, too, but I was smart enough not to marry a surgeon."

When Jack and I are finally allowed to get a word in, we tell her that her mother has been murdered.

Stacy's response is chilling. "What took so long?"

She adds, "I have no intention of coming to any funeral. Please don't call again." Wow!

Later in the day, we report on the Stacy call. Morrie is as astounded as we are. Then we get this further update from him.

"Guess where Kenneth Ryan went to on his almost-overnight short trips to very faraway places? Sydney, Australia, Fiji, Tahiti, and Hawaii. Sound familiar?"

To mail four postcards of a posing Seymour, to make sure the stamps were real! Very expensive trips as part of their devious plot.

Yes, the postcards stopped the day Joyce died. And Kenneth left the country. Seymour never got to travel, after all.

Why did Kenneth assist her? Who knows? Did he love her so much that he helped her plan the murder/suicide plot? Maybe blackmail. Did she have something on him that forced him to assist her? We may never find out.

Or maybe he did it for eleven million dollars and change.

We now know all we need to know except for one very important fact.

What did they do with Seymour? For the first time, I'm beginning to fear for his life.

41

A WONDERFUL DAY

We decide to make a party of it. We're dressing up. Cocktail party dresses. Makeup. High heels, sort of. The works. Guys are actually wearing suits. We don't care that it's only ten in the morning.

We're forming a convoy. Nine cars are in our parade, carrying four to six people each. The neighbors from all of the Phases are up early, busily making signs to wave and attaching balloons to each auto.

Yesterday a man arrived at Phase Three with what looked like his girlfriend. Why that assumption? He was obviously rich and old and driving a Rolls-

Royce. She looked like a Vegas showgirl. We doubted it was his daughter. They came to pick up Joyce's Jaguar and had the key and ownership papers to prove it was his. The papers were signed by none other than Kenneth Ryan. The showgirl moved over and drove their Rolls-Royce. He climbed in and took the wheel of his brand-new Jaguar.

Of course it reminded Hy of a joke. Very off-color, but the punch line was something like, Get out, you and the horse you rode in on.

After they drove off, that renowned cynic of Phase Two, our very own Ida, commented, "He's definitely a doctor. A surgeon for sure."

We had a good laugh at that.

Anyway, we're finally ready. Jack, Evvie, and I are in the lead car. Jack's car. Not a Jag, but his very old (he calls it vintage) Caddy. The girls are riding along with Hy and Lola. Third car, Tessie and Sol, Irving and Mary. Even some Canadians have joined us. Fatima and Elaine and Frances are with us, after sheepish apologies. Sandra rides with them.

Just about everyone is carrying a bouquet of flowers.

Jack leans his head outside our car window. "Ready," he calls out, waving his arm to signal the line of cars behind him.

A chorus of "Ready!" floats back at us.

Hy has to put his own spin on it. "Wagons ho!" he calls out.

We arrive at the Fort Lauderdale jail. We wait. Some stay in their cars, with the air conditioners on; others step out carrying their signs.

The jail door opens. There she is. Arlene is free. Morrie is with her. Horns honk. Signs are being waved. "Welcome home, Arlene!" Women bring her their bouquets, hugging her and filling her arms with flowers.

Arlene cries. Everyone cries. She is overwhelmed by an ocean of happy tears.

Hy meanders over to where Jack, Evvie, and I are standing. He puffs out his chest and says, "Too bad she lost all those millions. I was hoping she'd spring for dinner."

42

SEYMOUR

We are sound asleep. The phone rings. Jack, eyes still closed, groggily reaches for it. He answers.

"Yeah, hello?" He yawns.

What time is it? I squint at the clock: 6 A.M.!

I jump up into a sitting position and grab his arm. Any calls at odd hours must mean something's wrong. With someone somewhere.

"Who is it?" I pull at his arm. He slides himself up. "Will I accept charges on an international call? Where? Dubai?"

I hit him on that same arm. "Say yes!"

He might be too groggy to remember, but I bet I know who's calling. Who else could it be? We don't know of anyone else in Dubai. I lean into him and he lowers the receiver so I can hear, too.

"Yes, I accept." We wait through static and foreign languages until we hear a familiar voice.

"Mr. Langford?" he asks.

Early as it may be, Jack's sense of humor is awake. "Mr. Kenneth Ryan, I presume?"

Kenneth is all business. "Get a pen and paper," he orders.

"What time is it where you are?" Jack asks, waving at me, trying to make me hurry. I scramble for something to write on.

"Two P.M.," he says. "Cut the small talk."

I run my hands through whatever is on my bedside table. What I come up with fast is a bookmark holding my place in my bedtime reading. Then I scuttle through the drawer for something to write with.

"How's the weather?" Jack asks, stalling.

"Hot. It's always hot," Kenneth answers, annoyed.

"Come on back home and we can make it even hotter for you."

I punch Jack again. "Don't make him mad, he'll hang up," I whisper.

"Write this down." Another order.

Pencil gripped tightly, I write whatever Jack repeats. It's an address.

"You took your inheritance too soon," Jack says. "Your scheme didn't work."

"It worked well enough for me."

"You now owe Arlene Simon eleven million dollars, rounded out."

"Not gonna happen."

"You can never come home again. Ever."

Kenneth hangs up.

"Stay cool," Jack says sarcastically to the dead air.

"Oh, no! Why didn't we ask him where Seymour was?"

Then we look at each other and start moving. Fast!

I'm already out of bed and grabbing the first outfit I can get my hands on. Jack's right behind me. It's got to mean what we think it means.

"Where the heck is Mariposa Street?" I ask.

"Morrie will know. I'm calling him as soon as I'm dressed."

I'm ready. I don't care what I look like. I run my fingers through my hair. That's good enough.

"I'll make some coffee," I call out to him even as I'm running down the hall.

Morrie is used to getting up at all hours. He picks us up in about twenty minutes. We ride with him in his car, each holding a coffee cup to help wake us up.

I thought I knew our neighborhood, but I don't know this street even though it is only ten minutes from where we live.

It's an old neighborhood with small stucco houses. We're holding our breath, not knowing what to expect. I pray it isn't a dead body. Somehow, even though Joyce and Kenneth were willing to destroy Arlene's life, I hope they couldn't commit an actual murder.

The house is in the middle of the block. Rundown, peeling paint, shutters broken off, needing a lot more than just a new paint job. It looks abandoned, but we know it's not.

We move slowly behind Morrie, who is looking every which way, observing everything, to be ready for whatever might happen. It's a cop thing. His hand is on his gun holster, but he hasn't snapped it open.

The shades are all drawn in the front. We tiptoe into the backyard, pushing open a squeaking, broken chain-link gate. Those windows there are covered, too. We return to the front and climb up the three steps leading to the door. Morrie tries the knob. It's locked. We search around the obvious places for a hidden key. Kenneth didn't oblige us with that information. Nothing under a flowerpot with a dead plant in it. Jack feels along the top of the door frame, another possibility. Nada under the tattered doormat.

Morrie shrugs. "Might as well ring the bell."

A few minutes go by. Morrie is groping in his pocket for the tool he carries that will open the lock when we hear a voice from inside.

"Who's there?"

I breathe a sigh of relief. He's alive.

Jack nudges me to answer. A woman's voice would be less threatening.

"Seymour, is that you?"

A pause. "You're not Joyce."

"No, I'm not. Joyce couldn't come." Well, that's not a lie.

"Where's Kenny?"

Kenny? We look at one another. A nickname for a kidnapper? He knows both their names. In mystery books, kidnappers wear masks and hide their identity. If a mask falls off, their victim is a dead duck.

They never meant to kill him.

"Kenny couldn't come, either. He had to go on a trip." That's close enough to the truth.

"Who are you? Are you from the show?"

What's that about?

"It's Gladdy. Gladdy Gold, your neighbor from Lanai Gardens."

Silence. I can almost hear him thinking as he processes what this means.

Finally, "You didn't bring my sister, did you?"

His voice is tremulous.

"No, Leah is still at home. But I'm here with Jack . . . and his son, Morrie." No need to use the cop word. Yet.

We hear the turning of locks. One. Two. Three and the door is opened.

And here's Seymour. At long last.

43

A STAR IS BORN

Seymour, dressed only in baggy shorts and a not-too-clean undershirt, walks us through the apartment. Very little in the way of furniture. A musty smell from a house that hadn't had windows opened in a very long time. The fifties-style kitchen is sparse. Pockmarked linoleum. A portable mini-fridge only. No stove, but a small microwave. A plain wood table. One chair.

We pass the bedroom. Just as sparse. A cot. Period. Seymour's few clothes are in a neat pile on the floor.

And then we get to the living room. What a difference.

There is a video camera. Now we know where the death scene played by Lady Macbeth was taped. A screen covers one wall. On another, a backdrop hangs from ceiling to floor, featuring—lo and behold—a rear projection of the Sydney Opera House in Australia.

There's also a TV and many DVDs stacked on a table along with props, such as a fishing net and baseball caps, from four different countries.

How did they ever get him to stay here?

Seymour asks poignantly, "Did you bring any food? I've run out. Kenny was supposed to go shopping today."

Well, Kenny won't be doing any more shopping in the future, either.

What good chocoholic wouldn't have a couple of Hershey's Kisses in her purse? I offer my small supply to Seymour, who rips the silvery paper off and eats them hungrily.

Morrie contributes a Power Bar he keeps in his pocket for those times on duty when he can't get any food. It, too, is grabbed. "Shall we sit down and talk?" he suggests.

Seymour climbs into his moldy-looking recliner chair, the one in front of the TV set.

I sit gingerly on a scratchy, ratty-looking couch.

Jack takes the one plain wooden chair from the kitchen. Morrie stands.

This house reminds me of Seymour's apartment, only worse.

Which finally helps me remember what I was trying to recall a few days ago. Except for a few clothes, Joyce had nothing. Even her purse had been emptied. Kenneth's office was cleared out as well. They wanted to leave nothing behind. The two of them knew they were going away, permanently. How ironic. They both moved on to a place from which they can never return!

Seymour looks at Morrie. "You look familiar. Were you on one of the shows? Maybe the bachelor one where you got to pick a wife?"

Morrie says no.

Jack smirks at his still-unmarried son. "Don't I wish."

Morrie throws him a dirty look.

"Then are you another producer of our show?" Seymour asks Morrie.

"What show is that?" Morrie asks, feeling his way.

"Why, our new reality show."

Now it all clicks into place. Seymour's scrapbook in his apartment. All those DVDs. They lured him in with his passion.

"Would you excuse me for a minute?" Jack asks Seymour. "I have to make an important call."

Seymour is magnanimous. "Go ahead. You showbiz people are always busy."

I grin at him, knowing what my kind husband is going to do. Attaboy, Jack, call Leah and tell her her brother has been found.

Jack nods and walks back outside with his cellphone.

I ask, "Tell us, how did you meet Joyce?"

He brightens. "I was taking my usual walk in Lauderdale Park and this very nice lady comes up to me and hands me her card. I still have it here." He reaches into the pocket of his shorts and hands me a crumpled business card.

I read it aloud for Morrie. "'Joyce Smith.'" Smith? Well, that would work for a made-up name. I continue to read. "'Producer Survivor Productions. Hollywood, California.'" No address listed. No email. No phone number. They had him at *Survivor*.

Seymour is animated. "My very, very favorite show! Do you know it? These lucky people get to travel all over the world and have adventures!"

I remember turning it on once for thirty seconds where some grungy-looking people dressed like bad Tarzan imitations were eating fried ants. That was enough for me.

Seymour continues, wringing his hands in excitement, "She wanted me to try out as a contestant for her new show. Me, Seymour, going on TV!"

Morrie moves it along. "So she brought you here . . . ?"

"Yes. It was Kenny who picked me up that night. Kenny Jones." He grins, proudly. "In his fancy Jaguar."

They sure did choose original names. Smith and Jones. Poor Seymour. Because it was an expensive car, he got in with a stranger. The joke was on him and he didn't get it.

Seymour rhapsodizes on. "He's the other producer. It was so exciting. I was told that I had to keep everything a secret. Not tell anybody I know or else I was gonna be"—here he stumbles on the big words—"instantly disqualified."

"And what were you doing here?" I ask.

"Well, it's very complicated. They had to take pictures of me in different places to let the studio people see if I was photo— If I looked good in pictures. So they dressed me up and had those things on the wall. They didn't have the money to send me to those expensive places, so this was how they did it."

Little did he know Kenny was living his fantasy for him. Too bad they didn't let Seymour make those four expensive trips to four faraway places, just to make sure a postcard was stamped!

"Seymour, dear," I say to him, "why couldn't you share your secret with your sister, so she wouldn't worry about you?"

Suddenly, here's a different Seymour. Agitated. "Why should I? She would have said no. She always said no to anything I wanted. I was going to tell her after my audition was over. After I got the part."

"So your producers let you hide here, away from Leah," says Morrie.

And that's why he stayed.

Jack has returned and is smiling. I can't wait to hear what Leah said. Later.

Seymour is animated once again. "Yes, wasn't that nice of them? And they were willing to cover my rent till we were done with my screen test.

"When are they coming back? I want to know if

I made the cut. That's what they called it—making the cut. I want to know if I'm starring on their big new show, *Death Defiers*."

The three of us exchange glances. Who was going to break the news to Seymour that a Hollywood contract was not in his future? I didn't envy that person.

Seymour searches our faces eagerly.

I nod to Jack. You do it. I don't want to be the one. Jack nods to Morrie. He's not the authority figure here. His son is. Morrie shrugs. He has no choice. He takes the responsibility. He's works up his courage to give Seymour the bad news.

But Seymour beats us to it. He's been staring at each of us as we look unhappy. He jumps out of the recliner. He is near tears. "I get it. Joyce and Kenny sent you to do their dirty work, didn't they? I didn't make the cut. I'm not going to be in *Death Defiers*."

He scrabbles for his DVDs, grabbing for all of them, dropping some of them. "Get me out of here. Take me home!"

Showbiz is a cruel mistress.

44

GRADUATION DAY

Evvie and I are invited to the big event. We are seated in the front row on folding chairs with a few strangers sitting next to us. Rico sits there, grinning like a proud relative.

It's graduation day at the Mike Gatkes Private Eye Academy.

We were told by the girls not to say a word, no matter what we saw, so I'm predicting some kind of entertainment.

Ida pokes Bella and Sophie to straighten their backs as they stand at attention in front of the chalkboard. They smile at us.

Mike Gatkes, in speech mode, emotes as he holds their three certificates aloft. "Congratulations on completing your Mike Gatkes Private Eye Course with flying colors."

We politely applaud. This is the first time we meet Gatkes. What a character, what a phony. But if he made the girls happy and didn't soak them too much for his "expertise," it was harmless. Gatkes is a most unfortunate name. It means men's winter underwear with a back flap. In Yiddish.

Gatkes drones on pompously. "Go bravely out into the world of crime, knowing you are well equipped to stop any abomination, any abuse, any corruption, any evil, any felony, any illegality, any transgression, any wrongdoing wherever and whenever you come upon it. I salute you."

Which he does with a clicking of his heels. The girls are handed their certificates. And a huge print of the three of them holding what looks like a stuffed squirrel.

Happily, they thank their teacher.

Evvie and I are about to get up, but there's more going on. So we watch and listen. It's a bit puzzling. Evvie shrugs. Whatever.

Sophie mumbles, gazing at her certificate. "He spelled my name wrong. What's so hard about Meyerbeer?"

Ida shushes her. "Never mind."

For refreshment, there's cookies and punch.

As they imbibe, Ida corners Gatkes. "Mike, about the reward you got from Fleigel . . ."

"A mere pittance . . ."

"Not so. Harvey found three hundred dollars in quarters up on his roof. I suspect he was very grateful."

"You would deny a man his living wages?"

"We solved the case."

Mike grumbles, "A lucky happenstance. Whadda you want?"

"How about you cancel our credit card purchases and we'll call it even."

He sighs. "You really know how to hurt a guy."

Just as we're about to stand up, thinking the show had actually ended, the door to the office suddenly flies open with a slam bang against the inside wall.

We sit back down again.

Everyone turns to look. A very skinny guy who seems like he doesn't eat much fairly leaps into the room. He wears a gray sweatshirt with a hood that covers much of his face. There is fire in his eyes, a determination in his stride. He reminds me of that actor who always plays great slimeballs, Steve Buscemi.

"I've got you, Gatkes," he cries out in an unfortunately squeaky voice.

Mike throws up his arms as if to protect himself and backs farther into his room, trying to get away. "No, no," he gasps.

The intruder reaches into his jacket.

Sophie panics. "He's got a gun!"

Bella seems to faint, daintily, falling onto Mike's faded brown horsehair sofa.

Ida keeps her cool. She knocks the guy down.

A finger could knock that guy down.

Rico jumps off his chair, going immediately to

her side. They turn him over. Rico holds him down. Ida whips out the handcuffs. Sophie positions herself in front of him, legs and arms akimbo, brandishing a lipstick. A lipstick?

"Drop your gun!" Ida the "bad cop" snarls.

"You really ought to do as she says," "good cop" Sophie pipes up.

Rico is busy getting the cuffs on the squirming man.

"I got no gun. Get offa me," the intruder cries.

"Oh, yeah," Rico sneers.

"Take it out of my pocket and look, you idiots."

Rico reaches around and removes what's in the guy's sweatshirt pocket. He retrieves a narrow folder.

"Oops," Rico says, holding it high for all to see.

"It's a summons," the Buscemi double shrieks. "I work for a lawyer whose client is his wife and these are papers summoning Gatkes to divorce court. I've been chasing after this flake all week."

Embarrassed, they remove the handcuffs and help him up. Sophie attempts to brush him off. That rug really is dirty.

He pulls away from them and pushes the papers into Mike's unwilling large paws.

With that, the process server heads out the door. "I oughta sue," he growls.

Bella comes to. She stares at the quiet group. "What did I miss?"

Evvie and I applaud as we get off our chairs.

The girls turn to look at us as if we are nuts.

"Nice play," I murmur as I grab a chocolate chip cookie.

"Good theater," says Evvie, grabbing a Fig Newton. "Polish it up a bit and you could take it to Off Broadway."

We leave, giggling all the way down the long, dark staircase.

A week later Ida comes to us, the girls trailing behind her. "Too much paperwork," she says. "I'm willing to give up Ida Franz and Associates and return to the Gladdy Gold agency."

The girls are happy. Evvie and I are happy. I'll break the news to Jack later. After he's had a good dinner. We are a family again.

Acknowledgments

First and foremost, thanks to Lois Leonard, my *mechutainista*. She knows why.

Thanks to Betty & Roger Eggleston of Florida, yet again. Squirrels, indeed!

And to round up all the usual suspects:

Caitlin and "good" Nancy again and again and again

My sons, Gavin & Howard or Howard & Gavin. Get it? And Alison, of course

Camille, Peg, Jonnie, who help me get it right every time

Sister Judy and the Tucson Voyager fans

And all the great "sisters" in SinC and the pals in MWA

To Margaret and the Women Who (still) Walk on Water in Wisconsin

And lots and lots of friends and readers giving continuous support. Thank you all!